THE VALKYRIE

Also by Kate Heartfield

The Chatelaine
The Embroidered Book

THE
VALKYRIE

KATE HEARTFIELD

HARPER
Voyager

Harper*Voyager*
An imprint of
HarperCollins*Publishers* Ltd
1 London Bridge Street
London SE1 9GF

www.harpercollins.co.uk

HarperCollins*Publishers*
Macken House
39/40 Mayor Street Upper
Dublin 1
D01 C9W8
Ireland

First published by HarperCollins*Publishers* 2023

1

Copyright © Kate Heartfield 2023

Illustrations © Andrew Davis 2023

Kate Heartfield asserts the moral right to
be identified as the author of this work

A catalogue record for this book is available from the British Library

ISBN: 978-0-00-856773-6 (HB)
ISBN: 978-0-00-856776-7 (TPB)

Typeset in Meridien by Palimpsest Book Production Ltd, Falkirk, Stirlingshire

Printed and bound in the UK using 100% renewable electricity
by CPI Group (UK) Ltd

For my brother

PART I
FAFNIR

CHAPTER ONE

Brynhild Falls

Like all stories, I have more than one beginning.

Three hundred and twenty-seven years ago, I was born, in the days when Hadrian ruled the Empire that crumbles around us now. Eight years after that, my father gave me in tribute to his god: the one he called Wotan, the one I learned to call by many names. Seven years after that, I finished my training, took flight for the first time as a Valkyrie, learned to gather the slain.

The only beginning that matters came centuries later. My beginning was in you, Gudrun.

But you already know that story. You want to know what came before, what I was before you melted and reforged me. I'll go back one beginning, then, to my exile and my fall. It seemed like an ending, then. My last sight of Valhalla, a shard of daylight that closed in a moment, as the weight of my mail and helmet pulled me down.

I was a long time falling.

Somehow, in that void between worlds, there was light enough to see. I thought I saw other women, though who can say which worlds they were falling from, or to. A pale, wry face framed by short red hair, and a hand searching the

3

hilt. The golden hair of a girl, streaming as she floated, hands covering her face, her shoes kicking at nothing. We tumbled at different speeds, and sometimes they flickered out of existence while I watched. Perhaps I imagined them.

They were not Valkyries; I am the only Valkyrie Odin ever exiled.

The fall gave me time to think.

I imagined what would happen at the bottom. Perhaps I'd land on a pile of corpses, or skeletons; perhaps I'd add one more to the pile. All these fallen women must land somewhere.

But when I hit the ground, I was alone. Alive. Breathless, coughing, bruised. My cheek stung where it slammed into the edge of my helmet. When I pulled my helmet off and wiped my watering eyes, the back of my hand came away bloody from the cut. I wiped my hand on my green wool cloak, another brown stain for its collection.

I staggered to my feet and looked out at Midgard. My birthplace.

I barely remember my family now, and I did not remember them any better then. My father was something like a king, or so I recall him, but I do not think he is in any of your stories, Gudrun, at least none of the ones I heard in your hall. Kings gave their daughters to the gods, sometimes, where I was born. But where was that? Three centuries had passed since I left them, as a child, my small hand in the rough hand of the Allfather.

Valkyries age during the hours or days they spend on Midgard, but nobody ages in Valhalla. By the time I was exiled, I was a woman grown, but my body was much younger than all my centuries.

I stood on a cliff, looking out over brown land under a pale sky. A thin, dark river wound like an adder, far off. Kites circled and screamed over my head, chastising me for existing where I had not existed a moment before. Though I lifted my arms to be among them, the wind did not take me. I could fly no longer; I was a woman. That was my punishment; the very worst thing Odin could imagine.

It was spring, and the leaves were new-green. I walked, stiffly, helmet in hand, seeking shelter.

Down in lower places, I found that the water of the skinny river was clear as weak mead, with little brown trout darting in it, and a pink-skinned pine twisting overhead. I sat knapping a flint to the finest edge. Then I snapped the pine branch that leaned westward. *Westward wood for harming, eastward for healing.* And with my flint I sharpened the point.

Odin had taken my powers of flight. I had to assume (and I would be proven right soon enough) that he had also taken the other powers he had bestowed on me when he made me a Valkyrie. I would not be able to walk unseen among the humans of Midgard, now. I would not be able to perceive their secrets or prophesy their destinies. Very well. But I still had the skills I had learned, and I made a list of them in my mind. I remembered the runelore, and how to work spells for healing, strength, protection, and other things. I knew how to hunt and how to fight. When I landed and the kites screamed at me, I understood their speech, still. The language of birds was something I'd learned, and the things I had learned were still mine.

My flint bit the bark, and I carved the rune I needed.

The Tyr-rune is for victory with honour, as Tyr kept faith with Odin in the war of the gods. Just as Tyr did Odin's bidding, so your weapon will do yours.

Odin once spoke those words to me as though they were written by someone else, as though the name 'Odin' were not among his own. I was not yet grown to full height. He told me that day that a weapon pushes fear away but doesn't banish it, that the fear will still be lurking at the tip of your sword unless you speak to it and call its secret names. He said he had learned this himself at great cost.

'Who could the Gallows' Burden possibly fear?' I asked

him. I had adopted the practice of always speaking one of his names, of never saying *you* to my teacher.

'There is always someone waiting to challenge the Allfather for rule over the nine worlds. I cannot sleep,' Odin said, switching to the personal and looking off into the distance. 'I have seen a vision.'

That was not long before Odin took a rune for himself, the god-rune. Why should Tyr have a rune all his own, and even Freyja, Odin's former enemy, and not the Allfather? Why should warriors and healers not be able to call upon the source of all knowledge, the fountainhead?

I was a disciple down to my toenails. My comrades, especially the younger ones, came to me whenever they needed to dispel their doubts. Black-haired Hrist thought my faith must have been founded on certainty, and she wanted me to explain the things none of us could understand.

'But how can Odin be the source of the runes,' she asked me as we scrubbed our shields, 'if Freyja came to Asgard knowing them already? Wasn't that why the gods went to war in the first place, because Odin mistrusted Freyja's magic?'

'I don't know what stories the skalds tell in your father's court,' I spat. 'They had it wrong, or you misunderstood. Odin found the runes first, of course. Freyja must have stolen them from him.'

'Oh,' said Hrist.

'You have to be patient with Hrist,' Kara said, and as always, no one could tell whether Kara was serious. 'Her mother is a Persian, you know. With so many different stories in her house, how could she know that some stories are truer than others?'

My faith burned as bright as my sword, which is why I came to ride at the head of Odin's Valkyrie host.

But that sword stayed in Midgard when Odin banished me.

Cold and hungry, I made myself a spear. The soft tree-finger took the rune from my knife but I would not risk more than one invocation of Tyr; even two could splinter that weak wood.

My spear found a trout and I regarded it for a moment in my hands. Odin had thrown me out with what I wore but not what I carried, and he judged my tinder bag to be in the second category. But I would need fire eventually. I might as well start now.

So I cut the poplar hearth stick and carved the runes. As I worked the dry-reed spindle with raw hands, I found myself wondering whether Odin had taken the things I carried so that I would be forced into action. So that I would have something to do other than wander and grieve. In those days I was still accustomed to thanking Odin.

That first trout cooked on my small fire tasted rich, sucked off my fingers. I washed my hands and my bloody cheek with river water. There were markings of mortals on the land: hoofmarks in the dried earth, the sharp stump of a felled tree, a small pile of whitening dog dung.

It was the custom among the Valkyries to carve runes into our hands, give ourselves scars in remembrance of our fallen comrades. Valkyries did die in battle, more often than any song records. *We* recorded them. That's why I bore two dozen uneven runes on my hands, some stretched and red and some long faded to thin white, each one of them in remembrance of a warrior. I wondered what they would do about me: would they consider me a fallen comrade? Would they carve a rune for Brynhild on their hands?

I wasn't sure which I preferred; I thought I would like them to remember me as alive.

On that cold ground, I dreamt of Valhalla.

—*Get up, Rota, wake up, lazy Gondul. I see you're awake, Hrist. Clear the mead-cups off the benches and strew the rushes on the floor. We have a new guest coming this morning.*
—*Who is coming, Brynhild?*
—*A king.*

—*Is it one of our fathers?*

—*Why do you care, Hrist? Why should we care? We have not seen our fathers, none of us, since they traded us away to Odin.*

—*Yes, but I would like to see my father. I remember him, you know.*

—*You only think you remember him.*

—*What's the difference?*

CHAPTER TWO

Brynhild Speaks with a God and with the Birds

I never told you the reason for my exile, Gudrun, but I will tell it now. It makes a short tale.

Two kings fought on a green field. The young king was better, wiser, stronger. If he had lived, his people would have prospered. Odin eyed him like honey. He should have lived.

I chose the young king to live, and the other to die. And Odin gainsaid me, and when I railed at him, he cast me out of Valhalla forever.

Even if Odin had invited me back, I would not have gone. He'd shown me he did not value my wisdom or my strength, and that was over, now, forever. It could not be undone. Frankly, I didn't want it undone. I wanted no more of Valhalla.

But I did value my own gifts. I had spent three centuries learning to fight, to heal, to judge. Surely, I thought, I could carry on that work in Midgard. Midgard needed me more than Valhalla did; the dead had plenty of cup-bearers. Yes, I missed my comrades terribly, but I could carry on our work. I would walk until I found someone who needed me. A good fight is never difficult to find.

So my spear became my walking stick. We hardly ever

walked, in Valhalla, or on our journeys to Midgard on Odin's business. We rode and flew and danced and fought. I remembered very little of my childhood but I remembered walking away with Odin's hand over mine, the cold impression of my mother's final kiss on my cheek.

My mother was long, long dead. My father's kingdom was wiped from the world. I had nowhere I could claim as home, no people I could claim as mine.

As I rounded a great boulder, I saw a figure, leaning against the rock, a paunch over his belt and a broad-brimmed hat over his head.

I should have known he couldn't stay away.

'Well met, Wanderer,' I said. 'Did you think I wouldn't recognize you here?'

'This is my world, as much as the others. I wander, I give advice. I wanted to see how you were, Brynhild.' He touched his cheek, looking at mine. 'You might want to—'

'I have. I'm fine. Surely you are needed in some other part of this vast world, Allfather, or one of the others.'

'Not as vast as you might think. There are parts of Midgard where I cannot walk. I'm not welcome everywhere in it. The same is true in the other worlds, in Vanaheim, in Jotunheim . . . it is definitely true in Helheim.'

'Tell me where those lands are, then, where you don't go. I will make my way there.'

Odin looked away, gazed at the forest. The path forked, just beyond him. 'You pretend that I have wronged you, Brynhild, but you always knew that Valkyries only choose who lives and dies in battle as a service to me. The ultimate right to decide is mine. It always has been.'

'Yes.' I never said otherwise. He got his way, and the man he said should die went to Valhalla, and the man I fought to kill gasped his way back to life. I knew it wouldn't matter, in the end, what I decided. But I could not make a decision that was not a decision at all. It would have been pointless.

Just as it was pointless trying to stop Odin from lecturing

me. Sometimes the only thing keeping Odin from destroying several worlds is his joy at hearing himself talk.

'And yet you defied my orders and chose the wrong man.'

I chose, yes. I chose right.

'I cast the runes,' I said, telling Odin what he already knew, to repay him in kind. 'I saw their futures and their pasts. I made my judgment as my conscience led me. If you don't want my runelore and my wisdom, you don't want me. Fine. I am gone. I am not your problem any more, Baleworker. Leave me be.'

Odin stepped closer and put his hand on my shoulder. He smelled, faintly, of mead and warm bread. I smelled of fetid river water.

'*Your* runelore, Brynhild? Was it you, then, who hung by the neck from the world-tree for nine days, to learn wisdom? You disobeyed me outright, knowing what the punishment would be.'

It was Odin himself who'd taught me to use my judgement, to weigh the consequences of every human life. I'd disobeyed him by following the lessons he'd once taught me. But whether those lessons had been insincere, or whether I simply couldn't understand the mind of a god, what I understood and what Odin wanted were two different things.

'So I did,' I said. 'The punishment is done, Trembler. Leave me to it.'

'To what?' he asked. 'What will you do now?'

I stayed silent. I would be a Valkyrie, as I had been trained to be. I'd use my wisdom to find those who deserved protection, and I'd use the strength of my arm to defend them. The only difference would be that I'd do it without any comrades or allies. But that was fine. I didn't need anyone, I told myself. If I was to be exiled, then let me be alone.

'Go west,' Odin said at last, when I didn't give him an answer. He pointed to one side of the fork in the road. It was wider than the other path, sun-dappled, broken only by broad, mossy rocks. 'Three days' walk to a village that came through a plague not long ago. There are rich estates sitting empty because their owners died. Life there would be easy.'

'I don't need anything to be easy.'

'The easier it is to fill your belly, the more good work you can do. The head man there is a great bully who terrorizes the village. You would be their protector and their lady. It would be a chance for glory.'

'You give contrary advice, Dangler.' I eyed the other path, which rose along a pine-topped slope carpeted in golden needles. 'What lies to the east?'

'Death and politics.'

Even now, he was trying to take my choices from me. Of course I realized that Odin might have been steering me east by seeming to steer me west. But if I went west, I would bear his advice with me like an evil charm. It didn't take me long to make up my mind.

'I'll go east, Son of a Bitch,' I said, knowing that Odin was already gone.

For you, my love, gods are dead or distant. Your mother taught you to worship Christ's father, the god of the Jews, but you have never met the father or the son, have you? Nor have you met the gods who preside over the other altars in Vormatia, and you thought the gods of the Franks, Goths, and Romans who clung to their old faiths were as distant as your own.

It's true that most who ask for Odin's help have never heard a reply. He takes what he wants, and people follow him because he is powerful, not because he is particularly inclined to help. He is the master of rune magic, and he is owed many favours. He can move between worlds, and he claims territory in more than one. Is that what makes a god a god?

There was certainly a time – a very long time – when I thought of Odin in much the same way you think of Christ, I think. I thought he cared about my welfare, and the welfare of all his followers. And then I thought, *My god is a wild god, and not easily understood. Yes, one of his names is Deceiver, but he deceives to teach us. When his choices seem strange to us, the failure is in our understanding, not in his choices. He can see the future. Nothing he does can be without a greater purpose.*

Now I know a god can go wrong, and he can go very far wrong indeed.

The day I fell to Midgard, I still could not see all that Odin had become. But I was angry at him all the same. Or perhaps angry is the wrong word; it was something like a leaving a lover. I had not lost my faith; my faith had abandoned me, and some part of my spirit longed for it to return. How I wanted to be that girl again, the one who believed Odin was the source of light and love. But that girl had served him to the best of her ability, and Odin judged that service worthless. Fine, then. I would walk alone, for the rest of my mortal days. What choice did I have? None at all.

I walked hard for a long time after meeting Odin, until the sun was at my back, creek water to drink and smoked fish to eat.

Once, I saw the signs of a boar in the mud and gripped the spear I'd been treating as a walking stick. My comrades and I used to hunt boar in Valhalla: three would go to the right, three to the left, and I would ride down the middle, and harry the beast, until at last it would turn, and I would struggle with it, tusk against spear, and I would win. And everyone would eat: all the Valkyries and the gods and dead warriors. We'd all drink beer and eat boar meat. At sunrise, those very boars would rise again, whole, ready to give sport and give their meat again. There was very little distinction between Odin's miracles and Odin's punishments.

Whenever the newly dead arrived, they would watch the skies of Valhalla lit with Odin's green sky-fires and marvel at how deserving they must have been. After some time – hundreds of years, in the worst cases – they began to understand that they could never leave. That unlike the

Valkyries, who can move between worlds as gods can, the dead would never see the stars of Midgard again. They began to see the morning resurrection of the boars they'd killed the day before not as a miracle but as a sickening reminder of the permanent impermanence of their state. They grew reckless at this stage: breaking the drinking horns, cursing Odin, fighting each other without stopping for breath until they fell down dead and were resurrected themselves. Or they watched the departing Valkyries wistfully, wishing that they too could visit Midgard, if only for the space of a battle.

And then, after a very long time, they drew inward. They kept themselves company and made themselves better company. Their faces grew wise, and their limbs grew strong as they walked the green mountain meadows and tended the animals.

In recent years, some of the recently dead had taken to asking the Valkyries whether Valhalla was a reward or a punishment, a heaven or a hell. We didn't have any answers for them. It was an afterlife, one of many. It was where we took the warriors who wished it and deserved it. The warriors who wished elsewise, who believed in jealous gods, we did not take. Those who deserved some other task – a family to care for, a kingdom to rule, a lover to comfort – we let live, until their day would come, and they would be taken to Valhalla, or to Folkvang, or to Helheim.

But another thing had changed in recent years. Odin had taken to guiding our decisions about which warriors deserved Valhalla, and his reasons were unfathomable. Some of my sisters, especially the younger ones who didn't remember how it used to be, said that of course Odin, with his knowledge of the future, would have a deeper understanding of a warrior's destiny than we who were born mere mortal girls. I tried to reassure myself, until the day came when I no longer could.

In Midgard, the things that are dead stay dead, most of the time.

I could have killed that boar alone, but it would have

taken hours, and I would have been tired and, perhaps, wounded. And then I would have found myself with enough meat to feed a hall of warriors. Even if I'd taken the time to smoke it, it would be too much to carry, without a horse.

In the end, I contented myself with netting a scrawny squirrel. I skinned it with my flint and started a fire.

I didn't have the time or inclination to tan the hide, so I set it aside, and sure as sunrise, a crow came calling. She was an old crow; I could see the years in her eye. The two of us sat in silence for a while, the crow pecking and pulling bits of pink flesh off the red squirrel skin. I hunched on a log, watching my meat brown on the spit.

Some day, my Gudrun, I will teach you the language of birds. Some sky-creatures talk in weird poetry, or snatches of song, like oracles. Others speak almost as humans do. Crows are in the latter category.

'Poor meal,' the crow said, after a while. I don't know whether she knew me as a Valkyrie, or whether she was talking to herself. She didn't seem surprised when I answered.

'If I had the help of a hawk or a kestrel, I could have done better for both of us,' I said.

'Hmph. Crows do not talk to hawks. You could.'

'Not any more,' I said, and found my voice raw from the smoke of my small fire. 'I'm in exile. Just a woman, really. I can't fly now.'

'But you still hear birds. Still talk to birds.'

'I learned how to do that. Like the runelore. That, the old Deceiver couldn't take from me.'

A new voice trilled from the trees, a woodlark hidden from sight: 'Foolhardy damsel, hold your tongue! Ratatosk carries news skywards!'

'Asgardwise!' called a quail, from somewhere in the underbrush. 'Odinwise!'

'Thank you for the warning, friends,' I said, and meant it, though I didn't need them to tell me Odin loved to spy. I pointed at the tiny corpse on my spit, a scrawny, desperate, and now dead example of his kind, who had probably never so much as spoken with Ratatosk. 'I suspect Odin's gossip-monger will stay away from a hungry Valkyrie, even one who's no longer a Valkyrie.'

'Where will you go with no wings?' chirped a yellow-hammer, hopping onto the ground near the crow and the skin, but not too near. 'What will you do in Midgard?'

What indeed. I had never had wings; Valkyries fly by the will of Odin alone. 'I suppose I'll find a place to live,' I said. 'Until I die.' The birds just stared at me, so I carried on, more brightly: 'I'm walking east. What lies that way?'

Death and politics, I heard Odin say.

The crow made a rattling noise, tucking her beak into her wing. 'Don't go east. Any way but east.'

I peered at her, wondering whether she was one of Odin's. 'Why not east?'

'Lindworm,' she said.

That I had not expected. We had heard many tales of dragons, basilisks, vipers, and other beasts in the mead hall at Valhalla. There was even a lindworm depicted on a tapestry there: a great scaled serpent, with clawed feet and a head like a dragon's.

'What do you mean?' I asked. 'There's a lindworm to the east?'

'Poisonings!' called the quail. 'Dead hatchlings!'

'Its very breath is poison,' said the yellowhammer.

'It has wasted the land, and the eggs are thin, and the water is death to drink,' the crow explained. 'Everything is black. The humans there are dying. Birds are dying. It is cruel to everything in its path. Don't go that way.'

I took the squirrel, now brown and crispy, off the fire. It burned my fingers but I ignored that, and ate, thinking. Odin had told me once, on one of our walks in the woods in the days when I still counted every moment in his presence as a mark of grace, that Hel would occasionally complain to Odin and Freyja about the hordes of dead that flooded her land with every rampage by a dragon or a lindworm. Surely these ought to be considered battle-deaths, she would argue, but Odin countered that none of them had fought back. (What Freyja said about it, I did not know. I had not met her and did not want to.)

'How far is the lindworm from here?' I asked, at last.

'Two days' flight for me,' said the crow. 'Or a little less. But the lindworm has no wings.'

I wasn't asking how long it would take for the beast to reach me, walking on its four legs or slithering on its belly. I wanted to know how long it would take me to reach it.

And what would I do when I did? I had chosen not to hunt a boar; what made me think I could kill a beast as large and as fearsome as a dragon, alone, with nothing but a sharpened stick? But I wanted a fight. Needed a fight. My chance to prove to Odin, and myself, that exile would not stop me from doing what I knew how to do.

I had no weapons or comrades, but I still had all my knowledge.

We had many ways of increasing the chances that a chosen warrior would be the one to win, the one to live. The only rule was that we couldn't take away a man's chance to fight, to earn glory. But we could help him. We'd fly in the air unseen and bat away arrows. We'd guide swords and shields. And sometimes, when a warrior was weakened by hunger or wounds, or confined by his enemy, we'd visit him days before the fight. We'd carve the thorn-rune on his body and send him to sleep for days at a time. This thorn-sleep was a kind of magic of its own, and a warrior would wake from it hot-blooded and bear-strong. It was one of the ways to make a berserker.

I had no allies but after a few days of thorn-sleep, I'd have no need.

There was no one to watch over me, so I chose my sleeping place carefully. Up on high ground, where an overhanging rock face would keep the rain off me and the fire I'd build to warm my body and frighten any curious predators. I made a long oval out of rocks, the size and shape of a grave. Around it, I made another, slightly bigger oval, and in the space between, I laid hot coals. I drew the fire-runes on each rock with the end of a burned stick, to turn the rocks into food for the fire.

Then I stepped inside and sat on the cold ground. The flames licked up around me.

I hesitated for a moment with the tip of the thorn just pressing into my finger. I had to draw the rune carefully, in a puffy and bloody part of my body.

The backs of my hands were covered in runes already, scars to remind me of my fallen comrades. One finger that held the thorn ended in Eir's rune.

But the rune I'd carve on my fingertip would be for forgetting, to give my body strength enough to fight. I carved the rune deep, and then bound my finger to stop the blood, swearing a little. The bloodwell would close, but it would take days. Days of deep sleep, in which my muscles would knit, my mind would sharpen. When the wound healed, then I would wake, ready to fight the lindworm.

I don't remember falling asleep.

CHAPTER THREE

The Betrothal of Gudrun

If you're going to begin with the monster, let me begin there too. While you were sleeping, my shining Brynhild, just a few days' ride from our city, the lindworm came and destroyed my life.

But that morning, I already thought my life was ending, even though I didn't know anything about the monster yet. I knew that a stranger named Bleda was coming to take me away as his bride. And yes, that felt like the end of everything. Long before dawn on the day I was to be married, I lay awake, planning my final day in my city, with my family.

Final days are never big enough for what they contain, are they? When I can't find something big enough, I crawl inside something small, and take root there, like a worm or a snail. I puff myself up inside it and make it as big as I need it to be.

So, I decided that on this final day in my city, I would determine, I would *judge*, for all time, which fish sauce in Vormatia was the absolute worst. Oh, I know, you'll call me ridiculous. Why fish sauce? Why not fish sauce? I have always been good at unusual things. Useless things, I thought then.

The other thing to understand is how my brother Gunnar and I were in those days, still. He was lighter of spirit than when you knew him. We were so close in age, and had been through so much, we practically shared our thoughts. No one else knew me as well as he did, not even Hagen.

Gunnar, being one year older than me, remembered a little bit about the years before our people came to Vormatia. Or at least he said he did. Before I was born, our people, the Burgundians, slept in tents and spent their days on horseback. Some of our people never lost the taste for open spaces, but most were happy to settle once my father made it possible. He fought the battles that forced the Empire to let us settle just inside its border. The emperor promised us all the lands on the western shore of the Rhine from Mainz to Speyer, with Vormatia in the middle as our capital. Those who didn't want to live in the city were given estates out in the country, still within my father's lands, and he was king, and our lands were safe. The Huns finally left us alone, knowing the Empire protected us. My father even went to a feast at the home of the Hunnish king Octar.

When Octar woke up dead the following morning, the Huns blamed the Burgundians, and the long peace broke.

I never asked my father the truth of how Octar died. If he had a hand in it, he had his reasons. Anyway, I never had the chance to ask him; he died of infection not long after. And when the remaining Hunnish king – they always had two, then – died as well, the Huns and Burgundians both found themselves ruled by young kings, burdened with old grievances.

I knew my brother Gunnar better than anyone, and I knew he could be a good king. But unlike our father, he didn't have old comrades-in-arms among the powerful families. And after years of bad harvests, years of skirmishes at the edges of the kingdom, those families were not eager to fight for him.

So, he met with the new Hunnish kings, the brothers

Attila and Bleda. He apologized for the death of their uncle. And to seal the peace, he agreed to a marriage between his sister and Bleda, the unmarried brother.

It was fine. It was, in fact, my idea. It was what I could do, to keep the kingdom intact and safe.

Still, I hated to leave.

On my last morning in Vormatia, I walked past my brother's guards and pulled the blanket off him. 'We're going to find the worst fish sauce in the city.'

He sat up and rubbed his palms over his hair, which didn't make him look any less like a hedgehog. 'Today?'

'When else? It's my last chance. By tonight I'll be a Hun's wife, riding across the plains and sleeping in tents, and who knows if the Huns even eat fish sauce?'

'Everyone eats fish sauce.'

'But nobody would eat that murky business from Varro's cookshop if they had an option. Come on. We need to solve this definitively. I think Ansila's is the stinkiest, and that one from the cart by the harbour is the strongest, but we need a test.'

Gunnar hung his head dramatically, then looked at me. (He didn't have to lift his head much to do it. I'd been two heads shorter than him for years.) I can see his face now, how it was, then, worried but not yet haggard, still trusting in the possibility of joy. 'I am a king, you know.'

'Meet me in the atrium once you're dressed, and don't dally. I don't have all day.'

I strode past the guards, flipping the purse in my hand by its leather strings, my sandals tapping the tiled floor.

Vormatia is older than the Empire, which is why its streets are all a jumble in every direction. I don't know how the Empire's governor used the great stone square of the Domus. We moved in when my mother was pregnant with me. The western rectangle was the private half, with our family's bedrooms and weapons room at the north. I think my rose garden must have once been an open-air stadium of some kind, or an exercise yard, since it was next to the bathhouses. My mother's workroom may have been for storage in those days.

The eastern half, I expect, has always been much the same: the great banquet hall, the peristyle, the dining rooms, the library, the guest rooms, through the atrium and out into the main street of our city.

As I walked through the Domus, my fingertips skimmed the stone of fluted columns and broad fountain rims, and the cooler stone of walls in shadowed corners. I tried to remember everything while it was still in front of my face. There I grew my rose garden; there I trained with sword and dagger, book and cauldron. That stone palace, and the busy city around it, had been my world.

I stood in the atrium, where water dripped into the little collection pool, and I turned in place, looking at everything.

Gunnar tried to keep a sombre face as he walked towards me, but he couldn't maintain the act.

'The worst fish sauce is clearly the stuff from Ansila's wine bar,' he said as we walked out of the gates of the palace and into the street. 'I don't need confirmation of it. I had confirmation of it for three days after the last time I had it.'

'Then your memory of its taste cannot be trusted. Come on, show some courage. You're the king now!'

The guards watched us go, warily, but didn't follow. We'd been walking the streets of Vormatia since we were children. Besides, we were protected not by guards but by the sworn loyalty of every family. Every man we passed with a dagger at his belt was as good as a guard.

I think we knew even then that the circle of protection was not quite as strong as it had been when our father was alive. Since Gunnar became king, there were some heads of families, out in the villas and farms, who were slow and stingy in paying their respects.

But in the city, we still saw only courtesy in the faces of the people out in the streets that morning: the fishmongers and haulers rolling their empty carts towards the river, the slaves carrying night pots to the sewer, the children sent out to play before breakfast, to get out from under their parents' feet.

Past the old temple of Mars, past the new church, my brother and I walked our city. I knew the map of it by sound and smell and taste. In the southern quarter, the smoke from pottery kilns hung in the air. Brynhild, did you ever meet old Varro, the Roman with jowls and a beady eye? We bought a loaf of bread from him. His sauce was made of mackerel and he didn't leave it out very long – he did a brisk business – and it tasted as if it was still fermenting.

The vendors were still setting out their wares in the market. People chattered in all their various languages: the Goths, Franks, Burgundians, Ethiopians, Greeks, Syrians, some of them intelligible to each other, speaking Latin when they weren't. In the market, we bought a dash of a dark sauce made with anchovies, from the vats in a factory just a little way down the Rhine. It was harsh but interesting.

All things pass away but I remember these things. I hold them like a handful of smooth stones.

Between the barracks and the bathhouse, God, you must remember those smells of the oils and musks, the rich men stepping gingerly over piles of cow and horse droppings from the carts going in and out. The wine shop there – that was Ansila's. It was, in fact, in possession of the stinkiest sauce, but the taste was almost sweet, and rich, and golden.

That left only the harbour stall to compete with old Varro for the title.

The harbour was chaos in the mornings, then, when the city was still open to the world. Wooden docks and piers jutted into the Rhine. Boats come from Mainz in the north, from Speyer in the south. Guards leaned over the parapet of the city's main gate and watched the workers unload jars of olive oil and wine, barrels of eel, perch and shad, bundles of cloth and crates of silver. One boat from the south unloaded small horses, while one from the north brought half a dozen soldiers of the Empire from their nearby border fort, clutching their pay.

Everything smelled of rope and tar. We trotted down the ramp to the pier where an old woman sold roast meat, pies, bread, fruit, and nuts in season. She kept a jar of fish sauce potent enough to burn a hole through a shield. I don't remember her name, if I ever knew it.

But we never did test her sauce against Varro's. She was talking to a boatman as we approached, her hand smoothing the grey hairs at her temple.

I watched my brother change. How I wish you could have known him in those days, Brynhild. Kingliness was not something he put on; rather, it was his nature, and what he shrugged on and off was ease or nonchalance. He shrugged it off now, tossing his bread-end into the dark river and asking the woman if he could help with her troubles.

'My lord,' she said, bowing. 'I've had bad news.'

'I'm sorry to hear it.' He turned to the stranger, a boatman with a scraggy fur over his broad shoulders. 'And are you the bearer of the news?'

'I've just come from Ludgast's people,' the man said.

My brother and I glanced at each other. When my father was alive, Ludgast had come into the city from time to time, out of respect for his old comrade-in-arms, his king. He never pretended to like the settled life, though. He wanted neither soft villa in the country nor warm townhouse in the city. He took his family and his family's family and went north, to the edges of our new kingdom. After our father died, he stopped coming to the city altogether. We hadn't seen him in a council meeting in two years.

'They can't grow any food,' the boatman said, his big jaw moving nervously. 'There's a blight. The winter crops have withered, and they fear to start the spring planting, seeing the state of the land. The wild plants are dying too. It's some sort of witchcraft.'

As the children of a witch, Gunnar and I knew full well what witchcraft can do, but we also knew that many things are called witchcraft that are not.

'Will there be help for them?' the old woman asked. 'My sister's children are there.'

My brother nodded. 'Thank you for bringing this news,' he said to the boatman. 'I will send a rider north to Ludgast to learn more about this. Of course, they will have whatever help they need, and they are welcome within the city walls, should they choose.'

As we walked back to the Domus, I said nothing. I could feel how hard my brother was thinking.

CHAPTER FOUR

Gudrun Outside the Gates

My brother and I never did finish our conversation about the fish sauce. I spent what I thought was my last morning with Heva, a woman my family had enslaved in a battle before my birth. Like too many things in my life, I didn't question it.

By noon, I was dressed for my wedding. My hair was coiled and bound, my skin perfumed with an oil of marjoram, rose, styrax, and myrrh. I can still smell that perfume, although it's been years since I had anything to smell but my potions and brews and smoke on the wind. It was all I had to carry with me of my rose garden.

The garden was a bit of a consolation prize, you might say. From the time we were small, my mother tried to teach Gunnar and me to do the same sort of magic she could do. She told us magic was a gift from God, like the yeast in the bread and beer, or the clay under the earth that the potters turned into the wealth of our city. Earth, air, and water were all under her command, to some extent, although she was most powerful with water, especially river water. I didn't understand why, until later.

Gunnar gave up right away. He had no magical ability at

all – for reasons I was to come to understand. But maybe that's too simple. His magic was in the glint of his eye, his smile, his sword arm. It didn't bother him that he wasn't a witch. He wanted to be a king.

As for me, though, the more I tried to work my will on the elements, the clumsier the results. One day, when I was about seven years old, I tried to split a stone and succeeded only in giving myself a headache. My mother laid a cool cloth on my forehead, a cloth woven on her loom and dipped in Rhine water, and the headache went away.

'You do have your own skills, you know,' she said. 'They work a little differently from mine, that's all.'

'Ha! I have no skills at all.'

'Do you think I haven't heard you pleading under your breath with the buckets of water and bits of wood I give you for practice? And sometimes you manage to make the spells work. Or at least, nearly work.' She smiled kindly.

'Will I be able to do what you do, one day?'

She pursed her lips. 'I don't know. Maybe you won't ever learn to command the elements the way I do. But that's because your talent is in . . . something else. Diplomacy, perhaps.'

'Diplomacy!' I had listened to the Romans and Franks and Goths who came to eat with Father, but never imagined myself having such conversations. Father always grumbled afterwards.

'Of a sort. If you can negotiate with a bucket of water, you can coax a plant to grow. Softer magics, and subtler ones. Perhaps. Let's find out.'

She was right, and that's how the open space in the private half of the Domus, with its few old statues, came to be my garden. I loved the garden from the first. I challenged myself to grow impossibilities and surprises there: roses that hung upside-down from trellises. Roses in colours that no one could dream. By the time I grew to my full height, the garden was already called mine.

It was the last place I visited before the arrival of my bridegroom, on that chilly, dull day. The year was still too young for blooms. The ground smelled of earthworms and mulch. But there was some green already creeping between the flagstones and pushing through the old growth. One stone wall was nearly invisible behind thick rambling vines.

'I planted those dog roses soon after we arrived here, when you were still a child,' said my mother, behind me. 'How I struggled with them, until you learned how to whisper to them.'

I turned. 'And you'll tend them after I've gone.' A request.

My mother nodded, her mouth grim. Auda, queen of the Burgundians, was not yet fifty, and her hair fell in honey-coloured curls from the pinned mound on her head. How jealous I used to be of those curls when I was a child: my own straight, black hair seemed uninteresting and heavy. But I learned to bear the weight. On my wedding day, it hung down to my knees in two coils, wrapped in a golden snake on either side.

My mother tucked a vine into its lattice, gently. 'I want you to know, Gudrun, that there will always be a place for you inside these walls.'

She wasn't often wrong, but she was wrong about that, although neither of us knew why, then. I bowed my head, saying nothing, because on that day of all days I didn't want to contradict her. Only my absence, I thought, ensured that those walls would stand. My brother needed a few years of peace, and I intended to give that time to him.

'I've never seen a bride look finer,' my mother said. 'But I have one more gift for you.'

Between two fingers she held a single ring that I had never seen: plain gold. My mother put her lips to it and whispered, just barely loud enough for me to hear: 'Drip, drop, drink.' The ring suddenly looked molten: wet and gleaming, and some of its gold collected at the bottom like dew, and dripped to the ground.

A bit of weedy thyme on the path beneath sizzled, shrivelled into brown death.

'Poison,' my mother said, brightly. 'If your new husband turns against you, turns against *us*, a little of this in his drink will take care of him, and then you come home to us. It doesn't even look like a poison-ring because it's simple gold. A neat trick, isn't it? Three drops to make him sick. Twelve drops to dispatch him.'

I hesitated before I took it. Why? Maybe I was afraid it would be discovered. Maybe I was afraid, then, of the person I'd have to be to use it. But I knew better than to refuse my mother's gifts.

'I hope my husband will not require poisoning,' I said with a wry smile.

'Perhaps you'll even like him! I've heard he's handsome.'

'Bah, no man is handsome enough for me. Their beards hurt my face.'

'Well then,' came my brother's voice from the columns at the garden's entrance, 'it's a good thing I was shaved this morning.'

Gunnar stepped into the garden. His mail caught the weak sunlight. He had dressed for diplomacy or for battle – for men it is one and the same; I suppose for women it is too, but the other way around, for most of us. No, not for you, Brynhild: you don't ever dress for diplomacy. You wear your armour like skin and your skin like armour, brazen and bright.

Sometimes my brother was armoured and sometimes he wasn't. That morning, I think, was the last time I saw that old easy grin of his.

'Is it time already, Gunnar?' I smiled to let him know I was not afraid.

There was a new line between his eyebrows, as sharp as an axe-wound. I hadn't noticed it before.

'You look glorious,' he said. 'Turn and let me see.'

When I stopped spinning, Gunnar was holding two small

iron keys between his thumb and forefinger. Each key had a leather strap.

'These are to the chests you'll take with you,' he said. 'One of clothing and one of treasure. Soon you'll have an entire household's keys on your belt, but these will be the first.'

I lifted my arms so that Gunnar could tie the keys onto my belt.

'Not too heavy?' he asked.

'Not heavy at all,' I said, with what I hoped was the smile of a warrior.

'I don't know how to rule without you, Gudrun,' he said. 'Who will tell me when I'm wrong?'

'Assume you're always wrong and you'll be fine.'

He smiled sadly. 'I won't be fine.'

I wanted to open up everything I was keeping shut, and shout at him: *I'm the one who's leaving! You'll have Mother and Volker and Hagen and Heva and a whole city full of people you know. I'll be all alone among strangers.*

But I didn't say it, because I knew then he would say, *You don't have to go. We'll tell them the arrangement is off.*

I couldn't bear to have to make the decision to leave all over again. It nearly broke me the first time.

So, I kept myself closed, and I said, 'You'll simply have to take yourself a wife, brother.'

He lifted an eyebrow at that, and said, 'God help us.'

Because you only knew Volker in sadder days, I'll tell you what he used to be like. He was relentlessly cheerful then too, but he wasn't desperate about it yet. He hadn't made optimism his religion. Even then, though, he was in the habit of talking to God, although I seldom saw him at mass. Sometimes I thought all his songs were conversations with God, despite the fact he looked at everyone when he sang the war songs, and at Hagen when he sang the love songs.

I can still see the two of them standing in the courtyard

outside the Domus, waiting to escort me. Volker, with his floppy dark hair half-covering his face, his arms crossed like a restless teenager. Hagen, a head taller and broader, his golden skin and curly bronze beard a contrast to Volker in every way.

You know that Hagen was raised with Gunnar and me, as our foster-brother, but I don't know whether you know that he is our cousin, too. My father's father travelled with the Empire's army when he was young and took a Syrian wife. As these were my grandparents, they were also Hagen's, and the Syrian side was evident in him – he even followed a Syrian Christian rite, while Gunnar and I followed the teachings of Arius, as we'd been taught by our mother. I never knew my uncle and aunt, Hagen's parents; they died when we were young.

'You look beautiful in this light,' Volker said as I stepped out in my bridal finery.

'It's a grey day,' I answered him.

'Indeed. The best sort of light for lovers, and painters, and for exchanges of goods,' he said, smiling to show he was teasing.

Hagen elbowed him in the ribs. Hagen, my dear friend, never felt any need to pretend to be cheerful, and his face showed exactly what he thought of the fact that I was leaving Vormatia to go and live with the Huns. He knew it was necessary. But he didn't like it any more than I did.

Three steps up to the block and I gathered my skirts to mount a mare as heavily bedecked as I was: Clotilde. I suppose she is long dead now. Even in that cloudy day we glittered: gold and lapis and garnet everywhere. My eyes watered but I couldn't be seen wiping them, so I blinked violently.

Volker, Hagen, and the rest of my brother's guard arranged themselves behind us as we rode out into the city. The streets were full of people, and they cheered when they saw me, although I'd walked those same streets in quieter hours just that morning. They'd come to bid me goodbye.

Clotilde lurched forward, her ears twitching. She and I had never much liked each other since the day I'd stood on her back to prove to Gunnar that I could pick an apple that way, but we respected each other. She was a good horse for this sort of business: she knew how to look disdainful.

I kept her steady the same way I kept myself steady: I sat tall. We rode out through the wooden city gate built into the old walls, walls built long before we Burgundians came west across the Rhine. We rode past the harbour where Gunnar and I had been that morning, although I didn't see the old woman in the crowd. Our horses beat the stone bridge like a drum, all the way over the wide dark Rhine. My parents built that bridge, a few years after they burned the old one down.

Beyond the cluster of river-houses at the far end of the bridge was the open plain, with a few horse-tracks across it, leading to guardtowers on the Empire's frontier.

The Huns were already there, on the plain, waiting for us. Several dozen mounted men and women, arrayed in a horse-shoe shape. Three times as many as the Burgundian guard at our backs, but then, they were travelling, and we were at home. Behind the strangers were three tents: two small blue ones on either side, and in the middle, a long pavilion covered in felt dyed in whorling patterns of blue and white. I assumed it was for the two brother-kings. Soon I'd be in that tent myself, I imagined.

I peered at the most richly dressed mounted men, wondering which one was my husband.

As if he knew my thoughts (which he probably did), Gunnar nodded at one of the men, saying in Latin, 'You are welcome here, Bleda.'

Bleda had bright eyes and a sharp nose. Like many of his comrades, he wore a pointed horsehide hat with a broad fur brim. It was a nice enough face, with the trace of a smile. Compared to his brother, Bleda was slim in his shoulders, and he slouched a little on his horse. He looked more like a scholar than a soldier, despite the gleaming mail that bit into the leather beneath it.

Then my brother addressed the bigger man on the bigger horse. 'You are welcome, Attila. All of you are welcome.'

Some of Attila's retinue were Romans, some were Goths, some were Huns, and some were from farther lands. It took a keen eye to see the differences: the brooches that clasped the cloaks, the shape of the hats, the armour and weapons. Some were pale and some were dark.

One of the dark-skinned men was no taller than a child of six, although by his face, serious and cragged, he was well into middle age. That was Zerco, but I didn't know his name then.

Bleda said, 'Let us have peace from this day on. Is this my bride?'

He had a voice as deep as Rhine water. Although I was only marrying him out of duty, I thought that maybe he wouldn't be so bad. I bowed my head. I may even have blushed. I was supposed to blush.

'I am Bleda, and this is my brother, Attila.' He turned and gestured, and Attila brought his horse up alongside, so close that the tall, square saddles were nearly scraping each other. Attila was thicker and taller, and smirking of course, but I would have known by their faces that they were brothers. They were both handsome, with sun-brown skin and strong cheekbones. Attila was broader in the face as well as the chest. A neatly trimmed beard and moustache framed a smile that pulled back to show his top teeth.

'How beautiful you look, Gudrun,' Attila said. 'It is a pity you do not marry today. Or at least, you may have to choose another bridegroom.'

Very quickly, three things happened.

Bleda turned sharply to look at his brother, and opened his mouth.

Zerco drew his sword half out of its sheath, uncertainly, and walked his horse forward.

Attila wrapped his right arm around his brother's shoulders, and in his left, a blade flashed.

I screamed, and every horse flinched, so many riders' hands jumping in the reins, not knowing what to do. Several Hunnish horse-archers, at the edges of their assembly, nocked their bows. Zerco stopped with his hand on his sword, still half drawn. Whatever action he might have taken came too late.

Bleda slumped over, blood pouring from his throat, and his distressed horse stepped forward, a few dancing steps, then stopped uncertainly.

Attila brandished his blade, and turned from side to side, as if looking for any sign of dissent among the horsemen and horsewomen behind him. No one moved or said a word. I wondered, later, whether any of them knew what he had planned. At the time, I could barely see clearly.

I felt Gunnar bring his horse up close beside me.

'My brother is dead!' Attila shouted. 'I am the king. I alone. And I declare the peace agreement void.' He paused and turned a little. 'Do you object, Zerco?'

Everyone looked at the small dark man, hunched on his horse, hand on hilt, his gaze on Attila.

'The peace can hold, Attila!' Zerco cried, hoarsely. 'It could be amended. Bleda—'

'Bleda was a traitor who would not listen to wise counsel!' Attila shrieked. 'We are rid of him now, and I am sole ruler of the Huns. Between me and this rabble there is no arrangement.'

'This is dishonourable!' Hagen growled, behind my right shoulder.

My brother and I had not yet said anything. There was a weird hiss on the breeze, some artefact, I thought, of the way the wind curled around the city walls.

'We have seen what my brother would have done,' Attila carried on. 'Made common cause with those who killed our uncle. These leeches who've attached themselves to an empire because they lack the balls to create their own.'

At that, at last, Gunnar spoke. 'This is unforgivable, Attila.' I could hear the fear in his voice, but I knew him well. 'To murder a brother. To break the peace he forged.'

Attila rode closer, his horse thundering towards them. Doughty Clotilde stood her ground, and I looked my bride-groom's murderer in the face. Though he was not an extraordinarily tall man, he was strong and well-armoured, and he rode a large horse, and the overall impression was exactly as intimidating as he wanted it to be.

'I don't expect forgiveness from the dead,' he said, for our ears only. 'From him, or from you.'

The hiss on the air grew louder and suddenly all the horses were screaming and prancing.

The long blue and white tent in the middle, behind the Huns, rose into the air, as if a sudden breeze had lifted it from below. But it was not a breeze, of course.

It was the lindworm.

CHAPTER FIVE

Gudrun and Fafnir

We never talked much about Fafnir, you and I. Maybe I assumed the lindworm wasn't a subject you wanted to talk about; maybe I saw his shadow flickering in your eyes. Maybe because of what happened with Gunnar, afterwards. Maybe I felt that my own tale was smaller than yours; all I did was manage to save myself, really. I am the sort of person who needs to talk about the things that have hurt me, but I had Hagen for that, and you and I were busy with other things.

What I remember most about the lindworm was that terrible iron helm he wore. I see it in dreams: that sharp snout with the ring through it, the high crest with two horns curling above. When he shook himself loose, earth fell off the helm in broad curtains. The blue and white felt of the tent fell to his shoulders like a cape, for a moment, and then fluttered to the ground.

We all stood rooted: me, Gunnar, the men of the guard, the Huns, Romans, and Goths. I stared at the lindworm's body: thick and serpentine, with shiny skin that looked as if it had been slowly, slowly burned. Fafnir must have been as long as a house, wouldn't you say? I remember his long thin tail whipped as if of its own will.

He reared and showed his two front arms. They were almost like the arms of a man, I thought.

The horses were prancing and snorting. Someone shouted – I think it was Attila, giving a command – and the Huns and Romans scattered to either side, leaving no one between the lindworm and my people. I wanted to wheel my horse and ride back to the city, to lead my people back to whatever safety we could find, but all my limbs were heavy and I couldn't seem to do it.

Beneath that awful helm, Fafnir's jaw was long and pointed, the skin stretched over bone. Out of his mouth seeped something like smoke: a brownish vapour, the colour of old rust. It was heavier than air; it settled like mist on a lake, rolling towards us.

Horses screamed and crumpled, spilling their riders. The three men closest to Fafnir – Dancwart, Eckart, and Sinold the cup-bearer – all fell, slumping off their horses, choking and holding their throats, their skin burned. They were good men, all of them, and Eckart and Dancwart left behind wives and children. I'm sorry you never had a chance to meet them.

I don't know what happened with Volker, whether he rode towards the beast – it would have been like him – or whether his horse simply bolted. I heard him scream. Somehow, I recognized his voice in it – that voice that used to do impressions of all the old warriors behind their backs, that voice that sang so brightly in our halls. His horse spilled him right into that rusty fog. He wrapped his cloak around his head and I saw his fingers scrabbling, ballooned up in great pale blisters, thick as sausages.

At that, of course, Hagen was down on the ground, pulling his beloved Volker back, out of the cloud of poison.

The lindworm laughed.

It was a strangely human sound, and something about it shocked me into action. I didn't know what Fafnir was, then. I didn't even know he had a name.

'Ride!' I screamed, the reins quivering in my arms. My voice hardly made a sound and I felt both far too heavy and weightless in the saddle. Clotilde, stubborn but wise, wouldn't turn. She wouldn't run. She took a few small steps backwards, her ears flicking. That took me behind most of the men, but it was as far as my horse would go.

The brown fog rolled closer to the horses, rose around their knees, and they whinnied in pain.

I'll never forget the expressions on all the men's faces, as they stared at that horrible monster. Each expression was painfully private, as if I were watching them in some moment they expected no one to see. All of them as still as statues. My brother's loyal guard. Final days are impossible to contain but moments endure in the memory.

And then my eyes blurred and I started to cough. I held my beautiful cloak over my mouth, although it didn't keep out the smell, both foul and metallic.

I imagined it was rising around me, burning me. But it didn't blister me the way it did Volker. When the poison-breath rose around me, it would burn me away altogether, I thought. My outward shell of bright clothing and bright smiles would char to dust and all that would be left of me would be nothing. An empty saddle.

I knew this would happen the way I knew my own name. I knew it so thoroughly that I also knew there was no point in trying to stop it, in trying to escape. I could see my future and it was a moment of revelation, of an illusion punctured. What was I? Where was I?

Nothing and nowhere.

I heard the words in my mind, in a voice not my own. I know now that voice must have been Fafnir's.

Then I saw my brother riding towards the lindworm, brandishing his sword. My throat closed but I was able to blink my vision clear at last. I still don't know what Gunnar intended to do. At first, I thought he meant to kill the beast outright, and maybe that's what he thought too. For some reason, Gunnar kept riding, right past Fafnir, due east, away from us, away from Fafnir, away from Vormatia. His scream tore on the wind like a tattered standard, and that was the last we heard or saw of him that day.

Fafnir turned his head, to follow the path of the king. Maybe that's what Gunnar intended; it's what I pretended to assume he intended, later. If he thought Fafnir would follow him, though, he was wrong. Fafnir only shifted to watch him go. But he never stopped breathing that awful poison, which spread to new places as Fafnir turned to watch Gunnar. The poison rolled right over some of the Huns, who were still on their horses, off to one side. They screamed too, and some fell off their horses, trudging through the vapour as if it were tar.

I don't think Fafnir intended to kill any Huns, but I doubt he cared that he had.

I couldn't see anyone but the lindworm in that swamp of foul air. It settled in thick clouds, and little flames popped into life here and there like marsh lights.

My head ached and I knew if I coughed one more time, I'd vomit. With Fafnir's attention turned away from me, I thought, maybe I can move. Maybe I can make my horse move.

So I screamed: 'To me! Burgundians, to me!'

And Clotilde, to her credit, decided that was a dignified reason to run. She clicked and whinnied some message of her own to her comrades as we circled and rode towards the bridge. Fafnir was still close by; if Gunnar had intended to draw him away, he'd failed. But at least the monster was distracted, for a moment, which might be long enough to get back across the Rhine.

But what then? Would the lindworm follow us into the city, where the children and the old people would succumb to its poison and drop in the streets? I wept as I rode, praying to all the many gods that have ever been worshipped in my city. I probably prayed to your Odin, for all the good it did me, but to be fair, no other god helped us that day either.

But there was one answer to my prayers: my mother. Auda, queen of the Burgundians, stood alone on my father's triumphal stone arch at the far end of the bridge. She lifted her hands.

She lifted the Rhine.

As we rode, the river rose behind us, swamping the bridge, roaring, frothing. It made a sound like the death of mountains.

We barely made it across in time – poor injured Volker was slung across Hagen's pommel – but as the great oak doors closed behind us, we slid off our horses and scrambled to the walls.

The lindworm was still on the far side of the Rhine, the river roaring between us. For the moment we were safe. We had no idea then what had happened to the Huns, or to my brother. Whatever we each imagined, we kept to ourselves.

My brother didn't come home that day, or the day after. We looked for his body on the far side of the river, but he wasn't there. The only bodies were of Dancwart, Eckert, Sinold, and Bleda, and there were also four dead Huns whose names we didn't know.

We sent out riders in all directions. The river calmed down eventually, but the bridge was damaged, its stones shifting and cracked – just as you saw it, when you came to the city later. I posted a ferryman on the far side of the Rhine to watch for Gunnar, to bring him back to us, like a Charon in reverse.

We buried our own dead and the dead Huns in the cemetery outside the city walls. I didn't weep at my bridegroom's grave. I hadn't even known him, but I took his death personally, nonetheless. I took it all personally.

There were no weapons and very little jewellery left on the bodies. Scavengers might have visited them before our people did, but it was hard to imagine anyone wandering into that befouled land. Hagen said the lindworm probably took the spoils himself; after all, we had seen bronze rings on its arms and that terrible helm on his head, the red-stoned ring through his nose.

My mother grieved in her room. She'd done the same thing after my father died, her keening drifting through the stone walls of the Domus. I remember sitting perfectly still on one of those walls with an imperial helmet on my lap, a souvenir my father had given me. Looking down at that helmet and listening to my mother's wails, until Gunnar came to sit beside me. After a few minutes, he asked me why the helmet had a red coxcomb on it, and I started making up explanations, and the despair lifted a little. Auda did come out soon after, her eyes dry. There was a weird kind of loneliness in my mother all her life; it probably came of her command of wind and water, metal and stone. Something like that must tear at the mind. All I knew was that she needed to be alone. Unlike the days she spent mourning for my father, this time I didn't have Gunnar with me to weather it. I was without my brother and the city was without its king.

Still, Hagen was at my side. Hagen could have taken the crown then, had he wanted it. He was as good as a brother to me and Gunnar, raised in the Domus, and respected as a warrior. Maybe it would have been better if he had. Maybe we could have avoided everything that came later. But it's pointless to speculate. The fact was, he didn't want the crown, and I don't think I could have convinced him to take it, not if I'd begged him on my knees.

Besides, he was worried about Volker, who was feverish, drifting in and out of bad dreams. I made whatever potions and salves I could to heal the burns, but the lindworm spoke to Volker, I think. The poison had got into him, into his mind.

We put Volker into the room he shared with Hagen, in the family wing of the Domus. It had been Hagen's room all through his childhood. When he fell in love with the bard on a campaign to the north for my father, Volker's lute and sword took their places by his bed. Now, Volker lay in that bed with a poultice on his throat and hands, a cloth over his eyes, and the shutters closed.

Hagen may have been glad we had politics to discuss; it was something he could do. He and I sat together with a flagon of wine and a guttering candle to scheme and plot. We didn't have much time. The Burgundians had always chosen their kings, usually from the sons and nephews of kings but sometimes not. Gunnar's election had not been a certainty, and so many families had been holding back in the first months of his rule, waiting to see whether he'd keep the peace with the Huns, whether he'd keep the favour of the Empire, whether he'd fall to some challenger. Such a challenger hadn't appeared, but one certainly would now. We didn't know where Gunnar was, but we knew he was not in Vormatia, so my family's days in the Domus were numbered.

'Ludgast will see the kingship as his due,' Hagen said, tapping his cup. 'But maybe he won't want the hassle of dealing with the bishop and the patricians and the merchants and the soldiers. He's happy in his—'

'Shit. Ludgast!' I clapped my forehead. 'We had word, the day that – there were rumours of a terrible blight on his people's crops. I don't suppose Gunnar had the chance to send a rider. Not that it matters, now. I think we can guess what caused the blight.'

Hagen looked thoughtful. 'If the lindworm blighted his lands, Ludgast might decide that city life is not so bad.'

'But the city wouldn't take easily to him. My father was the sort of man who could play both the hardened wanderer and the clever politician. Ludgast isn't. He's just a wanderer, just a warrior, nothing else. He's got no interest in governing a city of many nations, and certainly no interest in bowing and scraping to the Empire. He'd have half of Vormatia up in arms against the Burgundians within a year, and our people would be sent out, homeless again.'

'There's always Snot-Nose, I suppose,' Hagen said, his mouth showing his distaste for the grandson of another of my father's old companions.

I laughed. 'Come now, Lothar is old enough to be king. And he's smooth enough to play the Empire like a lyre. But Ludgast's people won't call Lothar king. He speaks nothing but Latin and dresses like a Roman. And besides—'

Hagen finished my thought. 'And besides, he'd never be able to defend the city against the Huns, when they return. Which they will.'

I wasn't so sure. 'He's very clever.'

'Our people won't fight for him.'

'What about one of my brother's companions?' I asked. I didn't say, *and then if my brother returns, he can take up the crown again, as though he'd only asked a friend to hold it for him.* It was silly to hope that my brother would return. But I did hope it.

Hagen shook his head. 'Don't ask me to do it because you know I would rather die than be king. Volker – well, Volker will live, the healers say, but he won't hold a sword for some time yet. Besides, Volker's a bard.'

'And a bard can't be king?' I teased.

Hagen gave me a scheming look. 'The people might accept a queen, given the circumstances.'

'My mother won't come out of her room.'

'I wasn't thinking of your mother.'

I snorted, then shook my head. Of course, I'd had the thought already. It was creeping up the back of my neck.

Burgundian law is clear on the matter of inheritance: in the absence of living sons, a daughter inherits everything from her parents. But while the crown tends to pass within families – within my family, for the last few generations – the final word is always the people's. The king – or queen – is whoever can command the confidence of the people, for as long as he or she can command it.

But what could I command? I was a woman of small

talents, I told myself. I could still hear my mother's words, from years before: *I don't think you will ever learn to command. But that's because your talent is in . . . something else. Diplomacy, perhaps.* What could I do? I had a rose garden, and I knew where to find fish sauce and the names of every pet cat and how to win at knucklebones. Small things. Diplomacy was too big a word for it. I had tried to use diplomacy to help my family; I'd offered myself up in a marriage treaty. And I'd failed even at that.

'As you said, our people follow fighters,' I said, more bitterly than I meant to. 'I've barely spoken in council meetings. They might accept a queen, but would they accept me? Be honest, Hagen. You and I both know that I haven't prepared for this.'

'You've been taught by a witch, and you can wield a sword and spear – haven't we practised together many times?' He sounded sterner than I expected, but maybe it was the beard. The beard, you know, had that effect. 'You know this city better than anyone. You know how to keep the people fed and healthy and how to keep the walls standing. That's what Vormatia needs now. The Huns could return any time. We don't have time for politics. We need to get the grain stores full and the weapons sharp. You can do that, with me to help you.'

I did love my city, and all its people. Even in the midst of that grief and horror, some part of me was relieved to be still among them. I wanted to hear them gossip in all their languages, and laugh with their children, and celebrate their beautiful things.

'But Ludgast and Lothar will challenge me,' I said. 'They won't accept it, even if the people do. This is their chance, and they both know it.'

'Let them try,' Hagen said, spreading his hands. 'There's nothing we can do about it. And I'm not so sure they'd succeed.'

I shook my head. 'I don't have your faith.'

'In yourself, or in the people?'

'In anything.' I traced lines on the table with my finger, runes with no names. 'If one of them married me, then he'd be set. Everyone would acclaim him king. And they're both unmarried.'

I couldn't see through the shadows over Hagen's eyes.

'And if Gunnar came back then—'

I waved my hand. 'Don't worry, I'm not going to marry either of them. Even if Gunnar – even if we knew he was dead, I wouldn't do it. I don't think either of them would be a good king. But . . . The possibility would be too tempting for either of them to ignore. If they had to compete for me, it would occupy them for a while. And that would give *us* time.'

He took my hand on the table, in a brotherly way.

'It's a risk. A day will come when you have to tell them both they can't have you, and then they'll challenge you.'

'I know. All we can hope is that by then Gunnar's come home.'

'Or that if he hasn't,' Hagen said, 'by then you'll have made yourself queen in fact, and we can make you queen in name, whether Ludgast and Lothar like it or not.'

This seemed impossible to me, but I didn't contradict him. There was enough to worry about in the present without looking too far into the future. With God only knew how many lands blighted by the lindworm, I would need to make sure of the city's supply of grain. The old families on their country estates would be worried. The garrison would need to be fed, and the soldiers on the nearby frontier kept as allies.

As soon as my mother was able to give her blessing, I would send a messenger to Ravenna, to Galla Placidia, regent of the western Empire. Diplomacy, again. Nothing was possible without the Empire's approval, tacit or otherwise. Inside the city, the wealthy families would be an asset to me, if I kept them from panicking. The bishop could help me with that, although I didn't like him much.

'When Mother's well enough, we'll consult her on all this,' I said, cautiously.

'Good, then it's settled,' said Hagen. 'And you know that if they do challenge you, I'll be your champion.'

I stood up, took his curly head in my hands, and kissed his forehead.

CHAPTER SIX

Brynhild and Sigurd

If I had known Fafnir was killing people – your people – while I slept, perhaps I would have fought him there and then, unfortified. In all honesty, I probably would have died. Fafnir was too strong for me without my magic, and possibly too strong for me alone no matter how much thorn-sleep I hoarded up beforehand.

So, we come to Sigurd, and how he woke me when I wasn't ready.

The first thing I became aware of was a man's hands on my shoulders, shaking me out of a dream I will not recount. My eyes were still heavy with thorn-sleep, which is not an ordinary sort of sleep.

The tip of his sword at my throat forced my eyes open, as I scrabbled for him with hands that felt boneless.

I heard the rip down the front of my body; felt my mail shirt opening to the cold. Before I'd even understood what he had done, I roared up to my knees and bowled him over, my hand pressing his neck down to the ground and the rest of him following, and then I realized that my mail was cut in half, swinging free. The hammer-weaving that had saved my life hundreds of times. It had turned away arrows and spears and falchions and axes. I'd scrubbed every ring with sand, but I had never had to mend it. Since the day Svafa gave it to me and sent me into my first real battle, the day my training ended and I became a woman grown and a Valkyrie indeed, this shining shirt had never failed me.

Somehow, this stranger had sliced it in two, which should have been impossible. That was shock enough to loosen my already uncertain grip on his thick neck, and he pushed me off him. He'd dropped his sword, but he was reaching for a knife at his waist.

'What the hell do you think you're doing?' I asked. I don't know what language I said it in; possibly the language of my childhood. In any event, it was not a language he spoke. His eyes only widened in fear and confusion.

Like the language of birds, I still spoke most of the languages of humankind. I thought for a moment, through the ache in my brainpan, and had a look at him. I saw a full-grown man, but young, with hay-coloured hair and a short golden beard. Wearing simple clothes, with no armour. But he had a sword, and not just any sword, if it had cut through my mail. Never mind that, I thought: what is he? Goth? Roman? Frank?

I took a chance on Latin, and it came out something like: 'Put your fucking hands on me again and I'll rip your bowels out through your throat.'

That, he understood. He raised his hands, weaponless, palms outward.

'Are you a woman?'

'For my sins,' I growled.

He looked at me then as though I were a miracle he'd performed, as though he had done me a kindness when he cut my armour and woke me from my enchanted sleep.

I held the two flaps of my mail coat, sliced down the middle. 'How in the name of every god did you do this? And why? What the hell were you trying to—'

He interrupted. 'I thought you couldn't breathe.'

There was nothing to be said to that, which was just as well, because I was speechless for another reason by then.

My old horse, my dear Grani, was walking towards me, head down. He was wearing strange saddlebags. Gudrun, do you remember how beautiful he was? Dark grey, black mane, a long pale line like a sword blade on his forehead. A horse from Odin's own stables, taller and stronger than any of his Midgard cousins.

'Oof, that's my horse, sorry,' said my rescuer. 'Leave us be, Horse.'

I swung my heavy head back to look at him. '*Your* horse! I don't think so.'

'It is absolutely my horse,' he said, defensively. 'He bore me here.'

My finger still stung a bit. The thorn-wound had knitted together but was not fully healed. I'd not been asleep long enough to reach the full strength the thorn-sleep could bestow, but it had been several days at least: long enough to feel as though I was jumping to get out of my own skin. I was hungry, and breathing hard. There was a weird restlessness in all my limbs, and I wanted to run for days on end, or hit something.

Instead, I very steadily held out my hand and Grani walked up to me.

'Your hands,' he said. 'They're cut? Hurt? Or – is that writing?'

'Runes, and none of your business,' I said, flipping my hand over, so that he'd stop looking, and so Grani could nose my palm. 'Good boy,' I murmured, to the horse.

'You've seen this horse before?' he asked.

Seen him? Grani had been my horse since I came to Valhalla as a child. We'd flown together over many battlefields. But I saw no reason this man deserved to know any of that.

'He came from the stables, where I used to live,' I said. 'I'm no horse thief.'

'I didn't say you were.' No thief, except perhaps Loki, could steal a horse from Valhalla. And the old grass-cropper seemed to be comforting me as much as himself, standing quietly as though to reassure me that everything was all right. I had never known a horse with such a sense of justice. 'Let me guess. This horse was given to you.'

'He was indeed!' He seemed almost relieved that I believed him. 'I met an old man, yesterday. He gave me the horse. He said it belonged to a traitor, and that the other horses would have nothing to do with him.'

'Did he now?' It wasn't enough that Odin had banished me; now he was finding every way he could to hurt me, to remind me of everything I'd lost. Perhaps my rescuer knew little of the gods, to be so unsuspecting of a one-eyed old man, or perhaps Odin had altered his appearance. I was suspicious, but not suspicious enough. I thought Odin was merely trying to goad me, out of revenge.

'Well, then,' I said. 'I suppose the horse is yours.'

Grani lifted his head a little, stared straight ahead. A horse of Midgard, now. No more trailing his hooves through gilded clouds. I counted no more white hairs on his coat, but then, I had not been gone very long. Besides, Grani did not age in Valhalla; nobody aged in Valhalla. Like the Valkyries he was bred to bear, Grani grew older only while he was in Midgard. I miss him, Gudrun.

I supposed that my horse and I had both better get used to the idea of ageing at the usual rate. The centuries I had expected to live collapsed, deflated, a hideous jest. Perhaps that was what Odin meant me to think of when I saw Grani, I thought.

'The horse led you to me?' I asked.

'No, my eyes led me to you. Well, to your fire. I saw it from a distance.'

'And you chose to investigate.'

'Yes.'

He was sitting more comfortably now, knees up, one arm

draped over them. Broad shoulders and big arms, skin gleaming in the light of my coal-circle, which was still glowing red. Not rich, I thought, but not a woods-wanderer. A labourer. An adventurer? If so, it was a new adventure.

I asked his name.

He swallowed, as if it was a painful question. 'The only name I've ever known is Sigurd.'

Some close cousin to a laugh emerged from my throat. 'A strange answer.'

'And what is yours?'

I thought for a moment but could see no reason to lie. The name would mean nothing to him anyway. Valkyries are not as well-known as gods, and this fool hadn't even recognized Odin. 'I'm Brynhild.'

'And you come from the same place as this horse.'

He was looking at me more shrewdly now and I wondered whether I'd misjudged him. What would this stranger do, if he learned that he had found one of Odin's legendary warrior women? But truth be told, I had no desire to talk about Valhalla anyway.

'Yes. From my foster-father's halls. It is some distance from here. His name is . . .' I thought of a name for home. 'His name is Heimar. Who are your people?'

He looked away. 'Let's make an arrangement, Brynhild, all right? Let's not ask each other about what's behind us. Let's only talk about what's ahead.'

'All right. And what's ahead for you, Sigurd?'

He grinned. 'I'm going to kill a lindworm.'

I snorted, and Grani's ears flickered.

I couldn't reason out whether it was a chance meeting, or the work of Odin or some other god, or something else, or all of it. My sleep-sated brain didn't want to think. It was swimming in my strong body, like a drunken fly on the top of a mug of beer.

'Listen, Sigurd, I've been sleeping for days, and I want to run for about a mile, and drink from a bottomless horn, and do a lot of other things too, but first I really need to eat something.'

Sigurd had his endearing qualities. You saw them right away, I think, when he came to your door. My ways of judging character were harsher.

What I cared about most just then were his careful little bags of provender: salt pork, barley meal, oats, hard cheese, dried peas, wheat flour, and salt. I made a new fire and he made dough, and while the flatbread was baking on a rock, he handed me a ceramic flask shaped like a giant's finger-ring, with a bottleneck where the stone would be.

'To whose memory shall we drink?' I asked, holding it out. It was plain, with a few simple decorative lines in the clay made by the potter's thumbnail.

'Is that a custom, where you come from?'

'It's a habit,' I said. 'But I forgot. We promised to look forward, not back.'

'Then let's drink to being remembered,' said Sigurd.

I lifted the flask to my nose and sniffed. It smelled of honey and good dreams, but just to be sure, I dipped my non-scarred fingertip in and traced the beer-runes on the back of my hand: ansuz, laguz, uruz. Then I dipped again and traced the laguz on the neck of the flask, and the naudiz, the need-rune, on my fingernail.

'What in God's name are you doing?' Sigurd asked, his mouth wry.

He knew nothing of runelore. He looked genuinely curious.

'Have you ever had too much to drink, Sigurd?'

'I'm a smith's . . . foster-son,' he said, his voice speeding up and slowing down the way a voice does when the person using it is unsure how much it would be wise to say. 'I learned to drink deep to take away the pain, the first time I burned my thumb.'

'And later?'

He chuckled. 'And later, I learned to drink with the other boys, and the girls. Yes, I have occasionally had too much to drink.'

'And sometimes, you might find that it brings good cheer and good dreams. But other times, even if you drink no more than you did before, it makes you surly, makes your head ache, makes you forget things?'

He nodded. 'Once or twice, yes, I've had that experience.'

'The beer-runes take away the bad, and leave the good,' I said, and drank deep of the mead. It was sweet, and strong. I can still taste it.

I handed him back his flask.

'The one on the flask is for poison, and the one on the hand is for treachery. You don't need those, not with your own mead.'

'But you did?'

'As I said, these things are habit. But even with your own mead in your own horn, you can still make mistakes. Dip your finger in the mead and trace this symbol on your fingernail,' I said, and held up my hand to show him. 'It protects you from what you do to yourself.'

He squinted at it. 'I can barely see it, with all those other markings on your hand.'

I shuffled closer to him, and took the flask from him, laid it on the ground. 'Oh, for the love of Valhalla. Give me your hand.'

He complied, resting it on my left hand while I traced the naumiz on his nail. It was a short nail, broken and dirty. His hand rested on my own for a moment longer. Then with that hand, he took the flask up and drank. When he was done, he cocked his head, with a thoughtful smile.

'Hmm,' he said. 'Do you know any other tricks?'

I stood, and traced a few runes on my spear, paced away from him. His smile faded and he got to his feet, too slowly, as I sent the spear towards his right shoulder, where it pulled his cloak off. The ash-bolt buried itself in a beech tree, Sigurd's cloak flapping from it, Sigurd's plain iron cloak-pin on the ground.

'Christ's bones.' He rubbed his shoulder, as though the removal of his cloak wounded him there.

Under the cloak, he wore a wool tunic, undyed, and a little too snug. No mail. He was no kind of warrior.

I, on the other hand, could feel how the thorn-sleep had made me stronger, interrupted though it was.

'Are all the shield-maidens of Heimar's hall like you?'

'We said no questions about the past,' I said, and walked past him to retrieve the spear.

He fell into step beside me and put one hand on the spear-shaft, as if to help me, but I yanked it out before he could.

'Then I'll ask you a question about the future,' he said. I found him unsettling, this close, or perhaps I was easily unsettled just then. I couldn't look at all of him at once, and found myself fascinated wherever I looked. My eyes, like the rest of my body, were restless, and looking for an anchor.

So I deliberately looked at the spear, examined it for damage, plucked the torn cloak off.

'Ask,' I said, and handed him the cloak.

'Where are you going next?'

'To kill a lindworm.'

His eyes widened. 'Fafnir? My lindworm?'

'I didn't know it was yours, or I would have asked first.'

His mouth tugged. 'You're teasing me.'

'I swear to whatever you think is holy. I am on my way to kill the lindworm that's been harrowing this land.'

Sigurd gaped at me. 'Why?'

'Why? Because someone needs to dispatch it.'

'Yes, but why you? Why should it be you?'

I didn't have an answer, at first, and that bothered me, so I spoke quickly. He surprised me into saying more than I might have. 'Because the one thing I can do is deliver justice, and when I cannot do that any more they might as well put me in the ground. That's what . . . people like me are good for. That's what I can do.'

He nodded, thoughtfully. And then, as quick as sunrise, his expression shifted. 'And I'm good for burning the bread.'

He dashed to the rocks, swore as he tried to pull the bread off with his hands, then grabbed his sword and used it to lift the bread and place it clumsily onto a log. He looked up at me sheepishly.

I ate that charred bread still hot, tearing into it, not caring that it was burning my hands and mouth. I have never been that hungry, before or since.

We passed the rest of that night on my ledge, though the last thing I wanted was more sleep. We lay wrapped in our cloaks on the cold ground about a foot apart, and I listened to Sigurd dream.

The next dawn, I woke to see Sigurd brushing Grani, and talking to the horse under his breath. I smiled, only a little sadly. Grani would not suffer any of that if he chose not to. My old companion trotted over to me when his dark coat was gleaming like silver in the hollows, and whickered softly, until I patted his neck and told him that I had never seen his mane so smooth.

We began our journey to the lindworm, together. It pained me a little to see Grani walking behind us like a pack horse, but it was lovely to be able to walk without the weight of my mail and helmet, not to mention meat and bread and water. If the birds were right, we wouldn't be able to drink from streams as we drew near to the lindworm, and I suspected the hunting would be poor.

In any case, the terrain was too steep for either of us to ride Grani (and certainly not both at once, an arrangement neither of us suggested). So Grani walked behind, bearing the saddlebags, without complaint. Not that I could have said anything about it even if I objected. The horse, like my ability to fly, had only ever been mine through the grace of Odin, and Odin had apparently decreed that both horse and woman must walk.

Sigurd and I walked south-east, towards the Rhine. I hadn't known we were near the river, and I started to get my bearings a little. We slipped into a rhythm of walking, stopping, drinking, eating. Our language was curt: 'Tired?' 'Ready?' 'There's plenty.' 'That one's yours.' 'That way, I think.'

After a while, I felt as though I'd always be walking beside Sigurd, just as I had been nearly certain I'd always be falling. But things do change, don't they? They change more quickly than we can ever imagine. The unthinkable becomes the inevitable, and the ordinary becomes wistful memory. I am still not quite used to this swift-passing life.

At the end of a long day, we made camp. I was grateful the day wasn't too hot; it was not yet summer. The evening air was delicate on my cheeks, and there was still a little purple light at one edge of the sky.

'What's that?' Sigurd asked as we sat across the fire from each other. I was stripping the bark from a piece of ash wood.

'Another spear.'

'No, I mean—' He pointed to his own cheek to show me he meant mine.

I put my finger to my cheek. I'd thought perhaps the thorn-sleep would heal my wound entirely, but it seemed not. It no longer hurt, but the skin had knitted into these two thin lines I still bear. The mark of my helmet biting my cheek when I fell to Midgard.

'We said nothing about the past,' I said.

'Scars aren't the past,' he retorted with a mouth full of meat. 'They're the present.'

I didn't accept his argument, but after a few moments, I decided there was no reason to be quite so secretive. I got to my feet, pulled my helmet from Grani's packs and showed him.

'My own helmet. Here, see this cheek piece?' I held it near the firelight, so he could see the shape of it matched the angle and lines on my face.

He whistled. 'It must have been quite the blow, to do that. And your helmet is not even dented!'

'It was made by an unusually gifted smith. Like my mail.'

At that, Sigurd hung his head, and we ate in silence for a few moments. The first few stars had appeared. I stared at them, willing myself to enjoy the sight; I had so seldom had the chance to gaze at the stars of Midgard. Most of the time, Valkyries left the battlefield long before darkness fell. But I found myself wondering if I would ever see the green sky-fires of Valhalla again.

At last Sigurd said, 'I was raised by an unusually gifted smith, myself. He made my sword.'

I had been wondering about that sword. 'I would have said no mortal could have forged a blade that could have cut my mail.'

'Well, Regin is mortal enough. He's dying.'

'Ah,' I said, and added uncertainly, watching his face: 'I'm sorry.'

'And I'm sorry about cutting your mail,' he said, with the sudden change of weather across his face that I was to come to know so well. 'I can help repair it, if you like.'

I didn't know what to say to that. The thought of this man's thick fingers repairing these shining rings – I simply wasn't prepared for it.

He broke in, misinterpreting my silence. 'I really did think you were hurt. I don't know any witches.'

'I'm not a witch,' I said, gruffly. 'A little runelore can be helpful to a warrior. Of course, so can a sword. And there you have the advantage. I lost mine. Not that a sword would be much good against a beast who breathes poison. Spears will let me keep a safe distance.'

'As impressive as your spear-throwing is, I don't think any spear will pierce the hide,' Sigurd said, shaking his head.

'Regin made my sword after years of long study. He said it was the only thing that would do the job.'

'And how does a village blacksmith come to know so much about this lindworm?'

A scowl settled lightly on his face. 'He fought him, years ago. And lived. If you have better knowledge than that, I'd be happy to hear it.'

I had to admit I did not. 'All right. What else did Regin tell you, Sigurd?'

He took a moment before answering. 'I know the lindworm is named Fafnir, and that he has four legs and no wings, that his heart – that a lindworm has a heart like anything else. That he has a very thick hide, enchanted, perhaps. And I know that his breath is poison, which I why I think I'd better approach him from behind.'

I shook my head. 'You won't get at the heart from behind, or the guts or the head either. You'll be fighting with the tail, and you'll probably lose. A lindworm does have a tail, I assume?'

He shrugged. 'I didn't think to ask that. If I could get myself onto his back, perhaps? He would have a hard time biting or breathing on me there. I wonder. I could drop onto him from a tree.'

'How big is he, exactly?'

He shrugged. 'I don't know. Big. And somehow, we'd have to make sure he walked next to the right tree, without seeing me in it. Perhaps if he came at me—'

I shook my head. The first lesson Svafa taught me, when I was still a child and new to Valhalla, was that a fighter never waits for the enemy to attack. She was tall and grim, and had golden hair, and I still didn't know whether I was in love with her or just wanted to impress her. *Stop hesitating, Brynhild*, she'd say. *Don't respond. Make me respond.*

'It might be the best,' Sigurd continued, doggedly. 'I can't approach from the front or I'll be poisoned or bitten. From behind, well, as you say, chopping the tail won't get me anywhere. So I suppose that leaves from above.'

I was still thinking about Svafa's lessons. 'Rage above, regret below,' I murmured.

'Hmm?'

I looked at him, putting my memories away. The aphorisms I learned would have been ancient by the standards of Midgard; of course, he might not know them.

'Who taught you swordplay, Sigurd?'

He tightened his mouth. 'My foster-father. Regin, the smith. He taught me a few tricks. He wasn't one to tell me the names of things, or anything like that. Just showed me what to do.'

I took a deep breath. Perhaps this was why Odin gave the fool my horse, I thought, as a sign to me. To make sure I went with him and kept him alive. Why Odin should care about this tow-headed smith, I didn't know, but perhaps he'd heard a prophecy or seen a vision. The longer Odin lived, the more he seemed to live in the future.

'All right, then. Never mind the principles, but I've wielded a sword and shield for . . . a long time, and I can tell you that death often comes from underneath your guards. You don't want to be over your enemy. I wonder—'

'What?'

I spoke slowly, thinking. 'I wonder if I could get below the beast. He doesn't fly, I believe. Is that right? He's not like a dragon, that way?'

He nodded. 'But he might rear.'

'He might, but—' I thought again of the aphorism not to wait for one's enemy to move, and stopped. 'It would be a hell of a gamble. But I think there might be another way to get beneath his belly. If we dug a pit, and waited until he was overhead, I could stab upwards with a spear.'

He gave me a look, and I gave him one back.

'My spears are more than they appear, Sigurd.'

He shook his head. 'I don't care how many runes you draw on them. A bit of wood won't pierce the hide. Regin – I've watched him, for years on end, labouring over sword after sword, throwing away weapons that any king would covet, before he made this one.'

'Hmm,' I said, and then, 'May I see it?'

He handed it to me with no reluctance. The scabbard was wood wrapped in black leather, covered in line upon line of tooled runes. They were the usual sort of thing for swords: scraps of song about flame, about gifts. The sort of thing that made a sword ride true in its owner's hand, and not turn against him. Simple spells that might work and did no harm.

I stood, and drew it, and moved into three or four guards and a couple of attacks and counters. High, low, turning the blade, a wrath-blow from above at an unseen enemy.

'Hmm,' I said.

'What?'

I paused, uncertain what to say. To look at, the sword was certainly lovely. Its pommel was a wedge of silver, carved in the form of an interlaced serpent – or, perhaps, a lindworm. The silver was so new that there was no sign of tarnish; not even the faintest blackness rimmed the scales of the beast.

As lovely as the pommel and the matching crossbar were, and as welcome as the hilt felt in the hand, the blade was like nothing I'd ever seen. Pattern-welding, the steel rippling in waves like agate-stone. And all along the blade, runes crowded in four long lines on either side.

These, I couldn't read. They didn't form words, at least not in any language I knew, and I suspected not in any language. The meaning was in the selection of each in relation to its neighbour, bound together like the welded steel, some of the joins apparent and some not. I peered at them, thinking how I would like to make a study of them.

'Is there something you don't like about it?' Sigurd asked.

'It's the best corpse-piler I've ever held in my hand. Perhaps the best I've seen. And I have seen many.'

I ran a fingertip along the edge to test it, and swore when my skin parted, and three tiny drops welled up. I sucked my finger and sheathed the sword, handing it back to him.

Sigurd was chuckling. 'It's sharper than the new moon,' Regin said. It can part a bit of wool simply held up against it.'

'I don't doubt it. But I still think any sword is a bad weapon for lindworm-slaying.'

Sigurd sighed. 'If you want to risk it, go ahead and break your spear. I know that I'll kill the beast, with this sword.'

'How?' I peered at him, wondering again about his encounter with Odin. 'Did someone prophesy at you?'

He shook his head. 'I just know I will, because I won't accept the alternative. The name of Sigurd will be spoken with respect and remembered forever.'

With a sigh, I considered the situation. Even a man with no training could close his eyes and stab upwards. If he didn't strike true, it would at least distract the lindworm, give me an opening. And Sigurd would be as safe as he could be.

'Fine,' I said. 'You wait in the pit with your sword. I'll be the one to lure the beast over the pit, then.' He made a face, and I shrugged. 'This plan takes two people, and it's the best one we have. You need me and I need you, or else you need a different plan.'

'I don't want your blood on my hands,' he said.

'Then,' I said, 'I will try my best not to bleed on you.'

CHAPTER SEVEN

Brynhild and Fafnir

The birds chattered as I walked next to Sigurd. They told me sad stories about every lake and river we glimpsed through trees or mountain passes: histories in bird-poetry, refrain building on refrain.

The last thing they told me before we came to the wasteland was that the lindworm's home was called Hind Mountain. It was hard to believe that place ever had any deer grazing its slopes. It was all grey rock, tall pines, waterfalls and crags. No green. From a distance, one might have thought there had been a fire, one that had not left behind any ash. Everything was a heavy, soggy brown, cold and stinking. The trees looked as though they'd been tortured to death.

The lower slopes of Hind Mountain itself were steep and thick with fine, gravelly scree. I couldn't imagine us climbing them. There was only one way up: a rickety wooden stair built into the side of the mountain. We couldn't see the top; the air was thick with rusty clouds.

Nobody would have chosen to live in that forsaken land, unless they knew of no other way of living, unless they hauled that wasteland with them wherever they went. It made me shiver to think of the mind inside it.

Sigurd tied Grani to a withered tree. I started to tell him not to bother, that Grani wouldn't leave us, but he wasn't my horse any more, and it wasn't my business. Grani and I exchanged patient, knowing glances.

Sigurd glared at the top of the mountain. 'There's something on the top of it. Something bright.'

I squinted. He was right: some stray sunlight, filtered through all that brume, hit something at the cliff edge, in just the way I'd seen the sun glint off the shield-bosses of an approaching army. But no army could be that quiet.

No insects buzzing, no birds twittering. Nothing.

In that stillness, I could feel the thorn-sleep strength coursing through my body. We had been walking for three days, from before dawn to after dusk, but there was no stiffness in my legs.

While Sigurd watched me guiltily, I pulled my damaged mail shirt out of the pack and tied it up with some thin strips of leather so that it would at least stay on when I pulled it over my head. We had to be ready, now. The lindworm couldn't be far. The only sound was the trickle of a creek, clear water over polished rocks. Not a water-spider or a bit of moss to be seen. It smelled wrong, as everything there smelled wrong: like sour metal, like a sword left to rot in wet soil for a thousand years.

We drank only from the water we brought.

'Regin says Fafnir doesn't fly,' Sigurd said, uneasily.

'So I've been told. I am certain of nothing, until I see it myself.'

'Well, if he's at the top of that thing, he must get up and down somehow, and I doubt he uses that staircase.'

There were some scars in the scree, which I'd taken for landslide cracks. Perhaps not.

'He must,' I agreed. 'But I'm sure he knows about that staircase well enough.'

We had no intention of going up the mountain. For our plan, we needed time to dig and hide before the lindworm knew we were there, so we worked on the flat land, far from the slopes.

It took a long time, digging with brittle branches. We cleared the hole with our hands, pulling out clods of heavy clay studded with sharp stones. By the end of it, our hands showed bloody cracks through the pale grime. We ate Sigurd's cold smoked pork in silence. The hole was deep enough for Sigurd to stand in and just barely wide enough. On one side, we carved a rough step halfway up, to help Sigurd get out of the hole without having to pull himself out by his arms. We didn't talk about what circumstances might make that necessary, or what good getting out of the hole could possibly do, in those circumstances.

There was a half-dead willow copse at the side of the stream, and we cut a dozen withies to weave into a tight lid. Once Sigurd was in, looking like some ancient warrior buried upright, with his sword in his hand, I settled the lid and swept a thick layer of wet earth over it. The difference in colour was stark, at first, so I spent a lot of time gathering topsoil from near the hole and sprinkling it on top, until I was satisfied it looked the same as everything around it. I poked small air holes, on the leesides of pebbles so they'd look like shadows.

He assured me he could breathe, though his voice sounded far away. 'At least if I'm poisoned, no one will have to go to the trouble of burying me.'

'Yes, there is that.'

There was no one to bury me, I realized. Perhaps the lindworm would eat me.

I picked up my spears, one in each hand, and glared up at the mountain. Had the old monster been watching us, laughing at our plans? I didn't think so – a Valkyrie is so used to being unseen that she knows in her bones when she's being watched.

But then, I wasn't a Valkyrie any more. A thought wormed its way to the front of my mind. When we were walking and planning, I seemed to have been able to keep it buried, the same way that work kept the restless thorn-sleep strength from making my skin itch and muscles twitch. Now, there was only me and that mountain, and the thought.

When I died, I would not go to Valhalla.

Odin would surely not take me back, once I was dead. He would leave me on the ground for the shadowy Disir to carry off to Folkvang, Freyja's ghostly fields.

I shivered and told myself there was nothing I could do about that. Anyway, on that day, I was determined not to die. In that stinking waste, I remembered the voices of the frightened birds. This was an easy judgment, and a fight worth having.

All the same, I was very aware that I'd never faced anything like this creature. If I simply called him down from the mountainside, he might suspect a trap. The only idea that made any sense was to pretend I was trying to get up the mountain, to make it look like failure when the fight came down to the lowland.

So I started climbing.

I didn't get very far, but then getting far wasn't the point. I scrambled noisily up the slope, ankle-deep in gravel. I slid once, twice, right to the bottom. The third time, I managed to pull a great deal of rock down too, with a rumbling boom.

And at that, there was a scream from the top of the mountain: something like a hawk, but also nothing like a hawk.

I scrambled to my feet, brushing the rock and dirt off my mail coat. I donned my helmet.

Fafnir came slithering down the mountainside, a dark liquid line moving with remarkable speed. The gravel flared on either side of him as he slid headfirst, small stones ricocheting off his leathery skin. At the base of the mountain he stopped, four feet on the ground like a cat, and lifted his helmeted head.

What frightened me most, I remember, were the arms. They were so very human. They stretched out from that serpentine body, with bracelets on. And there was something human about the way he cocked his head beneath that terrible helm. The iron ring went through his nose and through two holes in the helm, and it shook a little every time he moved his head.

And then the creature spoke. This is the hardest part to tell, Gudrun, even after all this time. That voice is burned into my mind, and I can't forget a word of it, though I've never told anyone what he said.

The mouth did not move. The voice was in my head, as smooth as a creeping shadow, and there it remains.

A woman, said the lindworm. *Interesting.*

'Fafnir,' I said, and took a step backwards, casually, just as I would if I were afraid of a blast of poison from his mouth. And, of course, I was. But I was also thinking that if I walked twenty paces backwards, I would be standing over Sigurd. I just needed to bring the beast with me that far.

You know my name, but you haven't given me yours.

'You don't need to know it.'

It seems unjust that only one of us should know our killer's name.

At that, I was startled out of my backwards walk, and the lindworm lifted his head, snakelike, a triumphant glare in those glassy eyes. Poisonous fumes trickled out of his nostrils. Everything stank like death. If there had been anyone near, they would have seen me as a dark figure veiled in cloud. Consumed by the wasteland. A tormented soul. Certainly not a hero.

'You mock me,' I said. 'Or you'd have me believe you're a seer?'

Either you'll kill me, or I'll kill you, and either way it comes out the same. I knew when I took this form what my end would be.

As long as he was talking, I was alive. I told myself that was why I spoke, that was why I listened. To keep my feet under me and my lungs still moving. My spears rested uneasily in my hands, juddering on the ground as I walked.

'You were human once,' I guessed.

I took another step back, as though I were frightened, which did not take very much pretence. It took all my discipline not to look at the ground to gauge where I was. I'd lost track of my backwards paces.

I am human still. Why do you think I talk to every dolt who comes here to kill me? These conversations with thugs and suicides are no chess games, believe me. But life is very long and I am liable to forget what I am holding onto, if I have no one to tell it to, from time to time, before they choke to death on my poison and their vomit.

I couldn't be far from Sigurd now. And then what? We'd show our hands, Fafnir would stop talking, and our deaths would be ugly and painful and probably slow, but at least Fafnir would have stopped talking. And then my eternity would begin, in some unknown place. Perhaps nowhere at all . . .

'And what are you holding onto?' I barked, to shut up my own brain.

The slenderest thread, he said, and I learned that a monster could speak softly. *Grace.*

I snorted. 'Grace! Will you do penance, like the Christians?'

Oh, my grace comes from punishment but not my own. I am the scourge of God.

I resisted a shiver. It was damp and cold in that place. I could run, I realized. I didn't have to choose to kill him. I could run, but then I'd be a coward, and I'd let the lindworm live on to keep murdering innocents for sport. And there was Sigurd, waiting in his hole for me to keep my word.

'Enough talk,' I croaked.

My death will be my greatest accomplishment. I will be more dangerous when I'm dead. Because a great worm cannot die without inheritance.

'I don't want your gold.'

It will be yours whether you want it or not, but that isn't the inheritance I mean.

67

'You speak in riddles,' I said.

I'm only passing the time for you to get up your courage. You can stop my voice forever with your sword. Do you have a sword, by the way? I'm starting to wonder whether you're the one who'll kill me after all. The other one might be better for my purposes.

He lifted his head, sniffing the air, and I froze in place. Even my thoughts froze, as I worried they'd betray me.

'There is no other one,' I said, after too long. 'I'm the only one here.'

Fafnir snorted, lowering his head so that his eyes were on a level with mine. I scrambled backwards, my feet slipping in the gravel, not bothering to try to count my steps. At any moment I expected a blast of poisonous breath.

Instead, his voice in my mind came like a whisper, almost gentle, definitely pitying.

I am talking to the other one right now.

I froze like a hare. What did the beast know? Could he really be speaking to both our minds at once?

Sigurd told me his name right away. He has borrowed reasons to hate me. He carries his punishment with him. And you?

I remembered falling, the crack of light closing overhead, all chance of seeing my sisters lost, and Odin waiting at the crossroads, his face hidden by his hat.

'I have done nothing worthy of punishment.'

That means your sins are still to come. I will give them to you. It is my task.

I told myself Fafnir's riddling was all to goad me into making a mistake, into running and turning my back. His voice was a weapon, but I had weapons of my own.

'What will you do,' I said, taking a step back as though I were losing my nerve, 'if I turn and walk away?'

Walk? Mocking.

'Or run.'

He lowered his head, avuncular. *I will kill you. I will take that broken mail coat and put it into my trophy hall. I won't even mend it. It will remind me of you better, broken.*

'Why kill me, if I'm no threat to you?' I was still moving backwards, but the lindworm wasn't following, damn him. He didn't need to be close to be within striking distance.

You seek death. I provide it. Now shall I ask you the same question?

'You have killed others. The birds told me. You poison the land.'

I'm sorry to tell you what Fafnir said next. He said it was true, that he had just come from the gates of a city, where he had left bodies on the ground and poison in the soil.

I did what I had to do, but I was invited, you see. Just as you invite me now.

He had come from Vormatia, from his brief alliance with Attila, though I didn't know that then. There were many things I didn't understand yet, or didn't want to.

'Enough,' I croaked, but could barely hear my own voice.

I could see, though it was just a shape glimpsed out of the corner of my eye, a tree stump that looked like a falcon in silhouette. And then I knew where I was: nearly over Sigurd's hole. Another few steps and I'd be standing right over Sigurd myself, so all I needed was to make sure Fafnir came close to me, to give Sigurd his chance.

I told you I was the scourge of God.

Come on, beast, I thought.

But you didn't ask me which god.

If Fafnir could have smirked, with that terrible sharp jaw, he would have. I froze in place like spider-meat.

The lindworm's next words were a mere whisper in my mind:

Yes, I come from the gates of a city. I come from the Bale-worker's business.

Perhaps he could have told me more, if I'd kept him jawing. Perhaps many things would have been different, if I'd seen the truth in what sounded like lies and worked out the meaning behind it. But all I knew in that moment was that his words were poison, and I was dying of them. I raised my right spear and as Fafnir opened his mouth in response, I threw it into that void. I would have needed a great deal of luck to slide my spear down his throat just then, but for a moment I thought perhaps, perhaps. Then the spear struck the awful helm and fell away, soundless, and I was slipping backwards as the air filled with murderous brown fog.

My heels shuddered, each one landing a century apart, or so it felt. I stumbled right over the patch of earth where Sigurd waited, not slowing, not even allowing myself to will him to wait a moment, to strike at the right time. I let go of all my thoughts. I let desolation of purpose fill my mind, like pebbles fill a hole.

I would hold on to life long enough to kill Fafnir. I did not need to be a Valkyrie to take one evil out of this world. I swore it then, an oath on no god, and with my thundering heart as witness.

Between the burning tears filling my eyes and the brown fog filling the valley, I could see very little. Just the dark shape of my enemy, ever closer, looming higher. I kept my breath as shallow as I could, coughing on the reek in the air. There was not much time left before I'd succumb to the deep blackness that was already creeping at the edges of my vision.

Fafnir screamed.

First my ankle twisted, then the rest of me. I fell onto the dry ground.

The lindworm recoiled, lifting one of his legs, which were more beastlike and less human than his arms. Blood bubbled out of a ragged hole in his skin, blood pooled on the ground, red and bright against that dun landscape. But he didn't lie still or fall over; he was thrashing, gravel flying up from his tail, and he opened his enormous mouth. Rusty fumes curled all around us, and the smell of rotten metal filled my mouth.

I lifted my second spear and Fafnir moved his head, sharply, like an owl that has seen a mouse. But it wasn't me that caught his gaze.

Between Fafnir and me, Sigurd was hoisting himself out of the hole. He was covered in red blood, so that he looked like something being born from an unholy womb. Not his own blood. The lindworm's gore had pooled into the hole. He must have been nearly drowning in it.

The lindworm laughed, a rough, bubbling laugh, and lifted his tail. On the end was a large black leathery knob, like a mace. Sigurd was out of the hole but still staggering to his feet. I cried out and Sigurd crouched, coughing up blood that wasn't his own.

Not yet.

The tail whipped through the air and I ran.

With my right hand, I pushed Sigurd down, out of the way, and with my left, I stabbed at Fafnir's tail.

It didn't pierce the hide. I slammed sideways into the ground, my spear a splinter, and the tail slammed down just beside me. Sigurd crouched a few paces away, splayed on hands and knees, with the pale shape of a handprint in the middle of his back.

The palm of my own right hand was covered in lindworm blood, from where I'd pushed Sigurd to safety.

I rolled to avoid another blow of the tail. Fafnir had shifted, so that Sigurd was now closer to the great head.

I think I shouted at him to run, if I had any voice left. In any case, he did run, for a few steps. Just far enough to get out in front of Fafnir and brandish his fabulous sword, holding it too close to his ribs. He had a shield somewhere, but it must have been with Grani still, as he hadn't had any use for it in his pit.

Fafnir opened his jaw and bit down on Sigurd, lifted his body in his mouth, with Sigurd's feet sticking out horrifically comically, with his right arm dangling out the other end. His sword arm, but the sword had fallen from it.

Then Fafnir lifted his head and flung Sigurd out, far out, into the stream.

His body hit the ground with a thud.

My lungs and stomach both rebelled but I swallowed and ran low through a dark brown cloud of stink, towards the monster. The broken stick that was once a spear felt warm in my hand, my weaker hand, the one that did not have the lindworm's blood on it.

Not yet.

I knew when I saw you that I would inflict a just death upon you, Fafnir said, turning his head to me, a great dark bulk in the fog. I could see the peaked shape of the helm and feel it ringing in my bones. *I just didn't know whether it would be mine, or yours.*

I couldn't see anything, but I didn't need to see. I only needed to stay alive long enough to get close.

As the mouth opened, and the air thickened and closed down my throat, I fell. Face down, the broken spear beneath me. I grabbed it, but this time with my stronger right hand, the one still sticky with the dragon's own blood, from where I had pushed Sigurd. As the mouth closed around me from the right side, I writhed, twisted, and pushed the splinter of my spear into the open mouth. Elbow-deep I thrust it, my hand burning, gagging as I heard the lindworm gag, until I suffocated.

CHAPTER EIGHT

Brynhild Bathed in Blood

I woke to the sight of Sigurd's worried face looming over me, and I thought for a moment: *this already happened; I am a ghost, reliving the same moments forever.* But this time Sigurd was covered in dried blood. It matted his pretty golden hair and the stubble that was, by then, a short beard. It looked as though he'd wiped some of it off his face and hands, but not with much success.

I tried to speak, coughed, tried again.

'Alive,' I managed.

'Yes, you are.' His voice sounded nearly as raw as my own.

'Not me, you dolt. You.'

He laughed at that, and we both collapsed into coughing fits.

'Water,' he croaked at last, and half-dragged me to my knees. Clean sunlight and clean water from a flask. Fafnir's body was a long dark shape on the ground. Though I could still smell that poisonous miasma over everything, I felt as though a spell had been broken.

We walked over to Fafnir's corpse, and then I realized that the helm of terror had vanished. I asked Sigurd what he thought had happened to it.

'Maybe it was always an illusion,' he said, uncertainly. 'But wait – look.'

He bent to the ground and picked up an iron ring, too small to be a bracelet for Sigurd, and too large to be a finger-ring. It bore a large red stone, glittering, like a drop of blood turned to glass. 'Isn't this—'

'The ring that was through his nose,' I agreed, shuddering. 'All that's left of the helm, it looks like.'

'Then it's a trophy now. Proof.'

'You keep it,' I said, answering the question written on his face. 'I don't need proof, and I don't want it.'

Inheritance, the beast had said. I looked down at Fafnir's carcass and wrinkled my nose. He was still wearing six golden bracelets on too-human arms. We left them there. Sigurd, for the moment, was satisfied with his trophy. I didn't want to strip that horrible corpse.

Sigurd was staring at me as though I were a goddess, despite the fact that I'd nearly lost both of our lives. He was not wearing his tunic – he was dressed in nothing but trousers, the top half of his body bare. I'd hardly noticed, as he was so caked in blood. Fafnir's blood, from when it had flooded into the hole.

'I'm amazed that you survived,' I said. 'I saw that beast bite down on you, and fling you onto the rocks. I would have helped you, if I thought there was any chance you were still alive. And here you are helping me!'

'I thought it was a miracle, at first, but then I felt the pain in my back, and – well. Look.'

He stuffed the iron nose ring into a pocket somewhere, turned around to show me that one patch of red on his back was not the crimson of caked blood but bright, blistered flesh. I winced just looking at it. I pulled him over to the little creek. To Sigurd's surprise, but not mine, Grani was there, dragging the rope Sigurd had used to tie him to a tree. Grani looked up at me, worried, but then lapped a little at the water as though to tell me it was all right.

I splashed a little water on Sigurd's back to clear the blood. He winced, flinched, but kept still.

When the blood was washed away, I gasped. The red burn in the middle of his back was in the shape of a hand – of my own hand.

'That's where I touched you,' I whispered, and looked down at my palm, the one that had been caked with blood before I washed him. I held it to the burn on his back, not quite touching him, checking that it was indeed my palm print.

'Pushed me, you mean,' he said, and turned back to face me with a grim smile.

'Saved your life, as I recall it.'

'Yes. And you took some of Fafnir's blood off me there, before it could soak through my tunic and onto my skin. That place was the only place where the poison burned me. And look!'

He pulled himself to his feet and walked unsteadily to Grani, pulled a knife out of one of the packs. Then he jammed it, hard, into his own thigh.

As I cried out, the knife turned, glanced off his skin as though it were steel.

I blinked. 'This is new, I take it?'

'New? By Christ, of course it's new! It's the lindworm blood. It's done something to me, something magic. I wish I'd known the damn thing couldn't hurt me once I'd been in its blood. I would have—'

'What?'

'I don't know.' He grinned sheepishly. 'Something.'

I looked down at my palm, covered in the dried blood of Fafnir. I brushed off as much of it as I could on my breeches; I didn't want to waste the water in the flask. 'May I borrow your knife?'

The blade didn't cut my skin. I tried it gently at first, then harder, then jammed it down, wincing in anticipation. It bruised but didn't cut. I could hardly believe it. Immortality

– or even invulnerability – was not something Odin offered the Valkyries. We could be invisible, when we chose. We wore the best battle-clothing in the nine realms. But we could die, when the ones we were fighting against – or sometimes, the ones we were fighting for – stuck us with their swords. Eir died of her wounds on the borders of the Empire. Gondul died bleeding in a field in Gaul. But that came later.

'You have an invincible palm.' Sigurd looked towards the dead lindworm, towards the pit beyond it, filled with blood. 'Why don't you make the rest of you match?'

I didn't understand what he meant, at first, and then when I did, I gagged.

'Why not?' he said, almost petulantly, as if he didn't want to be the only one to have bathed in the blood of our enemy, even though he'd not made the choice.

I walked with him to the edge of the pit. It was still filled with blood, though the level was a little lower, and there was a thin, solid rim around the bright red froth on the top. We had been some time, dreaming on the threshold of death, as Fafnir crossed over it. My stomach was aching, empty. My muscles were still restless from the thorn-sleep, though my head ached.

'Skin that can turn any weapon is not something to refuse lightly,' he said, standing beside me. 'Imagine the good you could do, with such a gift. That we could do together.'

'Leave me alone for a bit,' I said, wanting him to stop talking, to stop echoing my thoughts.

'Why?'

'Because if I jump in that, I'm not jumping in with my clothes on.'

I looked pointedly at him.

He snorted. 'All right. I'll be in the creek, washing.'

He walked away, left me staring at the blood. It was not as though I hadn't been wet with the blood of my enemies before. A few moments of revulsion, and it would be done.

What kind of warrior would I have been, if I hadn't taken the chance to harden my skin? That's what I asked myself then, and though I know the answer well enough now, I would not have wanted the gift of prophecy, then or ever.

I stripped, pulling off my broken mail shirt, my tunic and trousers. One toe in. It was mercifully cold, not as thick as I'd expected. I sat on the edge, stretched out my legs, held my breath and slid in.

The blood came up to my nose and I felt for a moment that I was drowning in the stench of it. We have sworn to tell each other everything, love. What can I tell you about those moments? I felt no magic, only the blood. Corpse-perfume always smells like what it is and nothing else, even when it's fresh. My stomach revolted as I pulled my hands out, covered in clots like baby eels, and daubed the cold blood on my face, my head.

My bare toes scrambled for the step we dug out of the pit, and I pulled myself up to the surface, and vomited all over the poisoned ground.

CHAPTER NINE

Brynhild's Legacy

I waited until I had washed in the creek and dressed in my dirty but more-or-less dry clothes. Then I borrowed Sigurd's knife, gritted my teeth and ran the blade across my arm.

A dull pressure, leaving no mark on my forearm, not even a red line. The knife was sharp.

'We can't be killed,' Sigurd said, a little farther down the creek.

I walked over to where he sat dripping, shivering, with his elbows on his knees. 'Well, not with weapons. I wouldn't go drinking poison. Or, uh, swallowing swords.' I thought I'd seen that done once, at a banquet in my father's hall, when I was a girl. Perhaps I'd dreamt it.

'Speaking of drinking.' He stood up with a groan and picked up his mead flask from the pile of bags he'd pulled off Grani, who was eating some oats out of one of the open bags. Sigurd took a swig of the mead and handed it to me.

It was just what I needed to wash away the stink of the blood. I drank deep.

His brown wool tunic was so dark with water that I couldn't tell whether it was also still stained with blood, but I suspected it would take more than a cold dip in the creek to cleanse those stains. Sigurd's mail lay in a dull heap, and why should he ever don it again? This man, invulnerable to arrows and spears and axes and swords? This man, shivering with cold.

My own broken mail coat was draped over my arm. I laid it next to his, but I knew I would never give it up. My mail was more than protection: it was a promise, a warning, an honour.

'We should make a fire,' I said.

He stood up, shook his head. 'Not just yet. I can get warm just as easily by walking up those stairs.' He looked at me mischievously. 'I wish I'd had the foresight to go in naked myself, and keep my clothes dry.'

I looked at the side of the mountain, where the wooden staircase clung to the rock. 'I give those stairs an even chance of falling and bringing us down with them.'

'I've survived worse today. Come on. We should find out what he had hidden up there. There could be prisoners who need our help.'

I made a face, and half-wondered whether Sigurd was a hoard-chaser, and half felt guilty I hadn't thought about prisoners myself. Fafnir didn't seem the sort to keep any living companions around, but what did I know of a lind-worm's ways?

So we walked to the mountain. The stairs were weathered, grey – I can't even say what kind of wood they were. But they bore our weight. That mountain was higher than it looked. The fog was thinning. As we climbed, we could see dark wooded slopes rising all around us. The waste of Fafnir was not the whole world, not even very much of the world.

At the top of the staircase was a ramshackle wooden plat-form and a strange wall, made of gleaming metal, in colours that ran together like the markings on the fur of some animal: waves of bronze and gold, black veins of tarnished silver, verdigris bruises. Here and there we could see the half-shapes of half-things, melted and fused: the boss of a shield, the face plates of a helmet, a sword, and a scythe and a ploughshare.

There was no door or gate from our platform, which must have been built before Fafnir made his home there, before he built that terrible shield of shields, melting the weapons of his enemies with his poisonous breath and fashioning his fortress out of it.

'How do we get over it?' Sigurd asked.

I peered along the length of the wall. 'It's lower over there. Look, there's the path the worm took, leading from it. That must be where he went over, on his way up, over and down.'

We crept gingerly along the lip of rock between the wall and the steep scree-slide, and found that the wide, smooth dip in the wall was low enough for us to scramble over.

The top of the mountain was a double peak, with two horns of steep grey rock, one higher than the other. The wall didn't go all the way around the mountain but stretched from one peak to the other on either side, closing the gaps. I could just see in the foggy distance the second wall on the far side. In between the two peaks, there was enough flat ground that the mountaintop could have accommodated a small village. It was bare, though, save for one large hall at the far end.

I never learned who built that hall of gleaming oak; certainly not Fafnir. The walls were the trunks of mighty trees set on end in the ground. As we got closer, we could see the shakes of the roof, the carvings on the door pillars. I was staring at it, wondering, when I tripped on something, stumbled, and looked down.

It was a skull. A human skull.

'What in hell,' I muttered. There were more bones nearby: human, and horse, and what looked like pigs. All left to bleach under the sky.

'Come on,' Sigurd said. 'The beast has paid for his crimes already.'

We saw old blood splattered across and around the double door, which hung open. Sigurd and I walked into a hall that looked, at first, as though it had only recently been abandoned by some minor king and his court. It rose to the timbered roof on massive carved pillars, with stairs to a railed walkway halfway up the building's height. Benches were scattered haphazardly, and in the middle of everything was a stone-lined hearth a few feet across, with half-burned wood still in it. Over the fire hung chains and many-branched iron hooks.

'I wonder how long the worm was here,' I breathed.

There was a faint smell of poison, of rust, of decay, but it was bearable – or perhaps we were just getting used to it. I walked past the hearth, glanced up at the hole high in the steep roof. The ground was beaten earth, with little ribbons of metal in it here and there. As though the metal had run hot, liquid, and cooled again. But it wasn't from heat; the lindworm's poisonous breath could change the shape of metal, like acid.

At the far end of the hall, a doorway to one side brought me to a small room, low, split into two storeys.

And there, I gasped.

A mountain of metal, and unlike the wall, it was made of whole, undamaged things. Brooches, torcs, bracelets, coins, statues. Weapons, armour, and a mound of coins. Gold and bronze and copper and silver.

'This is ours,' Sigurd said, picking up a golden statue of a pig. 'You can have a sword, now, Brynhild. Hell, you can have six.'

There were so many beautiful swords, half-buried in coins and jewellery. I picked up a ring, small, gold, with a dull red stone, and slid it onto my index finger. It looked a little like the ring that had been through the nose of the helm that Sigurd had taken, only much smaller, and duller.

A lindworm cannot die without inheritance.

Fafnir might have meant that there was a curse on his pile, or on some part of it. He certainly wanted me to wonder that, and perhaps he even thought it himself, after all these years guarding it, twisting it into walls.

Sigurd was right, though: it was ours now, whether we walked away from it, buried it, or stuffed it into saddlebags. A hoard is only a hoard while it isn't being used. Here were tools and beautiful things, the work of human hands, the labour of hours. If I walked away, left it hidden there, I knew that it would always be with me. And I would always fear it. I had learned long before that what a person fears, they worship.

'We'll split it in half,' Sigurd said. 'Don't you think?'

It seemed like the only reasonable division to me, and I said so. 'There's no way Grani can bear it all, though.'

He nodded. 'We'll have to bury or leave the biggest things. Will you go back to Heimar?'

I blinked, remembered my lie. 'My foster-father? No, I don't think so. I think I'll just find somewhere to lay my head for a while, now that I have enough gold to keep me fed. Somewhere to think.' I lifted a sword, a short one, one that had belonged to a soldier of the Empire by the look of it. 'We do have many weapons here to choose from, don't we? I used to train . . . shield-maidens. I wonder if there are any unwanted daughters or angry widows near this place who might want to learn some things.'

His face twisted into a weird smile. 'You want to teach *women* to fight with swords?'

I dropped the short sword onto the pile, picked up a long battle-axe, its simple blade gleaming at the end of a red-painted haft. 'Well, I have heard it said that some women might not be strong enough to draw a bow. Or vicious enough to fight with an axe.' Suddenly, I swung my axe down, hooked him by the back of the neck with it, so that he stumbled towards me. The curve of the blade would have drawn blood from his neck, if he hadn't been protected by the lindworm blood. 'So it's useful to have swords available, in case I should come across any of those weaker women.'

That wiped the look off his face, and he raised his hands

in surrender. I let the axe-head fall to the ground. He was standing close to me, and his smile now wasn't the smirk I'd thought it.

There was still a little of the sleep-strength left in me, and it curled up my limbs like a vine, made my muscles twitch. I itched to run, or possibly to fly.

'I'll remember not to cross you or any army you might train, be they men or women,' he said. 'I'm sure any king or lord nearby would happily give a monster-killer a piece of land, in thanks for ridding them of the lindworm. Probably throw a great big banquet too.'

'You'll go back to Regin, and be hailed a hero,' I said.

He looked away, and said, 'Maybe we should make that fire now.'

There was a little unburned wood still in the hall's enormous hearth, though it was sandy and damp. The few trees on the mountaintop had been cut to stumps or were scraggly pines clinging to cracks in the sides of the peaks, far above. Neither of us relished the thought of cutting wood down on the plains and hauling it up that staircase, so we decided to walk around to the back end of the hall and see if, by some lucky chance, there was a woodshed.

There was, of a kind, and it took our breath away.

At the back of the hall, someone had built a tall and narrow addition with its own entrance. It was dominated by an enormous wheel, like the waterwheel in a mill. A cable wound around the wheel, and that led to a steep track running down the cliffside, just under Fafnir's wall, like a rabbit hole under a fence. Two wooden sledges leaned against the wall, along with neat piles of chopped wood, earthenware jars, and several large sacks.

'Christ's wounds,' Sigurd breathed. 'Is that for getting things up the mountain?'

I laughed for joy, tugging a bit on the wheel. It moved, rolling with a long creak. 'Amazing. The lindworm had no use for it, I see. Look: Fafnir's ugly wall goes right over the track, so it's closed off now.'

'Well, we know there's wood. Will you make a fire? I want to check on the horse.'

'Good, and bring up the food and mead, will you? I don't see a well, and I wouldn't drink from one here anyway.'

He nodded. 'I suppose we might as well spend the night up here.' He blushed, strangely. We'd slept side by side under the stars for several nights by then, but perhaps there was something different about being in a place with a roof.

I could feel the side of my mouth pulling into a grin as he walked away, head low, determined and swaggering.

You never asked me about my lovers before Sigurd. There were not many, considering I'd lived three centuries by then. Valkyries are warned about falling in love with mortals. That was how my teacher died.

Svafa was diamond-brilliant, with her long blonde hair and her tongue as sharp as her sword. I was so dazzled by her when I was a girl. Her arms! Those muscles! You smile, but it seemed like a miracle that she believed I could be anything like her. She taught me how to fight, how to perceive a warrior's true character, how to know the ways in which he served his people, or didn't, just by looking at him. How to change the path of an arrow or knock a shield out of a man's hand.

Most of all, she taught me that it mattered. The world is wrought by people's hands, and if you change the hands, you change the world. Kill the young men and let the old men live, and you nudge the future into a certain course. Kill the frenzied, arrogant king and save the lives of children.

I learned this from Svafa and I learned it from Odin himself, who told the tales of the battlefield in the mead hall at night. His visions told him that we, his Valkyries, had chosen well. He was pleased with our work.

That was the first century.

In the second century, for reasons I didn't understand, the

older Valkyries became cynical, dead-eyed. Perhaps it was only the effect of long immortality, working on their minds the way it worked on the dead. I saw some of them place bets on whether they could send an arrow this way or that; I saw some of them fight for sheer battle-lust, without any judgement or restraint.

And one day, I saw Svafa bat aside my sword, as I was about to dispatch a warrior.

I was shocked into stillness and was nearly run through. She pushed me aside, laughing. 'Get out of the way! You'll be skewered.'

'He is meant to die.'

'I like him.'

All around us, the din of battle. She kept one eye on her warrior and lifted his shield to parry a blow. I was confused. 'He – the Allfather expects—'

'The Allfather doesn't check up on every one of them, believe me.' She ran through the other one, the man who was meant to live.

She sounded bitter, but she was smiling her shining smile. Svafa took the man's arm, and pulled him into the forest, and kissed him. He could see her. He ran his hands over her body, and I stood there and stared.

Two weeks later, he was murdered by his brother. He never came to Valhalla. Svafa wandered by his barrow, and sat in the evenings with his ghost. She kissed those dead lips. She never came back to us. I don't know how or when she died, but I know where.

As for me, I chose Odin, and loyalty, and the law. One by one, the older Valkyries died or wandered away as Svafa had, and I found myself the senior member of our company. And I made sure that there were no more battle-games or love affairs. From then on, the Valkyries were as upright as I'd imagined Svafa to be. I set an example.

So no, I did not have many lovers.

By the time I met Sigurd, I had spent a night here and

there with three of my fellow Valkyries, two minor gods, two kings, one farmer and one priestess. Most of these affairs were brief, and some were over before dawn. Over three hundred years of living, that came out to many nights alone, but I wanted no entanglements.

But I wasn't a Valkyrie any longer. I could feel the rushing inevitability of Sigurd and me, or perhaps it was the thorn-sleep still working its way through my body, or the feeling of vertigo that comes after every bloody victory. Perhaps all of it. A bard, like your Volker, would say it was fate, that all of it was fate. But I know well enough that I made my choice, that I sat there in that hall and made my plans.

While Sigurd was gone fetching the food, I took a piece of charcoal and drew the fire-rune on a stick of dry beech from the pile. It burst into flame, and before long, I was sitting beside a hall fire like a king waiting to be entertained.

In walked Sigurd with his hands full of bloody meat.

'What the hell? Did you hunt?'

He shook his head. His face looked grey as he dumped the meat onto a bench and pulled out his knife, started paring fat away from it. I walked towards him, stopped, looked at the shape and size of it. 'Tell me that's not what I think it is.'

'Fafnir's heart,' he said.

I nearly gagged and shook my head. 'If you think I'm eating any part of that—'

He looked as ill as I felt. 'It's not for us. I promised to bring it back to Regin. He said that anyone who killed a lindworm could take the heart and eat it, and that would give them power to absorb knowledge from others. I have to smoke it so it'll keep.'

'Shit. All right. Set it aside until we've finished eating, will you? I can only imagine how it'll stink. It looks like it's already made you sick.'

We ate the last of Sigurd's bread and some nuts, a poor victory feast, but we'd lost our appetites. Then he sliced the heart into several pieces and hung each from the great iron hooks over the fire.

Somewhere, not too near, an owl hooted. The birds were coming back already, now that Fafnir was dead.

We sat on either side of the fire and watched the shapes in the flames and kept out of the smoke. It smelled like boiling vinegar. The hall was dark; the sun had gone, and the fire was our only light.

A bit of the heart-meat fell away from the hook, dangled over the fire by a thread, and Sigurd stood and grabbed it with one hand and moved it back, then hissed and put his thumb and finger into his mouth.

'It's hot,' I said, amused.

He took his hand away and looked at it. 'Do you know, I felt the heat, but no pain after. My hand isn't burned.'

'Well, we'll both be very sought after for stirring the soup,' I joked. 'If no one needs any monsters killed.'

He gave me a smile, and we sat in silence for a while. I didn't want to kill any more monsters, particularly. I was enjoying the quiet, for the moment. Somewhere, Hrist would be arguing with the others over battle tactics, and Kara would be complaining about the behaviour of the dead, and Odin would be making his plans and decisions and telling no one, listening to no one, save, perhaps, his ravens. And none of it was my problem any more. I was exiled; I was free. There in the hall I could see no frightening distant horizon; I could see only firelight and hear only wood-sorrows.

'Fafnir said Regin is my father, not my foster-father,' Sigurd said, out of nowhere.

I was startled. 'What would the lindworm know about it?'

'He said that he, Fafnir, was Regin's brother.'

'What?'

'Yes. That would make the lindworm my uncle.'

He looked at the heart on the hook, and a strange hiccupping laugh escaped him and he put the back of his hand to the corner of his mouth.

But you didn't ask me which god.

'Fafnir was a liar,' I said. 'He tried to turn our thoughts against us.'

'He knew things about Regin. And about me. I don't know. I don't know what to think.'

I was silent for a while, trying to think of anything that would help. 'He was probably just trying to make you reluctant to kill him.'

Sigurd tossed a bit of wood into the fire, not looking at me. 'He said he was one of three brothers. Two of them were shapeshifters. The youngest brother they called Otter, because he always took that shape when he could, so he could play and fish in the river. Fafnir was the middle brother. Regin was the oldest, and he couldn't change his shape. So Regin was jealous, and found ways to manipulate people, to work spells and tricks. That sounds like him, all right. One day, Fafnir found his brother Otter dead on the rocks, a wound on his temple, the water washing over him. Regin was there, and so were two gods.'

'Gods?' I asked, a cold feeling coming over me.

'Odin and Loki, Fafnir said. I'd heard those names, but I never thought to meet anyone who'd met them, any more than I'd expected to meet a man who met Christ. We don't live in a time of gods, do we? But I guess gods live for a long while. Some of them.'

I sat, thinking of the centuries that separated Sigurd's birth from mine, and waited for him to tell me what he chose to tell me.

'He said Regin somehow made everyone believe the gods had killed Otter,' Sigurd continued. 'That the gods believed that themselves and wrung their hands. Regin demanded compensation, in the form of enough gold to cover Otter's beautiful pelt. The gods were afraid to be in blood-debt. They piled gold on him, until not even a whisker was showing. Fafnir was angry with Regin for cheating the gods, and for killing his brother. He wouldn't let Regin take as much as a single coin off that hoard. He shifted into a terrible form, to protect his brother in death as he had been unable to in life. He made his breath poison and his fingers claws, and he swore there would be justice.'

I am the scourge of God, I heard in my mind. A scourge that belongs to a god, or the scourge that punishes one? I shifted on the bench to move closer to the fire, closer to Sigurd.

'You've lived with Regin your whole life. He raised you. Gave you that sword.'

Sigurd swallowed and poked the fire with a stick, stirring up sparks. 'Only because he had no one else. He told me so, often enough. He had wanted to train a hero, to rid the world of the monster Fafnir. That's why he took me in, when my parents died. Or so he said. But I was a disappointment to him.'

I screwed up my face. 'Was he kind to you?'

'Oh,' he said with a little laugh. 'No, kindness is not in his nature. Me, the cat he kept around to eat rats, the neighbours, the birds. We all disappointed him. How I longed to bring him this monstrous heart and show him he was wrong.' He looked up at me, through the firelight. 'But you were the one who killed Fafnir.'

'We both did,' I said honestly. 'We both delivered blows. If you hadn't stabbed him, I wouldn't have been able to get close to him.'

He shrugged.

'You have nothing to prove to Regin or anyone else, Sigurd. You have slain a lindworm. You can go where you like, make whatever life you like.'

Now I wonder what the bards would say about that? Is it fate that I chose to say those words, when I could have said something else? I could have sent him back to Regin, who probably would have eaten his prize, gained whatever power he could from it, gone off to be an evil wizard and left Sigurd to be a smith in a small town, with his monster-slaying story to tell at the tavern. I don't know whether that would have made Sigurd happy. Perhaps, if they had sung songs about him around their fires. Perhaps that would have been enough.

In any case, he would have lived. And I might never have met you, my morning star.

Sigurd was quiet, so I stood up and poked the fire. He looked up at me. 'You decide which way we ride, Brynhild, and wherever you go, if you want my company, you'll have it.'

I watched the shadows dance on his shoulders, his neck.

'You look like you're about to throw something at me,' he said.

'Actually, I was thinking about kissing you,' I said.

Yes, I know, you're laughing at me now, Gudrun. How awkward I am. We said we'd tell each other everything, didn't we? And anyway, you know you have my heart, as no one else ever has or ever will. Our love has infinite mansions; there is more than enough room in it for all our other affections. And we both cared for Sigurd, in our way, and I think we both have our regrets. That night is not one of them for me.

That night was a battle-night. I wanted to absorb him and be absorbed. We bit each other's invulnerable necks, scratched each other's invulnerable backs, as we dropped our fire-warmed clothing to the ground. He was warm against me and he smelled like sweet sun on dry grass. He smelled like mortal man, and by Valhalla, it was a scent I wanted to lick off him until all of it was mine. We spent that night entwined like two dragons on a brooch, the firelight playing in the shadows of our limbs.

It still hurts a little to think of Sigurd in those days, how he was, and how we were. I know it; I see myself in your face, as I remember my life and you remember yours. But this part of the story is an old wound, and mostly healed. I'm glad now that I can press on it to remember that it was real.

*

I didn't dream of Valhalla that night, or of anything. With the last of the thorn-sleep finally sweated out of my body, I drifted beyond all thought, as content as though I were lying on my back in a sunny poppy field. I had proven that I could still fight for justice, here in Midgard. I had a new ally, his body warm beside mine. There was a roof over my head, and a hoard of battle-spoil waiting for me, and a dead monster rotting at the foot of my mountain. Yes, I already thought of it as my mountain. I already dreamt of it as home. A warm hall, with a lover by my side. Everything I could want.

My exile was but a new chapter, I thought, and a better one. I would be a better Valkyrie here than I'd ever been able to be in Odin's service. Here, I had nothing to obey but my own conscience, and my conscience was clear. Not even Fafnir's poisonous whispers troubled my sleep that night.

Just before daybreak, the watery voices of ravens half-woke me.

I've gone back so many times in my mind to try to recall exactly what those ravens said, though at the time I thought nothing of it. Just chatter, I thought. Useless gossip that Sigurd would hear only as caws and clicks and grunts. But the raven-speech ran something like this:

Look. You see? This man was killed.

I don't think it was killed. If it was killed by the lindworm, how did it get up here? It is sleeping, just like the Valkyrie.

Is it a Valkyrie?

It must have helped her kill the lindworm. I saw it hold a sword.

It holds a sword like a cuckoo holds a twig. Like it doesn't know what it's for. No, this one has the look of a raven-starver. I know. I know humans very well. A bedfellow for the Valkyrie, that's all. Who else but a Valkyrie could kill a lindworm? No one with sense would believe he had anything to do with it. She has him under her protection, that's all. He spoke of Regin, the owl said.

Of Regin! The murderer?

The very same. He flees; perhaps he has displeased Regin.

Or he has done as Regin required of him, and is of no more use to him.

Either way he will end the same.

The same. Dead.

No wonder he is here, then, where the Valkyrie can keep him safe. She stays longer than they usually do. I thought she would be gone once she had killed the lindworm. Back to Valhalla.

'Let us sleep, friends,' I mumbled, losing patience. 'I will tell you all the gossip you wish to know in the morning.'

The ravens clicked, offended, embarrassed to be overheard; they don't like to be called gossips. I let my eyelids flutter open for a moment, caught the outline of Sigurd beside me in the dawn light, like the blue line of a distant mountain. And then I went back to sleep.

When I woke, Sigurd was gone.

CHAPTER TEN

Brynhild on the Mountain

I knew I was alone on the mountain as soon as I woke. Felt it in my bones, or perhaps it was only the chill. The fire in the hall had gone out, and the strips of foul meat were gone from the hooks above. I stood for a moment, looking at the iron, thinking.

When Svafa left, I found myself one of the oldest Valkyries. Eir, the healer, was the exception, but it wouldn't be long before Odin left her to die in Midgard too. One moment I had been the future and the next, I was the past. The younger Valkyries liked training with me, but they didn't confide in me. One day I realized that if any Valkyrie could help the young ones understand *why* we did what we did in the ways we did it, it would be me. All of them had their chats with the Allfather, but they needed to learn from someone who had also been taken from her home and family, who also knew what it felt like to see the surprise dawn on the face of a dying man who knows full well his enemy's blade isn't the one that pierced him.

It is a strange occupation.

I had very nearly left it too late. Most didn't care to even ask questions. They'd already chosen to revel in the blood, or compete with each other, or torture themselves with second-guessing. But there was one who had questions for me: Hrist. She was a rebel. She scowled at all the answers. And after a half-century, she became my right hand, and we led a troop of Valkyries that shone with righteousness and gleamed with joy.

In three hundred years or more, I'd sometimes felt lonely but I had never felt alone. And now, in the space of a few days, I'd been first exiled, then summarily abandoned. Abandoned by a man who had said 'wherever you go, if you want my company, you'll have it'.

It was a short walk across the top of the mountain to the wall made of molten weapons. From there, I could see the tree where Grani had been tied. The corpse of the lindworm was half-skeleton already. The golden bracelets were gone from its arms.

One of the ravens hopping around the carcass flew to me. It was a young bird, not yet mated. Part of a gang, and cocky, by the look in its eye. One of the same who had been squawking in our window the night before, I thought.

'You're awake,' the raven said. 'Thank you for the meal. It is not good, but there's a lot of it.'

Ravens speak with a complexity that eludes most birds. It makes them good messengers, when they choose to work as messengers. Most do not.

'Have you seen my friend?'

'The man? Yes. He rode away on the horse before the dawn.'

'Rode away?' The coldness ate at my bones, and I wrapped my arms around myself. He was really gone, then, not just rummaging around somewhere. 'Did something happen?'

'I could smell the fear on him,' the raven scoffed. 'But he had enough wit to pack his horse with gold before he rode off. He stripped the last gold off the lindworm, too. We don't want it.'

I nodded, slowly, and thanked the insolent bird, out of habit and prudence. 'If you see him, will you tell me?'

The bird cocked its head in a way that usually meant yes. Under the grey sky, I strode back across the mountain, swinging my knife in my hand.

The treasure room was not empty, but some of the gold was gone. The smallest things: the gold pig, and piles of coins and torcs. He'd left me most of the arms, helmets, coats of mail, from what I could see.

Perhaps out of concern for me, perhaps to make room in the saddlebags, he'd left his mead flask, and three sacks of food: peas and flour and nuts. As if I couldn't fend for myself perfectly well.

We'd agreed that we should each take half the hoard, and by the looks of it, he'd left me well more than half. He hadn't stolen from me. He'd simply left without saying goodbye. It irked me that I didn't know why.

Where would he go? Back to Regin, with the smoked lindworm-heart and the iron nose ring to prove Fafnir's death? Or somewhere else? To find a place where he'd be hailed as a hero, as a monster-slayer?

No matter. I wouldn't go looking for him. He'd made his choice. And I would go – where?

I sat on the bench by the ash-floored fire pit and thought. Valhalla was not open to me, but I had a hall of my own, now. I had gold, and weapons, and the strength of my hands. I remembered what I'd said to Sigurd, half-jokingly, about widows and unwanted daughters. I'd already proven that I could be a battle-judge here on Midgard. But to truly be a Valkyrie, I needed companions, and students.

Why not?

I began with water. There was a stone cistern not far from the hall, but it had green stuff growing around the edges at the top of the dark water. At least Fafnir hadn't been using it. It was too small for him; he had most likely gone down to the creek to drink, if lindworms need to drink. It was well built, though, and didn't leak.

I drained the water, scrubbed the inside with ashes. With a flint, I carved runes in every rock to purify the water that would fall with the next rain.

By the third day, I had venison hanging from drying racks, and I had pulled a withered tree trunk up from the plain below and set it into the earth to be a pell for sword training. Every morning I tested a different weapon against it from the treasure room, until I found the ones I liked best. The red-hafted battle-axe I'd used to tease Sigurd with, and a sword with the shape of a woman with upraised hands forming the hilt and pommel. You know those weapons well; that's where I got them. The runes that said 'Hrotti' on the blade of the sword might have been the name of the maker, but I took to calling the sword by that name.

I had been there five days, I think, when the raven returned to tell me he had seen Sigurd, in the company of several men.

'Were the men his friends?'

The raven said, 'He is a man full of fear. That's all I know.'

'Where is he?'

'About a day's walk for you, to the south. The opposite direction to the one in which he set out. But he's close to a village; that may be why. The village was half-abandoned when the lindworm was alive, but there are still some poor people there.'

I considered this. I wanted flour, seeds for planting, perhaps some chicks to raise into fowl. I wanted a fresh change of clothes. And soon enough, I'd be ready to start bringing students to my mountaintop. This village didn't sound big enough to have a market, but if its people were poor, they might well be grateful for some gold. Gold was one thing I had in abundance.

I don't know to what degree I was worried for Sigurd, and to what degree I was simply curious. After all, he was impervious to weapons. He'd defeated the lindworm at my side. There was no reason I should have been worried for him. But the raven's words – a man full of fear – made me itch to be off down the mountain, my sword in my hand.

And so that's what I did.

I met them well before the day's walk was done. They were sitting under a leaning ash tree, eating roast meat. Their horses were grazing. Sigurd was with them, and he wasn't shackled or bloody. He stood up when he saw me approach on a narrow track through the grass that hardly deserved to be called a road. That was hilly country, and the track wound its way through the passes, and so by the time we saw each other, we were already within speaking distance.

But we didn't speak.

One of the men did.

'Well, now,' he said, standing up. 'Where do you come from?'

I saw myself as they must have seen me: stained and torn trousers, stained and torn tunic. I had seen no reason to take my mail with me. My belt bore Hrotti on one hip, and my water-flask and a purse of lindworm-gold on the other. I had braided my hair all along the back of my head and left my helmet in the hall. I didn't look like a warrior, I suppose. I looked like a woman with a sword.

'I come from the mountain.'

They scoffed. 'The lindworm mountain?'

'Yes,' I said, my mouth dry. I took a sip from my flask and wiped my mouth. 'It's dead.'

'We know it's dead,' said another of the men, who hadn't bothered to get up. He pointed his elbow at Sigurd. 'This one killed it, a few days ago. Lucky for you, eh? But where did you come from before that?'

'Oh, he killed it, did he?' I looked at Sigurd, who met my gaze, more angrily than he had any right to.

'Yes,' said the first man. 'I suppose the hall's still up there? Convenient place to sleep, it must be, for a runaway . . . slave? Daughter? Wife?'

'I'm not running away from anything or anyone,' I said, though I owed them nothing. I lifted my chin. 'I was looking for a village. To buy clothing, seeds and flour.'

'The village doesn't have anyone with enough to sell,' said another man, grim-faced, who hadn't spoken before. 'There's nobody with food to spare around here. You'll have to walk to Mainz or Vormatia.'

'Perhaps I will,' I said, and hesitated, not wanting to venture far from my mountain. I looked at the saddlebags. If the people nearby were in need, better to trade with them anyway. 'Surely someone can sell me a bit of old cloth, or some beans. Some fruit, perhaps. Something I can plant. I can pay well.'

'Can you?' said the biggest man, with a sharp eye. 'Sigurd, did you happen to leave any of your gold behind on that mountain? I think this girl's been stealing from you.'

'It's hers, whatever she has,' Sigurd said at last, hoarsely. 'I know her, and I know where she comes from. She has an old family right to that mountain, and now that it's safe, she should live there. Let me see if I can help her.' Abruptly, he strode over to me, took my arm, and marched me a little way distant, where we could speak without being overheard. The other men hooted with laughter.

Somehow, I objected to his magnanimity, which I didn't need. I opened my mouth, though I can't remember what I intended to say. But he spoke again, for my ears only.

'As I said, I know where you come from,' he said, his jaw tight. 'I know exactly who you are. Valkyrie.'

Confused, I managed, 'We said we'd say nothing about the past.'

'I told you everything,' he said bitterly. Then, more softly: 'What the lindworm said, Regin, everything.'

'I don't understand. Sigurd, what happened? How did you even know—'

'The birds!' he said, frustrated. 'I can understand their talk, somehow, now. You're going to tell me I imagined it.'

Somehow, he'd learned the language of the birds. I thought back to the day when Svafa had taught me, the little speech she'd given me about all the ways to cheat one's way to knowledge. None of those ways would be ours, she'd said with her wry grin. We couldn't bargain or sacrifice or devour a magical beast. We couldn't even hang ourselves for nine days, come to that. We'd simply have to study.

I heard her say the word 'devour' in my memory, and it all made sense.

'The monster's heart. You burned your finger and put it into your mouth.'

'So?' He was defensive.

'So you said Regin said that eating the heart would give you – what did you say? The power to absorb knowledge from others. I, well, I understand the language of birds. I learned the skill long ago. When you sucked your finger, the night – that night, you gained knowledge. From me.'

He looked at me as though he hated me. 'So, I am even further in your debt.'

'What is this, Sigurd? What the hell has made you angry with me?'

'You're a Valkyrie! That's why you killed the monster so easily.'

'Easily! I assure you, nothing about that was easy.'

'You've been mocking me. Playing with me. Taking my victory from me. What did you say? That I could go anywhere I wanted, tell them I slew a monster, and have the life I chose? Unlikely, with a Valkyrie at my side ready to tell them that in fact, she was the one who killed the monster, while I hid in a hole.'

'I wouldn't—'

'Who would believe I had anything to do with it? Who would call me a hero, if they knew I fought alongside you? I can't even go back to Regin, now. He has tricks. He'd know the truth.'

I looked beyond him, to the men half-watching us.

99

'I'm certainly not going to tell anyone,' I said, coldly. 'And I'm not a Valkyrie any more, anyway. You don't have to fear—'

He shook his head. 'I'm not afraid.'

But he was. He was more afraid of me than either of us had been of the lindworm. Not of what I'd do but of who I was, and of what that meant for who *he* was. He thought my very existence robbed him of his right to call himself a hero.

'Go, then,' I said. 'I wish you good health and a long life.'

What had I really imagined, anyway? We weren't in love. I didn't want to make my life with Sigurd, and he certainly didn't want to spend his life with me. But we had been battle-companions, and lovers for a night, and, I thought, friends and allies. My only friend and ally in Midgard. I felt alone, and very disappointed.

'She's going back to her hall,' Sigurd said, walking back to the men. 'I'll send someone to sell her what she needs.'

'That won't be necessary,' I snapped. 'If any of you have anything you can spare, I'll happily buy it from you. Otherwise, I'll find my own way to what I need.'

There was a long silence. Then the grim-faced man stood up, wiped his hands, and rummaged in his saddlebags. While his companions jeered at him, he offered me a half-eaten wheel of cheese, some flour, some dried peas I could plant. He sold me a linen shirt that was too big, but I could make needles out of bone.

I pulled a gold coin out of the little purse I'd fashioned out of a saddlebag, and showed it to him.

'Would that be sufficient?'

He took it, looked at it, then looked at me, astonished.

I stared back. I did not know the value of coins but I could weigh a heart with a glance, and I felt his was trustworthy. Or so I told myself, anyway. My pulse was like a bird's, and I wanted to be gone, back to the mountain, and truth be told I would have happily dropped my whole little purse full of coins onto the ground. Back at my hall there was clean water and good weapons, and that was more than I had fallen to Midgard with, and more than enough. I had no love of gold.

'This is useless to me,' he said at last. 'Anyone would wonder where I'd got such a thing and accuse me of stealing.'

'I didn't steal it.'

'I didn't say you did.'

I sighed and opened the saddlebag. I'd only brought coins, leaving all the jewellery and other trinkets behind. But I didn't know anything about the values of coins, new or old, or how much anything ought to cost. I had never bought anything in all my three hundred years. Just at the edge of my vision, Grani was looking at me. I pulled out a few bits of hacksilver, some other coins.

'Take whichever of these you can use, then.'

Then I felt the bigger man's breath on my neck. 'What a fine dowry! It seems you're in need of a bridegroom. And just your luck; I'm in need of a wife.'

I pulled away from them, stuffed the coins back in my purse.

'I feel I should warn you,' I called as lightly as I could. 'My mountain has protection against thieves.'

'Your mountain, is it?' The big man laughed. 'Come now, you will have to yield to someone before long, up there all alone with your bags of coins you don't know how to spend. It might as well be me.'

'Get out of my sight,' I said.

'Will you really make us climb up there? Come with me now and save me the trouble.'

'Show me a man who can climb out of his own backside and I'll consider it.'

I thought I saw small smiles pass from one of his men to the other.

I looked at Sigurd, and spoke louder. 'Show me a man who has enough without hoarding. Show me a man who knows the weight of a heart. Show me a man who cannot be wounded. Show me a man without fear. Until you can do that, I have no wish to marry.'

Very clever, I thought it. A little poem, a little speech, and a final barb. How was I to know how they'd twist my words? There was never any point in saying anything to them. I should have saved my breath and turned around the moment I saw them. But I didn't.

I threw a few coins at the grim-faced man, took my small bags of goods, and walked briskly back to my mountain. When I got there, I paced the length of Fafnir's wall and I threw up a protection of my own all around the mountaintop: a wall of flame.

The idea of finding students or companions, I put away as a distant hope. Perhaps one day a student would find me. I only knew that I wouldn't go out into the world any more than I had to. From then on, I thought, I would be alone on my mountain.

PART II
THE ROSE GARDEN

CHAPTER ELEVEN

Gudrun Provides

When I was a child, a noblewoman named Maren took up residence at the top of a tower a half-day's ride away from Vormatia. Did you ever see it, Brynhild? She had it built out of sandstone for her purpose, which was to suffer. If you can build a house just to make yourself suffer, I thought, you must be very rich. But then, I was a child. My family hadn't even built the Domus. We'd just moved into it, like a hermit crab.

Inside, Maren's tower was nothing but a stone staircase. The top had a railing all around it, and a winch for a bucket.

Bishop Timaeus had a slave send food and drink up to her in a bucket every Monday, and she would send the bucket back down with her waste. I asked my mother what Maren did with her monthly rags, and my mother said she probably didn't have any, with her body so starved.

People came from far away to see her, to ask questions or to pray nearby.

Ten years she lived there, with the sky above her and nothing but an iron railing around her. Sometimes, when the weather was cold and there were no travellers around, I would ride out and watch her from a distance, to see what she did when she thought no one was watching. I stared at her one day for more than an hour. She was kneeling, her hands on her knees, her body perfectly still. For some reason it made me angry.

That was the last time I saw her. A month later, the bucket slave reported that Maren was gone. Many people believed she had vanished, ascended; some said she'd died and rolled off and her body had been carried away by animals. Some said she had simply climbed down and walked away. We never heard from her again, one way or another.

Once the river had subsided after Attila's treachery, my mother came out of her room and told me she was walking out to Maren's tower. She wanted to ask the wind for news of Gunnar, whether he was living or dead, and where he might be found. The wind doesn't like to answer questions, so my mother expected she'd be there several days at least. I told her I thought there were better ways she could use her time, and she said there is no better use of a mother's time than looking for her lost son in the best way she can, and that was that.

My mother took a basket of figs, nuts, bread, and wine, because her suffering was not of the bodily kind, and she didn't want to be disturbed. I told her I'd send someone for the waste bucket.

With the bridge still damaged, the boatmen did a brisk business, although the soldiers from the Empire's watch-towers grumbled about the delays when they came to the city to see their mistresses.

Ludgast came to the city that very night. I ordered rooms for him and his companions and ordered a meal for the two of us: soft cheese, olives, smoked mackerel, bright green asparagus. We ate off the red glass plates and sat across the table from each other. I would have liked to have had Hagen there, but we agreed it was best that there be no doubt about who was in charge.

We ate in the small dining room – not the triclinium, which my father kept for Romans when they came, but the one with the plain oak table and the wide chairs. Ludgast looked at the swords hanging on the wall as if they were his allies. He didn't look at me that way.

'It is hard not to have a body,' he said brusquely. He meant my brother's.

'We don't know yet that Gunnar is dead.'

'Then where is he? If he's alive, he abandoned his people. Either way, he is no longer king.'

'You might consider the possibility that your king is wounded and in need of your service, after risking his life to save his people.'

He nodded very slightly, like a man who's choosing not to argue with a woman he thinks is wrong.

'Sit,' I said. 'Eat.'

He sat, and wrapped some bread around some mackerel.

'Whether I wait for the king to return or not, my people need land to till now,' he said bluntly. 'And pasture for their animals, before the summer comes. My nephew will take them north.'

I was surprised. 'To Mainz? All those lands are already spoken for.'

'North of Mainz.'

'We have no sovereignty north of Mainz. We can't raid in provinces of the Empire.'

'We are Burgundians. We have sovereignty wherever we choose.'

I shook my head. 'The Empire will not tolerate us raiding within its borders. Now, of all times, we must hold on to what we have. Without the protection of the Empire, we can't stand against the Huns.'

'I have fought the Huns many times in my life, long before your father made his treaty.'

'And did they have a lindworm, when you fought them?' That was sharper than I intended. The stink of poison was still in my nostrils.

As it was in his, it seemed. 'My people will starve where

they are.' He made a fist on the table; he had eaten a few bites. I hadn't eaten much either.

'Then they can come into the city. We have storehouses here.'

He shook his head. 'They want their own land to till. And they won't wait for someone else to give it to them. They are Burgundians.'

'I am a Burgundian too,' I said quietly.

'Then show it,' he said. 'I will be king, and you will be my queen.'

I was startled; I don't know how I had expected it to come, but it wasn't like that. 'Is that a question, Ludgast?'

'It is the only choice that makes sense.'

I looked at him and thought that if the times had been different, I could have done worse for a husband than a man of fifty with broad shoulders and a narrow mind. He wore his scars proudly and his thinning hair long. Nothing about him would have surprised me, which would have been fine, as I am capable of seeking my own surprises.

But the times were not different. If I'd married Ludgast, he very likely would have made himself king, and he would have lost Vormatia. He didn't even care about Vormatia. To him, land was something to be raided, occupied, hunted upon. A city was simply in the way.

I cocked my head and smiled. 'You are not my only option.'

He narrowed his eyes. 'Lothar? He's no king.'

'He wouldn't have been in the old days, that's true.'

Ludgast shook his head, as if a fly were bothering him, but there were no flies in our dining room. 'If we were king and queen together, we would rule a great people, who took what they needed and were safe in their lands. If you choose another husband, you may find yourself called queen, but ruling what? This city, full of Romans, Egyptians, Franks, Syrians, and the gods know what else. I wish you joy of it. Make your choice, but I can't wait long. My people need to sow their crops.'

And I needed time. Time for Gunnar to return, time to fortify the city, time to make allies in case Gunnar never did come home.

'I will visit your people, Ludgast,' I said. 'Tomorrow.'

He looked taken aback, suspicious, but he said that I would be welcome.

I didn't have my mother's gifts, but I was good with plants. That was something I could do. And plants were Ludgast's problem, or at least the problem he was using as an excuse to go raiding. So I rode out, with Ludgast and his companions, to the lands poisoned by the lindworm.

Ludgast and the other heads of families gave me permission to work a spell, seeing that their land was dead already and I couldn't kill it any worse. Maybe they gave me more credit than I deserved, because they had heard about my mother's great works. I had no great works. But I managed to purify a few farm holdings. It took me three days, walking the fields with a sack full of loaves, breaking the pieces, casting them on the earth. I made offerings to the plants and coaxed them into believing the danger was gone.

I felt as if I were tricking them. By then, Fafnir was dead, thanks to you. But none of us knew that yet. He hadn't returned, but was Attila holding him back, making plans for another assault? We had no idea, and I couldn't help wondering whether I'd cured the land of a poison that would return any day.

But I smiled when I walked among Ludgast's people. 'You can plant spring crops now without fear of them dying,' I told them. I could see they doubted me, but then the birds came back to the fields and ate the remnants of the bread and they saw that my magic, small and slow though it was, was sound enough.

And Ludgast had no argument to make, then, when I told him he would have to wait for my answer to his proposal, that I had many burdens and much to consider. He couldn't protest that his people would starve. He'd be back, I knew, to insist on marriage and the kingship, as a final ultimatum before he split his people away from us altogether. But I had a little more time now.

Ludgast lent me two men to accompany me back to Vormatia. We rode home through the dappled forests, our hoofbeats on the pine needles soft under the warblers' songs. I was happy there, but I had to get back to the city as soon as possible. There was so much work to do.

Maybe, I thought, there would be a response waiting from me, from Galla Placidia, the regent of the Empire. It would take a messenger a fortnight to carry it to Ravenna, and then another fortnight to return. If I could hold off Ludgast and Lothar for a month, I could present my people with a guarantee of imperial help. There was a reason the Empire had made a treaty with my father, given our people our home on the inside of its border. We could help hold the Huns and everyone else at bay, but we would need soldiers and gold to do it.

What was she like, this Galla Placidia, this woman who ruled everything from Britain to Africa, from Hispania to Dalmatia? Maybe she would have some sympathy for a woman in my position; she'd taken over when her brother died.

My breath caught and I stopped the horse, holding up a hand to stop the guards. Just off the path ahead I thought I saw a woman, holding her skirts, looking off into the forest, perfectly still.

I looked closer, about to call out, when I saw the gleam of wood on her cheek. She was carved out of a wide, squat pine tree, the bark forming her jacket and the folds in her skirt.

'It's just a beehive, my lady,' said one of Ludgast's men. 'The beekeepers tend them inside the trees, and sometimes they carve them into shapes, like people or animals.'

I'd seen hives made of trees before; as a child, I used to

imagine all sorts of tiny creatures lived behind their doors. But never one carved to look like a woman. It was a pity; whoever tended this would be at the mercy of the lindworm or the Huns, if either came this way.

'Whose land is this?' I asked. 'We're on my brother's personal holdings, aren't we?'

'Yes, my lady, it is all the king's land, from that creek we crossed a little while ago, all the way back to the Rhine. That hive is one that supplies the Domus. There are many of them on this path, some carved like that, and some plainer. There will be fresh swarms looking for homes, too, at this time of year.'

I couldn't move stones, but I was very good with plants, and I was on friendly terms with the bees in my rose garden. These were my brother's hives, and I would take them home safe.

You can climb a branch all the way to heaven, my mother used to say, but it needs an invitation first. Plants crave pathways. I was good at guiding and suggesting; my mother wasn't. But it didn't matter, because if she wanted to, she could force a piece of wood into whatever shape she wanted.

I couldn't take the hive-woman by the hand, but I could give her something to hold. One hair from my head, plucked and laid upon her shoulder. One dark, sleek bee crawled near her nose, and I could hear them inside her. My hair was very long and black in those days. A nub of green on her bark grew into a tendril and grasped the hair just before the wind could whip it away. New-green shoots reached for me, for another hair from my head, for a pathway to me, and I smiled and turned away.

As my horse took a few steps, I could hear the hive-woman behind me, the rough drag of roots through soil. Moving, following.

'Don't look behind,' I told Ludgast's men. 'Just ride on.'

We passed two more women, a bearded mail-clad knight, and a bear standing on his hind legs, all of them buzzing with invisible bees. Like Orpheus walking out of the under-world, I led our shy wooden followers. I felt honey-drunk already, sleepy from the mead we'd make. I pulled hairs out with each hand and let them fly on the wind, and vines shot out from the shadows and wrapped around my wrists, and then their ends came free, and I moved my arms to twist them, to form wicker hives, skeps that hung from my shoulders and back. A slick of bees crawled up from the forest floor, over my body and into a skep. Another swarm dripped down from a nearby branch.

How my brother would have laughed to see me, and the trees dragging themselves along behind me, the bees obeying me too and scurrying in and out like eager children. It had never occurred to me to try something like that before. Too bad, as I could have made Gunnar a wager that I could do it and won.

I invited the hives home. They would be safe in the city: we would build them palaces for apiaries, and the city would tax their honey lightly. Their wax would light candles for prayers. I promised the hives that all around the city walls I would let the meadow flowers grow, that they would hardly miss their forest honeydew, that I would coax fruit trees to come near just as I had coaxed the hives.

The boatman didn't want to take us, when we came to the Rhine.

I nearly asked the bees to fly me over, but I could feel I had asked enough of nature for one day. So instead, I asked to borrow his boat, said that my guards would row me and my companions, and send it back to him. We could hardly hear our negotiations over the buzzing. I stood in the boat all the way over, holding my buzzing vine-skeps, not brushing away the bees that wandered onto my neck or arms. We hummed together. I walked out of the boat, my companions behind me, and although all eyes were on them now, they had come too far to turn back, so they followed me into the city.

As it turned out, the roots wrapped around the hull damaged the little boat, so later Hagen offered to pay the boatman to repair it. But by then the boatman was ashamed of denying us, and took no payment.

I never turned back, so I can't imagine what it must have looked like as we walked through the gate. A roar that must have sounded as if it came from the bear, moving so hesitantly on his two rooted legs. The wooden women with their wide skirts, the knight so indifferent. And me, with my twisted vines spreading around me like wings and a halo, crawling with bees. I stood as tall as if I'd been carved out of wood myself, stiff with fear of messing up the spell somehow at the last minute.

The children came running, laughing, pointing, with their mothers behind them, nervous. I smiled then and spread my arms wide and let the skeps drop gently to the ground. The bees had come into the city, to make us honey when the siege came.

And I had shown the people, inside the city and out, that I could provide for them.

As for protecting them, that was another question.

CHAPTER TWELVE

Gudrun at Pentecost

We doubled the watch on Vormatia's walls, giving every boy his first taste of duty. We set the fletchers making arrows and the dairies making cheese. Inside the city, the wealthy families gave over every space they could spare to planting cabbages, onions, beets, carrots, leeks, turnips, peas, gathering all their seeds in from their country estates, and we did the same inside the Domus. It sounds like abundance now, listed out like that, but I was worried about hunger. I built vegetable beds in my rose garden. Salted fish hung from clotheslines. We sent all our grain stores to be milled, and had the flour sent into the city. We told the carpenters to make ballistae and paid the potters to make vessels full of stinging potions to put on the walls.

A month after the lindworm came, we celebrated the feast of Pentecost. We garlanded the cows and goats and drove them through the streets and out through the gates to further pastures, although that year they would be kept as close as possible and guarded by armed men.

I wore a birch crown that I made myself. My dress was the colour of the tongues of fire that descended on the apostles, that lit their eyes and warmed their hearts and caused them to speak in all the languages of the world. In Vormatia we all spoke each other's languages already, at least well enough to be understood.

Birch wreaths hung from all the windows and we put a pole in the centre of the city, near the church, the synagogue, the temples, and the forum. There were some Romans who made sacrifices at the temple of Mars, and some Burgundians worshipped Tiu there. Most of the Burgundians had been Christians since my grandfather's generation but not all, and there were also some among the Goths and Franks in the city who were not Christians.

Still, everyone came out for Pentecost. Even my mother came down from her pillar. She had heard nothing from the wind that did her any good. No news of Gunnar. Our riders had not found his body.

Our people gave nervous thanks for the fact that we'd had no sign of the lindworm. But we knew the Huns could return at any moment, and we would be no match for them.

My mother set her mouth into its grimmest line and told me that Galla Placidia had given my father a promise on behalf of the Empire, and that such a promise would not be lightly broken.

Maybe my smile tightened too, as we walked through the blossom-strewn streets and smiled in the sunlight. Hagen was at my right, and our mother walked a little ahead of us. We kept a slow pace, partly so the people hanging out of their windows and up on walls could see us well, and partly so as not to tax Volker, who walked on my left. He had mostly recovered from his injuries, but his breath still came ragged when he exerted himself, and his voice was hoarse. That was the first Pentecost at which he did not sing. He slept most of the day, still, and Hagen weakly joked that it took a monster to get Volker to sleep for more than an hour. He had terrible insomnia, much of the time, and he walked in his sleep. I'd found him wandering in my garden more than once when I went there in the mornings, and sometimes he was awake, and sometimes not.

Anyway, our little family procession wasn't very impressive. Young Lothar must have smelled blood. He caught up with me at the doors to the church, after the bishop performed the mass. There was a crush of people, both coming out of the church behind us, and in the streets, where they'd been listening to the sermon as best they could.

Unlike Ludgast, Lothar hadn't pressed his suit right away, though I knew it was coming. I could see him steeling himself to the task of wooing me. So why hadn't he spoken sooner? Well, Ludgast had felt some urgency, I reminded myself. But the uncharitable part of my mind, which was probably correct, suspected Lothar had been waiting for advice from his imperial friends.

'My lady, I think it is time we had a talk about the state of things.'

'It's Pentecost, Lothar. Wasn't it a lovely sermon?'

'Bishop Timaeus is an embarrassment.'

Lothar's tongue was particularly sharp that morning; I glanced at him. He was good-looking, in an objective sort of way. Well-groomed.

'You want someone with more fashionable theology,' I said. 'A trinitarian.'

'I want someone who is not a heretic. Whose teachings are in line with the rest of the Empire.'

'He is bishop by the will of our people, and therefore of God. Many of those people revere the teachings of Arius, as he does. And Vormatia is not part of the Empire. It is simply inside it.'

'I think the time has come to let go of such fictions, don't you? The Huns could attack any day, and we need to be able to fend them off.'

I stopped, then, looking hard at his face. Lothar was always lusting after the Empire in his heart, but I'd never heard him speak so plainly before. I pulled him aside, away from the crowd. Hagen looked nervous, but I sent him a glance to tell him it was all right. 'Lothar, the Empire promised my father independence and protection in exchange for keeping the borders secure.'

'An arrangement that was made a generation ago with a usurper, a traitor whose skull still grins on a wall-pole in Ravenna.'

'Galla Placidia said our arrangement was not with the usurper Jovinus but with the Empire. She gave her word it would be honoured.'

'Her regency is coming to an end. Her son is nearly of age, and he's decided nearly of age is good enough. He's taken over. And Valentinian imagines an Empire without any barbarian kings inside it.'

I wasn't sure how much irony was in his use of the word 'barbarian' to describe his own people. Everything Lothar said sounded ironic. But I had no reason to doubt his information, when it came to the politics of the Empire.

No wonder I'd had no response to my letter to Galla Placidia.

I smiled at Lothar, trying not to look surprised, but in truth I wanted to lean against the nearby pillar for support. Without the Empire's troops, we were at the mercy of the Huns.

Maybe that was what this Valentinian intended. Use our enemies to get rid of us, pretend it was a dispute among barbarians, rather than an imperial project.

There was a commotion in the crowds in the street below the steps, and my heart seized. Maybe Lothar hadn't waited to gather the city fathers; maybe he was moving now, taking power in the old way, removing everyone loyal to me. Or maybe it was Ludgast – where was Ludgast?

A skinny young man came running through the crowd, his face as red as if the tongues of fire had lain on him. I recognized him as one of our scouts, and then my heart flipped again.

'Someone approaches the city on horseback,' he gasped, out of breath. A red-cheeked boy, more excited to have news than frightened by it.

I stepped closer to him, pitched my voice soft. 'An army?' The boy shook his head. 'A single rider. From the east.'

I wrapped my red cloak around my shoulders and walked down into the people. I felt myself walking like an old woman, tentative and unsteady, afraid my ankles would not hold me up.

We weren't far from the city gates. Someone shouted, 'The king! The king has returned!'

The crowd parted for him but didn't cheer. Everyone was silent, shocked at first by his return, and then by the look of him. He was thin and hunched over his horse, my brother, the great rider. I tried to shift my own expression into joy, but it kept itself frozen into a kind of questioning despair.

He rode to me and I put my hand on his leg. There's a story about one of Christ's first followers, a man named Thomas, who wouldn't believe Christ had risen from the dead until he touched him with his own hands. I felt a little like that.

'You're alive,' I whispered.

Gunnar nodded, although it was not very convincing. His dark hair hung matted with blood to his chin, and his eyes were coals.

I eased him off his horse and he stood, broken, and I put my arms around him.

'Where have you been?' I hissed into his ear, as the two guards looked on.

Something like a dry sob choked him, racked him. 'The beast spoke to me – made me believe—'

'Never mind,' I said, conscious of the people around us. I pulled away from the embrace and took him by the hand like a child. 'You're home now. You're king.'

'Is anyone left alive?' He looked at the people around us as if he thought they were an assemblage of ghosts.

'We lost Dancwart, Eckart, and Sinold in the attack, and a child, a relation of Ludgast's, died last week after a long illness from the poison.'

His face was shocked. 'So few? That's all who died?'

'That's all of our people. A few Huns died, and Bleda, of course. We buried them.'

'And the lindworm?'

'Has not returned.'

He nodded, shortly, ran his fingers through his hair. 'I'll need to make a plan for the city's defences, won't I?'

'The city is defended. You'll need a bath, a cup of wine and a joint of meat, and a bed. And then we'll talk to Hagen.'

'Hagen survived?' He looked up at my face for the first time. It was a nonsensical thing to say, as I'd just given him the list of dead, and Hagen wasn't on it. But Gunnar seemed unable to believe anything good in that moment. 'Well, that's something.'

The Gunnar who returned to us was not quite the brother I'd known before. His jawline was sharper, his expression darker. Whenever he could, he chose to be alone in his room. We held no great feast to celebrate his return, but when Volker was well enough at last to sing, we had a supper together, just the friends and family, in my garden. We set a wooden table with summer food and decorated it with flowers, and Volker sang love songs, softly as his throat was still raw, and played his lute.

Gunnar sat with us for a little while, then stood, said nothing, and went into his room.

The preparations went on, although with each day that passed, the city's fear of the Huns faded. Where were they? Maybe the lindworm had swallowed them all up, or poisoned Attila's court and left them all dying in agony. We hardly dared to hope for it, although it seemed a fitting end for anyone who would ally with a monster.

I couldn't rest. I walked through the city, seeing to the

bees and orchards and kitchen gardens. I mixed whatever potions might be useful, for hurting or healing. Mother and I walked the city walls, and she found the places that were weakest, laying her thin hand on the cold stones, and whispering to them.

Gunnar was quiet, but not idle. He ordered new armour, its shifting plates bright as beetles. He brought money to the families of the men who had died in the lindworm attack. There was no fault in his conduct, but there was also no mistaking that he had left part of himself in some land we would not find on any map.

It might have been ten days after he returned when we had word that Ludgast was in the atrium, asking to see the king.

Gunnar, Hagen, and Volker were in the bathhouse, sitting on the bench that ran around the edge of the water in the warm room. Two men I didn't know well were standing at the door, pikestaffs in their hands. I had never known Gunnar to use a personal bodyguard before, not even during negotiations with ambassadors or kings, but now these men came with him everywhere he went. There in the water next to Gunnar were two of the greatest warriors ever known, and Gunnar's most loyal friends, but he kept his guards at the door even so.

He told the guard to send Ludgast in.

Maybe fate brought Ludgast to us at that moment, instead of when Gunnar was poring over maps or sparring with Hagen – both of which he did, every day. But it was Gunnar's mistake not to make Ludgast wait, not to get out of the bath and meet him somewhere else. As it was, Ludgast came to see my brother when he was naked and oiled, lounging Roman-style in a bath with two men known to be lovers, with guards at the door. But maybe it didn't matter. He probably wouldn't have made any decisions differently, if he had found Gunnar in circumstances he'd consider more befitting his old companion's son.

I was tying up new plants in my rose garden, which of course Ludgast had to walk through to get to the bathhouse. So, I heard all that happened, keeping my head bowed under my enormous straw hat. It kept the sun off.

Ludgast stood at the door and bowed his head very slightly and reluctantly. 'My lord, I've come with a request from my people. May I speak with you tonight?'

My brother's voice, faintly, from within: 'You can speak with me now, Ludgast. I hope that my sister's work still holds, and there is no more trouble with poison in your fields.'

Gunnar never begrudged me my small skill with magic. He treated it like women's work, because in our family, it was. Ludgast glanced back at me, in a way that showed he didn't quite thank me for what I'd done. I smiled pleasantly at him, bits of rope in my hand. All talk of marriage had stopped, since my brother came home. Suddenly, I wasn't a path to the throne; now I was a symbol of loyalty to my brother and his family. I didn't miss having suitors.

'The crops are up already, and we expect a good harvest,' Ludgast said, turning back towards the interior of the bathhouse. 'The request is simply that you tell us what kept you away from your city for a month. Where you went, and what you did.'

A long silence. Then: 'I don't see what concern that is of yours, Ludgast.'

'The people will not be ruled by a king who runs away.'

The guard shifted in their positions, but Ludgast stayed steadfast.

My brother's voice was so low, I could barely hear it. 'Are you suggesting I ran away from the lindworm?'

'I am not suggesting anything. I am asking whether you did. If a man has a reason for running from an enemy, it behoves him to explain it.'

Another long silence. I gave up all pretence of tying the plants and stepped closer. I wanted to protest that the king

121

didn't owe any subject an explanation for his decisions during battle, but the truth was that I didn't believe that, and neither did my brother. I couldn't think of anything to say.

Eventually, my brother said something, although I couldn't hear what. Ludgast did, though. He straightened his big shoulders, in their fine but plain red tunic. His chest lifted his beard.

'Then I challenge you, Gunnar son of Gjuki, for the kingship of the Burgundians and right to tribute from all their lands and families.'

It echoed a little, in that garden surrounded by stone walls.

'What form does your challenge take?' I asked, sharply. 'Will you challenge him in combat? You are a great warrior, Ludgast, but you're more than twenty years my brother's senior.'

I suggested it on purpose. Combat wasn't necessary; Ludgast could simply have called all the heads of families and the city council together in the banquet hall and demanded that they choose their king. That wasn't a contest I was confident my brother could win.

Ludgast took the bait, but he was craftier than I knew. He turned to me. 'Combat would suit me well. And as for my age, well, a man may name a champion. The power of a king is not only in the strength of his own arm, but in the strength of the arms of the men he commands. In the strength of his character.'

'You'd name a champion, then?' I tried to make it sound pitying, but Ludgast just nodded.

My brother stood at the door, a linen robe around his waist, dripping between his bodyguards. 'Name any champion you'd like. Send Hercules against me if you can get him. I'm not afraid of any fight.'

'If I believed that,' Ludgast said heavily, 'I would not be here today.'

CHAPTER THIRTEEN

Gudrun and the Challengers

We set a day and a place for the combat: midsummer day, in my rose garden. It had a few advantages: we could feed people easily inside the Domus, and we could make sure that the combat didn't turn into an actual battle.

Ludgast sent his acceptance, and Lothar sent word that he would challenge for the kingship too.

We arranged to feed and house the two challengers and their retinues. Despite the short supply of livestock that year, we paid what it cost. It was a simple calculation: to be the king means to be more powerful than everyone else. To be powerful means paying fletchers, smiths, and carpenters, and sometimes it even means paying men to fight, or paying men not to fight. A king must be able to pay for all that and feed his people too. Gunnar might be able to survive a failure of his courage; he could not survive a failure of his hospitality.

So Hagen, my mother, and I sat down with tablets and worked it all out.

My mother oversaw the brewing of beer. She had a talent for anything that had to do with water, especially water from the Rhine. The poison in the ring she gave me wasn't made from any plants or insects, as other poisons are. She just told water to become something else, and it did. I say 'just', but her magic was difficult and taxing. I could see it on her face, as she walked inside the city walls, touching the stones to strengthen them. The breweries needed to work faster and make more, so my mother lent her talents, speeding up the transformation of water into beer.

I ordered bread and the slaughter of lambs from our family's own flock. The men would have full bellies, and, I hoped, foggy heads.

Gunnar's chances were good. He was young enough to be vigorous but old enough to know his own body, and to train with discipline. He'd always been a methodical, determined fighter, since we were children. I hoped it would be enough.

My mother had learned not to trust to hope.

She came to me in my rose garden, the morning of the day before the fight.

The garden hadn't always been a rose garden. After my mother gave me dominion there, in the way of thirteen-year-old girls I suppose I thought there was no point in planting anything else when roses were an option. People used to bring me cuttings, when they came to the Domus to do business.

I wrote the stories of the flowers on little pewter rings or plaques at the base of the plants, like: 'Alexandria, from a plant Hypatia once used as an example in her teachings, brought to me by Synesius in the year of the consulship of Theodosius and Valentinianus.' But there was one plant with no ring and no plaque. I had no memory of planting it, or when it came to the garden. It had flowers so pale pink that they were almost white, and very blowsy, so a bloom would last only a day before falling to pieces in the air.

I remember that midsummer day dawned hot, and the petals on that plant were curling into pale brown at the edges.

My mother walked up beside me and put her finger on the petals, very gently. 'Is everything ready?'

'As ready as it can be. Hagen's been training Gunnar so hard, he's one big blister. Volker's been writing songs of victory, so his voice will have to heal fast, or else we'll have to endure him croaking at us all night. What do you think the best roses will be, for the victor's crown? I think white, for peace, but there is an argument to be made for red.'

'The main thing is that Gunnar needs to win.'

'Against an old fool and a snivelling sycophant? I think he will.' I wasn't as confident as I sounded, but I wanted her to stop worrying.

'Ludgast is an old fool, but he's a man of honour,' she said. 'Still, he may choose a champion, so there is an unknown there. And Lothar, well, I don't trust that little weasel.'

'What do you fear?'

'Everything,' she said, and laughed. 'Everything rides on this one fight, tomorrow. Here in your garden. People know what I can do, Gudrun, but you – that feat with the beehives has me thinking. You can make vines and roots move.'

'I can ask them to,' I said, uncertainly.

'What about here in your garden? Could you ask a root to rise out of the ground suddenly, to trip someone?'

I frowned. 'Mother, Gunnar can win the fight fairly. He has to win it fairly. If he's seen to be cheating—'

'And if he loses?' Her face was drawn, tired. 'If he loses, we lose everything. The crown, first of all, and the Domus. And then the kingdom. If Lothar wins, by this time next year we'll be a mere province of the Empire, if we're lucky. If Ludgast wins, by this time next year, we will have lost our lands, and we'll be wandering again, hunting and hunted.'

'I know.'

'Then Gunnar can't lose. We owe it to our people. You know as well as I do that the beast wounded him in some invisible way. If he stumbles, if there's some trickery – we need to be ready. That's all.'

I nodded, but stayed silent. I felt like bursting into tears.

My mother put her arm around me. 'I never told you the story of how I learned to do magic.'

Surprised, I turned to her. 'I thought you always had it.'

'Oh, no. No, it was only when we came here.' She paused, and I felt her grip tighten on my shoulder. 'It isn't an easy story to tell, and I didn't ever plan to tell my children about it. When you were a baby, our people were hunted, starving, diminished. We'd been chased south-west for years by Saxons, Goths, Vandals, Huns. We arrived at the edges of the Empire and found ourselves with nowhere to go. We couldn't cross into the Empire without being slaughtered as raiders. We couldn't stay where we were, outnumbered and exhausted. Your clever father saw an opportunity: several contenders for emperor were fighting among themselves. He made a deal with the one named Jovinus: if the Burgundians could help him seize power, we would take a small kingdom within the Empire, as payment.'

'I know that part,' I said.

'But you don't know how we managed to defeat the rival emperors. There was an encampment on the Rhine that Jovinus couldn't take, because of its position, high on a rock overlooking the river. Our scouting party discovered that there was a pathway up the cliffs from the river, but people said it was guarded by a terrible spirit in the shape of a woman. She would not allow our men to sneak up on the encampment that way.'

'And were they right?'

'Of the dozen men in the scouting party, only one returned, badly injured, so we believed him. That night, I walked out of our camp alone, took a boat, and went to the cliff myself. I had a conversation with the guardian spirit of the Rhine. That conversation I will keep to myself, but it ended with me sticking a knife between her ribs.'

My eyes went wide. 'Mother,' was all I managed.

'The next night, we attacked from the river side, and Jovinus won the right to call himself emperor – for a couple of years. By then, our kingdom was established. Then Galla

Placidia, sister of the new emperor, told us her brother would honour our treaty with Jovinus. All was well. But by then I had learned that the one who kills the guardian spirit of the Rhine must take her place.'

I pulled away from her, staring, and looked around the garden. We were alone.

'All my power comes from the river,' she said softly, raising her hands. 'I know every inch of the Rhine as though it were my own body. I sigh with it at night and sing with it in the mornings. When I shape stone, wood or metal, I shape it as a river shapes it, bending it to the pressure of my will. When I speak to the wind, it is as the roaring of water. That's the truth of my magic.'

I shook my head, trying to understand. 'Then it was never possible for me or Gunnar to do as you do.'

'No,' she said, looking disappointed. 'It seems not. Gunnar was already a baby when the river took me, and though I tried to sing it into him, to teach him what I could, he had no talent for it. But you did, in your own way. You were in my womb that night, when I climbed the rocks and spoke to the guardian spirit, when – anyway. I think you have some power of your own. But it is not my power. And you feel no . . . affinity to the Rhine. Isn't that correct?'

I nodded, my brows furrowed.

'It means,' she said, even more softly, taking my shoulders and looking at my face, 'that I can never leave our kingdom. I am bound to the Rhine, as its power is bound to me. Until I am killed, I am the river's guardian. One day, I will go to the river to take my place there. It is patient. It waits. But I think if I went too far from it, I would die.'

At that, I pulled away from her, horrified. I asked her why she was telling me all this. She told me she needed me to understand, that we must all make sacrifices, that we must all do what was necessary. I tell it to you now, Brynhild, without hope of forgiveness, knowing that we are in a place far beyond that now.

I didn't know what to say to my mother, so I did as she wanted, while she watched me. A little conversation with my rose bushes. No false promises; you can't deceive a flower. All I could offer were true things: my desire to always be mistress of that garden, my plan to water and weed and tread lightly on the ground. I asked politely.

A root shot out of the ground and wrapped around my foot. With difficulty, I resisted the urge to ask it to pull me right into the ground.

My mother embraced me. 'Very good,' she whispered in my ear. 'Only if it's necessary. Your brother is a better swordsman than anyone I have ever seen. I don't think it will be necessary.'

The night before the combat, Ludgast's men arrived in time for our feast. There was a fire in the banquet hall, though it was midsummer and the day was still bright. I recognized the two men who had accompanied me through the forest, the day I saved Ludgast's fields. It seemed ridiculous now, my whispering to plants and marshalling beehives. They were looking for reassurance that the strongest warrior would keep them safe.

I could tell which of the men was Ludgast's champion. The other men walked around him, as if showing him off on parade. He wasn't tall, but he was broad and well built, with a short golden beard and smiling eyes. He looked exactly the sort of dimwit to be satisfied with winning battles for someone else, I thought.

Beside him walked a rangy white dog with a head like an anvil.

And that was my first impression of Sigurd.

That night, we learned that Fafnir was dead, and I heard your name for the first time.

It was well into the meal. The banquet hall was full: the four inner tables, set around the fire, and more tables beyond the fat stone pillars. Everyone had a leg of lamb, roasted with coriander and served with prune sauce, and a large piece of bread and a small dish of honey. That was Hagen's suggestion, a reminder of what I had done for the city. But it was from the previous year's hoard, golden brown, thick and malty.

My brother was not talking to anyone. He ate parsimoniously, sipped from time to time, and stared out into the fire as if he saw something in it.

I was afraid he'd seem sullen to everyone who didn't know him as well as I did. He should have been gracious, or at least confident. The combat wouldn't start until the morning but the contest for the kingship had already begun. And there he sat, silent.

My mother's face was like stone. Hagen kept rubbing hand and forefinger together in the way he had when he was playing tafl or training a new swordsman. Volker had his lute, and he looked at me once as if offering to sing, although I knew his throat was still raw.

Finally, unable to stand the weird deadlock any longer, I pushed my chair back and stood up. Talking was one thing I could do well. Little Chatterer, my father used to call me. Well, I thought, time to chatter.

'There are three men in this hall who claim the right of kingship.' The noises of eating, murmuring, rustling, all quieted to nearly nothing. 'My brother is eager to demonstrate that his life, his very blood, is in the service of his people. The roses are blooming at last in my garden, my friends. It is a wide place, with broad stone walls where people can sit and watch everything that happens. I invite any man who challenges my brother to meet him there, tomorrow, and match swords with him, each taking a turn. Any man who draws my brother's blood will win the right to be king; but if my brother draws his, that man must swear loyalty to Gunnar, son of Gjuki, on pain of death.'

None of it was new, but the declaration was a reminder that we were operating under rules, and I was the one setting them.

'And if more than one of us draws Gunnar's blood?' asked Lothar, with a snide smile.

'Then you must determine among yourselves which of you is the victor, either with another duel or by some other means.'

'I agree, for my part,' Lothar said. 'But Ludgast, you old worthy, are you sure about this? A single cut might be the end of you, if it's a bit deeper than intended.'

Everyone looked around, grinning. By then it was obvious that Ludgast had brought a champion, and people had been gossiping about him all evening. Lothar was goading Ludgast.

'I am old, it is true,' Ludgast responded evenly. 'I cannot hold a sword as well as I once did. But a king needs wisdom, and the loyalty of strong men. I believe I can match anyone here in either. And I intend to prove it when my champion takes the field.'

He gestured to the blond man beside him, who stood, a little awkwardly.

'This is Sigurd of Xanten,' Ludgast said. 'He is willing to take the field on my behalf. He came to live with us some weeks ago, after he killed the lindworm.'

At that, Lothar's smirk vanished, and Ludgast's mouth curled into triumph within his beard. A hush fell over the hall. No one dared believe it could be true, that the lindworm was dead. And that the man who had killed it was here with us! I didn't know how to feel: relief at the monster's demise, if we could trust the report. Fear that the man who did what Gunnar could not would be able to claim the throne himself, if he had the wit to do it.

We all looked at Sigurd, who looked uncomfortable.

Finally, Gunnar broke the silence with a low laugh. 'What trick has this pup played on you, Grandfather?'

'It's true,' said Sigurd, tensely. 'If I may have my sword from the doorkeeper, I'll prove it.'

I gestured, and a man brought him his sword. Sigurd stood and unsheathed it. At first, I couldn't see what he was

showing everyone, as he walked the inner circle, table to
table. But when he came close enough, I saw the ring forged
onto one crossbar at the hilt. The ring with the red stone,
which had hung from the nosepiece of the helm.

'You all recognize it, I think?' Sigurd said. 'You had a visit
from the lindworm, I understand.'

Gunnar was still seated, but his hand on his thigh made
a fist under the table.

'How,' he said. 'How did you kill it? When?'

'About a month ago, my lord. And with this sword. I
added the ring to it, afterwards.'

'It's true,' said a man from Ludgast's company, and all
heads turned to him. 'I have seen the carcass myself. It lies
at the bottom of Hindfell. What's more, a sorceress has taken
up residence on the top of the mountain.'

'A sorceress!' Gunnar said, leaning back, his arm on his
chair's arm rest.

Sigurd returned to his seat, his face grim.

'So it would seem,' the man continued. 'She is called
Brynhild and is very beautiful. She raised a wall of fire around
the top of the mountain. She swore on the old gods that she
would only marry a man who could show that he had no
fear and could ride through the wall of fire and best her in
feats of strength. I say no bitch is worth burning all the skin
off my body, so I will marry the alewife's daughter.'

There was laughter; this was the sort of tale that men like
to hear in halls.

'You are welcome, Sigurd of Xanten,' I said. 'The man
who killed Attila's pet will always be welcome at this court,
no matter the outcome tomorrow. Tonight, let us drink your
health.'

Everyone other than Sigurd drank the sweet golden mead
I made out of the same honey that was at their plates, and
I sat down, and looked thoughtfully at the champion. He
had eaten even less than Gunnar, and his cup was still full.

*

People watched from the peristyle, the banquet hall, and the arcade, all of which gave onto the garden from the west and south. They crowded into the garden itself, though we cleared a space for the combat in the middle, on a patch of gravel where I intended to build a fountain.

The three combatants filed in stiffly, as if they were in church. Lothar looked terrified. Sigurd looked wary. And my brother looked grim.

I knew he was fully capable of winning the fight. Lothar had studied swordplay the same way he'd studied mathematics. Sigurd, I didn't know, but I had a feeling just from watching him handle his sword in the banquet hall that he hadn't had much training. My brother could dance around ghosts with his eyes closed.

But there was a reason both Lothar and Ludgast thought this was worth their while. They suspected Gunnar was not the man they used to know, that he would panic, that he would make a fatal error. They remembered the way he rode away from us on the day of the lindworm, and they thought: here is a man with water for guts.

I was pretty sure they were wrong. I knew my brother. But in my heart of hearts, I knew he had changed, and my skin was clammy under my gold linen stola.

'You're all welcome to my garden,' I said, my arms wide. 'Any man who fights with honour here will be met with honour. Any man who acts in treachery or bad faith will bear forever the curse of my ill will.'

'And the victor?' growled Ludgast.

'The victor will take this crown,' I said, and gestured at a thorny crown with three red roses on it, which sat on a stone pedestal that had borne a vase an hour before. 'In a sign that he will wear the crown of the Burgundians from this day forward.'

'A crown is a lovely trophy,' said Lothar, looking nonchalant. 'But it can be taken from a man's head as easily as it's given.

We want assurances that the results of the contest will be respected. That the family of Gunnar, son of Gjuki, will not deal falsely and take up arms against us once this company has dissolved.'

'You have my word,' Gunnar said, in a low voice.

'Of course,' Lothar said with a short, insouciant bow. 'But the surest sign that the family has accepted the outcome would be a marriage with Gudrun for the victor, for the true king. That would ensure peace. Indeed, I would venture to say it's the only thing that would.'

I should have expected something like that, but somehow, I hadn't. I'd thought the whole business of my marriage was set aside now that I had no reason to keep Ludgast and Lothar from acting. They had acted, now.

I thought quickly, not looking at Hagen or my mother, definitely not looking at Gunnar. I wanted to think about what was best. Of course, I expected Gunnar to win. But if he didn't? I had to think of our people above all, as my parents had taught me to do. A marriage would ensure that our family still had influence over the king. It would keep me close to the new king – close enough to take him down, if that became necessary.

But on the other hand, a marriage with me would make it difficult for Gunnar to gather his strength, dispute the outcome, and fight back.

The truth was, I didn't want to marry either of them. Do you know what I thought of, in that moment? You. The story those men told about you, about the vow you made not to marry any man except one who could pass through a ring of fire.

Oh, I know, that wasn't precisely what you said, but it was the story I heard. And I thought that I would like to put up a ring of fire, like that possibly invented sorceress on the mountaintop. That was one way to put an end to all the demands of men.

I didn't have a ring of fire, but I did have a witch as a mother. Witches have reputations. They are expected to know things, to have visions and see portents.

'I'm sorry to tell you that I recently made a vow,' I said, not looking at my family, who knew when I was lying. 'I have sworn to God that I will not marry.'

There was a small rumble in the crowd, and wide eyes. I kept my own gaze on Lothar. I lied: 'Three nights ago, I dreamt about a wonderful falcon, a golden bird, more noble than any other. As it returned to my arm, an eagle came out of the sky and tore it to pieces. I know now that if I marry, my husband would come to no good end.'

There was silence, and people looked at each other. Finally, I got up the courage to look at my mother. Wonderful woman that she was, she nodded sagely, like none of this was new to her.

'And how do we know this falcon refers to a husband?' Lothar asked.

I spread my hands. 'What else could a woman dream about?'

'And if I win—'

'We will respect the will of the people in all things,' Gunnar said.

Lothar, who understood politics very well, looked from my brother's face to mine, and scowled.

The fight would end when someone drew blood. They didn't wear mail, or even gloves. They bared their skin, fighting in trousers and tunics, so that nothing would be tested but their hearts.

Lothar came first. For his weapon, he chose a seax. An odd weapon for a young man, but it was a clever choice. Lothar knew full well that he was seen as the Empire's man, not a true Burgundian despite his parentage. So, he fought with the sort of weapon his grandfather might have chosen. It was a little shorter than Gunnar's sword, with only one cutting edge. But that edge curved to an evil point. Both men carried large, round wooden shields, with iron bosses in the middle. Gunnar's had two entwined snakes painted around the edge, and Lothar's was rimmed in red.

I saw right away that Gunnar was gripping his sword like a man trying to prove something. I shouted 'fight!' and he brought his sword into the centre line, to cut up under the ribcage. He went in fast, but Lothar only had to bring his shield edge down so it scraped along Gunnar's forearm, and everyone leaned forward to see whether it bled. But while his skin was red, nothing welled up.

While we all looked and held our breath, Gunnar and Lothar hadn't paused at all. Pinning Gunnar with his shield, Lothar raised his seax high to stab the base of his neck. I put my hand over my mouth to stop from crying out. My mother grabbed my arm. Just as the tip of the seax was about to pierce Gunnar's skin, Lothar's feet slipped and he came in under Gunnar, just a little. That gave Gunnar the advantage and he knocked Lothar to the ground.

My mother's grip relaxed, and I realized that she thought I'd been the one to trip Lothar, that I'd called my plants into service. But I hadn't. Unlike her, I couldn't simply call on what I wanted. I had to persuade, nudge, cajole. So I closed my eyes for a moment and tried to calm myself enough so I could do that if need be.

A noise went up. Gunnar stumbled as he tried to keep himself from following Lothar to the ground, and his shield arm flung wide, leaving him exposed. Lothar thrust his shield up at Gunnar and caught him under the chin, but Gunnar was swinging his sword wildly at Lothar's knees. I saw the blood trickle down Lothar's skinny calf and I threw my arm in the air and yelled in triumph. I can't remember what words I used.

There was a short break, for Gunnar to catch his breath before his second challenger. I brought him water and a cloth for his face. I told him to stop gripping his sword so tightly, or he'd wear himself out. Stay high, stay disciplined. Gunnar's advantage would be in his training.

My brother, bless him, listened to me. He started with a high guard, forcing Sigurd to try to find an opening. Sigurd used his ringsword and a black shield. Their blades rang against each other and clanged against their shields, and nobody got anywhere for a long time. Finally, they grew tired, and came in close, grappling, almost wrestling with their hands full of swords and shields and their arms around each other, their bodies pressed.

Then Sigurd, frustrated and annoyed, pushed my brother off him, and while Sigurd's sword and shield were both low and wide, Gunnar sliced down with his blade right onto Sigurd's collarbone. It was a good hit, and I rose to my feet, my hands clasped.

But there was no blood. Sigurd didn't bleed. This won't surprise you, Brynhild, but it surprised all of us, I can tell you. No one was more amazed than my brother, whose body had gone lax with his victory and his relief. He'd stepped back, dropped his guard. Sigurd flailed with his sword and nicked Gunnar's ear.

I watched the blood trickle down my brother's neck. The blood of a king, spilled in my rose garden. There was no sound but that of a bird chattering nearby.

CHAPTER FOURTEEN

Gudrun's Feast

'I thought I had him,' my brother said, looking straight ahead.

'So did I.' I handed him a cup of mead, and then sank into a chair. We were in our weapons room, in the family wing of the Domus. It wasn't a comfortable place to sit: swords and axes lined the walls, and it smelled of oil and metal. But we kept a few chairs there, and there was something about the place that lent itself to our family councils of war. Hagen paced by the door, idly flipping a knife. He was always flipping knives.

My mother sat very still, her hands gripping the arms of her chair. The whites of her eyes were tinged with red. She was the first to guess there was more to Sigurd than met the eye. 'There's some trick here. That blow should have cut him.'

'You suspect magic, my lady?' Hagen asked. He turned to Gunnar. 'Did it feel—?'

Gunnar shook his head, as if confused. 'I don't know. I thought I had him.'

'We will fight magic with magic,' my mother said, lifting her chin. 'If Ludgast thinks he can take the crown from my son with a trick, sending some enchanted stranger to fight on his behalf, he's a fool as well as a coward.'

I bit my lip, angry with myself. My mother had suspected there might be trickery. She'd come to me first, and I'd failed her.

'However he did it, he beat Gunnar in a challenge for the kingship,' Hagen said. 'Ludgast's people won't let that go.'

'They won't have to,' my mother said wearily. 'They won't remember it. I have some beer brewing that should be nearly ready. Not quite ordinary beer. Tonight, we'll hold a feast where we'll concede defeat and proclaim Ludgast king. We'll raise a toast, and everyone will drink, and when they have drunk, they'll forget it ever happened. Not only that, but they'll forget why they came here at all.'

Gunnar and I both spoke at once.

'It takes more than half a day to brew beer,' Gunnar said, while I said, 'You planned for this.'

Then Gunnar accused her of expecting him to fail. I could have said the same.

'I have been a wartime queen for most of my life,' our mother said. 'I always make more than one plan.'

'Why didn't you just feed them the beer to begin with?' Gunnar demanded.

She hesitated, her bony fingers wrapping over themselves. 'Because it isn't the best solution. They'll forget what happened in the rose garden, yes, but they won't forget what happened with the lindworm. Trouble is still coming for us, now. I knew that if you had a fair chance, you could win the kingship. And put any doubts to rest.'

'Doubts,' he repeated, staring at her.

'How certain are you it will work?' I asked.

'Fairly certain,' said my mother with a thin smile and red eyes. I forgave her deceptions. How could I not. She had saved us from the lindworm, and she was about to save us from overthrow. She had given both of us a chance to use our talents, and we had failed her. I felt the heat in my face.

We all sat quietly with our own thoughts until my mother added, 'It's this or hand the city to Ludgast, walk away from our home, and spend the rest of our lives riding in fear at every sounding of a horn of war in the distance.'

It was midsummer night, and still sunny in the courtyard. But in the banquet hall, we lit the fire, and stared out at those glittering eyes.

Lothar looked distant, rather than disappointed; I suspect he was already planning a journey to Ravenna, where his talents would be recognized and his sycophancy rewarded. Sigurd didn't seem interested in politics, but he was sharp enough. I watched him watch the hands at knife-hilts, the taut mouths. Nobody felt safe in that room. He sat, his invulnerable bare arm gleaming in the firelight as it rested on the board, his fingers light and ready around his cup. He didn't eat anything.

I walked around the room, pouring my mother's beer into every cup. It smelled just a little grassy; she brewed it with myrtle, yarrow, rosemary, and God knows what else.

When every cup was full, my brother rose. 'I drink to the health of the new king of the Burgundians and ruler of Vormatia, Ludgast, son of Dietrich, my father's right arm.'

He still managed to sound like a king, even when giving it up. Especially when giving it up. But I couldn't smile at my brother just then; I had to look disappointed. Until they had all drunk, all forgotten, we had to go along with the pretence. I ran my finger along the edge of my goblet; it was made of green glass. How I miss that set! Heavy, olive-green glass, a cylinder narrowing just a little towards the bottom, where it sat on a squat stem. The outer layer of the glass carved with curling vines, but the inner layer so thin that the firelight shone through it and turned it red. There was something dragonish about it, this blood-red glow within a sickly green skin.

Everyone had to drink. I watched Sigurd sip, watched him wipe beer off his golden chin. I watched Ludgast and Lothar and all of them drink. And I drank from my cup, which I'd filled from the first pitcher, the unenchanted pitcher I'd used for my mother, Hagen and Gunnar too – and Volker, because Hagen couldn't keep a secret from him anyway. We all drank, and then I stood.

'And to my mother Auda, whose hospitality we enjoy tonight, who raised the river and saved our city.'

People drank now without the excuse of a toast, as I continued, a little hesitantly. 'We thank you for your support of King Gunnar after his return from fighting the lindworm. At a time like this, when our people have suffered so much, unity is everything.'

Nobody scowled. Nobody moved, except to wipe ale off their beards.

But Sigurd made a face. He put his hand to his waist and looked to Ludgast, but the old man was just staring slackly at me. Everyone looked a little confused, but no one contradicted me.

'You have each come,' I carried on, as steadily as I could, 'knowing that a traitor might rise up against the king in this moment, to stand beside him, one and all. Together we are strong. No single traitor could rise against all of us united. The king greets you with the same loyalty and love with which you have journeyed here.'

Then Hagen stood and toasted me, and then Ludgast got to his feet. I held my breath.

'We drink to the past and to the future,' said Ludgast thickly, 'and to the traditions of our people. We drink to King Gunnar.'

I tried to keep my smile from showing as I raised my glass.

All their eyes were glassy now, as they nodded and drank.

All except Sigurd, who still looked confused.

My smile perished.

For two hours, maybe three, while the feast went on around us, through storytellers and singers and a roast boar and several increasingly drunken speeches, Sigurd of Xanten just sat and stared at me.

I avoided his gaze.

No one else seemed to notice. I told myself we'd won, but as the evening wore on, I just felt shakier. Gunnar looked weak and uncomfortable too; our mother was the only one who seemed equipped to play the happy queen. She'd been playing a role a lot longer than either of us.

One by one, the people left, in little knots of sing-song or vomiting or uncertain silence. In the morning, they'd go home, believing the king had hosted a midsummer feast.

But the reckoning was at hand, anyway.

Even after Ludgast left, Sigurd stayed sitting there, arms crossed, smiling at me. His cup was still half full.

'Will you take anything else, Sigurd of Xanten?' I asked, smiling.

The only people left in the great hall were Sigurd, on one side of the fire, and on the other, my brother, my mother, Hagen, Volker, and me. A conspiracy and one quiet man.

He pursed his lips and shook his head. 'I have had quite enough of your fare.'

I was unable to say words that would break the impasse, unable to stand it any longer. 'Then say what you want to say. It's late.'

Beard or no, he had a face like a child's, a child confronted with an injustice. 'All right then. I'll say this: you have performed some kind of witchcraft here tonight. Everyone has forgotten why they came, and what happened when they did. But I remember. I remember that I won the crown of the Burgundians, and I won't forget it. I may be a simple man but I'm not a dupe.'

Gunnar rose, knife in his hand.

Sigurd showed him his own empty palms. 'I have no desire to fight you again, my lord. And I'm happy to keep your secret until I go into the ground. On one condition.'

'Name it,' Gunnar said, not dropping the knife.

'I want a place here, in your household. At your side. I want to be consulted about every decision. I want to lead your army. I don't want to be a king, but I will be recognized as a hero, one way or another.'

My mother's laugh seemed short, involuntary. 'Is that all?'

'That's all,' Sigurd said. 'I think I've earned your trust, with my silence here tonight.'

'Trust!' My mother smiled. 'Perhaps. But how did you know? Did you only pretend to drink the beer?'

'No, I drank it,' he said. His face looked serious for a moment. 'I have – I know some ways of preventing harm from drink. I don't want you to think that I suspected poison. It's just a habit of mine. I do it every time I drink.'

I know now that he must have used the rune you taught him, Brynhild. He wasn't lying about the habit. I've never known a man who feared poison as much as Sigurd did. Once his skin became invulnerable, he started brooding on the ways he *could* die. I think that's why he got the dog, Vigi, originally: to feed him scraps. But then, being Sigurd, he got too fond of the dog to risk him being poisoned, either.

Sigurd always was his own worst enemy.

'I'd make a good ally,' he said to my brother. 'I've shown you that I am a better warrior than anyone in Vormatia.'

'You've shown us that you have some magic about you,' my mother said sharply.

'I have – some advantages. Yes. You are a family in need of all the advantages you can get.'

'What are you asking for, precisely?' Gunnar asked.

'I ask to be your brother,' Sigurd said, standing up. He looked at me.

And at last I understood fully.

Two snakes were warring in my brain at that moment. I didn't want to marry the man, any more than I wanted to marry anyone. I was reluctant to bring anyone closer to the throne while my brother was still proving himself, and this stranger's so-called advantages only made me more wary. The man who killed the lindworm and married me would

be a terrible rival for Gunnar, if he ever decided that was
what he wanted to be.

All the same, it would be better to have him inside the
family than outside it. And I believed him when he said he
didn't want to be king. Sigurd wanted to be respected and
admired. That was all.

He carried on, like any suitor. He even blushed. 'I ask for
the hand of Gudrun, so that I may always have a place in
your family. So my name will be spoken with yours.'

I stalled, to give us all time to think. 'Maybe you've
forgotten something after all, Sigurd. Didn't you hear me tell
the company about my dream?'

'I'm not afraid of dreams.'

'What are you afraid of, then?' asked Volker. His face was
more serious, in the days since Fafnir attacked. He was fully
healed but never quite the same.

'Poison, it would seem,' Hagen said.

'And being a man without position,' Volker carried on,
answering his own question. He had his lute in his hand like
a weapon, and he advanced on Sigurd slowly. Volker understood stories, better than any of us.

'Being a man without use,' Sigurd retorted. 'Ludgast treats
me like a curiosity. All I ask is to fight for you, to bring
glory to your city and your family. It's a good offer. It's not
a trick.'

He was brave in his way. Invulnerable skin or not, he was
outnumbered, in our house, and we could have clapped him
in chains and seen just what poisons would do to him. But
he set his jaw and stared at us. He wouldn't ever back down
for his own good. I give him that much credit, and that much
blame.

'Give us a moment to discuss it,' Gunnar said.

We drew together at one end of the hall, while Sigurd sat,
watching us, feet on the ground, respectfully. Another man
might pace or put his feet on the table while making such
demands – but Sigurd took no glee in the power he held

over us. He just watched us, having decided that we were his new path to glory. It made me uncomfortable.

It was around that time that I heard the first clap of thunder, and the drumming of rain on the roof, and on the beaten ground of my garden, through the columns. There would be a terrible storm that night. I could hear people outside, the ones who'd been slow to leave the feast, laughing and shouting and seeking shelter. A few of the country people would stay in our guest hall, a little way from the Domus, and some would stay with the bishop, or in Lothar's house. Ludgast's men had their own arrangements; most of them kept houses in town, even though they hardly ever came there any more.

The candles were still lit but the fire in the middle of the hall had burned low. It was dark.

Hagen made the objection we were all thinking, but he made it half-heartedly: 'Marriage to Gudrun would give him power and position.'

Gunnar scratched his chin. 'He's a hard man to kill, it seems. If we don't take his offer, we have to find some other way of keeping the secret. Gudrun, what do you think?'

I swallowed. 'I'd rather have him inside our household than outside it. He's an asset.'

'Then marry him,' my mother said, and put her hand on my shoulder. 'A season ago you were ready to marry a Hun, a man who had killed our own people. A man you'd never met. Now you have a chance to marry a man who has done us no wrong, a hero and a monster-slayer, and, Gudrun, the man has pretty blue eyes and shoulders like two great rocks.'

I smiled, and glanced at Hagen. He was smiling too, which made me feel better. I trusted Hagen's instincts above everyone's.

'He wants to be part of our family,' Gunnar said, still serious. 'He doesn't want to take you away. Thank God, because I need you with me. Marry him, and I'll make him my counsellor, and you can live in the Domus. Nothing will change. And you'll have babies, and preserve the family line.'

'You can preserve the family line yourself, if you find a wife,' I said. I'm not sure whether I was teasing him, trying to recapture something of how we used to be, but in any case, he didn't smile.

'Yes, I've been thinking about that,' he said seriously. 'But it's best if we both marry. You said it yourself, with things as they are . . . if we have healthy heirs, it'll take one argument away from our rivals.'

I put two fingers in between my eyebrows, like I was damming a river. One long shuddering breath in, while I allowed myself to believe the future still lay uncharted ahead of me. But my mother was right. Although I'd avoided Lothar and Ludgast, I always expected to marry, and Sigurd was young, handsome, a hero. What more could I ask?

For some reason, I remembered Bleda's brown eyes in that moment. His stranger's eyes wide, while the red blood poured out of his throat and onto the ground before the walls of our city.

I exhaled. 'I'll do it.'

My mother clasped my hand and I leaned into her embrace. She was so thin, so small, and yet still the softest thing I can imagine.

Sigurd stood waiting, his impressive shoulders on display. He looked for all the world like a nervous bridegroom.

'We accept,' I said, before Gunnar could say it. It was my choice. If it turned to regret, let it be mine. Gunnar had enough to live with.

Sigurd nodded, nervously. 'I'm honoured, my lady. When?'

'Before the leaves fall,' Gunnar said. 'You'll be my brother. You will stay in the city, and pledge allegiance to me as the king.'

Sigurd nodded. 'I'll give you my sword, in the cathedral, if you like. Before everyone.'

Then Gunnar asked, 'Will you give me your advice on something now, my brother?'

'Gladly.'

'This sorceress who lives on the mountain. The one they told stories about, the first night they came here. The one who has sworn she'll only marry a man without fear. You've seen her?'

That was you, of course. The sorceress on the mountain.

I had no idea what Gunnar was up to. In the old days, he would have talked to us, but he was different after the lindworm.

Sigurd's smile dropped. He took a long time before answering. At last he said, 'I know her a little, yes. She is not – I wouldn't have called her a sorceress. She isn't wicked, nothing like that.'

'It's not her sorcery that interests me,' Gunnar said. 'We have enough of that. It's her vow that only a man without fear can cross her ring of fire. People know about it, yes? So if she did marry a man, everyone would know that man crossed the fire, and that man has no fear.'

Sigurd's face was pale. He realized part of what Gunnar meant, just as I was beginning to. 'You intend to cross the wall of fire. You want to go to the mountain.'

'I need a bride,' Gunnar said. 'And it seems some people need to be convinced of my courage. Will you help me win this sorceress? Will you help me cross the fire, my brother?'

'Gunnar—' I began, but he made a little movement with his hand, and I knew he didn't want to hear what I thought about it.

Sigurd looked nervous, but he said, 'It would be my honour, of course. My king.'

Gunnar smiled. 'Then we'll have a double wedding.'

Late at night, after the feast, we stayed up making plans.

Gunnar said, 'There must be some way to cross the fire. Maybe I could fly.'

'But then you wouldn't be a man without fear,' Volker said, with a wry smile. 'You'd be a man with wings.'

Hagen rolled his eyes at his lover, and leaned forward, elbow on one knee, to talk to Sigurd. 'Your skin turned away a blade. Can it also withstand fire?'

'Let's find out,' Sigurd said, and walked over to the dying fire pit. He picked up a charred and burning stick and drove the white-hot end into the back of his hand. We all winced, but he held it up to us, showed us there was no effect.

'What magic is this?' Hagen demanded.

Sigurd looked uncomfortable. 'It was an effect of the lindworm's blood, on my skin.'

'Useful stuff,' my mother mused. 'A shame the lindworm's been dead so long. I'm sure the blood has been scavenged by now.'

I pointed out that Sigurd's ability to walk through fire didn't help Gunnar.

'Is there some protection you can give him, Mother?' I asked. 'A cloak that will keep the fire off?'

My mother could only command what she saw in front of her. But she had one way to carve the air into new forms, even when she was far away: she had her loom. The magic was in the weights that pulled the warp: sometimes they were small stones with holes in them. Pierced cones. Bones. Rings of polished yew. She used to send Gunnar and me out looking for interesting things; I brought her an enormous bent nail once, so big I felt sure it was made for giants, and Gunnar found her a weasel skull.

With light things, like fishhooks, she'd have to tie several weights together, sometimes, to get the right sort of pull. And sometimes the combinations would have effects she didn't intend.

She cocked her head, thinking. 'Fire and I . . . are old enemies. I don't know of any weights that make such a cloak. But if we could find something that belonged to a shapeshifter, I might be able to bend the air and light and give Sigurd a form like Gunnar's.'

Sigurd's eyes went wide. 'You mean that I would go to the mountain, and Brynhild would think that I was Gunnar? I don't think it would work.'

'Why not?' Hagen demanded.

Instead of responding, Sigurd rose, and left the garden.

'He's no help to us,' Hagen growled. 'Gunnar, I think this is a dead end. You'll have a chance soon enough to prove that you're not ruled by fear. The Huns will come. We'll fight them. Then the people will acclaim you as king.'

It might have ended there, and the glitter in my brother's eye might have shrunk to a harmless spark. But then Sigurd returned from his room, carrying six rings of gold. The bracelets that had adorned the lindworm.

'Fafnir didn't always have that form,' he explained in a strangled voice. 'He was a shapeshifter. These bracelets belonged to him.'

Eagerly, my mother rose and took them, examined them. She didn't look surprised; she had probably had some idea already that Sigurd had something like them. 'These will make good loom weights. I think this will work.'

Sigurd looked ill. He was always so desperate to prove his worth.

I'd like to tell you I made some objection. Who was I to criticize the ways my mother found to solve our problems? Besides, you were a stranger to me then, and I thought of you and your vow as some ridiculous vanity. Why did it matter which man passed your test?

I would have thought otherwise, had I been the one being fooled into marrying a man other than the one I'd agreed to. Of course, I would have. Your anger was perfect and right, when it came. But at the time, I thought of you only as a way out. And unlike the contest in the garden, honour didn't seem to come into it. Asking for a man without fear was already an impossible demand. It did occur to me that, like my invented dream, your vow might be a way to keep suitors away. But I suppose I thought you could always refuse, if it came to that. No one had forced you to make your vow, and no one would force you to keep it. You were a sorceress! I thought you held all the power.

CHAPTER FIFTEEN

The Courtship of Brynhild

Those nights in the hall on the mountaintop were lonely. Lonelier than I had been in my first nights in the open. I suppose the place reminded me of the mead hall of Valhalla, where I was used to the company of comrades, gods and the dead. This hall I had to myself. My only comrade had left abruptly. Not even Odin showed his face, and if there were any ghosts in that high place, they kept to themselves.

Every so often I went down to see the lindworm carcass. Birds and beasts had cleaned its bones.

At first, each day alone seemed painfully unbroken. How strange, I thought (and perhaps I even said it to the birds, who would chatter with me for a moment or two but who lost interest in me quickly). How strange that centuries in eternal Valhalla, where our bodies did not change, should have seemed less relentless than my relatively brief sentence to mortal solitude. And yet. Each day was a reminder of everything I could not do. I could not fly away from my mountain. When I stared at the fire, there was no one's face on the other side of it. When I sang, I heard only my own voice, cracking and thin.

Gondul used to tell us the most hilarious, long-winded

tales. She was enormous, with long pale hair and a twisty smile. As beautiful as the morning. And she could make everything funny.

—*Gondul, tell us a story.*

—*I don't have any stories. I'm exhausted from dealing with that princeling last night. Every time I grabbed his elbow, he'd turn around and see a squirrel or something and he'd be off like an arrow. Kept me running around like a puppy after a snake. I'm not even sure we won the battle. I think it's still going on, frankly, and everyone's looking for him. I think we forgot to let everyone know he won.*

As the days wore on, the small breaks in routine came to seem like enough. One night, I went to sleep to a gentle rain outside the hall's open windows. I woke in the middle of the night to the crash of thunder, so close I reached for my sword. I opened a small window in the upper room of the hall and peered out at the play of lightning, illuminating distant hills. Thor showing his affection for the world.

I think it must have been the same storm that hit Vormatia on that midsummer day, when Sigurd fought Gunnar.

Before long, I was comfortable with the rhythms of the day. In the morning, I took my sword and practised against the pell I had set in the ground, calling out the names of the guards and attacks, over and over, precise as I could be. I hunted when I needed to. I carved myself a needle of antler and sewed new leather clothing for myself. I lit my fire. Cooked my food.

Ravens brought me news from a distance. A pair took residence on one of the blasted pines on the slopes of my mountain, and for the most part they chased the gang of juveniles away, though from time to time the gang returned to perch on the wall of melted weapons to make their presence known, and the older couple stared at them, and no one lost any blood or feathers.

On a day not long after midsummer, I was throwing axes. I used to stand on the flat ground near the hall and throw them at an old pine stump. Sometimes I would wonder about the last hand to hold each axe, before Fafnir killed its owner. So, between the thuds of the axes, and the far-wanderings of my thoughts, I was slow to notice the raven.

She was the female of the pair, standing on a stone and making a sound something like a knock, and something like a drop of water falling into a deep well, followed by a small click.

The language of birds is more than their speech. It's the angle of their heads, and the writing they make against the sky, together and alone.

The sound and movement this raven was making doesn't mean a word – or rather, it means so many words that it means only itself. It means listen, a beginning, a story, a warning.

I let my axe-hand fall to my side and greeted her.

'A man came through the fire,' the raven said.

Ravens are not given to parables or riddles; they're practical birds. So I was taken aback, trying to understand what she meant. 'What man? Where?'

The raven ducked her head. 'We haven't seen him before. He's lying on the ground and his clothes are scorched. He must have climbed over the wall and walked through the fire. We saw him from above; we didn't go close. He's moving and not dead yet.'

I thanked the raven. She bowed and flew off to her partner, who was waiting for her in the branches of a dead oak.

I half-expected one of the irritating men I'd met the last time I saw Sigurd. How greedy would a person have to be, to pass through my fire, just for a chance to steal my monster-leavings? Some smaller part of me wondered about Sigurd himself, whether he'd come back. He seemed pigheaded enough to try to walk through fire just to prove that he could. But I saw a man I didn't recognize: smaller than Sigurd, covered in sweat and soot and with half his dark hair burned away.

Like the raven, I didn't get too close. I yelled something to him, asked him whether he was alive.

The man lifted his head. Pulled himself up to his knees and croaked. 'I'm alive. I'm fine.'

'You're certainly not fine. Are you alone?'

He nodded, and I put my axe into my belt loop and helped him to his feet. By the cold fire pit in the middle of the hall I offered him a drink of his own mead and offered to make him a salve for his burned skin, but he shook his head. I asked him his name, and he told me in a fire-racked voice that he was Gunnar, king of the Burgundians. He said he had heard of my vow and come for my hand.

I nearly choked on the air.

'My hand?'

'Everyone says you have vowed to marry the man that would walk through your wall of fire.'

Of course, this was news to me. When I told him coldly he'd been misinformed, he said defensively, 'Only a man without fear would walk through that fire. You have to acknowledge that.'

Men! I had seen plenty of strength and reckless violence in my centuries, and I knew neither was courage. I can find a hundred pimply boys who'll jump off a jagged rock into a fast current just because it hasn't occurred to them not to. I can find another hundred who will goad a rabid dog. And I could fill the earth with the graves of all the boys and men who've fought each other to the death for no reason at all. None of these are courage.

I didn't owe this man anything, not an answer, and certainly not my body. I told him to drain his cup and then to rest, and in the morning, I would help him off the mountain.

To which he said, 'I walked through fire for you, Brynhild.'

I laughed at him. 'You hadn't even met me! You walked through fire to impress other men. Well, you can go and tell them whatever you want, show them your scars if you like, but you are not entitled to me.'

And then that man looked at me through your brother's brown eyes and told me a truth. Probably the cleverest thing he'd ever done, or ever would.

'You're wrong,' he said. 'I don't believe I'm entitled to you. I want to marry you because I'm a king beset by enemies, and they'll stop fighting me if I have you at my side.'

'As a trophy.'

He paused. 'It's true that your reputation as a sorceress who put a spell on this mountain would be valuable to me. Everyone in Vormatia thinks I'm a coward, you see, because when the lindworm attacked, I disappeared.'

'The lindworm?'

He nodded. 'Thank God Sigurd was able to kill it. All alone, I understand.'

He was looking at me curiously, as if to see what I'd say, but I didn't take the bait. I had no need to disillusion anyone; if Sigurd chose to leave me out of the story, that was his business. I wasn't interested in stories. And at that moment, I was more interested in Gunnar's lies than Sigurd's.

'So my fire is a test of your courage, and if you return with me, it proves you're not a coward. What a pile of horse shit.'

'It is,' he agreed, with an easy grin. 'But the point is, you're not just a reputation. You have secret knowledge. Sigurd told me. The people of Vormatia are safe from the lindworm now but they aren't safe from the Huns. They haven't had to fight in a generation – not a real war, anyway. Nothing but raids and skirmishes. Now they have to win a war against the Huns and the Empire might not help them. They're fighting to keep the land their fathers were promised. They need someone to help them win their fight. They need someone to deliver justice.'

That should have made me question how he knew me so well, to throw my own desires back at me. Perhaps I forgot that I wasn't able to weigh men's hearts just by looking at them any more. I thought: here is a man who is a warrior and a king, and so we understand each other. It came as a relief.

'Get some rest,' I said, and left him alone. I went to talk to the birds.

Aside from the occasional cough, the man seemed to be in no pain. He slept strangely peacefully, for a king. All of this I took as signs he was an unusual person; I didn't think of disguises.

I woke him up as the shadows were lengthening. He didn't need to ask me where the privy was, which I put down to him being observant, or the sort who would rather wander and waste time than ask where something is. It wasn't as though anyone could get lost on my mountain. He could try to raid my treasure hoard, but he wouldn't get far.

He returned, with no treasure under his coat. I gave him a bowl of nut porridge, which he ate with a good appetite.

'It seems I still have some skill at healing.'

'Mmm?' He looked up, and spoke with a voice still hoarse. 'My burns are not hurting as much. Thank you.'

'It's getting late. You can sleep here tonight, if you wish. Not with me.'

He inclined his head. 'Thank you. And in the morning?'

'In the morning we'll see how your wounds are healing.'

I was restless in the night, and it was cold. I covered myself in a bearskin some former occupant had left there; it still smelled of lindworm, but it kept the chill out. The fire sank to dull red coals.

I caught a glint of light beside the man: his naked sword, lying beside him where he slept. I couldn't make sense of it. In case of attack? A concealed knife would be easier and quicker than leaving a weapon out for the attacker to pick up. It made me wonder how soft he was, and what his life had been like.

At dawn, the ravens made a racket somewhere on the mountain, and I stood over him.

'Why is your sword out?'

He scrambled to his knees. 'I said I would. What I mean is, I made a vow. I wanted you to know that there was a blade between us. For your own – I mean, that you knew I would not try to take advantage.'

'Why in Odin's name would your own sword be any barrier to you raping me? I mean, it's your sword. You could just take it away again. Or use it against me. Also, I was sleeping over there.' I pointed.

He looked uncomfortable. 'I meant it to be a symbol, I suppose.'

I laughed at him. 'Just like you want me to be. Put it away and tell me about this kingdom of yours: who its enemies are, and its friends if it has any, although I suspect you would not be here if it did. Tell me which gods the people worship and how many men and women we can ask to fight, if war comes.'

It took the rest of that day for him to give me the assurances I needed, that my mountain would still be mine, that I'd have a seat on his council, that I would have my own room in the Domus and could bring my own weapons. He said nothing about the gold on the mountain, but said any property that was mine, I could keep, so long as I didn't bring it to Vormatia. He also said that among the Burgundians, the custom was for the groom's family to pay a bride-price, and he offered me twenty-four solidi.

He didn't try to kiss me.

In the end, all he had to offer me were a place and a purpose. Students to train, and allies at my side. He knew – he was the only person on Midgard who knew – those were the only things I lacked. He knew I was still looking for a fight.

CHAPTER SIXTEEN

The Betrothal of Brynhild

Hagen was waiting at the base of the mountain. A man like a hawk, I thought, with his golden eyes and a red-brown cloak, waiting quietly but seeing everything. He bowed deeply to us both, after a moment of hesitation. I thought it was reluctance to acknowledge his king's decision. Good advisers probably warn against proposing marriage to strange witches on mountaintops.

That was also when I met my bay mare, Sinir, a gift from Auda. The mare was slightly bony, but then so was I, after my weeks on the mountain.

It was two days' ride to Vormatia. For the most part, we rode in silence. When we stopped for the night, Hagen made the preparations while his king looked awkward.

I realized that I had missed the not-quite-silence of comrades. Small bodily noises in the night. A short 'watch out for that rabbit hole' or 'I think there's a stream near here', out of nowhere, without any need for politeness or introduction.

I was – do you want to hear about this? Not exactly eager for the wedding night with Gunnar, but not dreading it either. I felt nothing for him, but he was attractive enough and he had shown me nothing but respect. I had the half-sense that he was merely the shape of a man, and behind it there was some sort of struggle, to which I was not invited. I decided he probably preferred the company of men in his bed, which I thought would make our marriage no bother at all.

We followed the Rhine south, with the river on our left. On the far side rose high cliffs, crowned with green. The terrain on our side was hilly, forested, slow going for the horses.

At the end of the second day, we turned towards the road, and it wasn't long before the occasional house became a row of houses and shops, and then the walls of Vormatia rose before us. My first glimpse of your city. It struck me as a mix of old and new, the walls so straight, the roads inside such a tangle.

'I'm going ahead,' Hagen explained. 'To tell the men at the wall to send a messenger to the Domus. To prepare for your arrival.'

I was, suddenly, nervous.

'You're a queen now, Brynhild,' said my suitor.

It wasn't as bad as I feared. The streets of Vormatia seemed welcoming, with the late-afternoon sun warming the walls, and the smoke from homely fires. There were no crowds, but people did gather around our horses, and cheered for Gunnar as though he were bringing back a hunting trophy. Me.

As we reached the Domus and servants brought me a block to dismount, the white dog came running up and put his paws on my bridegroom's knees, tail wagging, mouth in a wide grin.

'Will you introduce your queen to your dog?' I said with a smile.

He looked up at me, then straightened. 'He's Sigurd's dog. Vigi is his name.'

'Ah. Sigurd.' I scanned the faces of the crowd, wondering where he was. I thought perhaps he was sulking. 'Will he stay for the wedding?'

My suitor's face was unreadable as he said, 'He will stay for good. He is marrying Gudrun, my sister, the same night you and I will wed.'

At that moment, rose petals fell from nowhere. They filled the air so that I no longer smelled smoke or meat or horse-hair. I smelled your perfume, or nature's homage to it. I turned around and I saw you.

Shall I describe the way I remember you, in every detail? Your hair, nearly black, braided in a thick coil around your head, from which ropes of seed pearls hung. You walked so lightly in your purple silk, and your expression was curious. It's always curious, but in this moment, it was most curious about me.

'You have saved us,' you whispered in my ear, before leaving a kiss to cool on my cheek. I kissed you too, but it was mostly air; I missed the moment, not knowing the customs. After that, I think I said something like, 'I under-stand I won't be the only bride.'

You turned to my suitor. 'Brother,' you said coldly, and you embraced him, though you pulled away quickly. I didn't understand anything.

'I think it's high time you changed,' you said to him, more pointedly than Gunnar's condition seemed to merit. He was only a little dusty from the road.

I liked the small dining room in the Domus. You'll say it was the weapons on the walls, but it was more than that: it was the colours, the warmth, the lines of chairs with arms down each side of the table as though every person there were a king.

And I liked the first sight of your family. You were chat-tering at your brother. People being people, but it seemed wondrous to me. Volker gave me a friendly smile, and Hagen I already had the measure of, and liked. A warrior like me.

Sigurd looked guilty. I thought that was because he had left me on a morning after and gone off to marry you, which

I didn't care about, and it irritated me that he thought I would care. That was all. I had an explanation for every expression, but my explanations were wrong, in the main.

Your mother was so beautiful, so graceful. I was a little afraid of her at first. I said, 'Thank you for the gift of the mare. I'll keep her well, and endeavour to be a good daughter to you.'

Auda put her hand on my shoulder. How I miss her! 'Welcome, daughter,' she said. 'I've prepared your room, but you must do as you like with it.'

She took my hands in hers, and asked me about the runes on them, in a way that showed me she was fascinated, not horrified. I explained that they were not magic, only memorials of people I had known.

Then Gunnar pushed his chair back, and walked to me, carrying something in his hands. He was examining my face as if for the first time. 'The promised bride-price will be delivered on the morning after the wedding, but here is a gift, to mark our betrothal.'

He opened his hand, and there on the palm was a plain gold ring. I took it from him and put it onto my rune-covered finger.

'It fits beautifully,' I said, which was true.

I handed him my favourite ring, the one with the small red stone, from the hoard. It never fitted me properly anyway.

Then I smiled at Sigurd. 'My friend,' I said. 'You look nervous. Am I so terrifying? Or is it marriage that has you so skittish? I would have thought the man who killed a lindworm, all alone, wouldn't fear anything.'

'Well met, Brynhild,' he said.

'Sigurd tells me you are a shield-maiden with a gift for magic,' Auda said. 'So you must feel free as well in the armoury and in the gardens and the library. We may be somewhat diminished, but we still have some books here, thanks be to God. Speaking of God, I don't suppose you happen to be a Christian, Brynhild?'

All eyes turned to me. I shook my head.

'We did not discuss any such requirement,' I said, looking at Gunnar, who looked back, wide-eyed.

Then you broke in, Gudrun, with your wonderful, bright speech about how in that city full of altars to so many gods, no one would expect it. 'Even among the Christians, we have our differences,' you said. 'Hagen is a heretic. So are we, but in a different way, and our way is the correct one.'

I didn't quite understand all your smiles and glances, but I understood the gist. I had quite enough gods in my life as it was. 'I will be happy to learn about Christ, in the coming years. But I have no desire to become a worshipper. Not now, at least.'

Gunnar nodded. 'Of course, if I wanted you to convert, I would have told you so,' he said, and glanced at Sigurd. 'It doesn't matter. Hagen has already secured the bishop's blessing for the marriage. We'll draw up the contract tomorrow, and the following day, those of us who are Christians will go to a celebratory mass, and then we'll have the wedding.'

Hagen explained then about the laws of your people, the scrolls you had taken from place to place that were now kept in chests in the Domus. Your family told me all the laws about wives and husbands, inheritance, children, fidelity. They talked of bride-prices and fees.

'I ask for no bride-price but to keep what is mine,' I said.

Everyone looked startled.

So, I continued, 'You have asked me to marry you, my lord, because people say it proves you are a man without fear. Because I have a reputation as a sorceress and as a warrior. You said you had no designs on my wealth. So be it. I'll keep my gold and you keep yours. I will give you my reputation, and you will give me the command of a company of warriors, at least a dozen. You will let me choose my fights, and I will promise not to join or begin any battles that would endanger your kingdom or your allies. That is the contract I will sign.'

Gunnar looked at Hagen. 'Is it possible?'

Hagen thought for a moment, looking at me. I liked him more and more. He said, 'We can find all of that between the cracks in our people's laws and the laws of the church, I think. We can draw up the contract. Bishop Timaeus is grateful for his seat here, and for our protection. He will agree.'

'Then let it be done,' Gunnar said.

I bowed my head, and when I raised it, you were looking at me. Your mouth was tight with concern, but there was a gleam in your eyes from the candles.

CHAPTER SEVENTEEN

Gudrun's Veil

When my mother wove my original wedding veil, she had weighted her loom with daggers.

For steel and sharpness, she told me. She was, after all, sending me off to marry Bleda, my enemy.

That version of the veil flowed to my ankles, and had a single border of gold thread, around my face. On the day after you arrived in Vormatia, my mother and I cut the veil in half, and stitched a border onto the cut edge of each piece. Two veils; mine fell to the small of my back, and yours to your shoulder blades.

We cut it in half for two reasons: first, to show the people how economical we were in these days of preparing for a siege. Not only would we re-use the same veil from my ill-fated first betrothal, but we'd cut it in half to fit two brides for the price of one. We'd show our people that, like them, we were making sacrifices. The second reason was that we really did need to save money. Every coin that could was to go towards weapons, defences, and food stores.

We didn't think to tell you any of that, I know. You weren't what I'd expected, Brynhild. A warrior-sorceress on a mountaintop should have been fearsome. And you were that.

I had to look up at you to look at you at all. (Yes, I have to look up at most people, I know.) But I didn't expect you to enchant *me*. And without even trying, that's the worst of it. Embarrassing, really. Even though Ludgast's men had said you were beautiful, I hadn't been prepared.

I hadn't expected to hate myself for agreeing to bring you down off your mountain.

In fairy tales, weddings were about lovers proving their courage, winning hearts, suffering for their doomed passion. But this was no fairy tale. Weddings were for diplomacy, and wealth, and stability. If you were fooled by the man who wooed you, I told myself, that was a fantasy you'd created on your own, anyway. Why did it matter which man walked through your fire? What mattered was the contract and the bonds of family.

These were the things I told myself.

When I took you the veil, you were in the garden, looking at my roses.

I made a joke about your height. 'I would have lent you one of my gowns for the wedding, but I'm afraid they would barely cover your knees.'

You laughed, and replied, 'Your mother has found me a gown. She woke me early to measure me. The last person who did that was an armourer, and he was gentler.'

'My mother can be gentle,' I said with a smile.

'She's a witch,' you said, which startled me. 'Is she a powerful one?'

'Very powerful, in some ways.'

'And you?'

I told you that I could make flowers grow and plants move, a little bit, and you asked me how the magic worked, and I found that I didn't want to talk about it. Why not, I wonder? Maybe I just didn't want you to think too deeply about what my mother's magic could do, and realize how you might have been tricked.

Is there anything I could have said at that moment, to

prevent you from hating me later that night? Believe me when I say I've had time to go over that question many, many times.

The fact is that I didn't say any of the good, true things I might have said. I chose, 'My mother has quick fingers with cloth. She'll make sure you look beautiful.'

How glorious the veil looked against your bronze-coloured braids, at the wedding.

There was honey in the cakes that we shared with our bridegrooms, each couple taking from one pewter plate. To share our first food, as a sign of willingness to share everything after. I remember breaking the cake with Sigurd, putting the pieces in our mouths, how we smiled and everyone laughed for joy. I remember, after the ceremony, you kissed my cheek with honey on your lips and told me that Sigurd, my new husband, was a good man.

CHAPTER EIGHTEEN

Brynhild and the Dog

Gudrun, you must have wondered who told me about the deception. It wasn't your brother. It wasn't Sigurd. Not Hagen, not Volker, and not your mother.

It was the dog. Vigi, as Sigurd called him.

To be fair, I think some part of me already suspected. Gunnar was quiet and peevish with me, nothing like the man who'd come to my mountain. But I wanted to be happy; I wanted to feel at home. That night, out on the plain across the river, there was music, and food and drink, and a hill-high bonfire. The smoke would perfume our hair for days afterwards. I think you were the one who told me that was the very place where the lindworm had attacked. We drove away its memory with that fire. You handed me a cup of wine and I kissed your apple cheek.

Gunnar was talking with Ludgast, joking and flyting, Ludgast's hand on his back. Sigurd was a little further away, staring into the fire.

Sigurd's bed-warmer came loping past and I recognized it as the same dog who greeted me when we came to Vormatia.

Gunnar was probably unbalanced from talking to Ludgast, from marrying me, from all of it. He called the dog to him,

bending and holding out his hand as though he had meat,
but he didn't. 'Come here, boy!'

The dog looked at him, and then walked on to Sigurd.

'Your dog fucking hates me, Sigurd,' Gunnar said, straight-
ening up again with a tipsy laugh. 'I keep trying but he never
comes to me.'

'He's a stubborn beast, my lord,' Sigurd said with a smile.
'Give him a week or two.'

Certainty gripped me, like cold hands on my shoulders.
That dog had greeted the man I thought was Gunnar with
such adoration when we arrived. Gunnar's voice, tonight,
was so clear; Sigurd's so smoke-hoarse. The glances, the
things I didn't quite understand.

I understood them all now. Or I understood enough. I
didn't know how the magic was done, but I knew you were
a family of witches and that Sigurd had taken things from
a shapeshifter: Fafnir's adornments, his very heart. What a
fool I had been.

My anger was so hot, I could have breathed on that bonfire
and lit up the entire world. But I was angriest at you. Why?
Because I thought you were an ally, a friend – because in
the few days I'd been at the Domus before the wedding, I
came to recognize the smell of your perfume, and every time
I thought I caught it in the air, I stopped and looked for you.

Besides, you had the misfortune of standing near me, still
smiling, in that moment when I saw the lie. I looked at you,
and I said, 'Tell me everything.'

You took my arm to try to lead me away, but I refused. I
said I would ask my husband to tell the whole world what
he did, that is, if I could identify which of these sons of
bitches was my husband.

You asked me whether it was so important to me to marry
the man who passed my test. Of course it wasn't, I snapped.
I wasn't the one who invented that story. Then why, you
asked, did I care which man had walked through the fire?
Why was I marrying Gunnar at all, if not for that?

Because, I told you, he was a king under threat, and I thought I could be some good in Vormatia as a warrior and a queen.

'So the manner of the proposal means nothing anyway,' you said. 'It isn't love. Is it?'

It wasn't. But I didn't like being tricked, and I told you so.

And you said, 'Then I will make you a pact from this moment, my sister-in-law. You and I will always be honest with each other.'

'You want honesty?' I demanded. 'Your new husband's good with his hands, if you like the hands of a blacksmith, and I do. I wish you a very good wedding night.'

It was the only way I could think of to hurt you, but I didn't think that it did.

One thing I hated about your beloved Domus was that to get to the family's private rooms, we had to cross through your flower-palace. It was like being with you, being in that rose garden. And I didn't want to be with you, not that night. By the time I passed through it, past the altar and into the little square courtyard ringed with the family bedchambers, I was simply exhausted.

I looked long at the weapons room. I considered leaving altogether. But I was queen, and that did serve my purposes. It was the best way I could think of to be a Valkyrie still, even in exile. At least, the best way that was open to me at that moment.

I was queen, but I was not part of the family that had tricked me.

So I went into the bedroom your mother had made for me. It was beautiful – a gleaming bed with a different animal carved on each post: a dog, a pig, a snake and a wolf. There were iron hooks on the wall for my clothes, though I had few enough to hang up at the time. A chair and a little table and even a bronze mirror. I thanked no god but luck that

Auda had guessed I would want my own room, separate from that of my husband. Still, Gunnar's door was right next to mine, and I assumed he would come to me.

So, tired though I was, I stayed standing, staring at my bedroom door, until at last Gunnar opened it and lurched in.

He was only a little drunk, but it was enough to make him bleary. He had an expectation for our wedding night, and all I needed to do was tell him not to expect it. I didn't set out to mock him, or for anyone else to know anything about our conversation.

'Husband, you were not the one who walked through my fire. I could walk away from this city now, telling everyone I met on the road about your treachery and your cowardice.'

He looked as though he'd been slapped, and he stood straighter, though he was still not alert enough to realize that the door was wide open behind him.

'Who told you?' he whispered.

'No one had to tell me. It doesn't matter anyway. I'm going to stay. But you and I—' I shook my head.

'Oh, come now,' he said, and smiled darkly, drunkenly. 'We're husband and wife now.'

The gall of it, the total lack of remorse or explanation, boiled my blood. So I picked him up, carried him to the wall and hung him by the back of his tunic on one of the unused hooks. He only dangled there for a moment before the tunic ripped and he fell onto his knees, beet-faced.

Outside, there were three or four men whose names I didn't know, and Sigurd, watching this with a mixture of shock, amusement and horror.

At least in Valhalla I always knew who my allies were. At least when I had my full powers, I always knew which side was right. What a fool I'd been for thinking I could find those same certainties in Midgard. But I steeled myself. I was a queen, with a hoard of gold and weapons. I could buy or train all the allies I needed.

'This is my room now, and mine alone,' I told Gunnar. 'You will not come here without my express consent, which I don't intend ever to give. You will give me full access to the stables, to the armoury, and a seat in every council of war. You will introduce me to every ambassador and let me interview every spy, both those of your own, and those you capture from others. I will begin training my company in the morning, and I will have my choice of all the warriors and would-be warriors in your kingdom. You will treat me with respect as your queen, and you will never, ever touch me.'

He stared at me for a moment, then nodded curtly, and walked out of my door. I know you've been at pains to tell me how your brother once was but believe me when I say I understood him well enough. I wasn't afraid of him, or angry at him. I held him in contempt.

His friends were drunk; they hooted, and called him unmanly, and said his wife had hung him from the wall like a dirty shirt. They clapped him on the back and offered to bring him somewhere better, but he threw them off and went into his room, and his friends stumbled away.

Sigurd, lagging behind the others, looked at me through the doorway. He must have seen in my face that I knew he'd used our brief time as comrades, friends, and lovers to make a fool out of me. Nobody else knew what we'd gone through that day with the lindworm, the stink of the blood, the voice in our heads. He had shared that with me, and yet he still treated me like a coin to be traded.

'I'm sorry,' he said, his voice still hoarse from the flames.

'War is coming,' I said. 'I don't need you to be sorry. I need you to be better.'

PART III

BATTLE-CRIES

CHAPTER NINETEEN

Brynhild's Walls and Bridges

You didn't see me much in those weeks that followed the wedding, I know. I wanted nothing to do with your family. I spent my time in the stables and armouries, talking to old men and birds.

The birds reported no movement of armies. As the summer faded, the city seemed to forget its fear. I saw people feasting for no reason at all, as though they didn't have to put up stores any more. Boys took to brawling with each other instead of practising with their slings.

At least your brother was as good as his word when it came to our marriage agreement. My company of fighters was a hundred strong, young men and women with willing hearts and sharp minds. Most of them were not Burgundians, and I came to understand that every family of your father's generation still trained its own fighters, as though they were still a wandering people, a people without walls. It made no difference to me. I took my Franks, my Goths, my Persians, my Romans, my Greeks, my Egyptians, and I taught them sword, dagger and bow.

Sometimes I caught sight of Sigurd watching them train, watching me, with his dog at his side. Some of my students told me Sigurd was advising the smiths on weaponry, and they all wore small brooches he had made for them, simple bronze pins with the shape of a running dog on the front. He was a wealthy man now; he could afford the metal. He was making himself useful and making himself known; the soldiers may have fought for Gunnar, but they wore Sigurd's badge. Both men and women. I remembered our conversation on the mountaintop, when he was so surprised that I wanted to teach women to wield swords. He didn't look surprised now. Wisely, he stayed away from me.

So did everyone else, except your mother.

One day, I looked up in the training yard and saw her: a small figure whose flowing blue robe seemed impossibly clean in that dusty place. We had a large open area between the barracks and the city wall, a private space where we could work in shadows for much of the day, which we appreciated in those late-summer weeks. Wiping my dirty hand across my forehead, I set the group of students sparring, and walked over to her.

'I've come to give you something,' she called, and held out her hand when I approached. 'An apology.'

What she dropped into my hand was a river stone, dark at first glance, with bits of gold and red that caught the light. It was flat, the size of my palm, as polished and shiny as a gem, but smooth and perfect.

'I didn't know apologies came in rock form.'

She shrugged. 'What do you give the woman who has a hoard?'

'Half a hoard.'

I tossed the stone a few times. It had a very nice feel to it.

'I accept your pebble,' I said. 'As for the rest, well, it doesn't matter. I'm here, I will fight. You need not try to placate me.'

'I can see that you're ready to fight. Your students look very impressive. I wonder, though, why. Why fight for us? You have made no secret of your hatred for my family.'

Hatred seemed the wrong word. Numb. I was numb. I used to dig my fingernails into my wrists to see whether I could make a mark. I hadn't realized something, when I went into the blood-pit after Sigurd. I hadn't thought about the fact that I could never again mark my hands for a fallen comrade.

I gave Auda an answer. 'I fight because that is what I trained to do. And I fight on your side because the other side is the invader, and the invader is always in the wrong.'

'Always?'

'In my long experience, yes.'

I expected her to ask how long, but instead she looked off to the side, at the city wall, beyond which was her river, and beyond that – Attila, before long. 'And your marriage to my son—'

'Gives me authority in this city.' I gestured to the students at their work behind us.

She nodded. 'We fight for our own reasons, so we fight with each other, even if not for each other.'

I had never fought for anyone; the idea struck me cold.

'But we fight with different weapons,' Auda continued. 'I have heard that you carved runes into your whetstone.'

And again, I was suspicious. These people seemed so eager to conceive an idea of me.

'It's a simple charm to keep it from doing harm to any weapon: chipping the edge or breaking the tip. The charm binds the stone to do the will of its maker.'

'And does it work?'

'I wouldn't use it otherwise.'

Auda smiled then, and said, 'I ask because I am having some trouble with stones, myself. We are rebuilding the bridge, as you may know. Without it, we are cut off from the imperial troops at the border wall, and from supplies.'

'And from your enemies on the far side of the Rhine.'

'Indeed,' she said. 'When they come. But I'd rather they come to this bridge, where we can hold them, than cross somewhere north or south and then approach from land. We need the bridge. It is a military matter. And so I come to you, and your runelore.'

I told her I didn't know any runes for building bridges. Anyway, I thought she already had magic to control stone.

'The river is the only thing I can command when I'm not touching it,' she explained. 'Stone and metal I can bend to my will – to the river's will, really, acting through me. I am the river, in a sense. I am not the bridge.'

'But you controlled the air around Sigurd, with the cloak you wove, and you were nowhere near him.'

'Yes,' she said. 'And I'm sorry about that. But this is different. The trouble is that the stones tremble. They remember what I did, when I brought the river up to drown them. Even new stones, from far away, have heard the tale, through the rumbles of the ground. They shift and shudder. I can't control them.'

The thought seemed to worry her. Her mouth was a tight line.

I knew a charm to bind a stone to its maker, and a rune for ships to keep them safe from the waves. I thought of all the magics that I knew. As I closed my eyes, I could see them, how they ought to be.

There was a young student named Drusus, with curly black hair and laughing eyes. He was the quickest and quietest, and my favourite student. I knew he wouldn't ask questions or gossip, so I asked him to bring me our smallest and sharpest iron chisel.

I carved the right runes on the flat river stone Auda had given me, and then I handed it back to her.

'Keep this with you at all times, and have your builders carve the same runes into every stone in the bridge. I think the stones will obey you then. I think they will no longer be afraid.'

She weighed the stone in her hand. 'If only someone could carve a rune into me to take away my fear.'

'There I can't help you.'

'No.' Then she looked up at me. 'But this stone was my gift to you.'

'I have said I want nothing from your family. I meant it.'

'Of course.'

And she was gone, leaving me wondering whether I had been tricked.

With my next visitor, there was no doubt.

A fortnight had passed since I gave your mother the runes. The bridge was rising before our eyes; the speed didn't come from my runes, but perhaps it came from some other magic of Auda's. Perhaps once she could tell the stones to lie still, the mere matter of joining them together was easy for her.

Very early one morning, nightmares chased me out of bed, and I went into the family courtyard, where I saw a familiar figure. A person, leaning against the far wall of the fountain, facing away from me. Despite the long black hair, I knew at a glance it wasn't you; the hair was thin and lank, for one thing. And that slouching posture. Everything about that person was long, from the folded arms to the pointed toes of the black leather shoes.

I took my knife out of my belt.

'You'll need a bigger knife for me, I think,' said Loki, turning around.

'What the hell are you doing here?'

The god of mischief grinned. 'Offering my congratulations. I love weddings. Especially when I'm not invited.'

'The wedding was nearly a month ago.'

Loki shrugged and put one hand to her round belly with a sly smile. 'I've been busy.'

'I can see that. Rolling around in the stables again?'

She ignored that. 'I am overdue on other congratulations too. I hear you met an old acquaintance of mine.'

Her tone was light, but her expression was serious. It took me a moment to realize what she meant. Fafnir. Sigurd had told me the story, of how his foster-father Regin tricked two gods into believing they'd killed the shapeshifter Otter.

The two gods were Odin and Loki.

I couldn't quite connect it all, but I was suspicious. 'I met a lying worm, so I suppose that is the sort of company you keep.'

'Ha,' Loki replied. 'Everyone always thinks the worst of me. The fact is, the lindworm was Odin's pet, not mine. The Bale-worker gave Fafnir what he'd always wanted: the chance to punish Regin, who had killed Fafnir's brother and, incidentally, tricked Odin into giving him a pile of blood-gold for it – and tricked me too, I don't mind saying. Respect where it's due. But Odin doesn't have a sense of humour. Never has. He helped Fafnir punish Regin, by helping him destroy Regin's champion.'

'Sigurd,' I breathed. 'But Fafnir didn't destroy Sigurd. It was the other way around.'

The memory came to me of Sigurd on the mountaintop, the stench of that roasting heart. Sigurd telling me the story the lindworm told him, about Regin's treachery. Sigurd saying, 'I don't know what to think.' Fafnir's deep whisper: *I am the scourge of God.*

It was true that Regin had lost Sigurd that day. How much of it had Odin engineered? Maybe Sigurd wouldn't have even made it as far as the lindworm if it hadn't been for the old man he met in the woods, who gave him a wonderful horse. *My* wonderful horse.

The bastard.

Still, it seemed a lot of trouble for Odin to take.

'I can't believe even the Blusterer would make common cause with that evil creature just because he held a grudge against Regin.'

Loki cocked her head. 'I didn't say that was the only reason. Why do you think Fafnir allied with Atilla? Why would a monster work for a man? The lindworm made a bargain for the information the Deceiver gave him.'

I frowned. 'So, Odin gave Sigurd a horse, and he gave Atilla a lindworm. Why?' Loki said nothing, and suddenly a thought chilled me: what had Odin given me, to manipulate me, to destroy me? The advice at the crossroads? The marriage to Gunnar? Or this visit from Loki? I snapped: 'If the Allfather sent you, you can—'

'Some of us are more than handmaidens.' Loki's smile was a snarl, or perhaps it just gave that impression. An effect of the small black dots around her mouth, scars from where it was once sewn shut, a long time ago.

I shook my head to rid it of all the thoughts and suspicions buzzing like flies. It was pointless to try to understand the ways of gods. But I had one here with me, for the moment, and I should make the most of that rare chance to learn what I wanted to know most.

'How are my comrades? How are the Valkyries? Have any died? Any wounded? New girls?'

'Not that I've heard about,' Loki said, falling back into a slouch. 'I don't keep track. The fact is that I am, as far as Odin knows, on Odin's business, but that business should not have taken me here, not by any path the crow flies. Vormatia was not exactly on my way.'

The sparks in Loki's eyes seemed sincere, but anger is no reason to trust someone. Anger is cheap and plentiful.

'Your way?'

'To Freyja.' At that, Loki smiled slyly, looking at me sideways.

'Freyja! If Odin is sending you as his emissary, he must be starved for friends.'

'I'm not his friend, and I'm not his emissary. He's asked me to do a little thieving.'

I whistled. 'From Frejya? Does Odin *want* to push her into war?'

'War with Freyja? No, not quite yet. I'm the distraction, don't you see? I'm the feint. I thought you'd like to know.'

'The distraction for what? What is Odin planning?'

'On that,' Loki said, tracing her finger around her mouth, those old black scars, 'my lips have been sealed.'

Loki was always infuriating, in all her many forms.

'Why bother telling me this half-gossip? Why bother with me at all?'

'Consider it a warning.'

'You're the god of mischief, not the god of warnings.'

'Warnings are the most useful mischief of all,' Loki said, loping towards me with one long finger raised. 'What if I told you that millions of people are going to drown in their own blood before your little human life reaches its ignoble end? What if you knew that before it happened? What would you say then, the next time some jackass of a king says, come, let's honour the fallen, pour out the mead. Pour one out for all the heroes. Raise the dead in a pile. Raise a flag halfway up. Plant a beanstalk. Climb to heaven. Look up, up, up, and see—'

She stopped, spreading her hands.

'What?' I asked, annoyed.

'Bastards,' she whispered in my face. 'At the top, there are only bastards. Get out your axe, Brynhild.'

And then she was gone, a mere shadow against the wall.

Why warn *me*? The idea that the Allfather's plans had anything to do with me, or with Vormatia, was chilling. Odin and his Valkyries choose the slain; they don't choose the battles. Or at least, they never had. And why would Odin care whether one petty king or another won the day? Why would he want to distract Freyja, of all people? None of it made any sense, and I reminded myself repeatedly that Loki might have simply wanted to watch me worry or drive me into doing something that would amuse her.

Still, I felt nervous. I watched the city breathe more freely, watched the first harvests come in from the fields. And I heard Loki's words in my mind.

The birds were flying in all directions by then, even over

the lands that had once been poisoned by the lindworm. So I asked them for news. For several days, they told me things that didn't concern me, of traders or of the Empire's border wall, raiding parties in the north, Romans marching in the south. No word of the Huns.

And then, one day, a very old raven came to me in the courtyard, just outside the stables, and told me that Attila was marching westward along the Danube, and he had two armies with him. An imperial army and a Hun army, the raven said. And there was a third army coming from the north, marching towards Vormatia.

'There are Roman men among the Huns, you mean,' I said.

The raven cocked her head at me. 'Roman *legions*, not Roman men. I meant what I said.'

This next part you will remember, my love. But you may not remember it the same way I do. In any case, I will tell it to the wind.

I walked through the banquet hall, through the peristyle, and into the family dining room where you all sat eating. The weapons on the walls seemed a mockery now. You all turned to look at me, surprised. You had knives in your hands and laughter on your lips.

'Attila marches on Vormatia,' I said. 'With an army of sixty thousand men. With imperial legions among them.' I hoped the bird's count was accurate.

Gunnar put his knife down and stared. 'Who says so?'

'I've heard it from a reliable messenger. There's an army coming west along the Danube, and a second coming from the north. Within a week, they'll meet each other.'

'What sort of messenger?' Hagen demanded.

I hesitated. You had all been told I was a sorceress. I didn't see any reason to hide the fact that I spoke the language of birds. Sigurd didn't meet my gaze. Perhaps he hadn't thought to ask the birds for news, or perhaps he hadn't been talking to them at all. Perhaps the dog kept them away.

'A raven,' I said, my chin held high.

Gunnar smothered a laugh with his hand, not very dili-gently.

Your mother did not laugh. She stood up, abruptly. Her hair was twisted in coils around her head, and she wore a stola of very deep brown, with a gold brooch dripping with amber beads at each shoulder. 'The wind will confirm it, if it is true. I must go to my tower and ask it.'

'There is no time,' I said, annoyed. 'We have a week at most before he is at the Rhine.'

'He will get no further,' Gunnar said.

'What certainty!' I couldn't believe anyone could be such a fool. 'Attila has had the summer to plan and to gather strength. Machines. Weapons. If he attacks Vormatia now, that will be the end of it.'

You did not smile, my darling, but you did tell me very soberly that the city was fortifying.

I'm sorry I snapped at you. 'It will not be enough! Last time he brought a monster. This time I don't think he will come with less.'

'What would you have me do?' Gunnar asked, spreading his hands.

'Ride east,' I said. 'Take everyone who can fight and ride out to meet him before he has a chance to put his plans into motion and gather allies. We might not be able to choose who wins and loses, but we can choose the battlefield. If we must fight, then let's fight far from the children and old people. We can choose who dies.'

Your brother snorted. 'Can we really? When we lose the battle, do you think Attila will spare the children and the old people then? He will ride into Vormatia unopposed. Why would we leave a strong, fortified position, with the river between him and us?'

Auda was shaking her head, her small hands gripping the back of her chair. 'Gunnar is right. We cannot ride across the Rhine. The Empire has sworn to come to our defence here, in these territories. It will not defend us across the Rhine, beyond even the Empire's border wall. And if we ride out to war in those lands, we may lose any claim we have to remain here, where we have sworn to keep the peace.'

Did I bang the table? I feel I must have banged something. 'By Odin's eye, the Empire is marching *with* Attila! They have turned on you. They've taken his side. Don't you see it?'

I looked at all your faces and I felt suddenly very old. I remembered the Empire of Constantine. I even remembered, dimly, the Empire of Hadrian. What remained of it now was scattered, uneven, dingy. Parts of it might easily go to war with other parts, without any warning. You were all acting as though it was a firm rock underneath you, but I had been watching it crumble for some time.

Sigurd wasn't even looking at me. He was fiddling with his napkin, folding it into something: a boat, or a doll, or some toy to give his dog or one of the village children. He was always making things. Useless things, for the most part.

You stood up, my darling, and spoke. 'My father used to tell the story of the girls at the mill. Two girls chained to a millstone, and they ground out the wealth of a kingdom. Very convenient! But when the king broke his promises to them, they revealed that they were giants, wonderful creatures of long lineage. The giant girls would not make wealth for the king any more, but they kept grinding. They never stopped. What they ground was an army, an army that just kept coming. If the Empire breaks faith with us, they will find us ready.'

Your face shone, telling your story. I was angry at your beauty, at your capacity to love your family and your home so faithfully. I was angry that you thought it was a time for telling stories. I thought I hated you.

So I said, 'Do you have a secret army ready to mill, then? Auda, have you readied this sorcery? If so, I'll go away, because clearly you don't need me.'

Sigurd said, 'I think—'

I snapped: 'I don't need to hear what you think, Sigurd. I always know what you're thinking. You are not complicated.'

Sigurd's face was red, and there were amused glances elsewhere at the table. I remembered how I had taunted you about the hands of a blacksmith on our wedding night, before everyone, and remembered that my past with Sigurd was known. I'd put it out of my mind, but how it must have galled Gunnar – Gunnar who had told Sigurd to sleep with a sword between us when he came to court me. Your brother did not love me, but he wanted to be a good king in every way, and in every way he failed, and that was what he saw when he looked at me.

'That's enough,' Gunnar said then. 'This ends here. You may be a sorceress and a shield-maiden, wife, but you know nothing of strategy.'

And Sigurd said, his voice choked, 'She is a Valkyrie. She does know.'

It was strange to see your family stunned into silence. I hadn't been sure whether they'd even know what a Valkyrie was; there were so many stories coming in and out of Vormatia in those days, and no one in your family spoke of the gods I knew. But it was clear in your faces that you knew the word.

Volker leaned forward. 'Sigurd, friend, comrade, I know you're not given to speaking in metaphor, but do you really mean – you don't mean one of the battlefield demons from the old songs.' He looked at me with an apologetic half-smile.

Sigurd answered: 'Brynhild has fought with the old gods, and with creatures that I thought were only stories. She killed the lindworm.'

'We killed the lindworm together,' I said, as though that mattered in that moment. 'Yes. I was a Valkyrie. I was not a demon. We – Valkyries – are humans, but trained to be warriors, and given some skills. I am . . . older than I look.'

'All this time, we've had a flying warrior-woman in our midst,' Volker said, with a low whistle. Then, after a moment's thought: '*Can* you fly?'

'Not any more.'

Gunnar glared at me suspiciously and gripped the edge of the table. 'You say you *were* a Valkyrie. And what are you now?'

It was uncomfortable, giving an account of myself to this man who'd wronged me. I didn't owe him that, and I had no desire to explain anything. I glanced at Sigurd. He looked petulant, vindicated; he'd taken my side, in his way. I'd come to that meeting to win an argument, and he was trying to show the rest of you why you should listen. I didn't thank him but I couldn't deny that his strategy seemed to be working. I had everyone's attention. Your mother was smiling, looking oddly satisfied. Hagen's eyes were as wide as a child's.

'I am your wife,' I said at last. 'And I've fought more battles than would fill all your sagas. I've slaughtered kings and guided the arms of heroes and caught arrows in mid-air. All the history of the world had me and mine moving behind it, for as many generations as most of your stories remember. I can still work the runelore and I can still talk to ravens and I can still wield a sword better than any man here. If I say we have a better chance riding to meet the enemy than waiting for him to pen us here, it's because I believe it to be true.'

I hoped, with every breath in my body, that I wasn't leading you into a trap. Some mischief of Loki's, or Odin's, or both. Or some stratagem of Freyja, who terrified even Odin. But all I could do was choose the best of the options that lay before me.

There was a long pause. I could see Gunnar thinking hard with his head bowed, while you and Hagen waited beside him, waiting for him to ask your opinion or your advice, I suppose. He never did. Finally, your mother said softly, 'It explains many things.'

Gunnar lifted his head then and said, 'If it's true, it also changes many things.'

'It changes everything,' Volker said, grinning. 'The Huns will tremble before us. We have a Valkyrie!'

And then Volker stood up and sang, the beginnings of the song that would be ringing from the city walls by morning: *How it startles, Brynhild's arm, flashing, fiery, Brynhild's arm!* He stopped, looked around, said, 'Eh?'

Hagen pulled him down into his chair, but he, like everyone, was smiling. Thinking that now they had a secret weapon, a god's weapon, that I would save everyone. Who could stand against Vormatia with a Valkyrie in its ranks?

'I know Brynhild's runelore to be as sound as her heart is,' Auda said. 'We can't ignore this warning.'

And that was that.

You were the one, I think, who asked Hagen how many days it would take to gather all of Vormatia's fighting men.

'They're already gathered, for the most part,' Hagen said. 'Ludgast's men could be ready in five days, maybe even three.'

'Will he fight for us?' Gunnar asked.

'He'll fight the Huns,' Hagen answered, carefully. 'And there are others who would fight too, farther north and west. Warriors who have kept their blades sharp for weeks, but who feared to leave their estates and families.'

'I can ride north,' Sigurd said. 'My horse is fast. I'll go to Mainz and all the estates along the way, and then to Ludgast's people, and meet you on the road east.'

At last, Gunnar looked at me, one raven-feeder to another. 'Where exactly did you say Attila is now?'

I told him what I had learned from the birds. 'Attila has city-breaking weapons. He has horse archers, ready to encircle and bring down any sorties. He wants us in one place, with open land around us. We must meet him where he can't pin us down, and before has all his allies with him. Somewhere with hills and forests, where he can't aim at us. Is there anywhere like that between the city and his position?'

Hagen shrugged. 'It's all like that, for the most part. A day's ride due east from Vormatia takes us into Odin's Hills.'

'What?' I nearly choked. 'What do you mean, Odin's Hills?'

'It's just what the people call it,' said Volker. 'A patch of low mountains, all wooded, for the most part. Crisscrossed with small rivers. Exactly the sort of land to confound an army of horsemen and machines. It's perfect.'

Almost too perfect, I thought. My mind spun like a spindle, wondering how the old man was playing with me. But I tried not to let him into my head. I told myself that Midgard was littered with hills and caves and lakes named for Odin, and it meant nothing. What could I do but my best? I was in Midgard, a human woman, and could only act on the knowledge I had. If I was going to make mistakes, they would be my own.

At some point, during the talk that followed, we decided to meet Attila at the Mimling River, in the heart of the hills, two days' ride from the city.

CHAPTER TWENTY

Gudrun in the Courtyard

I remember it differently to you. When you burst into our dinner, we were all terrified of you. Gunnar needed you so much more than you needed him. In fact, you didn't need him at all. You were a wealthy warrior witch – and a Valkyrie! You had no reason to stay, as far as we could tell. We were all waiting for you to turn on your heel and make Gunnar a laughing stock again.

But that wasn't the only reason you frightened us. Your face was grim, your hair bound up like a crown, and you *did* bang the table, so hard that Volker's cup sloshed. He was always spilling or dropping things. I think he half did it on purpose, when he was young, to make us laugh. And then it became a habit, or a fate.

I told my story about the millstones to assure you that I was on your side, but you didn't understand – or, no, it was a silly way to do it. I should have just said it straight out: Brynhild, you're right, we'll do what you say. There was never any doubt in that room. You didn't need to convince us. But we were a family, with years behind us to develop a silent language of glances and grimaces, smiles and sighs, and what was obvious to us was probably not so clear to you.

Anyway, I admit I was relieved. Those weeks when you were furious with us – for good reason, yes – unsettled me, for reasons I didn't quite understand.

The way our rooms were arranged, around that little central court, made for a farce, didn't it? How you avoided us, Brynhild. Avoided me. And your husband most of all, of course. It helped that Gunnar liked nothing better than to spend hours alone in the library, reading old books in Latin and Greek, and making copies of the scrolls that had travelled with our people. On more than one night I saw Gunnar go to his room and then heard your own door open not long after; you waited so as not to meet him, not even to pass in the halls. We were used to hearing doors open and close, since Volker walked in his sleep. We pretended everything was normal.

But that night, after you'd convinced us to go to war, your guard was finally down. You walked into the courtyard while I was still there.

That came as a surprise to me too, I admit. Your eyes went wide, and it took me a minute to remember I had put on the imperial helmet, the one with the ridiculous red brush like a sideways coxcomb on top. My father brought that back for me when I was a small girl, and I used to wear it to tramp around the Domus, with it down around my eyes. As an adult, I'd found a way to make it fit better, with my hair coiled under it. I felt comfortable in it because it was so silly. I'd put it on that night as I was watering my plants, out of old habit. And because I wanted to remind Hagen, Volker, and especially Gunnar of who we were. Who we'd been. Me with my flowers. Hagen with his knives, Gunnar with his books, Volker with his songs. If we could just hold on to something of that, we couldn't lose everything.

But you looked at me as if I was a creature without a name, and not deserving of one. Before you could stride off to your room, I crossed the tiled floor in my bare feet and caught your arm.

'I've wronged you, Brynhild,' I said.

You looked from my hand on your arm up to my face, your eyes like deep water. 'Yes.'

'I'm not saying that because we know who you are, now. What you are. It would be true whether you were a milk-maid or a princess or anything else. We shouldn't have deceived you.'

'But you are glad to learn I'm a Valkyrie,' you said. 'Nonetheless.'

I was surprised into a nervous smile. 'Are you immortal?'

You waited a long time before saying, 'No. I grow old like anyone else, but only when I'm on Midgard. In this world, I mean. In Valhalla, nobody ages. Nobody changes. It is like a dream there; time doesn't pass in the ordinary way. Odin took me from here when I was eight years old. I don't know how old my body is now.'

I dropped my hand from your arm then and surveyed you. Your hands were calloused from hafts and hilts, as mine were calloused from trowels, but there the resemblance stopped. How breathtaking you were! You were wearing one of the stolas that my mother had woven for you. It was the colour of marigolds, and you wore two round brooches like suns on either side of your collarbone. I wondered what it would be like to run my fingertip along that collarbone and slip that linen off your shoulder.

I think that was the moment that I knew. I was unsettled by you – not by our trickery, or your reaction to it, not my brother's marriage problems or the politics of it or anything but by your breath in the wind, by your shadow on the floor. The world with you in it was a different world to the one I had known, and there was no going home again.

But you were looking at me with the same disdain you'd shown for weeks. Maybe I could make you my friend, I thought, wordlessly. I liked a challenge, after all.

'I have about twenty-five years behind me,' I said. 'You look about my age.'

You shrugged. 'All right then, say twenty-five years. That's the count of hours I spent in this world when I was a Valkyrie. I'm as old as my battles.'

'Aren't we all,' I said.

I saw a glimmer of something in your green eyes. But it was probably just more fury. You said, 'Do not fool yourselves into thinking you have your own monster now. I'm just a woman. I can fight well, and I have some other skills: the language of birds, the runelore. But I do know warfare.'

'And you are certain this ride east is the best thing to do?'

'I have fought many battles.'

'Yes,' I said. 'But you have never had to protect your own home. Have you?'

I meant that as an offer, but you heard it as contempt, or something like it, I think. Anyway, you drew away from me. 'You should get to your room,' you said. 'Sigurd will be joining you there, I'm sure.'

You too must have heard the doors open and close. I probably blushed. My marriage with Sigurd was comfortable enough; it was no great love, and we didn't talk much, but you were right that he did visit my room. Part of the point of the marriage was to give our family heirs, especially since neither Gunnar nor Hagen seemed likely to do that.

'Do you hate me?' I asked. Succeeding in saying something head-on for the first time that day, despite my many attempts.

Your voice was thick when you said, 'No.' And then you laughed a little, and you said, 'I want to. I would like to say that I do, even now. I'd like to pretend that to myself and to you. But you said we should be honest with each other, did you not? Go on, then. Go to your husband.'

You opened your door and slipped away from me. Befuddled, I glanced towards the guards set at the entry to the courtyard and saw them smirking. They thought we were two jealous women, squabbling over Sigurd. They didn't understand anything.

*

Sigurd did come to my room that night, as it happened. But all we did was sit across from each other and play the game called Brigands – the one where you can capture the other player's pieces by putting a piece on either side. A game of ambushes and quick changes. Sigurd was not much good at it, but he was distracted that night.

I remember we drank yellow wine and ate pistachios and rich dates, off a pewter plate (and Vigi had the first one, as he always did). We talked about the battle to come. Gunnar had asked Sigurd to ride through the northern reaches of our kingdom, collecting men from Ludgast's people and the other families. He was under orders to engage the army riding down from the north before it met up with Attila's main force, and from there, to come to meet us if he could.

My husband asked me whether I believed in destiny.

Vigi snored under the table, and I reached down and scratched him behind the ears. I told my husband I believed in consequences and found myself repeating a speech my mother had given me many times: the Rhine follows the path that seems best, but that doesn't mean it makes its own path.

Sigurd found this unsatisfactory. 'God can shift the courses of rivers. If something is meant to be, it will be, no matter what obstacles are in the way.'

'What do you think is meant to be?'

He said, very seriously, 'I know that I will be great. I am just wondering how that's going to happen.'

And then he conceded the game, kissed my forehead, and patted his leg for Vigi to join him, as he went off to his own room to sleep his last night in Vormatia.

In the morning, I said farewell to my husband. Hagen, Gunnar, and my mother were already in the courtyard, down near the stables.

Sigurd embraced me again, this time more stiffly, a performance and a ritual. He said, 'Keep the city and yourself well. We'll come back victorious.'

'I have no doubt, because I'll be at the battlefield,' I retorted.

Gunnar wheeled on me. 'Will you indeed?'

But I stood my ground. 'I'm not staying here. Mother can manage the city without me well enough.'

'If I recall, I was the one who saved the city from the monster last time,' she said, but mildly.

'Yes. And you may have to save it again, if we fail. I'm needed at the fight. If Attila has any other surprises in store, we may need someone who knows a little magic.'

Mother didn't contradict me, and I didn't say what we both knew to be true: her magic was tied to the Rhine, and so she was too.

'You're right, Gudrun,' said Gunnar, still fiddling with Sigurd's weapons and belt. 'I need you with me. It's settled, Sigurd. Don't worry. Gudrun won't be in the thick of battle, and she won't be with the camp-followers. Gudrun and Brynhild can share a tent, since I have no wish to share one with my wife and she certainly won't share one with me.'

There was pain behind my brother's face, but no anger, at me or anyone else. He looked like a man resigned to something, and I wouldn't have said it was victory.

But when he was finally satisfied that Sigurd's belt was proper, he stepped back, took Sigurd's face in his hands, and knocked his forehead hard against his, and all the men roared with laughter. Gunnar and Hagen were prone to butting heads out of love, and now Gunnar was greeting Sigurd that way too, and sending him away that way.

'Bring me an army, Sigurd of Xanten,' my brother said.

CHAPTER TWENTY-ONE

Brynhild Does Not Sleep

In Valhalla, we played a game like the one you call Brigands. I recognized it, although the rules were different, when my students played it in the training yard in Vormatia.

It didn't take long to get them ready to march. A hundred young men and women, with shining faces and shining blades. I was not a flowery speech maker. I said I was proud of them, that they were ready, that it was time. I told them that if their hearts were set on wisdom and justice, their quick hands would not go awry. I told them that if they died, they would live forever in songs. After all, most of these young people were Christians. When they arrived at Valhalla or Folkvang, or whatever they might call the place they landed. Or they might well refuse an invitation to Valhalla; I had seen that happen. And I wasn't sure what I could promise them in that regard. But I felt I had to promise them something.

In other words, I told them something like I would have told the young Valkyries I had once trained. But these young people were not Valkyries. They would be all too visible on the battlefield, and they could not fly out of danger. And, as you had reminded me, they were fighting for their own homes and families. If we lost, it would be more than an injustice. It would be doom for the kingdom.

And yes, I was fighting for that kingdom too. I couldn't say whether Gunnar was a king worth fighting for, but I had heard the tales of Attila bringing the lindworm, and I had decided that Attila was a king worth fighting against. Whatever Odin's plans were, or Loki's, or Freyja's, none of that was my concern. I knew of a city where people sang songs and children played, and I knew of a monster that had threatened them, and I was ready to draw my sword.

I felt strangely elated once we left the city, riding along the imperial road, then due east across the plain. That first night, we made camp at the feet of the Odenwald, with flat open country behind us, and the hills rising ahead.

There was woodsmoke in everything: my clothing and yours, the horse blankets, our own blankets inside the tent we shared. It was in your beautiful hair, as you combed it before you slept, those long locks of silken black. I could hear the low music of conversations in other tents, every so often a cough or a laugh. Some of those people would have spears through them tomorrow. Some of them would be . . . elsewhere, soon.

And you and I were under the same tent, alone together, for the first time.

You asked me to tell you about Valhalla. I tried.

'Surely the Christians don't go there,' you said. 'Or anyone who follows gods other than yours.'

'Those gods aren't mine. They just . . . are. Other gods don't know me, luckily.'

That made you laugh, though I didn't intend it to. 'But is there not a heaven, then?' you asked.

I thought for a moment, remembering how to explain something that I had learned centuries before. 'What comes to Valhalla is not the whole person that used to exist. The form, for example – the body. It stays in the ground or burns in a fire. What lives on after that depends on what the person made of themselves. For some people, what lasts is their – well, I've heard it called fortune, I've heard it called other things. The balance of a person's choices, their way of moving through the world. That part, sometimes, becomes someone new. An inhuman creature, like Fafnir, or something less terrible. Or sometimes, it is reborn into a new child, some- times a descendant. That happens.'

'And for others?'

'Well, for some there is the force of will. Many magic-users depend on that so much in life that it lives on, sometimes in this world, or others. I don't know much about where those dead go, to be honest.'

'Magic-users. Like – my mother,' you said.

'Yes! I suspect that's the part that Auda uses to command water, wind, stone, and metal. But those of us who use small magics – like runes and potions – we don't need the will to be so strong.'

I saw you frowning, wondering which one you would be, and where the will of your mother would live after her death. I didn't have an answer to either question and didn't like my guesses. So I carried on: 'But what we invite to Valhalla is a sort of memory – the impression the mind made on the world, and the world made on the mind. The mind is what frees a warrior from being something other than their choices, Odin says. It's what distinguishes a warrior from a killer. So the mind is what we mean, when we say we're taking the battle-dead. But they don't have to come with us. They can go elsewhere; I don't know all of the places they can go. Folkvang is one. But some don't come to Folkvang or Midgard. All I know is that when that part of a person stays in *this* world, it twists into horrible forms. The body is meant to stay, but the self is meant to wander. For most people, only part of the self – that aspect of the self they made strong in life and that lasts in death – can move between worlds. The body is stubborn, like wet clay, and tends to stay where it's put.'

It was Eir who had taught me all of this, long ago.

'And what about the soul?' you asked.

'That I don't know. If it exists, perhaps it goes to a heaven, or somewhere else. Perhaps the other gods take parts of the dead. Perhaps they're all scavengers, picking off rings and cutting hair. I can't say. Odin has given me to understand that none of it lasts forever, anyway. Everything will come to an end. He's probably right about that. He usually is, about the future.'

You turned to me and put down your brush. 'You speak so casually of talking with gods and walking in other worlds, but I don't get the sense you were happy there.'

'Happiness isn't quite the word. I was incapable of being unhappy there, which is not the same. Valhalla is beautiful and peaceful, but unending, unchanging, and that makes it feel faded, unsatisfying.' I stopped, and tried again. 'All that is fleeting in a phrase of music, sung around a fire, belongs to the worlds of the living.'

'Do people fall in love there?' You had your face turned to me by the light of our one candle.

'There is a kind of love in Valhalla,' I said, uncertain how to explain.

'And sex too?' Your eyes twinkled.

'And sex too,' I said, smiling. 'But no *falling* in love. No yearning. There is eating but no hunger. We learn nothing there, because, like the boars we kill who rise again the following morning, we are no different from one sun-journey to the next. There is no risk there, and nothing to risk.'

Somewhere not far away, Volker struck up a sad song. You turned towards it, the edge of your profile illuminated in gold.

'I can't decide whether that's like heaven or hell,' you said.

'It's neither, as I said.' If I sounded impatient, I'm sorry. 'It's Valhalla. It's not like Midgard. The honour in a warrior's death is not in its reward. The things that matter can only happen here.'

But that wasn't quite true. My friendships mattered. My comrades. We'd fought in Midgard but we'd also trained in Valhalla. We'd taught each other how to forget our first families. I missed my comrades more than anything. And I was afraid of the battle, I realized – not afraid of dying or being hurt, especially since I had the same invulnerable skin as Sigurd. But I was afraid that I wouldn't be able to see the Valkyries. They would be there – they come to every battle – and if I couldn't see them there, that meant I would never see them again.

That night, while you slept an arm's length away, I heard the chirring of a nightjar outside our tent, with a message from Sigurd: *We met a group of Huns and fought them. We won. We meet you tomorrow.*

I went out of the tent, groping with my bare feet on the ground. 'Tell me how he is,' I asked. 'Tell me what you saw, and all that he said.'

'He fought as though he sought death,' the nightjar said in its long low poetry. 'His shield dragged him down and he left his neck long and exposed. Again and again their blows landed but he still lives, without a scratch. He wheezed with laughter and drove his sword into the men who should have killed him. Felt the smack of bone and blood on his knuckles. Scraped sweaty shoulders with dirty fingernails and grappled, bit, and wailed. He screamed, hoarse as a crow. No one can cut him down. He is a hero decorated in blood. He will be with you tomorrow.'

The talent of birds is to tell appalling news in sweet music.

I gave the nightjar my thanks and went back inside, listening to you breathe. I'd caught a chill out in the air, and I never got warm all through that night.

CHAPTER TWENTY-TWO

Gudrun at War

Did you think I was sleeping, when you slipped out of the tent, and slipped back in? Half-dreaming, I heard you talking to the birds, and I barely even wondered at it. By then, I already thought you could do anything.

I believed everything you told me that night, Brynhild. You told me the body, will, mind, and soul were separable; what else would death be? I saw no contradiction between your unseen worlds and the unseen heaven and the heaven of heavens, the words that flowed through my chest when I stood in church, like the river that flowed through my mother. All worlds and powers were equally real – or unreal – and made no difference to my actions in life. Or so I believed then.

And honestly, have my beliefs changed, in these long years since? I don't think so. Not really. Belief implies certainty but all I have ever believed in is possibility. It's because I'm a diplomat, my mother would say. Always ready to listen, to hedge. I didn't believe Valhalla was real as much as I believed the world I knew, no matter how much I loved it, could not be everything. I knew that I was seeing the universe through a pinhole, that everything around me was

199

a mere stream running to a sea. And I had never seen the sea.

But for the first time, I was about to see a battlefield.

Hagen had timed everything perfectly, so that we met Attila's army in a rumpled valley, wooded hills shot through with gullies and ravines. Sunlight glinted off the imperial shields in two of the ravines, and in another we saw Attila's own infantry, with siege towers and other machines of war, and another two were filled with rivers of mounted men.

But his horse archers and siege towers wouldn't help him here, where all the fighting would be close.

Thanks to you and your birds, we knew that Sigurd and his men were near, that Attila would soon find another enemy bearing down on him from the north instead of the reinforcements he expected.

It was a glorious bright morning, and for the first time I was glad that we had ridden out to battle. My city was two days' ride behind us, protected by the Rhine and its witch.

You, my dear, were otherwise occupied and didn't see me ride up over the ridge in my chariot. Around my neck were ropes upon ropes of clay and glass beads, in all colours, but mainly blues and greens. They had been gifts from my brother, on every birthday since my thirteenth. A private joke, because he'd beaten me at marbles, and taken my favourite one, a blue swirly wonder. He never did give me that marble back. I wonder what happened to it.

I could feel strength in my thighs, and in the staff I held mostly for show. This time, I was determined that my magic – such as it was – would not fail. These trees were strangers to me but I would charm them, make them move for us. By God, if all I could do was attack Attila with bees, I would do that. It might be silly and strange but I would not be useless.

But for the most part, I was simply watchful. The lindworm was dead, but *surely* Attila must have brought something.

Something more than this very ordinary army, spreading in the cracks and crevices of the mountains, spilling out of the forest.

I glared down at the force Attila had mustered to sack my city as it poured into the valley and met our attack. At the back the siege towers stood, abandoned. Most of the army was on horseback but the archers couldn't get their shots away before Gunnar's men pulled them down with nets, skewered them with spears, grappled with them and forced them to stand and fight.

And though you didn't see me, I saw you, riding at the head of your company, on Gunnar's left. I saw your gory sword in your hand. There was a moment when you glanced back, up to the high ground where I stood on my chariot. You were shining like a spear, your helmet hiding your face from me.

You wore your mail and helmet – to keep the enemy from guessing that you were invulnerable, I suppose. To protect any parts of you that weren't. Or because that was what you wore to fight.

I saw Hagen and Volker, back-to-back near Gunnar, with their men around them. Hagen had a blade in each hand.

There was an archer at my side, watching, keeping me safe. I could see what he thought: that he should be down fighting too, covered in glory, not mud from my chariot wheels.

But where was the monster, the magic, the hideous surprise? For that matter, which one of these horsemen was Attila himself? I couldn't recognize him anywhere, but then, it was hard to see in the crowd, and most people were fighting in the trees and ravines.

Then, a sound like a tornado. Every head turned to see a soldier racing his horse up and down a sloped gully, up and down, over and over, in a way that would be foolish if it weren't for the noise he was bringing and the standard he held.

A draco: the bronze head of a dragon, with a long golden

silk tail rippling out behind it. One of the Empire's standards. This was not just a reminder of Fafnir, and the shaming of my brother. There was nothing magic about it, but it was a reminder that Attila was there with the Empire's silent – or not so silent – blessing.

'Lend me your bow,' I shouted to the boy beside me. He turned, confused, and I grabbed it from him.

I'd trained with bows as well as swords and knives. But a bow always took more strength than I remembered, and I was slow and shaky drawing it back. So I whispered to the wood, to whatever part of it still remembered life. I begged for its help. Whether the wood helped me, or the wind did, I didn't miss. I aimed the arrow squarely between the shoulders of the man bearing the draco standard, halfway up one of his ridiculous runs up the gully, and he fell off his horse, and the damned thing went quiet at last, leaving only the roar of hatred and the clash of weapons and the screams of death.

'There,' I said, and gave the boy back his bow.

CHAPTER TWENTY-THREE

Brynhild's Battle-cry

I had wondered whether I'd be able to see the Valkyries on the battlefield. I could, it turned out. It was worse than not seeing them.

I saw Kara, her curly hair floating as though in its own gale over her head, while she guided a sword arm, kicked a man out of harm's way or slashed an artery. They were fighting on both sides. Choosing man by man who would live and who would die. Choosing whether Gunnar or Attila would win? Surely, but I couldn't work out their plans in the chaos. I couldn't tell whether they had chosen the same king I had – or whether Odin had chosen for them. The only thing they seemed intent on doing was ensuring that any victory came at a cost.

Whatever their goals, these Valkyries I had trained acted swiftly and decisively. They showed no sign of questioning Odin's foresight or their own rightness. Why should they?

Sinir had taken an arrow in the withers. It would heal, but I whispered to her and sent her away. On foot, I sheathed my sword and fought with my axe. I didn't need a shield.

Kara turned to me, with something like soured friendship in her face. As though I were an old acquaintance, someone who had made a choice that took me away. And so I was, but how my heart hurt. How I wanted to go fight at her side.

Then Kara, still looking at me, drove her elbow to the side, and knocked the arm of one of my men so that he stumbled into a Hun's sword, thrust into his gut, spilling him onto the ground.

And then I saw that it was Drusus, one of my best students. Sigurd's bronze dog on his breast. His beautiful black curls all coated in blood. Why had he been the one deemed less needed on Midgard? I didn't know the Hun he had fought, of course. Perhaps that man had a family. Perhaps he was destined for greatness. Odin always had his reasons, or so I had long believed.

Kara crowed over him for a moment, marking him for Valhalla. Then she strode away, off into the forest after other quarry. In the morning, young Drusus would wake, and find himself holding a cup of mead, content, never changing. No more fear, no more regret.

I had always pitied the dead; how could we not? But now I mourned him. Now I knew grief as I had never known it before. And I was angry. For the first time in my life, I had not merely chosen a side; I had taken one.

So when I caught a glimpse of Hrist, striding over the bodies of the dead with Gunnar in her sight, I rushed at her. As Gunnar raised his sword and hacked off the head of a frightened young man, I put my arm around Hrist. I'm not sure whose life I saved, but probably Gunnar's. Which of them deserved to live, Gunnar or the boy he slaughtered? I didn't have to care. Justice was no longer my task. All I could see was fairness, which is so much cleaner. Hrist turned her face to me in shock, and I smiled, brilliantly.

A black-toothed man leered at me, swung his sword. It whacked my shoulder.

It would have been enough to make me bleed, if I could still bleed. Hrist's eyes widened, seeing me.

One of the reasons Odin taught us the runes was that we'd often need to heal ourselves and our comrades, after battles. The Spearshaker always left wounded Valkyries on Midgard to heal, because there is no healing in Valhalla. Those who couldn't heal in a day or two, he'd leave with old women in huts, or in the barns of monasteries. People who owed him favours, or who would one day. Sometimes he'd forget to go back, for years and years, and then he'd return and the Valkyrie would have aged twenty years while the rest of us had aged a few days. That was what happened to Eir, our most skilled healer; she never fought as well after that and died soon after she came home to us.

Sometimes he'd forget them altogether. We Valkyries would try to remember our wounded sisters, but they'd slip away from us, into dreams. Valhalla is a place for remembering the past, not the present.

Dead Valkyries are given a place in Valhalla, but like all the other dead, they are unchanging echoes of themselves. Some of them sit in the mead hall like old men, speaking only of their battles, unaware of what is around them. Eir was one of those. Svafa became part of the landscape, a shade between birches, a whisper by the creek. Sometimes she walked in her body, and she would talk to me about whatever I liked, in those moments. But she would have no memory of the conversation the next time. Being a living human in Valhalla is like keeping a wound open.

I had thought it a privilege. To walk those halls, to serve those heroes, to stall my own death. But Midgard came as a strange relief. Life was so changeable; people were so unknowable. It was frightening; it was exhilarating.

I pulled the black-toothed man towards me and opened his throat with the edge of my axe. By the front of his bloody battle-clothing, I dragged him while the life drained from his eyes and deposited him at Hrist's feet. I breathed the chill air of Midgard and no sword could cut me.

'This one's free,' I said. 'With my compliments.'

Hrist looked at me, and looked down at the man at my feet. She looked up again, then glanced away, as though she could hear a battle horn I couldn't.

'Mark him!' I shouted, disoriented, ill at ease.

Hrist, lovely Hrist, who learned everything from me, said, 'That one's not for us.'

I was stunned. Odin never refused a raven-feeder. We took ours and the Disir took theirs, but we didn't work together. Freyja was entitled to claim half, but her Disir had to come and claim them if she wanted them. She always had.

'He died in battle,' I objected. 'He isn't for Hel.'

But Hrist was looking past me, into the trees. I followed her gaze.

And then I felt my battle-smile stiffen, peel off my face like bark from a dying tree.

In the distance, in the shadows of the trees, I saw a Dis.

Even when I was still a Valkyrie, I didn't always see the Disir in battle. Oh, I knew they were there. They were always there, just as fear and shadow and rot are always there.

The Disir carry no weapons. They wear no armour. This one was tall, and old enough to wear her glowing skin on her bones like a coat that she knows is beautiful. Young enough that she stood as lithe as a tree. Her hair was silver like bark and flowed behind her, lifted by the wind of battle. On her lips, a word that I could not quite hear. Behind her, there was a glint of sunlight, and suddenly I remembered what it is like to lie on a field of yellow grass beneath the sun and feel the heat of the earth beneath me. What it is like to lie in an oak-crook and feel the warmth of the wood. Solid, silent, alive.

The Dis invited me home. She was speaking to someone. At first I thought it was me, then the man I'd killed and offered to Hrist.

But I was wrong on both guesses. She spoke to a still-living man with a hole in his belly. It was Lothar, young

Lothar, looking haggard instead of sleek for once. Standing close to the Dis. Two men were yelling at him and pulling him away from the fighting, but he was staring at the Dis.

The Dis reached for him and I could hear my comrades scream. *Odin should have this one. Odin should have them all. Let them come home warriors. Don't let them go with those spell-spinners to whatever illusions Freyja has for them. Such a waste.*

'You come late,' Hrist said, to the Dis. Triumphantly.

'That we are here at all is a surprise to Odin,' the Dis whispered back. I'd never heard one of them speak before. 'But Freyja is not so easy to fool. We will take the half that is ours, as we always have.'

Hrist reached for Lothar but the Dis had him by the hand. I ran forward. Which one was I going to help? Which one was I going to hinder? I can't tell you now, and I probably couldn't tell you then. It doesn't matter. I stumbled.

When I looked up again, both Valkyrie and Dis were gone, and my bloody axe sagged in my hand. At my feet, Lothar lay breathing raggedly. His face was coated with sweat. Hrist had not called him, the Dis had not taken him. He was dying but unclaimed. He was not leaving this world. But he was dying.

A cold half-understanding gripped me.

With shaking hands, I carved a healing-rune into a bit of birchbark, and placed it over Lothar's wound, and pressed his hand over it. 'Don't die,' I said. Not the most impressive magic words, but there must have been a power in them, because he lived. I chose him to live.

And then I ran into the woods, calling the names of the Valkyries. I had questions for them.

But I never did find another Valkyrie in that battle. They kept themselves hidden from me after that. I wandered through those woods too long and missed my chance to warn you that something was very wrong.

CHAPTER TWENTY-FOUR

Gudrun After the Battle

By the time Sigurd came riding through a gap in the hills with his group of men from the north, the Burgundians already had the upper hand. I watched him from my chariot. It was difficult to watch anyone else. There was no fighter like Sigurd in this valley; no fighter like him anywhere. He was clearly untrained. He'd never spent time in the imperial army. He'd never been on a raid. He fought with no technique at all that I could see, but he came away alive from every encounter.

I watched a spear double him over, then clatter to the ground as he staggered onward. I lost count of the number of swords that slashed him. He didn't bleed, though I shuddered to think what was happening to the bones beneath.

The magic that had protected him against my brother still protected him, and even though I knew about it, it was astonishing to watch.

It protected you, too, but I didn't realize it. You, my astonishing beloved, fought by the book. Every time a sword came at you, it seemed to miss you by the breadth of a hair. Like a dragonfly, you appeared exactly where you wanted to be. You seemed to see the battle differently to anyone else.

So, I used what magic I could to help the other fighters in our ranks. I called on the tree roots to trip our enemies, and I even asked the birds to spy behind our enemy's ranks, knowing that you or Sigurd would be able to understand their reports. I whispered to the wind and shifted it to favour our archers. Half of it didn't work, or didn't work as well as I wanted, but I played my part. I was trying to learn how I could be useful.

In the meantime, whenever wounded men crawled or were pulled out of the action, I'd go to their side and chatter to distract them and hold their hands. I had several salves with me, and healing potions: some ordinary recipes of my own, some my mother had made.

I came to Lothar, clutching a piece of bark to his side. He'd drifted into sleep. Not death. And I saw your rune. As I bathed his wound, he woke, and smiled weakly.

'You'll live,' I said. 'It's all right, Lothar. Rest now.'

'I won't rest until the Empire begs forgiveness for its double-dealing,' he said hoarsely. He said it in Latin, even then. Lothar, who had loved the Empire so much. Who wore Roman clothing and ate Roman food. But the Empire had spurned him, and mistreated his people, and from that moment forward every breath he took would be for a strong and independent Vormatia.

But he wouldn't take many more breaths if he didn't calm himself. I told him to rest, and helped him to a safer place.

As I walked the battlefield, I kept track of our victories and losses in my head, to tell my mother when I saw her. Who fell in saving someone else, who killed the most before he died, who fought hardest to the death. I muttered it to myself, over and over, adding new verses every minute. Some names I didn't know. And some of the stories I collected were about Huns or Romans, too; Auda would want to hear them all.

As the shadows thickened and the fireflies darted in the trees, clumps of Burgundian men gathered by my chariot uncertainly, looking for enemies and finding none. We'd won the day, against all hope. People called out Sigurd's name, and yours; it was clear who we had to thank for our victory. My brother just smiled grimly when he heard that.

Three people claimed to have seen Attila, to have recognized him by his armour, his horse, his sword, or his hat. No one claimed to have killed him. He was out there, somewhere, still. We knew that.

But it was hard not to revel in our victory. We thought we'd saved Vormatia, proven to the Empire that we could defend our territory even without its help, and that we made better allies than the Huns. I wiped the blood off my brother's forehead and for just one moment it seemed that everything might be all right.

Volker sat on a tree stump and pulled a small lute from somewhere and sang a slow, sad song, a song of triumph and loss. One I had never heard before. I'm not sure whether he came up with it on the spot. Maybe he'd written several different songs, in secret, days before the battle, so he'd be ready for anything.

But Hagen, being Hagen, was nervous. He pointed out that the downside of choosing this terrain for the battle was that now we found ourselves, exhausted, in a place without defences, where the dark hills all around could spawn bands of Huns at any moment, not to mention wolves. We weren't entirely sure how many men Attila had left, or if he had any more in reserve. Maybe he was only waiting for the moment we let down our guard.

I looked around for you but couldn't see you anywhere. They said you were alive, and I didn't doubt it. I'd watched you fight.

There was no time to bury the dead, not even to sort out which of them were friends and which were enemies, though some of them we recognized even in the half-light. I knew some of the faces we should be looking for. Gunnar gave orders for all the dead to be piled in one heap, at the foot of the valley. We stripped the weapons and the armour. Hagen was charged with giving permission for taking things from bodies, for the families. The rest went into the king's war chests, to be distributed.

We set a watch around the bodies, a ring of men with their swords in their hands. This wall undulated on the sides of the hills, snaking in and out of the trees. We stuck torches in the ground to let the men see a little, and to keep away wolves. The torchlight caressed the faces of the dead.

The rest of the living walked for an hour or two, up the hill to a rock outcrop where we had a view of the valley. Twinkling in between the gaps in the hills were distant fires: Attila's army. Not far away. Licking their wounds? Planning something for the morning? The fires meant, we told ourselves, that they wouldn't attempt a nighttime raid.

Hagen, Volker, and I found Sigurd in the king's tent, with my brother. They were all filthy. Gunnar pulled off his shoes, rubbed his feet. Hagen stood by the door.

And Sigurd paced, like the dog that followed him everywhere, even into battle. He still had his sword in his hand.

'They should heat baths for you,' I said.

Sigurd stopped pacing and looked at me. 'For me?'

'For all of you. Should I give the order?'

Gunnar shook his head. 'Food and wine are all we need. I don't want to be caught naked and wet if Attila decides to send a raid tonight.'

'Oh, I don't know,' Volker said, pouring the wine. 'I think we'd make a terrifying sight, bearing down on the Huns with our shrunken peckers swinging in the wind.'

Hagen rolled his eyes affectionately, and Sigurd laughed, too hard and too long. He went to Volker, put his arm around him and butted his forehead.

'Ludgast died today,' Gunnar said, throwing a cleaned pork rib onto his plate. 'I saw him fall.'

'He lived many years,' Hagen said. 'A longer life than his father or his grandfather.'

None of us spoke the thought we shared, that his death, and Lothar's wound, made it easier for Gunnar to rule. And Gunnar had led his people to victory in battle. Everything was resolved. But somehow none of us felt easy. Maybe it was Sigurd's presence, as he paced back and forth.

The wine Hagen poured was a pale watery red like blood. It smelled like sap and needles, or maybe everything did, there. But I drank a cup of it and then poured myself another. It had been a very long day. And the longest night of my life was about to begin.

There was a commotion outside the tent, and Hagen slipped out to see what it was. A moment later he returned, with a boy holding a dead crow.

Not just dead. Burned. It was a hooded crow, but even the pale parts of its head were charred as dark as its wing feathers. Its wings and head dangled strangely, as if every bone in its small body had been broken.

The boy was old enough to grow a scraggly beard, barely. He was covered in dried blood and he had a fresh cut on his cheek.

He said his name was Adebert, and that he'd been set in the ring of men guarding the dead down in the valley.

'And you brought us a bird,' my brother said, questioning, not quite mocking.

'They're all like this,' the boy blurted, and then looked from face to face, and added, 'my king. All the birds have dropped dead. The carrion birds, I mean. All the birds that are eating the dead.'

Charred feathers fell off in his hands.

'They can't all be poisoned, can they?' Sigurd asked. He said the word 'poison' like a man who was afraid of it, and I thought about how he drew the runes on his cup, of how he always gave his dog a little of his food first. Vigi was outside the tent even then; I'd seen him sitting on the dark ground and thought he was sleeping, but as I approached him he'd looked at me with steady brown eyes.

'It must be something else,' Gunnar said. 'Some sort of illness.'

'Why did you burn it?' Hagen asked.

'We didn't, my lord. We found it like this. All of them are like this.'

There was a silence.

'Adebert,' I said, 'you have done well to bring this to us.'

'Your comrades will want to know you're safe, and that you delivered this,' Gunnar said. 'So I want you to go back. But first, have a cup of wine and some meat.'

I looked at Hagen, and at Gunnar, checking first that they knew what I was about to say, that they'd agree. Hagen's agreement was, as always, given before it was asked. It was in his face, in every movement of his long limbs.

'And you'll take Hagen with you,' I said. 'He'll accompany you and help you keep watch below.'

Out of the corner of my eye I saw Volker stiffen, shift his body a little, but he said nothing. To love Hagen was to watch him go into danger and say nothing. The same is true of loving you, I have learned more than once.

'Is it witchcraft?' the boy whispered. He asked me, specifically.

But my brother was the one to answer him. 'Not ours,' Gunnar said briskly. 'These birds ate from Attila's army. Those filthy Huns must have had some enchantment on them. For all the good it did them. Don't go eating the Huns, and you'll be fine.' He smiled at Adebert, put his hand on his shoulder. He had become, somehow, a smooth and confident liar. When did that happen?

At that moment, my love, you came into the tent and told us that the dead were about to rise.

CHAPTER TWENTY-FIVE

Brynhild and the Dead

We had heard stories in the mead hall, about the dead whose minds stayed on Midgard, a world that could not easily accommodate the thoughts of the dead.

Some, like Svafa's lover, were ghosts; usually they'd been murdered, and lingered out of spite. The abandoned, recalcitrant or captive dead are never at peace, and they become unlike themselves in life. They become their own delusions, stiff and hungry as dry wood. These dead we call draugar. You know them now, as well as I do. I had never seen them before that night.

But I was afraid, when I saw that the Valkyries were leaving some of the dead behind. The Disir would never take more than half of the slain; they couldn't, or they'd risk breaking the treaty that kept peace among the gods. So if the Valkyries were taking less than their due, some would be left behind. There had to be a reason.

I sought the Valkyries everywhere, but either they hid from me, or I simply had bad luck. I roved far from the heart of the battle and ended up on the far side of the Huns, near their camp. It took me a long time to work my way back, quietly, in the darkness, and by then I was nearly too late.

'We already killed them once,' Gunnar said.

'And now they will be much harder to stop,' I said. 'We can keep them at bay, down by the mound. Away from the wounded who are here in the camp. But if we don't want them to haunt our every step and slaughter us before we can ever reach Vormatia again, we'll need to trap them.'

'You mean magic,' Sigurd said.

'I know runes to bind the dead in their graves. But these men have no graves yet.'

You said, 'Leave that to me.'

Hagen blew his horn: a long, thin cry like a wounded animal.

There were a dozen of us running down from the outcrop: me, Sigurd, Gunnar, Hagen, Volker, and several others – more every moment, drawn from their tents by Hagen's horn. We had our weapons drawn and Sigurd was in front.

The mound of dead was glowing blue.

All the men we had posted as guards had drawn backwards, facing inward now. But their enemies could be anywhere. Some of the corpses turned to black smoke and drifted down into the earth, then rose again behind the men with the torches, and slit their throats.

There was a sliver of moon, but the only real light came from the draugar. A weird and sickening light. They moved as quickly as thought, expressionless save for the kind of curiosity a bully has for a cricket or a mouse. They were ready to tear apart their own bodies and ours, to see what would happen. And they could; they had unspeakable power. I saw the young student named Drusus, the one with the curly hair and the bronze dog-pin. He held out his thin, nut-brown arms, as if examining the flesh. Then he was growing before our eyes, his skin cracking like thin ice. His chest expanded and his legs lengthened like a cricket's. When his body bloated to the size of a giant, behind hands as hard as two bones, he crushed the head of a strong warrior whose name I never knew. And then Drusus, still growing, split in three, his body breaking, his face bored. His head lay with one massive shoulder and arm on the ground, like a toppled and broken statue. But he was still moving. He reached out his hand towards a young boy who approached him with his sword shaking, and Drusus grabbed for him, and the boy drew back like a scared dog.

This was an enemy I couldn't beat, and I knew it.

There was little we could do against an enemy that could change to rock. We couldn't burn them with fire; they'd simply turn to smoke, and drift through the air. Sigurd and I might be proof against blades but not against being picked up and hurled off a cliff, or torn to pieces. It was night, and we were outnumbered, and the dead were seeking revenge.

I called out to stop Sigurd and tell him not to go ahead alone, but he didn't listen. He had the scent of blood in his nostrils.

We followed him, our blades high.

In the darkness, I did not recognize any of the dead, but Gunnar did; I could hear him, a little to the east of me, crying out in a particular way when he saw a face he knew. Some of them no longer had faces at all, pecked by crows that paid a heavy price. A few had no heads, but they walked forward anyway. The legless crawled, shifting into shapes something like Fafnir's.

Draugar draw their power from hatred. Most stay on Midgard out of revenge, torturing themselves so that they may torture others. I'd only ever heard of lone examples: a single draug staying behind to curse his murderer or simply make a plot of land miserable for all who came to it. A draug is fuelled by deep, bitter vengeance, stronger than the pull of the Valkyries or the Disir on the battlefield or Ran under the waves or Hel's minions by the sickbed, those little birds that call the dead downward. There are not many who have enough hatred to resist all of those calls, refuse all those invitations, and stay on Midgard for ages without relief, unable to feel anything but rancour.

But here we had an army of them; a heap. Everything was chaos. The only thing I could do was try to protect the living from the dead. There were a few hundred of us, those from Vormatia who could still fight, after that day's terrible battle.

We formed two lines with our backs to each other, though sometimes a draug still crept up in the middle and stuck a knife in someone's back. I felt the knife poke me, more than once. Sigurd and I stayed on opposite ends of the line, he with his sword and me with my axe. I suppose we both felt that we were our friends' guardians. We couldn't be killed as easily as they could.

But neither could the draugar. Even when we could get a sword through a gut or neck, that wouldn't stop them. Not all of them seemed able to change their shape, at least, and those we could stop from fighting, by hacking them to bits. I saw half of Drusus's face, his eye so much bigger than it should be, lying on the ground staring at me. At one point I looked over at Gunnar and saw his face wet with tears, his mouth set in a grimace.

One woman turned herself into a kind of dust storm, a maelstrom of long fingernails and dark hair, her mouth open and rust-red with dried blood, and the rest of her a column of dark flying dust that was nearly invisible in the night. I think she had been in our baggage train, or a wife to one of the fighters. I didn't recognize her anyway, and she seemed to have no weapon. But then, most of the draugar had lost their weapons or had no use for them.

We must have fought for hours. I couldn't be cut, and my enemies didn't care if they were. My forearms ached, and my thighs, and my back between my shoulder blades. I could feel the bruises under my invulnerable skin. Very soon, we would fall down from exhaustion, those of us who were left alive. Sigurd came to my side, late in the fighting, and put his left hand on my shoulder, saying nothing. Both of us kept our weapons drawn. That pressure of friendship in his hand helped keep me standing. His face was drawn and contorted with grief. In his hand, Regin's sword was slick and filthy, right down to the lindworm-ring he'd forged onto the hilt. Sigurd wore no armour, and his loose clothing was night-dark with blood.

Though I'd left my helmet in the tent in my haste, I was still wearing my beautiful bright mail shirt. Mended, with a line of brass rings down the front, to mark the place where Sigurd had cut it. I don't know why I did that. When he first sliced my mail, I was annoyed, angry even. Later it came to seem like a battle scar worth keeping. Perhaps it was only because I couldn't earn any more on my skin.

In any case, I couldn't see the line that night, because every ring of my shirt was thick with the blood of others, blood I couldn't repay. I began to wonder whether we were all dead, even those of us who thought we weren't.

In the hour before dawn, I heard your nightjar.

'Gudrun says go go go north, to the bent pine, drive them there before you! North to the pines! Go go go go! Their graves await them there!'

Sigurd caught my eye – there were fewer people between us than there had been. The light of the draugar was no dimmer, and dawn was not far off. I could see his expression and saw there was hope in it. Your name brought us both hope. I may have even smiled at him a little. We had fought our way to hope once before, together. Perhaps we could do it again.

The message could have been for either of us, but it didn't matter which. It could have been a trick, but that didn't matter either; we were as good as dead either way.

The draugar paid the nightjar no mind; such understanding is not among the gifts they gain from death.

So we drove them north. A bent pine cut through the purpling sky, and we drive the draugar to it, though it cost us. We had to push into their ranks instead of just defending, and that meant our own ranks loosened, and the draugar's claws and blades were among us. I could smell rank death.

And then I felt the ground shudder.

It opened up, one long fissure. In the morning light, it was as dark as the void into which I'd been exiled. Like a reverse image of the wedge of light I'd seen as I fell. But this was not opened by Odin, or by any god. It was your magic, to trap the draugar. A messy, uneven pit, right in the midst of our battle.

Several of our own fell into it, and we pulled them out as best we could, though some nights as I try to sleep, I wonder whether we got them all.

'Bury them!' I heard you yell.

I looked for you and there you were, exhausted and pale, bent over the ground, your palms to the earth. A stream of pale greyish brown raced past you and I lunged with my axe but your expression stopped me, and I saw what it was: dozens of badgers, and a fox or two, all leaving the hole they'd dug for you.

'Bury them!' I screamed, understanding. I turned back to our men. 'Bury them!'

We had nothing but swords, axes, hands, helmets, but we threw the earth over the top, and pushed them back down into their trench, their grasping hands, their elbows. When they grew big, we'd fight them until they tired, stumbled, returned to their human form.

As the last handful of earth hid them, I took my knife and scratched the binding-rune on three rocks, and placed one at either end of the trench, and one in the middle.

We stood there, panting, bleeding, weeping, in ordinary dawn light. None of us said a word for a long time. We sank to our knees or lay down on the ground, too exhausted to be afraid.

There, Gudrun. There is the story of the most harrowing night I ever spent on any world. In those hours when we were apart, I felt as though I'd been dismantled. There was nothing of me left, just the pain and exhaustion, holding me together like sinew inside my gore-stiff mail.

But when I collapsed on that cold ground and crawled to you, I found you very still. The look on your face was so calm, so determined.

It was only when you reached your hand out to it, and your finger came away with blood that was wetter and lighter than the rest, new blood, my blood, that I realized my lip had been cut open. My mouth had not been touched with that hideous blood. A small part of me could bleed after all. That was one thing I shared with Sigurd.

CHAPTER TWENTY-SIX

Gudrun's Offer

There were tears mixed with your blood, Brynhild. That was why it ran so light, so pale. I might have thought you were something out of a dream if it hadn't been for your bleeding lip. It reminded me that there was still work to be done, and I had a few pots of salves in my little bag of tricks.

I dabbed your mouth with rosehip honey, and my heart quickened as I felt your lips beneath my fingertip, then watched your tongue tasting what I left on your skin.

'No cuts anywhere on the rest of you?' I asked, amazed.

Your expression darkened and you told me that if we were being honest with each other, you couldn't pretend it was chance that had kept you intact all through that battle. The same magic that protected Sigurd protected you. Or, as you said with a small smile that made your lip start bleeding again, most of you.

For once in my life, I didn't ask any questions, because I had too many. Maybe because I was afraid to learn more about your history with Sigurd. My husband, who'd fought like a berserker through a day and a night, and who was now missing.

What can I tell you about those hours you spent in battle?

I was so slow, finding my allies. Seeking the burrowing animals and asking them to talk to me, when they were all frightened out of their wits by the monsters who'd sprung up in their hills. Monsters that humans had conjured.

I wish I could have spoken to the badgers the way you speak to birds. It seems easier than whatever wordless negotiation I'd learned to do. But I made my case, eventually, and they heard and did what they could, because they saw it was their only chance too. I was left, that terrible dawn, with an uneasy feeling, as if the hills were looking into me. I'd opened myself up to things with fur and claws. I was in their debt and they weren't about to let me forget it.

There were two boys who'd been wounded in the first battle, and so couldn't fight the draugar, and couldn't keep up with the group of walking wounded I'd sent home to Vormatia. I told them to trap mice and pluck earthworms and beetles out of the ground, and to lay the food out in the lees of rocks. Payment for our friends.

After the night I had communing with wild things, I was relieved to find that I was still me – once I found you. That should have told me that you were not merely fascinating to me. You were, by then, everything to me. I suspect I already knew that. I don't think I'd put it into words. I only knew that you were alive, and it was morning.

Together, we walked through that terrible corpse-strewn place, tending the wounded. You bound a man's broken arm, fixing a stick onto it with willow bark. You showed me the rune for healing. The sun sailed into the middle of the sky, banishing bad dreams.

Hagen found us and told us that Sigurd hadn't been seen since just before the badgers came. A dozen men who came with him from the north were unaccounted for among the bodies of those we'd lost during the night. We were fairly sure they hadn't fallen into the draug-grave, but couldn't think where they might be, and had no one to spare to send after him.

I saw your face as you listened to Hagen tell us this, and I didn't know how to interpret the worry on it. I wasn't sure, then, what Sigurd meant to you. I wasn't sure what he meant to me, either.

But I didn't have much time to sort it all out. Everything moved so quickly: the morning brought Attila, at last. Zerco, the small African man I'd seen on what was supposed to be my wedding day, rode in to say the king of the Huns was willing to accept our surrender.

I remembered Zerco's hand on his hilt, the pain on his face, in the moments after Attila killed Bleda. His expression betrayed no emotion now, as he waited for us to return an answer. But he knew, and we knew, that there was no honour in Attila. Whatever agreements Attila made us now, in return for our surrender, could not be trusted.

Still, what choice did we have? We had defeated the draugar, but the draugar attack had badly weakened us, shifting the balance between our forces and Attila's. We couldn't meet Attila on the battlefield again right away. All our available fighters were there on that hilltop, and most of them were wounded. Meanwhile, Attila would have more allies streaming to him like flies to a dung pile. He had turned many nations into tributaries on his side of the Rhine. It was clear that he had secured the backing of the treacherous Empire in his war against the Burgundians. Besides, he might have more surprises in store. After all, he had sent a lindworm against us, and somehow he had raised the dead.

Our victory felt like defeat. We needed to get home safely to Vormatia, to heal and rebuild. Attila had no intention of letting that happen.

I left you, Hagen, and Volker to give Zerco a meal while he waited, and I went to see my brother.

Being in a room with Gunnar when he was sitting very still was like being in a room with a different sort of man when he's pacing. Gunnar was never a pacer. He would sit, and

223

watch, and take everything in, gather information, gather strength. Then he would act, quickly.

He was sitting in the middle of his tent, staring at the entrance, when I came in.

That day there was no joking about fish sauce, no affectionate bluster. I told my brother he had fought well and that our father would be proud.

Gunnar just looked at me. 'Our father left me with a single task: to hold Vormatia for the Burgundians. All the western shore of the Rhine from Mainz to Speyer. The Empire recognized our right to that land. I won't let Attila or anyone else take it from us.'

I nodded, but countered, 'Attila wants to show the world that we're under his thumb. He wants a permanent marker on the board. If we don't give him our land we will have to give him something else.' I paused, and joked darkly, 'And now that I'm married, I suppose we can't offer him me.'

Neither of us said what we were both thinking, that my husband was missing the morning after a battle, and that he might very well be dead, or gone away forever in the grip of some grief or madness.

'Tribute, then,' Gunnar said bleakly.

Having slaughtered so many of our fighting men with his treachery, now Atilla would weaken our ability to feed and protect their families. Our coffers were already bare from all the preparations we'd made for war, and from helping the farmers whose crops had withered under Fafnir's breath. But we could make a promise of annual payment to Attila, which would mean we'd have to raid territories elsewhere, which would make us even less welcome inside the Empire.

There was no other choice. Gunnar and I worked it all out.

And then you and Hagen came into the king's tent and told us *you'd* worked it all out.

You must have left Volker to entertain Zerco; I wonder what the two of them talked about. It didn't occur to me to wonder, then. I was just amazed by the sight of you, your braid unruly and your eyes dark from battling through the night.

'After Sigurd and I killed Fafnir, we each took roughly half the gold that was piled on the lindworm's mountain,' you said calmly. 'I have not counted it all, but I suspect it is more than you could gather in all of Vormatia. So you have enough to buy peace from Attila.'

Gunnar's brows knitted in confusion. 'But the terms of our marriage contract—'

You said, 'I have no use for that hoard. If I can buy peace for a city, I will consider it a fair exchange.'

'A city', you called it. Not 'home'. I didn't want to think about what that meant. You'd cast your lot in with us. Given your wealth to Vormatia. For once in my life, I was tongue-tied. When Gunnar accepted gratefully, I didn't argue against it.

'Will you come to the negotiations, to describe the hoard?' Gunnar asked.

You shook your head. 'I've told Hagen everything I can about it. He's written it all down. I'm going to look for Sigurd.'

And you turned and left the tent before we could offer you any help or ask you any questions.

With Sigurd missing, and you in search of him, that left Gunnar, Hagen, Volker and me to take care of the politics.

We met our enemy on open ground. None of us was on horseback this time, and there on the ground, one could see that Attila was not very tall. Still, everything about him said strength: his broad shoulders, his heavy black gauntlets, the Roman brooch holding a fur-trimmed capelet over shining mail.

I didn't recognize most of the men who came with Attila, except for Zerco. I was most curious about the Roman general at Attila's side; Gunnar whispered in my ear that this was

Aetius, the man the new emperor trusted the most. He was a man of middle age, with kindly eyes and an artistic set to his mouth. And no mail, just a dark grey tunic under his cloak. He seemed more politician than soldier, but looks can be deceiving.

The Empire was showing its hand, finally. All of this – Vormatia on its knees, Attila triumphant – was what the Empire wanted. I don't remember how long we talked there on that gloomy morning, all of us standing on the damp earth. I thought about asking the badgers to open up the ground right underneath them, and wondered who would come for us then. Was there ever going to be an end?

Attila still wore the neat square of black beard and moustache, but this time it didn't frame a smile, not even a smile of triumph. He looked at us as though our very lives were a nuisance. Attila claimed he had vast armies, which he hadn't even brought to the battle, which was probably true. He said he could still crush Vormatia, now that we were weakened, that most of our best fighting men were dead or grievously wounded. And that was definitely true.

Gunnar countered that we'd shown we could face any monster, any army. Twice, Attila had thought he had us, and twice he'd been proven wrong. He might take the city, on a third attempt, or a fourth or a fifth, but what would it cost him?

'I will do what I must to get my due,' Attila said, in a voice of terrible faith. 'I am the scourge of God.'

Flagellum dei. That makes you shiver, I know. If you or Sigurd had heard him say that, if you had seen then that he was being goaded by the same malice that once goaded Fafnir, what would you have thought? But neither of you were there, and the phrase meant nothing to me then. Just more of Attila's arrogance. Your story and mine diverged in all the wrong moments, our paths knotting like snakes.

Aetius the Roman cleared his throat and said some nonsense about the Empire being concerned about these constant disputes on the border, as if he hadn't let it happen – encouraged it to happen, most likely. It was only fair, he said, that the Burgundians give Attila tribute. With a little smile, he glanced at Attila – there was something in that look that reminded me of the way Attila had looked at Fafnir. Aetius was feeding Attila like a man feeds his meanest dog. And we were the meat.

The Empire had some use for the Huns, but the Empire didn't want to pay the Huns with tax money, so it offered up the Burgundians as a source of tribute. It kept Attila from turning on the Empire itself. And it kept our people weak; Ludgast's raids at the edges of our territory must have made the Empire nervous. So, Aetius, knowing the new boy-emperor in Ravenna would not stop him, happily tore up the promises we'd been given, promises that were no longer expedient.

It was sickening.

'The question is how you will pay,' said Aetius, officious, offensively calm. 'We know that warmongering has cost you dear. You will make an accounting of all your people's estates, and we will tell you what the reckoning is, and give you sufficient time to make it all ready when Attila sends to collect it.'

We could well imagine what that collection would look like, Attila's men looking for any excuse for violence.

My brother, red blood still seeping through the bandage on his arm, said that we had gold enough to pay out of the royal family's wealth, right away.

How satisfying it was to see surprise on Aetius's face, and anger on Attila's.

'I see the tales of your people's hardship were invented, or else that hardship came from the greed of the rulers,' Aetius said.

Gunnar responded that the gold had only recently come to us. With a withering look at Attila, he said it had been Fafnir's hoard. When the killer of Fafnir had joined our family, the gold came too. All of that was true, although we let them misinterpret it, and assume we were talking about Sigurd.

I remember thinking, just then, about you, and whether you'd succeeded in finding Sigurd yet, and what condition you'd found him in. I wondered whether I still had a husband.

That's when we heard the screams.

CHAPTER TWENTY-SEVEN

Brynhild's Choice

As I searched for Sigurd, I cursed my own wilful ignorance, my inattention. Just as I had missed the signs of the draugar until it was too late, I'd failed to stop Sigurd from becoming what he became. No one in the world understood Sigurd as I did, and I knew he was going wrong.

I walked down a gentle slope where pines stood like pillars, their golden trunks only spreading into green far, far above. Every so often, I called his name. I even called Vigi's name. Then, off to the right, I saw one crooked oak tree in the midst of those pines, and a figure I recognized, leaning against the trunk.

He saw me, and lifted his hat, and his one eye winked at me. Then he slipped behind a pine tree and did not emerge on the other side of it.

I stopped short and screamed all of Odin's names. But he wasn't there for me – he'd let me see him only because he wanted me to witness his triumph. The Battler needed all his victories to be laid at his feet. And Sigurd he saw as a victory.

Just as Loki had visited me, Odin had visited Sigurd. Where and when, how often – we may never know. I don't know what words he poured into his ear, but knowing Sigurd, they were words about how he was a hero whose songs would be sung for centuries. Odin could make such promises. I could imagine them: *A true hero doesn't bandy words with politicians or conclude a great victory over the draugar by offering tribute to the one who raised them. Gunnar can't be the one to avenge his people, not openly. He relies on his brother-in-law, his brother in blood. Sigurd, the hero.*

I think that is likely what he said. I think he probably sounded a great deal like Regin had sounded when he goaded Sigurd into killing.

Sigurd was lost to us from that moment. But he was not a creature like Fafnir or the draugar. He was still a man and had been my comrade. There was a reason, a true and honest reason, that Sigurd had earned the love of Ludgast's men – the missing dozen. I thought I could convince Sigurd to stop, to think.

Perhaps I could have, if I'd been a little faster working everything out.

By the time I found him, he was holding a bloody sword in each hand and ignoring the arrows and spears that rained into his body. He and his men had slaughtered a score of Huns who had been licking their battle wounds in their camp in the woods. They hadn't even had time to pick up their weapons. Sigurd had massacred them, and thus rekindled the war between Gunnar and Attila and snuffed out any hope of peace. He was beyond all reason, slashing at anyone nearby. I saw him wound one of his own men and carry on, unheeding.

The screams and shouts of war brought everyone down from the higher places: the Huns, the Romans, the Burgundians. I didn't see Gunnar at first, but I heard Burgundians shouting his name.

And suddenly it was around me: Romans shouting commands, and the beating of hooves, and arrows flying over my head. I ran through the woods, looking for cover or a fight, or both.

For the third time in two days, battle was joined in the Odenwald.

Hagen's horn called all the Burgundians who could still hold a sword. We heard the Huns' horns too. Surrounded by enemies, I couldn't search for Sigurd or even distinguish the Burgundians from the Huns, there in the forest where no battle lines were easy to spot. But they all recognized me. I suppose there were not many axe-wielding women with scars on their cheeks and runes on their hands, on either side.

I didn't see Gunnar fall. There was a cheer of triumph from the Huns, and then the screams of Gunnar's men. It distracted the two men who were attacking me at that moment, so I was able to brain one with my axe-head, wind the other in the gut with my axe-haft, and run towards the sound.

Your brother – my husband – lay crumpled, blood seeping out onto the pine needles. I rushed to him, seeing you in my mind, knowing how much it would hurt you to lose him forever. If I'd ever had a brother, I'd forgotten him, but I'd had comrades, and I bore their runes on my hands. If I could have saved your brother, I would have, for your sake and his.

But he was already gone. Claimed for some god or other. And although he was my husband only in name, I mourned him then and I mourn him now. His face in the peace of death looked like a stranger's: the man he was before Fafnir got into his mind. Gunnar tried to be a good king, in a difficult time. I hope he has peace in whichever world he has found.

The fighting around his body had paused, as everyone waited, uncertain what this meant. The death of one of the warring kings had to change something. But then downslope from us, we heard Sigurd's men, clambering up towards us, and they slashed our enemies, crying out 'Avenge Gunnar!' and 'To Sigurd! To Sigurd now!'

And Sigurd led them on, his teeth clenched, his blond hair wild, no armour anywhere on him, his sword drowned in gore.

Hagen drew me aside, to a place where we could be heard, deeper in the forest.

I knew what he was about to ask me. He was asking it to spare you having to make the decision, and I answered it for the same reason. Don't tell me now whether we did right or not. It doesn't matter. Whatever you said, I would do the same thing again if I had to. There was only one choice that remained to us, and it was a horrible one.

Hagen's face was contorted with grief for Gunnar and fear for his people. He pointed to my lips, still sticky from the honey you'd placed there, or perhaps it was sticky from blood; the wound had opened up again.

'You and Sigurd both bathed in the lindworm's blood. Am I right?'

I nodded. Hagen did not miss much.

'But it looks as though you missed a spot,' he said. He paused, then said, 'Did *he*?'

A cold hand clenched my guts. I thought about Fafnir's heart; what had Sigurd done with it? Eaten it all, in the hope of more wisdom? Burned it, muttering curses about Regin? Given it to Odin? Buried it somewhere? I wished I'd thought of it sooner; we could have given a taste to every one of the Burgundians, and the world would have known a whole people who could understand the birds. But then the birds of Midgard would have had no peace.

Sigurd came riding into those forested hills bearing a sword too heavy for any hand, his eyes bright and his hair rumpled. He wanted only to be what he thought he should be – what he'd been told he had every right and duty to be, first by Regin and then by Odin. Never in all of that had anyone wanted him to be a humble blacksmith who honoured his friends and married a wife who loved him. He would have been good at that, and he might have been content. He might have listened to the fireside stories without needing to be the one named in them.

But didn't he have his chances? He had a chance to be honest with me, and he'd chosen a coward's path instead. He had his own mind and a heart of his own. It was his choice not to trust either of them.

I was used to choosing who should live and who should die, and I knew that this choice was one of the simplest I'd ever faced. If Sigurd lived, the war would not stop until every Burgundian man was slaughtered, with the city of Vormatia in flames, with all its Romans and Franks and Syrians and Egyptians all massacred or fled. The Huns had a much larger army and they had an empire at their back. Sigurd was fighting a losing battle, as heroes love to do, at any cost.

It was simple, but it wasn't easy. I loved Sigurd the way one can only love a brother in arms, someone whose nightmares you've shared. I understood him. And I was about to kill him.

'On his back, just under the left shoulder blade,' I whispered to Hagen. Because of course I remembered the imprint of my own hand on Sigurd's back. I looked down at my palm, which was bloody again.

When I looked up, Hagen was gone.

CHAPTER TWENTY-EIGHT

Gudrun and Brynhild

I felt no affinity for rivers, the way my mother did. Rivers are deep and dark. In those days, I was sunlight on rocks and shining gold. I was shallow creek beds, still. I swear I heard the creek keening Sigurd's death before his body floated to us, a spear through his back.

We thought it was a trick.

But then I saw you approach from one side, and Hagen approach from the other, and your faces told me what had happened. Then someone said, 'the king is dead', and I would have crumpled to the ground if everyone hadn't been watching me. I felt that somehow I had failed my brother, that he had needed something from me, these last weeks, and I hadn't known what it was or how to give it. He had died fighting for his people. He'd proven his courage.

A few of our men were still fighting, tears wet on their cheeks, determined to avenge Gunnar or Sigurd or both. But they stood down when Hagen asked them to, and when he shouted at our enemy to lay down their arms and call their king, they did.

We began that day negotiating with Attila and Aetius, and we ended it the same way. I wasn't surprised that this time they made us go to them. I didn't like to leave Gunnar's body. It felt like an abandonment.

I was glad you were with me, standing with us as my brother's widow. Glad for Hagen's presence, too. Our people hadn't yet had a chance to choose their ruler, but with Lothar wounded, and Gunnar and Ludgast dead (and Sigurd also, a small voice said in my mind), I was the most likely; for Hagen didn't want it. Maybe they'd kill all of us with knives from their sleeves, I thought, and my mother would have to rule as queen, and have no more time to weave at her loom or brew potions in her workshop or walk the banks of the Rhine.

So that was the state of my mind when we left Volker in charge of our army and walked to Attila's camp. We had very little left but promises and grievances, but I intended to make the most of both.

But Aetius crowed over us with that look of tragic regret painted on his face. We'd broken a truce during negotiations, and proven we had no honour. So we must compensate Attila with double the gold we had promised that morning. Which, of course, we had, now that Sigurd's hoard came to me as his widow. How did Aetius know we could pay double what we'd promised? Did he know that both of you had split Fafnir's hoard, or was he only trying to make us pay more than we could?

'I will accept this payment for the wrongs done to me,' Attila said in his flowing Latin, with the beginning of a triumphant smile. 'But it's no guarantee of peace. The Burgundians have taken every chance they could to stab my people in the back. First, their father killed our king. Then they turned my own brother, Bleda, against me. Turned him into a spy. Forced me to execute him as they watched, to save my own life.'

I could feel Hagen's expression, beside me.

Attila wasn't finished. 'As long as they squat on my people's borders, they're a danger to me. Once they have paid me my compensation, I demand that they leave the Rhine, and all the lands they occupy.'

I kept myself very still as I said, 'The Empire promised my father that the people of Vormatia and the surrounding lands would be undisturbed, and under the rule of the Burgundians, who may choose their own king or queen.'

'Well,' Aetius said, slowly and snidely, 'the trouble is that you've broken faith with the Empire too.'

That was when my composure cracked. How did he dare to say that, when the Empire had turned its back on us and sponsored an enemy attack on us? I remember Hagen's hand on my arm, restraining me from hurling insults at him.

'Your father was given residency in Vormatia,' Aetius carried on, 'inside the Empire, on condition that he keep law and order among the people. I'm sure he was a good man to know. I've heard Galla Placidia sing his praises. But he couldn't keep control of his own people. So many stories of raiding parties on your borders, year after year.'

I thought of Ludgast, lying dead, blissfully unaware of the trouble he was still causing me.

'And sons and daughters,' Aetius continued, 'well, they don't stray far from their fathers, do they? There's no respect for the law among the Burgundians. Your treachery here today only confirms it. You're lawless barbarians who can't be entrusted with a territory inside the Empire.'

'You lie,' I said.

But he still wasn't finished. He twisted the knife: he said that Sigurd of Xanten had been found with a Burgundian spear in his back. He accused us of murdering our own, over a quarrel. He suggested ambition, or lovers' jealousy.

I started to argue. Why would we murder our greatest hero? Besides, there was nothing about our spears that looked any different, and anyway, anyone from the other side could have picked up a stray spear from the battlefield. But then I sensed Hagen, beside me, and I glanced at your face, your face that kept its promise to always be honest with me. There was no winning this argument. It didn't matter that the accusation was true; Aetius would have used it against us even if it weren't.

Aetius pronounced that my people had forfeited all right to remain in Vormatia. We were to be evicted. In his kindness, Aetius said, the emperor was willing to find us a new homeland within the Empire, but further to the west, where we wouldn't be so much trouble to the neighbours. South and west, in the mountains. But that was contingent on one thing: we must find and punish the murderer of Sigurd, to prove we were not barbarians.

Maybe he knew something of the truth; I didn't know then that gods were roaming our world for purposes of their own. Maybe he just wanted to see us turn on ourselves. He had a smile like an eagle's beak.

I could barely speak in my anger. I wouldn't give up Hagen and I certainly wouldn't have given up you. If these were their terms, I thought, we would have to fight on.

Hagen, beside me, said, 'And if we agree, and move our people away from the Rhine, to these new lands deeper in the Empire – it will take time to gather the livestock, heal the wounded, make provisions.'

'You may take three days,' Aetius said.

'Bring me my gold, and go,' Attila said, grinning.

I held up a hand. 'We have agreed to nothing. We'll take the night to consider your terms, and give you an answer in the morning.'

Hagen, of course, offered himself up right away. Predictable to the last. He followed me into my tent – the tent I had shared with you, a night and a lifetime before – arguing with me so hard he barely paused for breath. He moved a sheathed knife back and forth from hand to hand.

'Someone must have seen me,' he said. 'They wouldn't play this gambit without some evidence. Maybe they're holding it back, seeing what we'll do. It was my choice to kill Sigurd, and I will pay the consequences.'

I shook my head, and the movement made me want to vomit. Sigurd was lying dead. Gunnar was lying dead. And Hagen and I were in charge of the peace, but the stink of blood was everywhere, and I didn't think I'd ever smell anything else. 'You did what you had to do to save your people and stop the bloodshed. I won't hear of it.'

Volker thrust aside the tent flap and strode in, his face full of fury. 'What's this I'm hearing? Hagen, people are saying the terms they've offered us are an insult. Tell me.'

Hagen spread his hands. 'My love, we don't have a lot of choices.'

Volker, somehow, brought me back to myself. His face was just as it had always been: open and angry and loving and full of sunlight. He'd been through lindworm poison and battle, and he'd just lost his king, his friend. But he was still Volker. There was work to do.

I put my hands on both of their shoulders. 'I don't think Attila cares about punishing us for Sigurd. That's Aetius; he wants to assert the Empire's control. If we give Attila what he wants, then I don't think the Empire will fight us, alone. They have civil wars enough without making new ones.'

And then you were at the door, saying, 'But if we give Attila what he wants, that means . . .'

I didn't look at you. I said, 'I think there's something he'd accept in exchange.'

Volker shook his head. 'No. I refuse.'

'It isn't your choice!' I yelled. 'We have to drive a wedge between Aetius and Attila. We have to make a separate peace with one of them; God knows we can't afford to placate them both. And I refuse to let him drive my people away from the Rhine.'

Then Volker stood and said, in his calm, clear voice, 'Gudrun, I sit and sing with the people every night, here in the camp and back in the city. I know what people are saying and thinking. There are many who would jump at the chance to leave, to go to a new homeland far from Attila.'

I could hardly believe my ears. To leave Vormatia? After all my father had done to establish us there? After a generation of peace and prosperity? I was queen of Vormatia first, and queen of the Burgundians second. But I couldn't find the breath to argue. I knew Volker had to be right. He did spend more time with people, just talking and laughing. My brother and Hagen and I had been so concerned with defence and battle, with the challenge, with you – we hadn't had much time for anything else, lately.

Finally, I said, 'Anyone who wants to leave, can leave. And that includes the two of you: lead them to safety. But I'm going to make sure that Vormatia is still a home for those who wish to stay, Burgundian or otherwise.' When you all started to argue, I yelled. I know, I don't yell often, but when I do, I shatter skulls. And I did that day. 'Go, all of you! Leave me alone to think. Hagen and Brynhild, see to the wounded. Volker, all our fighters will be gossiping and worrying, and you love talking to them, so go and do it. Reassure everyone. I need time to think.'

My brother was dead, my mother was two days' ride away. I was alone. I needed to make this decision myself.

Volker and Hagen listened, and left the tent. But you didn't.

'I said go,' I growled.

You walked past me and around me, like a cat stalking a mouse, your arms crossed, your axe and sword hanging from your waist. Out came the sword, out came the axe, and you put them against the tent wall. Then you lay on your mattress, arms behind your head, and looked at me.

'It's my tent too,' you said.

I gave up. 'And what would you suggest we do?'

'Give Attila the gold. Both mine and Sigurd's. I don't want mine and Sigurd can't use his. But don't leave your city. He doesn't want it anyway, not really. What does he want with running a city? He's happy for a chance to regroup. Give him his gold and send him away.'

'He won't be satisfied. He has his pride.'

'It's a negotiation, so make him a lower offer, that's all. And he can't fight you again soon anyway, not without Aetius's support, which he won't have. You can see that Aetius just wants to make a show of imperial control over Vormatia, with this business about punishing Sigurd's killer. To show that the Empire's word is still law. He doesn't really want Attila ruling bits of the Empire either.'

'But he can't back away from his demand.'

You turned your gaze away from me. 'Let me worry about that. I'll sort out Aetius. Don't worry. I won't kill him.'

'Brynhild. I won't give Hagen up.'

'Hagen?' You looked back at me. 'Hagen is not to blame for Sigurd's death.'

'I agree.'

'Then we are in agreement.'

'Don't treat me like a child. And don't try to hide things from me. You aren't any good at it.'

'No,' you said, shaking your head. 'Not like you. You're good at so many things. I learn about new ones all the time.'

I tried to be angry at you, how pigheaded you were! But I was exhausted. All my anger had drained out of me. I had only sadness left, sadness for our past and our futures. I crossed the tent, I sat on the edge of your mattress, by your knees. The fierce look left your face and I saw all your worries there.

'Brynhild, I'm not good at the things I wish I were good at. And I'm so afraid.'

'Things will be better in the morning.'

'How do you know? Did a bird tell you?' I joked.

'Trust me, that's all.'

'I do trust you,' I said, and I realized I was wringing my hands like an old sorceress, I was so heartsick and worried. I very deliberately stopped, loosened my hands, and put one of them on your leg. 'I trust you and I need you to look after my people. No matter what happens to me, in the future.'

'I can't promise that,' you said, softly.

How quiet our two voices were, once we had both made our plans. A private conversation. It felt as if I was always having private conversations with you in my mind, but they were so rare in reality.

I told you I had no right to ask you for any promises.

'And I don't need to make you any,' you said, stubbornly. 'You will take care of Vormatia as you always have. I'll make Aetius back down.'

'Do you have power over Roman generals, then?' I asked, amused despite myself at your certainty. I didn't guess what you planned, or I didn't want to.

'We'll see what tomorrow brings,' you said. You trickster.

There were things I couldn't fool myself about, even if I didn't have the courage to put them into words. I knew you and I were likely to be parted. You must have been thinking the same, because you lifted your head, and put both hands on my shoulders, and finally, finally, you gently pulled me down.

'I don't want to hurt your lip,' I said, and laughed once, nervously.

'Then kiss me everywhere else.'

But then you kissed me anyway, mouth to mouth, and I tasted your blood. We scrambled at each other's clothing, our rough wool and leather, all filthy and stinking from battle.

Down, down, you pulled me, tracing a path open-mouthed, neck, armpit, breast, a tongue-pattern more whorled and tangled than the border of a manuscript. You pulled me like a scabbard pulls a sword.

I remember as we lay with our breath shuddering in unison, calming, how you said 'yes', just like that, though I hadn't asked a question. I thought you were talking in your sleep.

CHAPTER TWENTY-NINE

Brynhild's Bargain

When I woke, the morning birds were singing songs of battle, though it was still dark. You were no longer next to me, Gudrun, no longer in the tent. For a few moments, I allowed myself to lie there, staring at nothing, listening to the birds, feeling for the first time in centuries that I was home. There in a tent on the field of battle, I was home at last. And I knew either that home must burn, or I would. The choice seemed simple. After all, I'd had more than my fair share of years.

But I didn't let myself lie there too long. I reckoned you had gone to find Hagen and Volker. I seized my chance to slip unseen out of the camp in the gloaming. I left all my weapons behind.

Aetius seemed to know who I was, and that made me nervous. He was overjoyed to hear me declare myself Sigurd's murderer, and it didn't surprise him. That made me nervous too.

'You want me gone,' I said. 'Away from Vormatia, at least, and preferably dead.'

'We've heard many reports of your skills. You are a dangerous unknown, and I don't like dangerous unknowns, no matter which side they fight on. When they fight against me, I like them even less.'

That was enough to make me tell myself there was nothing more to it, that none of this had anything to do with gods and their plans, or my own exile. Aetius was a strategist, and I was in his way.

'And once I am gone, the Burgundians will be down one Valkyrie. They can go into your new homeland if they wish, but anyone who stays behind should be left alone, to live in their city as they have for the last generation, to choose their own king or queen.'

'And under the protection of their local witch,' he said with a condescending smile. 'I have heard it said that Auda never leaves the Rhine.'

'And Gudrun?'

'I don't worry about Gudrun.'

I wondered at that, and felt offended on your behalf, but didn't want to get drawn into some politician's word-trap. He offered me a glass of Roman wine, and I took it. I didn't fear poison, the way Sigurd had. What did I have to lose?

'And if Attila attacks Vormatia again?'

He shrugged. 'That is between Gudrun and Attila, but the Empire will have no more quarrel with Vormatia so long as it remains peaceful and lawful. So long as the Burgundians pay compensation for their treachery and obey the law by punishing the murderer in their midst, I am satisfied.'

'Then we have an arrangement,' I said.

You want to know whether I thought I would survive. Sigurd had ridden through fire, with the same blood-magic that protected my skin. But to ride through fire was not the same as to burn on a pyre for hours. My skin might survive, while I cooked and suffocated within it. I knew that.

I expected to die. I'm sorry, my love.

The only thing I knew was justice, in choosing the slain. It had been necessary for Sigurd to die but it was just for me to follow him. He was my brother in arms, and I had betrayed him and caused his murder. But I would not betray the home I had come to at last through you. In my final act as Gunnar's widow and as queen of Vormatia, I would make sure that the people who had taken me in had a safe place to live, and still had Hagen to keep them safe. You would lead them, I assumed, and you would need Hagen.

These were my thoughts, when Aetius ordered that two pyres be constructed, one for Sigurd and one for his murderer. They laid Sigurd on his back, so that his body appeared unwounded and he looked as though he were sleeping. Like a statue in gold and ivory.

They crossed his arms on his chest and laid his ringsword upon it. His pale dog Vigi sat and stared at the pyre. He didn't whimper or sniff; he just sat on guard.

The second pyre was empty.

I was there waiting when you came at the arranged time, and Aetius and Attila approached with their retinues. You were dressed in a clean linen stola, as blue as the Rhine and your hair was braided around your head and wrapped all around in your beautiful blue and green beads. I was wearing my torn mail shirt, though it was no good to me. I was a warrior and I would die with my mail and my sword and my axe, even though I hadn't earned a battle-death. I had my helmet under my arm, and my sword and axe at my belt.

You looked at the two pyres, and at me.

'Where is Hagen?' I asked you, before you could speak.

'Gone to fetch the gold. Attila has sent men to meet him at the gates of Vormatia.'

I was glad Hagen was gone, but less glad at the implication that you had spoken to Attila.

I didn't know you had gone before dawn, to bargain with him. We both made our sacrifices, to save the city that you had always loved, and that I had learned to love by loving you. We each made a separate peace. And we both broke the one promise we'd made to each other: we had not been honest. Sometimes I think love is the worst trickster of all.

Before I could say anything more, Aetius approached, and said, 'Attila, are you satisfied with your treaty with the Burgundians?'

'I am satisfied,' Attila said, his mouth curling.

'Then all that remains is for the murderer Brynhild to pay for her crimes and demonstrate that the Burgundians will behave as a civilized people within the borders of the Empire.'

I heard the muttering of our comrades behind us, and shouts from the young people I had trained.

Your face went white. 'No,' you said, a suppressed scream behind it.

'Tell us of your crimes, Brynhild,' Aetius said.

I turned away from you, and never looked back. I needed to keep my nerve.

As loudly and clearly as I could, I told them I'd met Sigurd before he came to Vormatia, and that we had been lovers. That I had seen him bathe in Fafnir's blood, and that I noticed the bare spot on his back, where he wouldn't be invulnerable. That he had left me with no word of explanation. That he had later tricked me into marrying another man, and that he had married you instead of me. All of that was true. I didn't lie. If they chose to believe that I was jealous of you and Sigurd, if they chose to believe that you and I hated each other because two powerful women could not be friends, then fine. Let them believe what they liked.

I told them I was responsible for his death. We had agreed to be honest with each other, and I saw no point in lying to the rest of the world either.

The last thing I heard was your angry screams as they tied me onto the pyre, muffled only a little by the helmet over my ears. They laid my sword and axe across my chest. Before long, all sound was lost beneath the cracking of the wood and flame around me, and my own coughing and retching.

The wood shifted underneath me as the fire took over.

I could see nothing but the colour of Fafnir's blood, and I breathed harsh poison, and pain racked my midsection, and skewered the muscles of my arms.

More wood shifted, and I dropped into the heart of the fire. When all the wood had burned, my body would fall into the grave beneath the platform.

Deeper into red pain, until my lungs stopped breathing altogether. Wood shifted; I fell. Pieces of flaming wood fell over my body.

Then another shift, another drop, another shift, and I fell into nothingness. For a very long time, I drifted downward into blissful darkness with no fire in it, my arms still folded on my chest, the smell of my own death in my nostrils.

CHAPTER THIRTY

Gudrun's Bargain

I screamed myself raw as the flames took you, and then I
felt Volker's gentle hand on my arm. Your choice would do
no good to us if I showed that I'd been unwilling. That you'd
tricked me. I suppose we were even.

Volker, bless him, made a big show of comforting me over
Sigurd – that was my husband, there on the other pyre, and
I had a legitimate public reason to scream and weep. I was
a queen, and it was in my people's interest for me to acknowledge that Aetius and Attila had finally broken us in the
ways the Empire wanted us broken.

My life stretched out in front of me, empty and cold.
Before dawn, when you were making your promises to
Aetius, I'd promised myself to Attila. This was my choice: I
would offer tribute and myself in marriage, so Attila would
leave Vormatia alone, independent and free. With me as his
hostage-bride, he could say he now had protection against
the treacherous Burgundians. He'd take what my brother
had once offered Bleda, the brother whose name he couldn't
even bear to speak without grimacing. A marriage to me
would satisfy Attila's pride, and he wouldn't even have to
go to the bother of running a city. Oh, I knew he wasn't a

man of his word, and he'd attack again if he felt like it. But I could buy Hagen time. And with time, I reckoned, the Empire would tire of Attila. Aetius would see he was too dangerous a dog to keep off the leash. (As for that, it's now clear I was right.) I just had to get Vormatia out of danger, for a year or two.

What choice did I have? I didn't want to lead my people to a new land, fleeing from one danger into who knows what else. If any of them wanted to go, let them, and I wished them well. But I had other duties. My people were all those who made their homes in Vormatia: the Burgundians but also the Romans, the Persians, the Franks, the Goths, the Alans, the Greeks, the Egyptians, the Syrians. That had always been my dream, that city, with all its people. If I led the Burgundians away in exile, what would happen to Vormatia and everyone left in it? Attila had no interest in ruling it, but he might keep it in constant terror, out of revenge or because he found it useful to have a terrified source of food and fighters at the edge of his influence.

Grief was all I wanted. Grief, and revenge, when the moment came. Because I thought my marriage would buy my time for that, too. I didn't know how, but I would have revenge.

I tried not to think about my mother. Had the wind told her yet that her son was dead? When I dressed that morning as you lay sleeping, I wore the deep blue dress she wove for me on her loom. A dress to call my fate to heel, she called it; a river-dress. She said it would help me make decisions. That was why she had given it to me when I left for battle, although I certainly wasn't thinking when I took it of the decisions to be made *after* battle. Maybe she was, though. My mother had depths.

Leaning on Volker's arm, I told him he must lead the remnants of the army back to Vormatia, where he and Hagen would hand over the tribute. After that, things would be difficult. The food stores would be low, even taking the deaths of so many people into account. And we'd spent so much preparing for war that the city's coffers would be empty too. My family had counted on using Brynhild's wealth and Sigurd's, but now we were losing it, handing it over to Attila. So the first order of business, after healing, must be to house anyone in the Domus who needed a place to live and food to eat. And then open up new trade routes to the west. Match workers to work, and collect food for those who couldn't afford to buy it.

And I told Volker he must give the choice to every resident of Vormatia to stay or to go, but if they stayed, to assure them they would be protected. All those who had been enslaved in my father's day were to be freed, in the Domus, in the city, in our lands beyond. All citizens would be equal in Vormatia, and face their fate together. Attila was trying to drive wedges between the Burgundians and everyone else, but he would not find it so easy. Most of the wealthy men who would have argued and clutched their purse strings wouldn't argue now; they had already lost their own lives or those of their children or slaves, all pieces of bodies down in the badger-pit. We had finally lost enough to build the city we needed; or so I hoped.

Volker listened and nodded, and even smiled at one point.

For once, Hagen didn't want to talk strategy. He spoke hotly in my ear. 'I've already watched one friend sacrifice herself this morning. I won't make it two.'

'I'm not dying. But you can think of Gudrun as dead. She is dead, really – the person you know. Sing songs about me.'

The wood shifted on your pyre; the stink of smoke was everywhere.

PART IV
THE TOWER

CHAPTER THIRTY-ONE

The Whetting of Gudrun

Brynhild, I've never forgotten watching you burn on the pyre, not for one moment since. I never turned away, and I knew the moment you were gone. The absence of you was like a gash in my world. The flames were so high and so bright that I couldn't see your body. But I knew you were gone.

My vision went black at the edges and I could feel my body weakening, a loss of control. I swear I felt my mother take my arm and whisper in my ear that we would have our revenge, although my mother was far away from me, back home in Vormatia. I wondered whether the wind had told her that her son was dead, or whether it would be left to Hagen to give her the news. Whatever really happened then, my vision and my mind cleared. When Attila said we'd be married that very day, I smiled. I twisted the ring my mother gave me.

Attila was, somewhat inconveniently for his Christian imperial allies, married already, to a woman named Khreka, and they had three sons. He didn't need me for any of the usual reasons a man might want a wife. But marriage is the easiest way for a man to say he owns a woman. He was taking whatever spoils he thought he deserved from my people and ending my father's line. He was happy to take me as a second wife.

First, he'd planned to watch my brother and me die, suffocated by the lindworm's poison. The slow agony of marriage to him, knowing my people were wandering and broken, would serve his purposes just as well. There was one way in which Attila and I were alike: we both understood revenge, how to wield it and how to wait for it. Your death gave me a challenge and a purpose like nothing I'd ever imagined I'd want. You were my whetstone, and I was ready to be your blade.

I suppose I expected his wife Khreka to be either vicious, like her husband, or a subservient victim. But she was neither. She was a tall, brown-haired and brown-skinned woman, grey at the temples, with a beautiful face. A proud queen. She offered to braid my hair, and I accepted.

'You will miss your family,' she said, in Latin.

I lifted my chin. 'My mother has always known I might be married to a foreign king one day. She thought she would lose me two seasons ago, to Bleda, but then your husband killed him.'

'*Our* husband,' she corrected me, unfazed. 'In the spring, your mother hadn't yet lost her son. Things were different then.'

'She has her foster-son, Hagen. And she has the love of all our people. My mother is strong.'

I remembered what my mother had told me: *I can never leave our kingdom. I am bound to the Rhine, its guardian, as its power is bound to me. One day, I will go to the river to take my place there. It is patient. It waits. But I think if I went too far from it, I would die.*

'I am sure she is. And now she can stay in your city, thanks to your agreement with my husband. What do they make there? Pots, isn't it?'

'Yes,' I said, thinking of the smell of the hot kilns, the sound of arguing in five languages, the taste of fish sauce, the bright clothing drying between the houses, the feel of the sun-baked paving stones under my shoes. 'They do make pots there.'

I wasn't a threat to Khreka, or at least, I wasn't a rival. She wasn't unkind to me. She told me that Attila did not hit women, that he treated his three sons well and equally, that he suffered from bad dreams and sometimes yelled in the night. Khreka and I both spoke Latin well although it was not the language of either of our hearts.

'What is the custom of kingship among the Huns?' I asked, lightly. 'After Attila, will his oldest son be king? Or sons, if there are two kings again?'

'Your sons will have as much right as mine,' she said, though she didn't look worried.

That wasn't on my mind. I had no intention of bearing sons by Attila or anyone else. I only wanted to know what would happen after I killed him.

As far as I was concerned, I was already dead. I had died when you burned.

I only needed to let Attila live long enough to make sure the remnants of our army were back safe in Vormatia, under my mother's protection, and that anyone who wanted to leave and go west had been given a clean start. I needed to give Hagen and Volker a few days, weeks at most, to take care of business. And then? Attila's sons were mere boys. I'd seen the way Zerco and the others looked weary when Attila spoke. They had no desire to fight us. We had so little to give them, now. Once they had the gold, once their king was dead, once there was some distance between the armies, I didn't think the Huns would go to much trouble to bother my people any more.

In other times, Attila might have ridden east with me, to marry me in the lands where his people planned to spend the winter. As it was, I think he was eager for the deed to be done, to reduce the chance of a rescue attempt.

The Hunnish camp formed a kind of circle with the largest tent, the king's tent, as the jewel in the crown. In the centre was a wide-open space, and as the sun set, they held games there to celebrate our wedding. Horse-archers competed to hit targets, and storytellers made people laugh. When I think of that night, my most vivid memory is of a man who made wonderful things out of fire with his hands, so bright against the violet mountains and the first few stars of evening. Cold was setting in, although there was no snow yet. They dressed me in a heavy wool cloak, as red as blood, redder even than the gown I had worn the day I thought I would marry Bleda.

Then they stoked the great fire and as the sparks flew upwards, Attila stood and declared that I was his wife. I didn't ask for a priest, and they probably wouldn't have offered one if I did, and most priests wouldn't have married me to an already married man. I was Attila's prize, not his partner. My family's religion, like the other parts of me that made me anything but a trophy, had been stripped away.

Then came the cup of friendship, and my chance.

It was a heavy golden goblet; one needed both hands to lift it. Attila drank from it himself, then offered it to one of his family or retainers, then drank himself again, after each one. Only the inner circle drank – about a dozen people – but still, Attila drank deep every time. The drink was kumis, mare's milk, fermented but not very strong. Attila handed it first to Zerco, I noticed; reminding his dead brother's lieutenant where his loyalties lay?

I drank last.

I had to add the poison while Attila was watching me, but the night was dark, and my mother's ring was devious. It was plain gold; how could it conceal any poison? I took the goblet, drank deep. It was thick and sour on my tongue. As I took the cup down from my lips, my mind spoke to the ring, and poison collected on it like dew. I drank just long enough for a few drops to fall. A line of kumis trickled from one corner of my mouth down my chin, to show that I didn't fear him, and so he would not fear me. That was, after all, the point of the cup.

I handed the poisoned cup back to my husband.

Three drops for sickness, twelve drops for death, my mother had said. Sickness was all I wanted: enough for him to suffer, and to leave me alone. His death would come after Hagen and my mother were safely far away. And if he sickened first, his death would look more natural, when it came.

For the next few hours, I sat by his side at a great table, our fronts warmed by the fire and our backs turned to the cold night. He asked me to tell him my people's stories, but I had already given him enough, so I invented things. Strange tales of cannibalism and monsters to haunt his dreams. He laughed at me, at my people, at what he thought were our fears. I kept him laughing, kept him drinking. Khreka watched me.

He was already sweating and putting his hand to his chest. Khreka watched that too.

What would she do, I wondered, when she realized I was poisoning her husband? Thank me, kill me, or simply make conversation as stoically as she seemed to do everything?

I sat in that hostile company, not eating or drinking, staring into the fire but listening with every inch of my body. I listened to the rustling, to the small conversations all around. I noted who was concerned, who was wary, who was entertained.

Attila stumbled when he stood up, and he said nothing to me. He just pointed at me, then pointed at the great tent. I obeyed.

Inside, there were low tables and felt cushions. The back of the tent was curtained into several partitions, for Attila's guards, I assumed, and perhaps whichever wife would be deemed superfluous, assuming he didn't want both of us at once. I started thinking of ways to delay him: fighting, talking, weeping. I wasn't sure any of it would work.

But my mother's poison was sure. He stumbled into the tent, stinking from every pore, and past me into the partition.

After a while, Khreka came in, looked at me where I sat on a cushion, and walked past me. I stayed where I was. It was nearly dawn when I fell asleep.

Attila spent the next three days in the tent, though nobody looked very worried. He was a man who often needed time to recover from feasts, I gathered. I spent those days trying to look unthreatening. I asked Khreka if there was anything I could do to make myself useful, and she showed me to a basket of wools and some carders. So I sat dutifully outside the tent and combed the wool into fine, neat strands, and watched and waited.

Other than Khreka, the only other people whose names I knew were Zerco, who avoided me altogether, and Aetius, the Roman. In the afternoon of the third day, Aetius came to sit in the plain wooden chair next to me.

I kept working, but every muscle in my body tightened. This man, with his pretty mouth, his spotless Roman clothing and his tight jaw – this man sent you to your death. I had no desire to sit next to him and chat.

Just as he opened his mouth, hoofbeats interrupted him. A messenger rode right up into the circle and slid off his horse. He was a young man, coated in sweat, and he staggered into the king's tent.

Aetius watched him, thoughtfully. 'Now we shall see.'

It might have been a death, a war, a disaster of any kind. There was no reason it had anything to do with my family. But somehow I wasn't surprised when Attila emerged from the tent, strode over to me, and grabbed me by the arm. He pulled me into the tent, where the young messenger was stooped – not because the tent was low; it was not. His whole body spoke of his fear.

'Tell her,' Attila said.

The messenger swallowed. 'Our people met Hagen at Vormatia and took ownership of the tribute. As they were crossing the Rhine again to bring it here, the bridge collapsed.

All the gold that belonged to the warrior Sigurd and to his murderess Brynhild – it has all fallen to the bottom of the river.'

I wanted to burst out laughing, but I didn't. Hagen and my mother had surprised even me. How you would have grinned to hear it, I thought! All the runes you had shown my mother, so carefully inscribed on every stone of that rebuilt bridge. They had robbed Attila of one triumph. I intended to rob him of another soon.

Wonderful though it was, though, I worried this would make Attila call off the truce and slaughter my people. Hagen would have had the same thought, surely. He must have felt it was safe. And my mother? My mother, I knew, wasn't going anywhere.

'I hope many lives were not lost,' I said.

'Four,' the messenger said as Attila put up his hand to silence him.

'The witch drowned them and stole our gold,' Attila spat. 'They did not honour their word.'

I gazed at him calmly. 'It sounds to me that the gold was handed over, and when it was lost, it was in your people's possession. I don't see what my mother had to do with it. Bridges do collapse, you know. The wagons must have been very heavy. Brynhild's wealth was legendary—' and here I stopped talking, because my throat closed. I'd been too clever, trusted my nerves too much. I couldn't talk about you.

Attila saw that, and his gaze sharpened. 'Every ounce of gold your family has stolen from me, I will exact from your body. They've broken their word, and they've broken the peace. Again. We'll be at their throats by nightfall tomorrow.'

Aetius coughed; he was standing in the doorway of the tent. Uninvited, I noted. 'The peace will hold. The terms have been met,' he said.

'The Empire has sworn to support me,' Attila growled.

'The Empire had a mutual concern about the growing power of the Burgundians on the borderlands,' Aetius responded smoothly. 'That power has been diminished. The Empire does not have any interest in an army of Huns chasing the Burgundians across the Empire, pillaging as it goes. This ends here. We have other uses for you.'

Attila cough-laughed, holding his side, still in pain from my poison. 'You think I'm a dog to be called to heel.'

'Nothing of the sort. I am discussing strategy with an ally.'

'Go fuck yourself.' Attila grabbed my arm, hard, and threw me down onto the cushions. 'Tie her up,' he said to the guard at the tent's door. 'If they want my spoils to go into the Rhine, so be it. We'll send Gudrun to the bottom along with the gold. We'll drown the witch. Unless you object,' he sneered at Aetius.

'Far be it from me to tell you what to do with your wives,' said the Roman parasite.

CHAPTER THIRTY-TWO

Gudrun in the Fire

The Huns marched me towards Vormatia by the same route that had led my own army west, only a few days before. They didn't give me a horse and made me walk with my arms tied behind me, flanked by two men with spears. Attila rode behind me, and though he didn't say much, I could feel his hot stare on the back of my neck.

How I wished I had given him more poison when I had the chance! He was already healing; already able to ride. I needed to escape. On foot and a fugitive, I would be slow, but I would find my people, and help them make their home in exile. All I had to do was get out of Attila's clutches.

I remembered the badgers, and considered trying to call eagles, or wolves, or bears. What stopped me was fear. Would the distraction be enough to let me get away? Or would they kill me on sight, once they realized what I was doing? Would it even work as I hoped? The badgers had answered my request, but I was not at all sure I could count on such a thing happening again. I could negotiate, not command.

So I did nothing. One foot in front of the other, towards the setting sun.

They stopped for the night at the very place where we

had made camp, where you spoke to the nightjar. It still smelled of our fires. They put me into a tent and threw me onto the ground, with three guards watching me. If Attila came to me, I decided, I would find some way to kill him. I'd bite his throat. I'd call a venomous snake.

But you came to me instead. In the slippery ways that grief creeps in. I tried to imagine your smile, but what I remembered was the wary expression on your face one day soon after you'd arrived in Vormatia. You were in the peristyle, looking up at the roof of the Domus, taking the measure of the place. I tried to imagine your touch and it came too fiery. Your smell was the smell of the ground where we slept. Your voice was husky with smoke.

None of it was any comfort, and it filled me with pain. Tears streamed down my face into the rough felt underneath me. I couldn't wipe my nose or my eyes, because my hands were still bound. The guards laughed at me, but I couldn't bring myself to care. You were gone, you were haunting me now. Every piece of you dissolved when I tried to look at it, to remember it properly. I gritted my teeth, I wailed.

Outside, the rain started to fall. I offered it my pain. Let the whole sky weep for Brynhild, I said. Let the rain that didn't douse her funeral fire pay the price of its guilt now, and pour itself on the ground like a temple sacrifice. Let the sky crack open and the lightning strike. Let the wide world burn down to ashes, as mine already had.

Did my mother look eastward, see the lightning break the sky, and think, at last, my daughter has learned to let go?

Because I had, and I did. It was my lightning. It illuminated every inch of the world and ignited the tent over my head and sent a line of red fire down it, opening it up to the gale.

My guards ran outside, but they weren't afraid yet. Surely with so much rain, the fire wouldn't spread far. Surely with her hands bound and the weather so punishing, their captive would stay where she was.

They were wrong about both things. In the shadows of

that terrible fire, in the sounds of screaming horses and shouting men, I staggered into the blackness of the woods. The mud slipped under my feet, stones cut them, roots grabbed at my ankles, branches slashed my cheeks. I didn't stop until I couldn't hear the screams any more and couldn't see any red on the eastern horizon.

I woke up one morning, days later, in my mother's arms. She was cradling me and singing a song in a language I didn't quite understand. It made me realize just how hungry, sore, and exhausted I had been.

My mother looked older, even more majestic. She was wearing a dress in the same grey as the rocks where she sat. Her beautiful hair had turned green, and it was always wet, running into rivulets down her back. Her eyes were two old stones.

I sat up and looked around. We were on a flat, warm outcrop, with forested hills falling away from us on all sides, and the Rhine flowing far below. It was one of those comfortable mornings when the lazy sun sleeps behind scraps of clouds, neither bright nor cold. The height made me dizzy, and I wrapped my mother's hand in mine.

'You aren't in the city,' I said.

'My place is here,' she said, smiling. 'I've always known I would come here, in the end. The river is patient.'

I listened to the quality of that silence, above even most of the birds. The river was a whisper.

I said, 'My place is with my people.'

There was a long silence. She said, 'But?'

'But,' I said. She knew me too well. 'But I have lost all my joy and I don't think I'd serve them well. Maybe they're better off with Hagen and Volker. If Attila learns that I'm alive, I'll be a danger to our people, not a help to them.'

She was silent for a moment, and then she said, 'After we made the bridge collapse, Hagen and Volker and I called everyone to the old forum and gave them a choice, to stay or to flee. I told them I would never leave the Rhine, and that I'd protect the city as much as I could. But many families chose to go west. They don't want to guard a border any more, and I can't blame them. Truth be told, most of the ones who went were Burgundians. So I had Hagen take copies of the oldest scrolls in the library. And cuttings from your rose garden.'

'Hagen?' I was shocked. 'Hagen and Volker left, then?'

She nodded. 'I asked them to. The ones who left were the most vulnerable, the old people, or those with young children who didn't want them to be taken by Attila to serve in his army. I knew I could protect Vormatia, but there was no one to protect the families looking for safety on the road. They'll take our songs, our laws, our stories. The wind carries me news of them. They are safe on the road, so far.'

I felt alone, sick, dizzy. My city was still there, but who would lead it?

'They'll choose someone,' my mother said, answering the question I hadn't asked aloud. 'You have done all you could, and your presence might be more danger than protection to the city. Now you have time to think and heal. Time for Attila to forget you. Maybe he'll die.'

'We can always hope. I used your ring, and it helped me. Kept him away from me. But I should have let a few more drops fall.'

I still had the ring, on my hand.

She chuckled, a bit sadly. 'I'm glad at least one of my tricks was of some use to you. When you're ready to leave this place, I have another.'

I spent another day and night on my mother's rock, sleeping beneath bright stars. Then we walked a long secret path down to the shore. The sun was dancing on the water. She cupped her hands, and laid them on the water, and then there was a boat there, made of nothing but light. I thought of the gold that was now far beneath the glassy dark waves. Your gold, my darling. It waits for you still.

'Talk to the wind, and I'll be here,' my mother said. 'And whenever you need me, you know where I'll be.'

The little boat bore me dutifully, and I felt better once I was on the western shore. My father's kingdom. I couldn't quite see the city walls; I was too far north. My body had passed through hunger to the other side, and now I just felt ill and weak. Maybe I could have called an animal to me, and asked it to give up its life, but I had nothing to offer in return, and somehow trickery seemed like a bad idea.

After a half-day more of walking, I found a place I recognized, and saw a landmark on the horizon: Maren's tower. The place where my mother had asked the winds for news of her son.

It took me a very long time to climb that tower. I had to keep taking breaks, to rest my sore feet and recover my strength.

At the top, I found a cedar chest. When I nestled the padlock in my hand, it opened: my mother's work. Inside were two dry cloaks, woven on my mother's loom, so they kept out the rain and kept me warm. There were baskets of nuts, dried fruit, dried meat, and two bottles of mead. I laughed through cracked lips and had a little feast, sitting cross-legged on the tower.

Your birds seem to speak to you plainly. But the wind isn't that clear, and it's stubborn. A sharp negotiator. I offered it whatever news I could: everything that had happened to me, everything that I knew. In exchange, I asked the wind to tell me where my people were. They were farther than I thought: at least a week's journey, with many of them on foot.

And where is Attila, I asked, and held my breath.

A whisper came to me, in Attila's own voice, hoarse and hateful: he swore he did not believe I had died in the fire, and that he would find me wherever I was, and if my people sheltered me, they would rue it.

But where is he? I demanded.

I am everywhere, his voice replied. *I am the scourge of God.*

I slept on that tower, under the moon. The safest place I could think of; my mother had used it, and I suspected she had laid traps.

How desperately I wanted to walk to my people, to feel my mother enfold me in her arms, to see Hagen's wry smile and hear Volker sing. I wanted to help them build their new home and defend it. They could hide me, I told myself.

In the morning, I left the tower. One of the cloaks my mother had left there was a deep purple, a queen's robe, and the other was a very dark green. I chose the green one, to help keep me hidden, just in case, and I put my hood up over my head. There was a little food left, which I wrapped in the spare cloak and tied to a stick.

Attila's voice was still in my ears.

I walked all that day and finished the food. Just before nightfall, I came to a small village – a collection of three farms and a small disused temple, really – called Grimstadt. This was near the edge of my father's kingdom. It seemed quiet; I assumed the people who lived there had gone west with Hagen and Volker, but they might have left some food behind. The first farmhouse still had chickens running around in one pen, and a horse in the other. They had left in a hurry indeed, I thought. I walked carefully around to the back, and then heard someone say behind me: 'I'd rather not have to stick this sword into you, but I will. If you're hungry, I'll feed you.'

I put my hands out to show they were empty, and turned slowly to see a woman, with a large pregnant belly, and a sword in her hand.

Ingund lived with her ancient father. Her husband had died in the battle with Attila. Pregnant though she was, she might have made the journey west when my people came marching, leaving Vormatia behind. But her father was racked with tremors and haunted by visions. He was in no condition to walk any farther than the privy.

They believed me when I said I had no desire to steal from them and was just trying to survive on my own in the woods. They fed me and offered me a place to sleep by the embers of their fire.

In the morning, I went out in the mist and looked eastward. Had Vormatia chosen a new king? I asked Ingund if she'd had any news, when she brought me a bowl of porridge.

'Lothar,' she told me. 'The Empire's man.'

'Not any more,' I said, and laughed. 'Lothar. That's perfect. I'm glad he's healed, and I'm glad he's king. The Empire won't find him easy to deal with.'

Ingund just smiled bitterly and said it didn't much matter to her who lived in the Domus in the city. Life went on as much as before on their farm, and they paid their taxes. But this year there would be no one but Ingund to work the field, and she would have a baby to feed, and her father to care for. Her best choice was to go into the city and find herself a new husband. She did not look joyful at the prospect.

The baby came that day, and the birth would have killed her if she hadn't held on to life by her teeth. I found mugwort and nettles and stopped her bleeding as best as I could. Her daughter was pink-faced and healthy, but Ingund herself was weak. There was no choice for me but to stay and help. I was her queen, though no one would acknowledge that but me. She never asked me my birth name and I never gave it.

It was deep winter by the time she was well enough to cook for herself and her father. It would be a long and dangerous trudge for me to find my people then, and anyway I had decided to stay. There were people in my father's kingdom – in Lothar's kingdom, now – who needed me. If I had gone west, or to the city, I would have been Gudrun again, and I might have brought danger to my people.

When Ingund was well enough, I took the payment she offered of cured meat, bread and beer, and I walked back to Maren's tower. It was the safest place for me.

Hardly a week passed before an old woman came to me complaining that her butter wouldn't churn, which was really an excuse to complain about the new taxes and her children recanting their Christian faith.

Then came the man with the infected leg.

Before long, they started calling me the Witch of Grimstadt; Ingund told me that, with a smile, on one of our chats at her farmstead, when I came to help her with the young sheep.

'You can't complain if you refuse to give us a name,' she teased.

'This place is where I live now, and what are names after all but reminders of our homes?' I said.

'And our people.'

And our people, I thought. I'd heard some stories about your deeds and Sigurd's from the people who came to me, seeking my help. All the stories were already wrong. I was the only one who knew you, who kept you in my heart.

'You can tell them my name if you wish,' I said. 'You may tell them I am called Grimhild.'

CHAPTER THIRTY-THREE

The Hel-Ride of Brynhild

When I burned, I fell. This fall was mine alone. I saw no other women falling, no one else at all. At one point, I laughed, wondering which parts of me I would scar this time when I hit the bottom, and remembering that I couldn't scar anything, because I had bathed in lindworm blood, and also because I was dead. But laughing hurt. To laugh, I had taken a breath, which also hurt. That pain frightened me, in some way I didn't want to understand.

I realized my eyes were open when a cliff face loomed to my right. My hand shot out on its own, to catch a lump of rock. That rock would have cut my hands to ribbons, if they'd been hands that anything could cut. At last I came to a stop, hanging by my screaming fingers from a ledge. Below my dangling feet, a rough path cut into the mountainside. Below that, cliff, and below that, deep grey nothingness. I dropped to the path, and my bones jarred just as though I were alive.

It was an odd mountain, with no plants growing on it at all. Just bare dull rock the colour of old mail. (My own beautiful mail, cleaned just that morning of all that blood, was now black with soot.) Everything else was uniform

269

pewter sky, without clouds, without birds. The air was chill and my tunic and trousers were half-burned into rags. As for my axe and sword, they didn't seem to have accompanied me. I thought they were still on the pyre, blackened and twisting.

Wherever I was, I wasn't in Midgard or Asgard. That much, I was sure of. It might have been any of the nine worlds, but given that I'd got there from dying, I could only assume it was Helheim.

The silence consumed everything and threatened to consume me. I yelled, and there was no echo. That place seemed to absorb my voice like wool.

And it absorbed all choices. There was only one direction to the path, which began just under the outcrop I'd grabbed, and sloped slightly upwards along the mountain edge. I wonder what would have happened if I had jumped off the cliff? Would I still be falling today?

I didn't jump. I walked, very slowly. My lungs hurt with every breath. It seemed unfair that I still had to breathe through injured lungs, when I was dead. Was I dead? Perhaps, I thought, death wouldn't take me until I reached the end of this road. With one hand skimming the rock face to keep me steady, I walked. The only sound came from my footsteps and my wheezing, and both sounded quieter than they felt.

There came a time when I had to stop and rest, sitting with my legs dangling off the edge of the path. My lips were cracked and thick with dried blood. The taste of your honey was only a memory now, forever. I whispered your name. I didn't want to shout it in case it was swallowed up by that place. I wanted to keep it small and close to me. It gave me the reason to clamber to my feet.

As the path rose, the air got colder and the path grew slick with frost, until I reached a point where my feet slipped and I slid on my hands and knees, losing much of the ground I'd gained. At that point, going forward seemed pointless.

But what other choice did I have? Again, I looked down at oblivion, but it didn't call to me.

I sat there for a long time, catching my pyre-charred breath and gathering my strength. I needed something to help me walk on the frost and ice. Hrist would have laughed at how long it took me to realize this. Everyone knows you can't walk to the land of the dead without the right shoes.

The only metal I had was my helmet, which had been through so much with me. When I pulled it off, I cringed. A hand to my head showed me why: most of my hair was gone, burned away, and the skin on my scalp and the tops of my ears was scarred and bloody; another place where Fafnir's blood hadn't reached.

How gruesome my shade would be for all eternity.

The cheekpieces came off their hinges after a few prises with a chunk of flint. It was perhaps an hour's work to twist them into spikes that would wrap around my charred leather shoes and stay on well enough that I could walk.

It worked – not well, but well enough.

As I climbed higher, the path turned to scraped and pitted ice, lined on both sides with old snow. The spikes on my shoes scraped and slowed me down, every time I slipped. I wished for a staff. I wished for many things. My face and fingers had gone numb with cold by the time the path evened out and a high meadow opened before me, all dead brown grass standing in the windless air. The icy path became a hard, frozen road. It led to a low, curving bridge made of the same stone as everything else.

Under that bridge flowed a river full of weapons: swords and axes, poles and spears and arrows, all jostling in the dark water like salmon to the sea. But it was silent. The whole world was silent.

A high house stood on the far side of the bridge. Its walls were of unbroken stone: no doors, no windows. The place seemed empty, but not unguarded. For one thing, in the middle of the bridge a stone statue stood vigil, stretching from one wall to the other, as tall as a giantess. In the stories told in the mead hall, trolls lived under bridges, and warriors walked on top. But this stony creature stood in my way, while the weapons of human monsters wriggled and swam underneath. She gazed at me. One step more, one step more. The stone was cold to touch. When I spoke to her, the stone giantess only gazed at me. I screamed curses at her.

The silence was getting under my skin.

Beside the river of weapons, I knelt, and thrust my hand into the cold water. I pulled out my own sword, gleaming as though brand-new, forge-new, fire-new. I reached in again and pulled out my axe.

The giantess was gone.

One step more, one step more.

There was a palisade of old, dark wood around the high house: a tight ring of poles sharpened like spears at the top. Rising just inside it were two terrible tree trunks, high as cathedrals, with the skulls of horses grinning on top. I chopped my way through the palisade with my battle-axe and walked through. Again, this should all have been louder than it was. I called out a few times, screamed really, in all the languages I knew.

There was nowhere else to fall, and no way to climb back to Midgard. Was this to be my eternity? No hall of heroes for me, no cups of mead. Only silence, a forbidding wall, the chill and silent mist.

The wall of the house did not yield to my fists. I tried to scratch runes in it with the tip of the sword and with the death-shoes I wrenched off my feet, but they made no marks on that shining black stone. There were no cracks in the wall, no joints.

Finally, I banged on the wall with my axe-haft, trying so hard to make a blow that would ring through that valley. Tears flooded my face, choked my mouth and nose. Cold and wet, I stood for as long as I could, and then I knelt, still flailing against the wall. How long did I spend there, deafening myself with the sound of futility? I don't remember when my sight went black, or when my body collapsed at last.

Like most people, you have probably never expected to find yourself in Hel's house. For one thing, you were raised a Christian, and had made other plans. Believe me when I say I never expected to be there either. A Valkyrie must go very far wrong to find herself in such a place.

My second exile began in an ice-blue hall with high ceilings, prone on a cold stone floor. Hel stood before me. There was no doubting who she was. Odin had described her in his campfire tales: tall, pale, grim. One half of her face was young, her skin gleaming, her black eye bright. The other half was decayed corpse, with a hole for an eye. (It occurred to me I probably didn't look much better, with my clothing charred, my head bloodied, my limbs bruised brown and purple beneath my perfect skin.) She was dressed in a shroud. One of Loki's misbegotten children. If there was a family resemblance, it was in the length of her body, and the long black hair as straight and shining as the walls of her house.

'You know where you are,' she said. Her voice sounded rusty, as though she hadn't spoken in some time.

'I do,' I said, and my voice sounded even worse. Burned from the fire, raw from screaming. My hands went to my throat, to the pain there.

'You are not in very good condition.'

'Am I dead?'

'That remains to be seen.'

I hung my head and shook it in confusion, which just made it ring all the worse. 'I don't understand. My body – is it still in Midgard?'

'No, you travelled here in your body, which is not recommended. Don't you recognize it? The dog brought you.'

Only then did I notice Vigi, Sigurd's white dog, sitting still as a statue beside her throne. She put out one long hand and stroked his head.

'Vigi,' I croaked.

'His name is Garm,' Hel retorted. 'A gift from my parent. I send Garm out into Midgard to be my eyes and ears, and sometimes he brings me things. Sometimes he brings me things I don't want.'

'If you don't want me, perhaps you can show me the way out.'

She stared at me for a long time, with those empty eyes. 'All right,' she said, and patted the dog, who padded away behind the pillars that seemed to stretch on endlessly in all directions.

He came back with Sigurd.

The dead don't hurt, but they do dream. In fact, their very existence is a kind of dream, full of impossibilities and sudden shifts. What they did in life, they do in death, but without joy and without cease.

So Sigurd walked through Hel's hall with his hand on his sword hilt and determination in his eyes. With a little cry of affection or pity or both, I saw at once that the battle frenzy Odin had laid on him in his last days was gone, and he was the Sigurd I knew again, watching and listening. But he was sad and confused.

He thought the dog was still his and patted him as he watched me.

'Do you know me, Sigurd?' I asked.

'I know you killed me,' he said, in the least accusing tones possible, and that sent another stab through my heart.

I didn't argue with him. Understanding sometimes comes to the dying, and I had no right to try to take his from him. He knew that though I didn't throw the spear that killed him, I might as well have.

Hel leaned forward on her throne, resting her chin on her folded hands, and watched us with amused interest.

'I had to do it,' I explained. 'You wouldn't stop fighting. You wouldn't make peace.'

He shook his head, agreeing with me. 'I wouldn't make peace.'

'But you died a warrior.'

Then he cocked his head, and looked at me in that child-like way he had. 'If I died a warrior, why am I here?'

'An excellent question,' Hel said.

'You died with a friend's spear through your back,' I said, through gritted teeth. 'And the only reason your back was turned was that you didn't expect the betrayal. You were not a coward and you didn't die in your bed. You ought to be in Valhalla.'

He swung his sword, thoughtfully, as though only to see it gleam in Hel's half-light. '*He* did say I would have a place in Valhalla. That's right.'

'Who did?' All amusement dropped from both halves of Hel's face.

'Odin,' I answered, exhausted and certain. 'He was goading Sigurd, egging him on.'

'He told me I was a hero,' Sigurd said, in a tone that was almost aggrieved but couldn't quite find the energy. 'He told me there would be a place for me in Valhalla. He gave me a horse.'

'He gave you a horse!' Hel stood up; she was even taller than I'd imagined. 'Whatever for?'

I shook my head to show my confusion. 'I don't know. He has plans for Midgard. Sigurd was part of those plans, I think, but I got in the way. Again.'

'You got in Odin's way? Explain yourself.'

I let out a breath. 'I was a Valkyrie, once. He cast me out. Sent me down. Exiled me, to Midgard.'

At that, Hel was very quiet. She stepped towards me, walked around me like a dog sniffing a dead animal.

'He exiled me too,' she said at last. 'Cast me down. Do you know, I think you are very much still alive, now that

I get a look at you. I think you should return to Midgard.'

I glanced at Sigurd, but Hel said, 'Oh, not him. He is definitely dead. He stays.'

'What if I made a bargain,' I said. 'If I die in battle, he can take my place, and I will take his.'

Hel's laughter was like nothing I've ever heard, and I hope I never hear it again. 'Your place! Where in all the worlds do you have a place? You've just told me you were banished from Valhalla. And do you think Freyja will welcome a former Valkyrie?'

I shuddered to think of it, remembering the ghostly Disir. I imagined Folkvang as a realm of haunts, misty and vast. Even then, Odin's lies shaped my mind. I didn't know what to say to Hel; she was right. I was not destined for a mead hall or an eternal battle. But Sigurd should have been. That much I knew.

'He shouldn't be punished for my mistakes.'

She spread her hands, palms up. 'He isn't being punished at all. He is dead, and now he is where dead people go. This isn't such a bad place, you know.'

I looked around those gloomy halls.

'Well,' she admitted, 'this part of it is a punishment. But it's a punishment for me alone, and as it happens, I have grown to like my house anyway. Sigurd's house will be whatever suits him.'

He stood, listening, saying nothing.

'It ought to be Valhalla,' I said.

'Well, are you not a Valkyrie?' she asked, surprising me. 'If you want to build him Valhalla, by all means, be my guest.'

I cut the wood myself, while Sigurd's shade watched me. He had led me through Hel's halls out into a rocky landscape, and from there to a wide, green slope at the foot of a mountain, dotted with pines. It was a lovely spot, and I was glad that he wouldn't have to spend eternity, or something close to it, in a terrible place.

My axe bit the pine cleanly, and I shaved every board. I made myself new tools out of flint and scratched out my plans with charcoal on a granite boulder. I knew Valhalla's mead hall like I knew my own heart, and I recreated it perfectly. It was ridiculously large for one solitary ghost, but I relished the soreness in my muscles.

After a time, Sigurd started helping me. We hefted logs together and without saying a word about it, he carved the doorframe, though it was nothing like the real Valhalla, which he'd never seen. His carving was of a long-tailed lindworm, and of roses wrapped around swords. That door-frame was our story, as true as Sigurd could make it.

We said very little to each other, but our silence was the silence of old companions.

When the hall was complete, I stood and surveyed what we had done. It was a good hall, but a desolate one. There were no bonfires with dead warriors gathered around, telling tales. There were no squeals of undead boars to be hunted. The sky was not painted with green fire. There were no meadows full of mad bees, and the forest trails I'd walked so often were not there. It wasn't Valhalla at all.

Hel appeared beside me, stepping up as though out of thin air.

'If he wants the rest of it, he can make it,' she said. 'Death is a dream you know you're having, for the most part, and you can change it if you like.'

I held out my hands, which would have been bleeding and blistered, if not for the lindworm blood. 'If he could make it however he liked, himself, why did I have to chop so much wood?'

Hel grinned. 'It amused me. Besides, I didn't know what to do with you. Garm doesn't usually drag me things for no reason, so I was loath to send you back to Midgard before I got a sense of you. As I said, Valhalla won't take you, and I assumed the Disir wouldn't take you either. But come to think of it,' Hel said, scratching her chin, 'that isn't a bad idea.'

What isn't a bad idea, I opened my mouth to say, but before I could form the words, I was lying on my back, with the sun on my face, and the smell of fresh grass all around me. I was no longer in Helheim, but I wasn't in Midgard either.

CHAPTER THIRTY-FOUR

Brynhild in Folkvang

Lying on my back on the ground, again. Another world, another exile. But this one began like waking in bed. I can't explain what it was like, Gudrun. I'd spent enough time lying on the ground, in my three centuries, to know that usually it is not very comfortable, even when one hasn't been beaten, burned and made to chop wood in the underworld just beforehand. There is always a stone, a root, a patch of mud, an anthill, stubbly grass. Not in this field. I was lying on soft rye stalks, trampled flat, over even, sun-dried earth. It smelled like high summer.

The flat area was a kind of path cut through the rye, which was growing tall and ripe on either side. That path was only one of many, cut into that great golden field. I thought at first it was a labyrinth, but I came to think of it more as a piece of art: knotwork stamped on the world.

There were no insects, but I thought I could hear a kind of whispering. The wind in the rye, I told myself. If it was a wind, it was warm and soft on my cut hands, my bruised body, my burned skull. I could feel it – or rather, them – healing my body. A strong feeling came over me that I was wholly welcome and wholly wanted, which I had never felt to be true anywhere before.

After a very long time – years, perhaps – I stood up. My body felt strong and all my pain was gone. I started walking.

The lines cut through the field intersected quite often, and they were seldom straight, so I kept note of where the late-afternoon sun hung, to keep some sense of bearings. The other side of the sky was purple and flashed every now and again with heat lightning.

Two pathways in the rye field crossed, making a wide circle, and in that circle a dozen people sat on stones, talking with each other. They were people of all kinds and ages, staring down at a pattern of bones cast upon the ground. One of them, a man of middle age with a beard and old-fashioned Frankish dress, looked up at my approach.

'Oh, someone new!' he exclaimed. 'Please, come, break the tie.'

'But step carefully,' a nervous young woman said, holding out her arm. 'Please step around, so you don't disturb the pattern.'

The pieces were knucklebones, dozens and dozens of them, of the kind that children throw in the air and then catch on the backs of their hands. Each one was painted on two sides, red and blue, and some had landed with the blue face up and some with the red.

An old man walked towards me, took my arm kindly. 'Now see the picture they make – the blue and red we have already interpreted. We knew which man would become bishop of Rome, and what he would do, and how long he would be pope before dying. But what we can't fathom is the method of death. See that shape over on the westward side? I say it is a venomous snake opening its jaws.'

'And I say it is a bow, strung and ready to loose its arrow,' piped up a woman from the far side of the circle.

'I'm sorry,' I said. 'I don't know this place, or what you do here. Why do you need to know how this man will die?'

'Oh, it's idle curiosity,' said the kind old man, with a bashful laugh. 'We've done it for all the kings, the queens, many bishops, some fishwives and saints and weavers and a merchant or two. But we got stuck on this one, you see. We cast the bones forty-four years ago and have been arguing about it since.'

'We'll find out who was right soon enough,' said one woman who hadn't spoken yet, darkly.

The old man said, 'We need a tie-breaker, you see. So which do you think it is? Will he be shot by an arrow, or bitten by a snake?'

I looked at the bones that formed the shape. From where I stood, it looked like a bell, opening up a little near the gap that might have been a snake's mouth. 'To me it looks like a foxglove flower,' I said.

'Poison!' a woman gasped, putting her hand to her heart. 'I might have guessed.'

'Well, now that you say it, that curve is all wrong for a bow, or a snake,' one mousy young man said. 'I think you're right. You're remarkably wise.'

I felt confused, but pleasantly, like a million bees were buzzing in my head.

'Will you stay with us?' A grey-haired woman smiled at me. 'Or do you seek Freyja?'

I did seek Freyja, I realized. I named the place then in my own mind at last: Folkvang. The place of shadows, the home of the Disir. I'd shuddered to hear it named for so many years, and grieved for the dead who went there, the half of the warriors we couldn't take to Valhalla, under the terms of a treaty Odin had signed with Freyja before any of us were born. Where did I get the idea that its vastness was bleak, windy, lonely? I couldn't recall anyone telling me that, but someone must have, once.

It was one more of Odin's lies. The place was vast, but it was the opposite of lonely. It felt like a place where one could be happy in one's own company. I felt I had amends to make, though Freyja probably wouldn't have cared what some Valkyrie thought of her home. Still, I felt that perhaps I should ask permission to stay there, since I hadn't come in a conventional way.

Only a very small part of me cared, in that moment, about returning to Midgard, and that part of me was sleeping. What had Midgard held for me, after all? Death and politics. I had tried to be a lone Valkyrie and I had learned that such a thing cannot exist. As wife, as queen, even as your lover, I had failed utterly. Perhaps here, in these fields, there was a task for me. I was wise, they said. I was strong, too. And the sunlight smelled of honey.

'I do seek Freyja,' I said. 'Which path do I take?'

'Any path!' a young woman exclaimed. 'Any one will do.'

So I set out on the closest one, and out of sheer jubilance, I started to run. Through the labyrinth of knotwork, crossing, turning, making choices based on nothing but whim, or instinct. I ran and I never tired.

Freyja did not sit on a throne. I found her working, in the most remarkable place. A wide opening in the rye field, with brightly coloured tents all around, like a camp of war or an entertainment. It was encircled by a palisade, and from the top of every pole there hung a very long, shining banner in red, blue, yellow or green. The opposite of the horse-skull poles in Hel. Every so often, a breeze would lift a banner free, and it would float into the sky, and the pole would grow a new ribbon, like a tree in bud.

The air above the field was filled with these banners, gliding like clouds.

In the centre of this circle were horses: lovely horses, but ordinary, from what I could see. And walking among the horses were women made of light.

Freyja was not made of light, and looked ordinary enough, except that she was a foot taller than any ordinary person. She was stocky and strong, with gold and silver curls loose around her shoulders, half-braided above. She was wearing a plain quilted shirt without sleeves, and a simple linen skirt, and sandals. But around her neck was the famous Brisingamen, a massive torc of flaming, twisted gold wire, set with shining broken stars. It left no doubt who I was talking to.

She held a long, thin dark wand in one hand, nearly as long as a staff. Freyja pointed it at me and said, 'You're not dead.'

It seemed I would have to get used to that greeting.

'No indeed, but I was sent here by Hel, and I come to ask for safe passage.'

'Sent by Hel! That hasn't happened in a very long time. She is not generally one for sending presents. What are you called?'

'Brynhild.'

'Ah,' she said, and let her wand drop. 'The former Valkyrie. Loki told me about you. You've played your part, then.'

Had I played a part? I'd done what Loki wanted, I supposed; I had caused some small mischief to Odin.

I was shocked just then by the sight of one of the women of light calling a horse – and the horse running to her and then leaping into the air, leaping so high that it was flying, up over one of the ribbons in the sky.

'What magic is this?' I gasped.

'A Valkyrie, surprised by flying horses? Didn't you ever wonder where Odin gets them? He pays me dearly for them, and I take full price. The horses are living, breathing creatures, taken from Midgard. My Disir whisper to them, call to them. It's how they train for the battlefield and calling the newly dead.'

There was so much in this that it made my head hurt. I thought of Grani, Odin's gift to Sigurd, who couldn't fly any more. Odin took that gift from him out of spite, then, or to serve his purposes. But that was the past, and another world. The world before me was too wonderful for words.

'These women – these bright women – they cannot be the Disir.'

'But of course they are. The dead are always brighter in the places where they ought to be, than in the places they haunt. Unlike Odin, I don't steal living people to do my work for me.'

I shook my head again. 'Nothing is as I thought it was.'

'Of course not. You were taken by the Liar as a child. But you got away. That does make you interesting. Why did Hel send you to me?'

'She seemed reluctant to return me to Midgard, and reluctant to keep me in Helheim. She said you would not accept a former Valkyrie, but she sent me here anyway.'

'Did she say that? Always very sure of herself, isn't she? Well, she is wrong, as usual. If you choose to stay in Folkvang, you are more than welcome. In fact, tonight you will sit at my right hand.'

I imagined, from that invitation, that Freyja must have a hall, like the mead hall in Valhalla. If she does, that is not where she brought me.

At sunset, we walked through waving rye higher than my head, and the ground beneath our feet began to rise into a sort of causeway. As it carried us above that golden sea, I gasped. There in the midst of the great field sat a ship, larger than any I had ever seen, as though it were becalmed, but there was no water anywhere I could see. It was built of silvery wood, and its prow rose higher than any cathedral. There was no mast or sail, and I saw no oars, but the gunwales were lined with round shields.

The earthen ramp brought us onto the deck, which was lined with benches. In the middle, where a mast would have been, was an iron cauldron hanging from a tripod. At the prow of the ship sat a beautiful carved chair hung with red tapestries.

That was Freyja's seat, and mine was on the bench next to her. The Disir came in: some walked up the ramp, some flew or floated down from the clouds. A fire sprang up in the cauldron and the last sliver of sun melted into the flat horizon.

All I could see, on either side of the ship, were waves of deep yellow. The sky was darkening, with scraps of cloud still lit by a sun I could no longer see. And then I felt the ship begin to move and grabbed the bench. Freyja chuckled.

'It's not the ship that's moving,' she said. 'Look.'

She pointed to the sky, and I realized that the clouds were streaming past us as quickly as thought, and forming bright pictures. It was something like the green sky-fires of Valhalla, but in all colours, and sharper. I saw scenes of birth and death. Faces so close I could stroke their cheeks, and scenes from high above of fortresses and cities, busy markets and working farms. All the people were strangers.

Then the images changed to a landscape of green, dotted with brown, with rivers running through it.

'Disir, listen and see!' Freyja called. 'Tonight, before you look for your loved ones, I must tell you of our next battle.'

The landscape tilted and I felt as though the ship were flying over it. It made me dizzy, and amazed.

'Attila will make his stand at a place called Maurica,' Freyja continued, 'with Aetius approaching from the west. We expect the armies on both sides to be extremely large, and though the Romans have allies among all the people of this part of Midgard, so do the Huns. This part of Gaul is quite flat, but the fields here rise to a sharp ridge on one side. The battle will not begin until late in the day, and we can come in the shadows.'

I froze, confused for a moment. 'Odin has tricked you,' I blurted.

Freyja looked at me, placidly.

'Attila is nowhere near Gaul,' I said. 'And he and Aetius are allies, not enemies. The Huns and the Romans are fighting together. This is another deception. This is Odin's work.'

'Odin has been busy indeed, convincing Attila that half the Empire is his,' Freyja said. 'But Odin cannot deceive me using my own magic. I think perhaps you have lost track of time, Brynhild.'

Lost track of time? My fall to Helheim, my walk, my construction of Sigurd's hall: it was hard to have any sense of time in all of that. I stammered, 'How long has it been, since – since the Huns fought the Burgundians, east of Vormatia?'

'Oh, I don't know. Ten years. Something like that.'

Ten years. Ten years in which you had lived, thinking me dead. Ten years of war and politics, of marriages and children – were you even still alive? I felt as though I would faint.

'Ten years,' I repeated. 'I was a very long time falling, then.'

'So it would seem. I've never gone to Helheim by those roads.'

'And what—' I licked my lips, trying to steady myself. 'What has happened on Midgard in the meantime?'

'A great deal of death.'

The ship flew farther over the land, towards a city, burning. I saw people running wounded, children weeping, animals with black wounds and desperate faces.

'Are they real?' I asked. It was a foolish question, for someone who had seen so many marvels in many worlds, but Freyja didn't mock me.

The terrible sights went away, and the sense of movement slowed, and now I saw a whole jumble of faces, for the most part kinder and happier.

'They are the images of real people, but seen from afar, in space and time. Some are living and some are dead. What you see now are the people the Disir choose to share with their sisters. You may choose to see anyone you wish. Old friends. Loved ones. Your family. If it's not too painful.'

I didn't remember my parents and didn't want to understand them or know more about what I had lost when they sent me away. There was only one living person who held any interest for me: you.

'What do I do?'

'Just think of the person, and they will appear. No one else will see it, unless you choose to share your vision.'

I thought of you; I called your name. My nails bit into my palms as I hoped to see you safe, and among your beloved people. I hoped your grief would not hurt more than you could bear. I hoped for a glimpse of your face.

Instead, I saw a tower.

The scene was dark, shadowed all around the edges, as though unwilling to show itself. A pale green sward, some trees nearby, and a lonely tower of stone, looming.

I blinked, and tried to see your face, candlelight on your collarbone, the bend of your fingers, the twitch of your smile. Tried to remember the last thing you said to me, before I went onto the pyre.

The tower changed its shape, into a stooping figure, cloaked. I couldn't see the person's face, but she seemed to be aware of me, somehow. She had been walking through the forest but now she paused, still as stone.

'I don't understand what I'm seeing,' I whispered.

'Try something else, then,' Freyja said gently. 'There are many kinds of magic in the world, and perhaps you've happened on something that is trying to keep itself hidden. Go to a different time, a different place.'

I thought back to the pyre and cringed with remembered pain. How you had stood so still, poised like a bowstring. I kept my mind's eye on you, as the fire raged, as it turned to embers. I followed you into a tent, and I saw you captive, saw you – married to Attila. Crying out, I rose up to stop it, to free you, but there was nothing I could do.

I saw you lying where we had lain, together. Your hands were tied. Lightning cracked the fields above Folkvang, and I saw your tent in flames.

'This was not supposed to happen,' I cried. 'I sacrificed myself so that she would be safe. To stop Attila from attacking her people.'

Freyja put her warm hand on my arm. 'Attila? Attila has

done nothing but wage war, and he will continue. He's being goaded, you see. He has poison in his ear.'

The skies cleared of that terrible fire, and in its place, I saw Attila's face, his glittering eyes. Behind him, a little to the side, I saw the Allfather.

'Odin,' I muttered. 'What does Odin want with him?'

'The same thing he wanted with the hero you killed.'

And here I saw Sigurd, wandering through the forests of the Odenwald, his face distraught, his head in his hands. Tears running over his cheeks. At his side padded the white dog Vigi – or Garm, as Hel called him.

And there was Odin, behind a tree. And behind another tree. Behind every tree. Everywhere Sigurd turned, Odin stood. He was speaking, but I couldn't hear the words. His mouth was cruel and mocking, sometimes; sometimes he smiled kindly. It was as though he were playing many different parts.

'The same thing he wanted with the lindworm you killed.'

Fafnir reared in the sky, and I stumbled back, seeing him. So the monster had not lied; he had been working at Odin's behest.

The sky went dark, and I sank onto the bench.

'But why would he loose Fafnir on the world?'

'To harvest more dead.'

'He gets half the dead,' I said, dully. 'Half the dead in war.'

'He has seen a vision, of a terrible battle in which he will die. Yes, even Odin can die. He suspects his opponent is me. I know he's wrong, but he won't believe me. So he's trying to increase his army, at my expense. Stirring up battles or making them worse, telling his Valkyries to make sure the best warriors die, and die quickly. Distracting me so that my Disir arrive late. It is all disgusting and quite pointless. He fills his hall, and meanwhile the leavings come to me, because of an ancient treaty he can't break. But I don't mind. My field is vast, and it can welcome all who die in pain. I have room for them all.'

She looked out at the ship full of bright Disir; I looked too, but I had to shield my gaze from them. When I looked at them, the pictures in the sky faded, and the sensation that the ship was moving through the waving rye stopped.

'He doesn't understand the dead, you see,' she said, distantly. 'Gods seldom do. I don't understand them either, but that's what makes them fascinating to me. Odin simply hates and fears them, and yet he gathers them to himself, more and more, because those are the only army he has.'

Drusus's face, so blank in death. The heap of corpses that Attila had turned into draugar, with Odin's help. Odin was using Attila, as he had used Sigurd, and Fafnir. So much pain, so much grief, because Odin was afraid. My act of defiance had been selfish; it had helped no one. He was about to unleash Attila on the world, just to get more dead men for his horde. I had failed to make a difference in Valhalla and in Midgard. I'd failed to save you. Nothing I'd ever done had mattered.

And now, I was in a ship for the dead, but I was not dead. Not yet. I could still fight.

'How can I stop him?' I asked.

Frejya laughed, a boisterous *ha* that rang in the night air. 'You cannot stop him. You're a mortal woman. He and his Valkyries will take more and more, until Midgard is emptied. He will make little children fight if that is what is left to him. Odin is insatiable.'

'I would like to try,' I said.

Her face grew serious. She said, quietly, 'You cannot kill the Allfather. It simply cannot be done.'

'I don't want to kill him,' I said, all my limbs cold from the very words. 'But he's not the one who chooses the slain. Help me find the Valkyries, and I will convince them to stop this.'

'And where would the war-dead go, if not to Valhalla? The terms of our treaty are clear. I can't take more than he takes.'

I thought for a moment. Here I was again, bandying words with a goddess about where the dead ought to go. Hel had shown me that afterlives were not as simple as I'd thought. People build their own houses, in death as in life.

I had lost track of time, she said. How long had my last journey been, from Helheim to Folkvang? What had happened to Sigurd in that time, if anything could be said to happen to the dead?

I asked Freyja if I could see one more thing. She pointed to the sky, and there was Sigurd again, in a green wood, with the white dog at his side. But this was not the Odenwald, and Odin was nowhere to be seen. This was Helheim, where Sigurd and I had started building Valhalla. And he was carrying on that work, free at last from the prickling whispers of the Deceiver. There stood Sigurd, whistling. Whistling! And beating a bit of red and black iron on an anvil. A little bit of dirty bone he'd made into a beautiful hinge, curved and lovely and strong. For a door, I imagined.

He looked happy.

Where would the war-dead go, if not to Valhalla? A very good question. An idea tugged on my mind. But I would need both goddesses on my side, and the Valkyries too. And where to begin to persuade a goddess who had, as she said, room for as many dead as would come to her?

But Freyja did have an interest in this business, if I could just show it to her. I had learned some useful things from the Allfather.

'Odin lied to me so frequently,' I said, as the image of Sigurd vanished into stars and darkness. 'I don't know what's real. Some people told me that he had no ability to weave magic or to see the future before you taught him, Freyja. Was that a term of your treaty too?'

I saw new pictures in the sky, and recoiled: a head dripping with blood.

'It was,' she said, a storm on her brow. 'Our first truce held with the exchange of hostages. But then one of our

people, in a frenzy, beheaded one of the hostages Odin sent
to us: Mimir. To hold the peace, I offered to show Odin how
to make Mimir's head speak again. I taught him the runes,
and how to use them. I taught him charms, potions, and
incantations.'

'And how to see the future?'

The dripping head disappeared, and I saw Freyja and Odin
standing opposite each other, their postures defiant, their
chins raised.

She laughed shortly. 'No. That he found for himself, but
only because the head of Mimir told him where to find a
magic well, and how to drink from it. His visions of the
future are few and dark. It's one reason he's so afraid. He's
seen a vision of a war in which the gods themselves die, but
he doesn't know where or when or who starts it.'

'And you do?'

She shook her head. 'I'm wise enough not to look where
my gaze is not required.'

'But if he can't see the future, how does he know where
the battlefields are, when he sends us?'

'He can see a little way into the future. What he sees, for
the most part, is what you have seen tonight: the present
and the past. He sees where troops are amassing and where
they are heading.'

'And now he is using the magic you taught him to harvest
as many men from Midgard as he can. Insatiable, you called
him.'

Freyja's gaze turned on me like a falcon's. The sky went
dark. I could hear the Disir whispering to each other down
the length of the ship, like the wind in dry grass.

'You're trying to say that it's my fault.'

I put up a hand, placatingly. 'I'm saying that Odin is abusing
the gift you gave him and turning a pact of peace into a
different kind of war. He thinks you're his enemy, whether
he's right or wrong.'

She shook her head, her masses of gold and silver hair

catching several different rays of light, an echo of her great necklace. 'You'd have me fulfil his prophecy, and start a war?'

'I would ask you for two things, goddess. First, that you accept that fewer dead will come here, but I will give you evidence that they have chosen a new home for themselves.'

Freyja looked sceptical. 'I don't see how that's possible.'

'That brings me to the second thing,' I said. 'I would ask you to talk to Hel.'

She rolled her eyes. 'And just when I was starting to think you had a head on your shoulders.'

CHAPTER THIRTY-FIVE

Brynhild and the Valkyries

I didn't ask Freyja how her conversation with Hel had gone, but she came to me some days later – time in Folkvang was liquid – and handed me a cloak of golden feathers, shot through with silver. It was long but strangely light as I settled it around my shoulders.

'With this, you can fly as well as any Valkyrie,' she said. 'This will help you find them on the battlefield.'

I was speechless. Eventually I managed to say, 'I will return this to you.'

'Yes, you will,' she said drily. 'I always retrieve the things that belong to me.'

Unlike Valkyries, who come down from the air, the Disir approach from the edges of reality. A relentless march into noise and stench. I was not a Dis, but I took their paths into Midgard. At first, everything was dim; my eyes had been blinded by the light of Folkvang. The first thing I saw was a man playing dead, face down in blood. I saw his padded leather rising between his shoulder blades. He was clinging to the hope that no one would strike him down if they thought he was already dead. Trusting to luck to save him from trampling hooves or from a flight of arrows.

There is no luck on the battlefield; there is only us. Valkyries and Disir, choosing the slain, and then taking them home. Beside me, a Dis reached out one shadowy hand, and tilted the man's chin up until he saw her. He looked at her like a man in love, and he rose off the ground, his feet dangling. Just an inch, he rose. Just high enough that the arrow which might have given him a painful skull-graze struck him in the brain instead, and the light went out of his eyes.

One for Folkvang.

Arrows rained from the Frankish contingent, all in a line. And then, more arrows, haphazard, like a windstorm. The Hunnic horse archers, trying to break through the middle.

It was a battle of many armies, and two uneasy sides. The Empire had its allies. Attila had his. There were Franks and Goths on both sides, but the Burgundians and Alans only fought with the Empire. Somewhere, in that vast mess of tens of thousands and living and dead human bodies, there might have been some old friends.

I turned, getting my bearings, careful to avoid the slashing swords, the knives, the spears thrusting up and the horses barrelling down on me. Then I remembered my cloak, and flew straight up to the sky.

The air was full of Valkyries. Like dancing birds, they were swatting arrows one way or another, laughing as they grabbed them in their teeth and then threw them down with more strength than any bowstring.

Swirled in my cloak of feathers, hanging in the air, I finally had a good view of the battlefield. There was no end to it, no horizon. The world was full of the thunder of hooves and the whine of arrows. The clash of steel against steel, against wood, against bone, a never-ending percussion. Screams and the smell of hot blood.

On the ridge to the east, the Roman forces were pressing

the Huns back. Here in the midst of the field, it was hard to
see any movement or change at all.

Then I realized that my former comrades, who could make
sense of any battle, could make no sense of this one. It was
too big; it was chaos. Their faces showed a desperate kind
of glee, like drunken children running to leap off a cliff.

Gondul fell like a shot bird, with a spear in her side.

She lay flat on the ground with men fighting oblivious
around her, stepping on her arms and on her matted dark
hair. Red blood seeped out of the wound. I sank down into
the gore, to comfort her. There was no way she could escape
death, not with a hole that size through her. No runes would
knit that hole together, no incantation would pour her blood
back into her body. Perhaps Odin might have done it, but
Odin was not here. He never came to the field of battle.

'You came back,' Gondul said as I bent over her. 'A little
late.'

With the fluttering of wings and a blast of air that sent all
the arrows flying in a circle away from us, the other Valkyries
descended, and stood around her, mourning her while she
was still alive, which would not be long. She turned her face
into the mud and then she was dead, a body like any other.
A mere woman. The worst thing Odin could imagine.

'This is a slaughterhouse!' I screamed at them. 'There is
no skill here, no judgement, no wisdom. You are collecting
corpses.'

'You *left*,' said Hrist, spitting, cynical, a different woman
to the one I'd trained. 'You have no rights here.'

'Go, before you distract another of us,' said Rota, pointing
at Gondul as though her death were my fault.

A soldier backed into her and she thrust her spear into
his back, leaving him bleeding on the ground. Casual killing.
What did it matter? Valhalla would get so many warriors in
that bone-harvest that they didn't need to be selective.

I looked at my sisters, covered in blood. Their eyes were
haunted and their teeth were bared. Freyja's cloak clung to

my sweaty skin and I itched to fly above all of this, to find blue skies and white clouds and a mountain somewhere. But I had a mountain once, and it had brought me no peace. Nothing had.

How Gondul had danced, and laughed, and walked in the forests of Valhalla at sunset. We'd laughed ourselves sick at her funny stories. I loved her. I loved all of them. I even loved Odin, and I loved Valhalla, still. I loved it all enough to light its funeral pyre.

I pulled the golden cloak around me and I shot up high into the sky, but not to escape.

Valkyries do not carry the dead; they mark them. The dead sleep for a short while, then wake in Valhalla. We have always seen it as a conferral of favour, and we saw the calling of the Disir as trickery, seduction, witchcraft. Now I was neither Valkyrie nor Dis, but I intended to give the dead a choice. I called to them, my voice lost utterly to the living in that din of battle. I told them the story of how Sigurd lived on a green slope, how his hall was new and empty. I spoke of the forests without anyone to walk the paths in them, of the empty hives that needed to be filled with bees. I could promise no eternal battles, no undead boar. I could not even promise Valkyries to bear them the cup of victory in the mead hall. But I could promise them no more generals to obey. Tales around a fire, rest, and peace. And the company of the most renowned hero the world has ever known, Sigurd the monster-slayer.

I offered them a door. I had to hope Hel would open it.

Even high above the battle, a few arrows turned against my mail coat, which was forged by a very clever smith. Some turned against my blood-hardened skin. I paid none of them any mind.

A sword blade knocked my helmet and I went flying to one side, the cloak keeping me aloft though my head was ringing. With more desperation than grace, I righted myself so I could see my attacker: Kara, raising her sword again.

I drew my sword and tried to get into a guard position

but not even Valkyries train for battle in the air; we fight mortals, on the ground. It almost made me want to laugh: there were no names for these positions, there was no perfect positioning. There was only what Svafa had taught me long ago: *Your sword is thirsty. Let it drink.*

As Kara's blade came down from above, I got underneath her. I thrust up at her ribs and kicked furiously at Hrist as she came stabbing at me from the other side.

Then in my peripheral vision, I saw Rota bearing down somehow from above, shield-first. Others joined them; some of them I didn't even recognize. I braced, and whirled, and prepared to acknowledge that I couldn't fight them all.

'Stop,' Hrist said. 'Lay down your weapons.'

It took me a moment to realize she wasn't talking to me. She lifted her visor, and her face was grim, but her words were not. 'We have lost one sister today already.'

'And you'll lose more,' I said, with blood in my mouth. 'Odin wants more battles like this one, bigger than this one. Wars unceasing in which you will all be torn apart.'

Ignoring me, Kara turned to Hrist. 'It's treason.'

'We serve *them*,' Hrist replied, gesturing at the field of broken bodies below, the dark blood pooling in the hoofprints and footprints. 'I haven't forgotten that, even if you have. If they wish to come to Valhalla, I will bring them their cup with great joy. If they wish to go to Brynhild's new place, then I won't be the one to stop them.'

There were bodies as yet unmarked and uncalled. Freshly felled. They were not yet bound for Folkvang or for Valhalla. And all of them opened their eyes, and they looked towards a patch of sky between the paths of the arrows, the door that Hel had opened for them.

Weeping, I fell on the ground with the dead men, and watched their eyes close again. The Valkyries stood around me and did nothing. There was nothing left to do. And there was nowhere for any of us to go, for we were not dead, and we would not be welcome in Valhalla.

CHAPTER THIRTY-SIX

Gudrun's Revenge

The wind told me all about the war, although in its indifferent cruelty, it breathed nothing about you. I knew that Attila's army of many nations had met Aetius's army of many nations in Gaul, and both armies had been slaughtered. Attila now marched east with the remnants. He was making his way to Italy, but first he wanted to pick up more men in his own lands, or the lands of people already living in terror of him. He was seeking new allies, and he planned to take a new wife from among the Goths.

The wind also told me that some Burgundians had travelled north, out of their new kingdom, to fight Attila. I asked the wind for news of Volker and Hagen, and it told me they had wandered to the south, after the refugees were safely settled, expanding their territory. I asked for news of my mother, and it gave me her love. Every night, she sent me dreams of her river. I knew it now nearly as well as she did. I've never been sure whether she meant to send me those dreams, or whether they were an accident, something that happens when a river-guardian worries about her witch-daughter. Traders told us that Vormatia was, if not thriving, then at least feeding itself, and living at peace under Lothar.

Everyone I had known was carrying on without me – and the me they had known was no more. I had almost forgotten the name Gudrun, or rather, I remembered it like a name in a story, of a princess who had a rose garden.

To be honest, I loved being a witch. I always had a potion fermenting, or a plant growing in unusual places or shapes, or a pot of something curious and strange bubbling in a corner. It wasn't as lonely a life as one might think.

It wasn't unusual for my old friend Ingund to visit my tower in those days, to bring me food and news, or tell me about someone who needed a witch's help. Her little girl usually came with her, the girl I'd helped deliver, who was now nearly ten years old. Ingund had stayed unmarried after all, thanks to the other women now living on her farm. Ingund had a gift for finding lost people. She would wander the forests and come out again with a widow or a stray.

So I didn't wonder too much when I saw Ingund approaching one evening with a girl I didn't recognize.

'This is Ildico,' Ingund said as I ushered them in.

I had made the base of my tower into a little room where visitors could come, or at least, those visitors I let through the magical traps first my mother, and then I, had laid all around the place. There were stools, and a few cushions. I offered them warm goat's milk and waited to hear what the problem was.

'Her father has promised her in marriage to Attila.'

At that, my eyes widened, and I sat down on a pile of cushions. 'How old are you, my dear?'

'Fifteen years old, Mother Grimhild.'

'And would you like me to help you hide or escape?'

She shook her head. 'If I did that, the treaty would not hold, and Attila would slaughter my people.'

I looked at her appraisingly, reminded of the girl I had been, once. 'Oh, I don't know about that. He needs all the fighters he can get, or so I hear.'

'He would force all the men to fight, then, and slaughter the old, the young and the women. I know he would.'

She gazed at me, defiantly, with big black eyes.

'All right, then if you don't seek my help to avoid the marriage, why are you here? I do have some things that help with the prevention of children, which I would recommend, at your age.'

'I would like to buy some poison.'

I frowned. 'I am not a murderer of children.'

At that, she was confused, and made a face. The kind of face only a fifteen-year-old can make, while talking to an adult who makes no sense. Then she understood, and said, 'Oh no! I won't take my own life. I'll take his.'

How long had it been since I'd laughed? The sound was quite terrible, even to my ears. The old witch cackling in her tower. But I couldn't stop. Here at last was my chance to rectify my mistake of so many years before. Here at last was my revenge, and it came in the form of a slim, wide-eyed girl.

Ingund smiled nervously, to reassure Ildico, I suppose. But Ildico didn't look as if she needed reassurance. She understood that I wasn't laughing at her.

At last, I said, 'As wonderful as the idea is, I'm afraid it's just as likely to lead to your murder. Do you think you'd escape so easily? And what would stop the Huns from taking revenge on your people?'

'Attila's three sons hate each other and will be most occupied with fighting over the throne. I don't think his generals want more war. And as for me,' she said, staring me full in the face, 'I think they'll all be happy to believe me incapable of killing the scourge of God. I'm just a girl. If I'm wrong, then let me die, but at least I won't go alone.'

I was afraid Attila, or someone in his household, might recognize the ring. Khreka was sharp-eyed. But there were other ways. I had learned all kinds of witchcraft in those years in the forest, and I knew my poisons as well as my

poultices. On the third floor of my tower, I kept everything
I needed in jars on shelves. Ingund came with me, up the
steps, ostensibly to help me but also to talk about the girl.

'You think I'm doing the right thing?' I asked her, softly.

'I wouldn't have brought her otherwise. She doesn't have
good choices.'

'Neither did you, once.'

'And neither did you,' she retorted. Ingund had probably
guessed who I had been by then, but she might equally have
meant that I had once been homeless and friendless. That
was true.

'And we're both still alive,' I said.

'For our sins.'

I pulled down a jar of mouldy woodruff, lifted the lid,
sniffed and winced. It smelled sweet like the breath of a
dying man. This was what I wanted: a poison that would
act throughout the body, and cause bleeding. Vomiting by
itself was an unpredictable way to cause death, and besides,
it looked suspicious.

A little vomiting, though. And a little coughing for good
measure.

I handed the jar to Ingund, and took a sprig of lavender,
and a bit of liquorice root. Then the jar of wolfsbane, the
purple helmet flower, to make sure of the business. A chunk
of yellow orpiment, so useful as a pigment, and so deadly.

And finally, my jar of rosewater, and a bit of honey, to
mix the paste into.

'That will do,' I said as we were laden with jars and odds
and ends. 'I just have to crush these and mix them and boil
a little. It won't be long, but night's falling. You can both
stay here tonight. I have food and a fire.'

Ingund nodded. She was standing behind me on the stairs,
but she wasn't moving.

'Is there something else?' I whispered.

'Not about the girl,' she said, uncertainly. 'But I saw something else in the forest, a short walk from her father's farm.

In a clearing, there's a small lake – the place you and I went to collect lilies, last year. I saw – women. I think they were women. But they were – please don't laugh – they were flying. And heavily armed.'

'Flying!' I thought immediately of Valkyries; I thought of you. But you were dead, ten years dead. And if these were your comrades of long ago, I thought, then what did that have to do with me? Besides, by the time I caught up with them, they might be gone again.

'I thought you would want to know. I thought you could tell us whether we're in any danger from them, whoever they are. If they're witches, or – well, I thought you might have an idea.'

Ashamed, I realized my first thought hadn't been about the people I lived among, the people I devoted my life to protecting. I had forgotten Grimhild and become Gudrun again, for a brief moment. How easily I shed my witchskin.

I shook my head. 'I'm sure they are no danger, but I'll go and see them anyway, if I can. There are many frightening things in the world, my friend. But we have one of the most dangerous creatures anywhere downstairs, waiting for me to bring her all this.'

When Ingund and Ildico were asleep, curled up like two little grubs in their blankets, I took a jar full of fireflies to light my path and walked in the direction of Ildico's family. It was hours before I reached the lake Ingund had described, and by then, the sky was light with the coming dawn. I freed the fireflies, set down my jar, and watched.

They weren't hiding. The Valkyries were having an argument; it seemed to be a council of war, and it probably was. All I could see were the tall women, their bright mail coats. Next to them were a pile of swords and helmets.

One of the women was wrapped in a cloak of golden feathers. It was so dazzling that at first I didn't recognize you; I looked at your heavy bronze braids and I thought,

Brynhild had hair like that. I looked at the way you stood and I thought, *Brynhild's shoulders made just that angle.*

And then you turned towards me, and dropped the cloak of feathers, and I cried out.

What I said, I don't know. You froze, and all the Valkyries froze too, watching the woods. I ducked down behind a log and tried to stop my heart from hammering. Why was I hiding? I suppose I didn't know what to think, or what to say. I didn't trust that it could truly be you.

Maybe my cry brought Odin. Or maybe he knew exactly where you were all along and had been waiting for this moment.

After an eternity, the Valkyries all seemed satisfied that the noise they'd heard was nothing but a forest creature, and they weren't entirely wrong about that. They pulled off their mail and some of their overclothes and they sank into the lake, disappearing from my view as the sun rose. You went in with them. I could see your shoulders, above the waterline, in a white shift.

And then I saw a movement: fast and low to the ground, like a squirrel or a weasel. I saw the cloak in someone's hands, and then I saw the someone. A tall man, standing by the lakeside, a wide-brimmed hat on his head. He'd taken your cloak of feathers, while you bathed.

His voice was that of a concerned friend, although he addressed no one in particular. 'Valhalla is quiet. The dead await your company. As do I.'

'We did not think we would be welcome,' said the Valkyrie with the darkest skin – it must have been Hrist, I think.

'Why would I fail to welcome the sheep home, just because they've been attacked by a wolf in disguise? Brynhild I will deal with. The rest of you are needed.'

There was the sound of something crashing through the woods, and I ducked down again. It blew past me: a great golden chariot, pulled by two great cats, like lynx but bigger. The goddess stood, a staff in her hand, and I remembered how I had driven my chariot to the battle with Attila. How confident I was then, and how sure of my place in the world. I grow less sure with each passing year.

'Freyja!' Odin boomed. 'And outfitted for war. Is there a battle I don't know about?'

'You tell me, Warmonger,' said Freyja.

'It won't be long,' Odin said. 'Attila will wage another battle soon enough, and another. He won't stop. And next time, there will be no interfering with my harvest.'

Attila, I thought, would soon be dead, at the hands of a girl.

'I'm only here for what is mine,' Freyja said.

Odin stepped towards her, so that for the first time I could see his face, although most of it was shadowed. 'You can't claim the living.'

'I don't intend to. Give me my cloak.'

Odin looked at the feathered cloak draped over one arm as though he'd forgotten it was there. 'You gave it away.'

'I lent it. And not to you or any of yours. Try sending Loki to steal it from me, if you like. That's worked out well for you in the past.'

Odin hesitated, but one of Freyja's cats, somehow loosed from the chariot, jumped and took the cloak in its teeth, as though it were hunting a bird. It brought it to Freyja, who laid it at her feet.

'I have no right to your cloak,' Odin said, the voice reasonable and a smile emerging from under the hat-shadow. 'But I have a right to my own traitors, to deal with as I wish. That is one of the terms of our old agreement.'

You spoke, then, coming to Odin's side. 'I've already been exiled. I've even already been killed. Send me to Helheim again if you wish. I have friends to visit there.'

'I want you to come home,' he said, still smiling, and a chill swept over all my skin. 'Your exile is ended, Brynhild. Your father gave you to me, many years ago, in fulfilment of an oath. Let us all leave here with our belongings. Freyja has her cloak. And I have my Valkyries.'

Freyja said, 'Your Valkyries chose to leave you. Are they slaves?'

'Valhalla and everything in it is my concern, as you well know,' he snapped. 'If you break the terms, Freyja, we will have war.'

She laughed brightly. 'And how will I know the difference between that war and this peace?'

I was on my feet before I really understood what I was doing. All I knew was that I couldn't stay crouched behind that damp, mossy log a moment longer, hiding while gods discussed your fate. You had sacrificed yourself once for me. I had let you die and let Attila live. One mistake was in the process of being corrected; now for the other.

'You can't take her,' I said.

For you, my love, conversations with gods are all in a day's business, but I felt myself shrink as Odin turned his shadowed face towards me.

'Gudrun, daughter of King Gjuki, daughter of Queen Auda River-Warden, Sigurd's wife, Gunnar's sister. Or shall I say Grimhild, Witch of the Woods?'

I quavered. 'Do you know everything, then?'

He glanced at Freyja before he spoke; maybe he would have lied if she hadn't been there. 'I can see how events are tending, if I turn my gaze on them. I can find out what I need to know.'

It wasn't quite the same thing. Even I recognized that. It meant that Ildico had a chance to kill Attila without Odin knowing, if he had no reason to turn his gaze that way.

'So there *are* things you don't know,' I said as lightly as I could, as though I were playing a game.

'Very few. Are you bargaining with me?'

'Yes,' I said defiantly, as though that had been my idea.

Do you think I didn't see you frowning at me? I saw you well enough, but I couldn't make myself look straight at you because I knew I would crumble if I did.

'You ask for Brynhild. And what do you offer in exchange for the traitor?'

I didn't know much about Odin; I was raised a Christian, so instead of stories I heard scraps and oaths and allusions, bits of poetry, bits of song. He had sacrificed an eye for wisdom, I knew. He talked to dragons about family lore and giants about magic, and he went out seeking riddle contests just to learn the riddles.

I gambled, and said, 'I know something you don't.'

It seemed to work. A wider smile broke on his face, and he said, 'If you can tell me something I can't know by any other means, I will give you your lover back. But no one and nothing else.'

'Gudrun—' you said. The Valkyries spoke too, but I didn't hear any of it. I had come close enough now that I could look into Odin's face, and I saw his one eye, the eye of a young man, blue flecked with red. We had an accord.

The sun was up, and not too far from here, Ildico and Ingund would already be on their way back to her parents' farm, to dress her in her wedding finery. Birds were singing. Maybe everyone in that glade understood what they were saying, but to me, it was just birdsong, the same as it had always been. But I had my ways of knowing things. My mother and I both spoke to the wind, and the wind spoke to us, and we shared secrets we would entrust to no messenger.

'I know,' I said, 'where the gold that once belonged to Fafnir lies.'

'So do I,' he said, smirking.

'But I know *exactly* where it lies,' I said. 'I can map every coin, and every torc, and statue, and every weapon. I know the secrets of the Rhine, and the Rhine guards its secrets closely. Even from you.'

The shadow deepened across the top half of his face.

'Tell me, then,' he said.

He didn't want the gold, but he wanted to know where

the gold was, because no one else knew that, and because he couldn't see it for himself. He was greedy for knowledge the way Fafnir had been greedy for metal and death. Odin was always his own scourge, and the truth was that he liked it. He loved to sacrifice himself in exchange for scraps. After so many years being a witch, I was a good judge of character.

I looked around for something to draw with and picked up a broken branch from the forest floor. Between where I stood and the lake, there was a long slope of sand, and it began with some high grassy patches, and there were ants living there. They gave me an idea. I drew the shape of the Rhine, or at least, one stretch of the Rhine. I marked the bridge and the cities, and my mother's rock. And then I knelt and whispered to the ants. I spoke to them with my mind, and they marched into my river-drawing, and made a pattern there. Then they stopped walking, which was one of the oddest things I've ever seen: ants, alive, but not moving.

Odin sniffed, as though he didn't like the smell.

'Are you satisfied?' Freyja asked, but quietly, calmly, as though she were speaking to a child.

There was no response. Odin was gone. Where the old man had been was only the shadows of trees, moving in a little wind. I'd fulfilled the bargain, and bargains have power. Whatever use Odin might have had for the knowledge of where, exactly, to find the Rhine gold, I can't say. I suspect it was no use to him at all. I suspect it is still there, the property of Attila. Sometimes people who wandered through my forest telling stories said that the lindworm's gold was cursed, that it explained all the bad luck that befell the people who touched it. But we all made our own luck, just as Fafnir had. Fafnir had chosen to listen to Odin's whispers. So had Sigurd, and so had Attila.

Odin was gone, but the Valkyries were still there. A small group of women in wet clothing, wringing out their hair. They made me shiver, but not from cold. To think of all the deaths they had chosen, and the lives they had saved. How the world might have been different if they'd marked other people for death. And in the end, despite their powers and their skills, they were all just women, making decisions as best they could. That little lake in the forest was a place for believing in gods and monsters, but what made me shiver was that *everyone* was a god and a monster, that there was no law passing out the power to change the world.

'He hasn't forgotten us,' said one of the Valkyries, the one with the curls – Kara, was it? 'He has left us here to wait and to wonder.'

You, my love, took Kara's hand, and said, 'I won't abandon you.'

Hrist said, 'If you leave us, you aren't abandoning us, Brynhild. I'll return to Valhalla with him when he comes for me. I have a duty to the dead. And I have a duty to the new girls he will bring and train. But I won't serve his whims any more. If he brings me to Valhalla, he brings a revolt with him.'

The others all nodded grimly, and you laughed, and then I saw your eyes were full of tears.

It was only then that I dared reach out my hand and touch your arm.

CHAPTER THIRTY-SEVEN

Brynhild and Gudrun

So we come at last to now, and you, and me, and this tiny boat.

Freyja put it in my hand when she left. A toy of honey-rich wood. I thought it was a keepsake; it reminded me of the great boat in her field.

But you, wise witch, took one look at it and said, 'That boat wants the sea.'

I thought you'd miss your tower, but you said the tower belonged to Grimhild, and you were ready to be someone else. Gudrun, I asked? Gudrun and Brynhild, you said.

And besides, Vormatia was safe under Lothar, and Ingund kept an eye on the forest, and Odin's war was over, for a time, anyway. The Valkyries would keep an eye on him, in Midgard and in Valhalla. Freyja would match his every move. And Loki would make useful trouble wherever it was needed. There was nothing left for us to burn down and build up, nothing to fight. Nothing to poison and nothing to heal. For the years left to us, we would find our homes in each other, and our work would be in telling each other all the things we hadn't made time to say.

'We have earned a little time for ourselves,' you said,

determined, and that was that. You were, then and always, my queen, and I would be ruled by you.

We followed the Rhine north for a long time, eating what you gathered and I hunted. We slept in each other's arms at last and woke in the morning to birdsong. I started to teach you the language of birds, and you taught me some of your magic. I told you the meanings of the runes – but not the meanings of the runes on my hands. We didn't speak about the past, very much. We avoided people and you stopped asking the wind for news.

One morning I woke up and saw you standing on the shore, looking across the river to a high rock. You were standing very still. Saying goodbye to Auda, I now understand. On that day, I only knew not to interrupt you, although I was eager to get moving. The gold that lay at the bottom of the Rhine belonged to a story that was over, and I wanted to leave it behind.

Finally, we came to a low country, and then to the sea. And you were right, as you always are. The little boat grew on the water until it was big enough for you, and me, and our food and water. Your tree that bears a different fruit every day, your jars of honey and mead, your breads that stay fresh, your sudden cheeses. The fish we catch, when we want to. Blankets woven by spiders to keep us warm.

You asked the wind to take us to a safe place, where we could live.

The wind asked for payment.

It asked for our stories.

So we have told them, to each other and to the greedy breezes. We are a nation of two, a witch and a warrior, a warrior and a witch, and we lie under the stars at night so close that our pulses kiss. Our little grey boat bobs on the waves. When our words fly past our ears, they become mere scraps on the wind, rumours told now only in the language of seabirds. I don't have Odin's gift for prophecy and I don't want it, but I have travelled between worlds and fallen through time enough to have a sense of how the future crouches in the shadows. Someday, there will be shapes like us in stories forged out of old swords and older rings. Let them say what they will, but let them remember that we burned down the world to save it, and the nature of the world is that it can always burn again.

Acknowledgements and Author's Note

This story began when I was reading Norse tales at bedtime to my eight-year-old son, and I started to wonder what Brynhild's version of her ill-fated affair with Sigurd might be. Then I read *The Song of the Nibelungs*, translated by Margaret Armour. I was struck by the descriptions of the kisses of greeting between Brynhild and Kriemhild (Gudrun), and of the way the two women stared at each other at feasts as though they could look at nothing else. And a new version of the story started to take shape in my mind.

My other main sources were translations of *The Prose Edda*, *The Poetic Edda*, *The Saga of the Volsungs*, and *The Rosegarden of Worms*, in addition to histories of central Europe in the fifth century CE.

The old stories span languages, cultures, and centuries. They contradict each other in several ways. Timelines and geographies shift. Characters divide, collapse, and change their names. Known historical figures walk the same pages as gods. Exactly how any of it fits into the real history of the Burgundians, the Huns, and the Roman Empire is difficult to say. The earliest manuscript versions of these stories were themselves historical fiction that dealt with events long past. I've taken some threads from all those sources for my own version, one in a long line.

I am in the debt of the writers, scholars, and translators who work with these tales. Mistakes and misinterpretations are my own.

I thank my agent, Jennie Goloboy, for her wise feedback on the early draft and for all her work. Thanks as well to my wonderful editor, Jane Johnson, for her vision and thoughtful suggestions. Copy-editor Susan Opie made the manuscript shine. I'm grateful for the hard work of the whole team at HarperVoyager UK, including Natasha Bardon, Vicky Leech Mateos, Elizabeth Vaziri, Millie Prestige, Robyn Watts, Terence Caven, Felicity Denham, and Sophie Raoufi, as well as my proofreader Linda Joyce. I count myself very lucky to have had my work graced by Andrew Davis's cover designs. And thanks to Jack Renninson for his support of me and of this book.

My first attempt to tell Brynhild's story was a 750-word flash piece for a weekend writing contest with the Codex Writers' Group, of which I've been a member for ten years. I thank everyone on Codex for all their help over the years – and for telling me that what I had was the beginning of a novel.

I thank my son Xavier, my partner Brent, and my whole family for their unwavering support. This book is dedicated to my noble-hearted brother Ian, who, I'm pretty sure, walked into our world from an old tale.